Lufts

Also by Leo Stapleton

Thirty Years on the Line
Commish
Fire & Water
Jakes
Ffops

Lufts

by

Leo D. Stapleton

dmc associates, inc
Dover, NH

This is a work of fiction. Any resemblance between any charcter in this book and any individual, either living or dead, is purely coincidental or in the mind of the reader.

Copyright © 1998 by Leo D. Stapleton

Published by dmc associates, inc.
PO Box 1095
Dover, NH 03821-1095

All rights reserved. No part of this work may be reproduced or transmitted in any form whatsoever, except for brief passages that may be used by a reviewer. Requests for permissions should be addressed to the publisher.

ISBN: 1-879848-13-9

Printed in the United States of America

2 3 4 5 6

to Jack Stapleton

Acknowledgments

I would like to thank my faithful supporters:

My wife, Doris, and my brother, Jack, from my generation.

Leo, Jr., Edward, Garrett, Jennifer, Amanda, Scott, Kathy and Gene from the next generation.

Jocelyn, Jordan, Courtney, January, Brian, Mary Kate, Laura, Luke, Hayley, Emily, Sydney, and Leo III from the one after that.

Lufts

One

Donald scanned through the General Order, picking out the pertinent information, his hands trembling as his eyes skipped down the page:

General Orders #34. October 31, 1996
The Fire Commissioner announces the retirement of the following members, effective November, 1, 1996:
Fire Captain Henry M. Fallon, Fire Prevention Division.
Fire Captain Nathan L. Tyree, Engine Company 55.
Fire Lieutenant James K. Brunick, Training Division.
Fire Lieutenant Arthur N. Rialto, Training Division.

In addition to the notices of the officers' retirement, the order gave brief histories of the retirees' promotions and concluded with the time-honored phrase, "All of these members leave the department with the best wishes of their associates."

Donald chuckled. It could have added, "Yeah, and especially those guys listed below." Donald had never known the two captains who were going out, but he had very fond memories of his two drill school instructors, Lieutenants Brunick and Rialto. While each had their own unique personalities, they had one common element—they were terrific teachers of recruits. Between them they had helped to graduate about half the guys on the job. If the Boston Fire Department is as good as we keep telling ourselves, then these two men certainly played a major role in that achievement.

The next part of the order caused Donald's eyes to mist over a bit:

The following named members are promoted to Fire Captain and are assigned to the Personnel Division, effective November 1, 1996:
Fire Lieutenant Joseph M. Desmond, Tower Company.
Fire Lieutenant Andrew L. Novak, Tower Company.
The following named members are promoted to Fire

Lieutenant and are assigned to the Personnel Division, effective 0800 hours, November 1, 1996.
Fire Fighter Donald F. Holden, Tower Company.
Fire Fighter Alan R. Hitchcock, Engine Company 32.
Fire Fighter Cassius X. Murphy, Ladder Company 23.
Fire Fighter Richard C. Foster, Engine Company 10.

What a score! Four members from the same drill class promoted together. Wonder if that ever happened before. Well, probably. A zillion guys must have moved through the ranks in the last hundred fifty years, so just about everything must be a repeat of something else. Lieutenant Brunick—known to Donald and his fellow Ffops as "Bulby"—used to say, "Lissen, you stiffs, ain't nothin' new under the sun, nor under my piercing blue eyes. Just shut up and climb that ladder." Or, Donald thought, drag that line, or chop that floor, or whatever we were doing when he chewed us out.

If anyone had told me four and a half years ago that I'd be making lieutenant now, I would've told them they were daffy. I felt so lucky to be on the job, I'd have signed to remain a fire fighter forever. But that was before I started working with Lieutenant Desmond. He never even mentioned studying the first two years I was with him, although he and Lieutenant Novak were always swapping information about the books back and forth. He concentrated on making certain all of his jakes were learning the job itself. His main concern was our safety, and his opinion was, the more you know, the safer you'll be. He compared the job to a team sporting event but with far more serious consequences when you lose: "If you're the Bruins, Celtics, Patriots or Red Sox, you can shrug your shoulders and say, 'Wait 'til next year'—and our heroes seem to get to say that more than anyone else. But here," he continued, "it can really mean life or death, either to you, your partner or the people in the building."

Donald nodded to himself. Yeah, I guess I can relate to that all right. He had some hairy memories of his first year on the job. He'd been flattened trying to rescue Mikey Sikorski and the poor wino at that multiple on Boylston Street. If it weren't for Desmond and Gap Keefe, I certainly wouldn't be being promoted tomorrow. I'd be pushing up daisies at the Fireman's Lot in Forest Hills Cemetery. Teamwork saved the day there. But the job on East Newton Street a year and a half ago in '95 was even worse. Donald shivered involuntarily as he thought about that weird day in June.

He'd actually begun studying for promotion back in 1994, about eighteen months after the excursion to Disneyworld with Monty Hall and his group. What a great time they'd had. Every promise Monty had made with his salesman's pitch had come true. The Caribbean Beach Resort inside the park was terrific. When the group arrived from Orlando Airport on the chartered buses, check-in was accomplished promptly and bellmen hustled everyone to their rooms in golf carts. And the rooms were spectacular, designed to handle large families with plenty of closet space, a huge bathroom and enough full length towels for a much larger group than Donald, Gena and Nancy. Nancy was thrilled that she was issued her own room key card, which also served as a charge card and transportation pass. "Oh, Daddy," she chirped, "they make me feel like a grown-up!" "Naw," Donald replied, "they make me and your mom feel like kids. Know why? Because these people know you kids are much more important than we are."

The rest of the week was a blur in Donald's memory because it sped past so rapidly. The entire group met at the main swimming pool as quickly as they could don bathing suits. Nancy was soon part of the mass of fire fighter's kids her own age. It didn't take long for Donald and Gena to slip into the water, some distance from the shrieking children and in the midst of other couples from their tour. A few of the fire fighters were from Donald's firehouse, but most he hadn't met before. Jakes and their wives have no trouble assimilating and in no time the men were talking about the latest fires and the women were talking about anything but fires. Since they had arrived in mid-afternoon, it wasn't long before the sun started its descent to the horizon on this bright February day. Suddenly a shrill whistle pierced the air, causing many of the kids—and some of the adults—to cover their ears, but it got everyone's attention. At the head of the pool stood Monty Hall, his head encased in a Mickey Mouse hat. He was wearing a Goofy T-shirt and a pair of multi-colored pantaloons that made him look like a swami from India.

"All right, all right, everyone gather around," he boomed in his tour leader's voice. "I have your orders for the week, and they are as follows: Your admission tickets are in your rooms. They will provide you all day unlimited access to the Magic Kingdom, Epcot Center, MGM Studios, Typhoon Lagoon, and for you older kids, Pleasure Island, where you gotta be eighteen to get in.

"You must be on the plane when we return to Boston in a week. Other than that, I have no instructions for any of you. Just have a great time and that will make me very happy. See you all later."

That magic formula was all the group needed. By the time they got on the plane—and everyone made it—they were exhausted.

Donald and Gena had started off bravely enough trying to keep up with Nancy and her friends, but it was soon obvious that the best course was to let the kids fend for themselves, extracting a promise to meet at a specific location at a certain time. The adult couples managed to enjoy many of the rides, but at a much slower pace. Goat Hitchcock from the drill class was there with his wife, his son, his daughter-in-law and two grandchildren. On the last day, as they were lining up to board the plane, he turned to Donald and said, "You know, Donald, yesterday I was on three mountains—Space, Splash and Thunder. I've got back and chest muscle aches that I have never felt after a fire. But...this is a trip I will never forget. If Monty Hall runs for president of the union, I'm with him."

I'll second the motion, thought Donald. Wonder where his next trip is!

When the vacationers returned to Boston, reality set in as it always does. On the return flight the pilot announced, "Hope you Mouseketeers had a great week. The good news is we have a strong tail wind and will be arriving at Boston's Logan Airport twenty minutes early, and the weather is nice and clear. The bad news is the temperature in Boston is fourteen degrees and there are six inches of nice fresh snow on the ground." A reality check, mused Donald, just like Eric Engberg gives on CBS every week.

The next day Donald reported for duty at the firehouse, stamping his feet to knock off the snow he had accumulated on his walk from the bus at the South Station. He'd left his car at home because everything in the city was screwed up from the storm. Of course, he'd also been too lazy to dig it out when they got home yesterday. He put his gear on the apparatus, attached his facepiece to his mask, went through the routine procedure to insure the unit was working and the cylinder was full, then he trudged upstairs to the locker room. His partner, Nick Deliago, was just coming out of the shower room. "Hey, Nick, I'm back and I'm in. Have a busy night?" Donald asked.

"Naw, we didn't do shit. Never turned a wheel after midnight. The whole city was dead. Now I gotta go home and tell the bride I'm exhausted."

"Absolutely the most important thing they taught us in drill school—never been a quiet night on the job yet!" Donald wondered silently if firefighters' wives actually believe their husbands.

He sauntered into the kitchen, grabbed a cup of coffee and joined some other jakes at one of the long tables in the mess hall. He sat next to Fred Keefe and Steve Tucker, both of whom had made the trip to

Disneyworld. Keefe tried to smile, showing his separated teeth which gave him his nickname, "Gap", and then said, "I'm disconsolate, Donald old pal. That Monty Hall never mentioned we hadda come back from the trip."

Steve nodded in agreement and said, "Yeah...after the first coupla days of sunshine, I forgot all about winter. I met some jakes from the Reedy Creek Fire Department while we were down there."

"Reedy Creek! What the hell is that?" Gap asked.

"The outfit that protects Disney. They got an aerial Tower just like ours, a lot of special stuff and all kinds of ways of getting into the theme parks. I was just wonderin' if they'd be interested in a kind of an exchange program—you know, like they do with the kids from Europe in school."

"Sounds good to me," said Gap. "How about January, February and March?"

Since this wasn't going to happen, the conversation tailed off into discussions about the local sports teams and their continuing and painful lack of success. Eventually, Lieutenant Joe Desmond, sitting across the room with Captain Hardy of Rescue 1, shouted over, "OK you superstars! None of you are on strike, are ya? Start moving those brooms around now that you've all been goofin' off with Goofy for a week."

Reality sometimes sucks, thought Donald.

The city remained quiet throughout the morning, and Donald, who was driving the Tower this week, asked the lieutenant for permission to pull the truck out onto the apron and operate the unit for a while. The sun had elevated the temperature to thirty degrees and it felt strong on his face, but he didn't attract any volunteers except Rick Foster, his pal from Engine 10.

The firehouse is the largest in the city of Boston, housing the Tower Company, Rescue Company One, Engine Company Ten, the department Haz-Mat Unit and the division commander of Fire Division One. It occupies the bottom two floors of a thirty story office tower and faces the Central Artery Expressway at a point where the roadway dips to enter the quarter-mile long South Station tunnel/underpass. Beyond the Expressway, Atlantic Avenue is lined with some old office buildings and they border the Fort Point Channel, which is an inlet of Boston Harbor.

Donald and Rick had been appointed together just over a year before. Jakes develop close friendships with their drill class members, but in most cases the members are assigned to different firehouses and run into each other only sporadically throughout their careers. But since Donald and Rick were assigned to units in the same house on the same group and even lived in the same neighborhood, their relationship flourished. Donald had even been Rick's best man at his wedding a few months earlier.

Donald set the automatic jacks, raising the entire apparatus off the ground and manipulating the levers until a green light indicated the twenty-five ton unit was properly balanced and ready for operations. Both he and Rick ascended to the turntable, transferred the power from the pedestal to the bucket, and soon were raising themselves up vertically, rotating and extending until they were at the full ninety-five foot level. The view at this height is spectacular, with the Boston Harbor Hotel to the left and just beyond it, the sunshine reflecting off the water making the harbor far more beautiful than the pollution reports indicate. The cold weather did produce some chunks of ice, but they only served to enhance the beauty of the scene.

The two jakes never noticed any of it. They were concentrating on maneuvering the Tower into various positions trying to imagine where they would place the bucket in the high rise to either rescue occupants or attack a fire. Donald prided himself on his ability to feather the controls so gently that the ladder would creep by inches into a window sill. When Rick attempted to do the same, the Tower would jerk back and forth and keep swaying after he neutralized the handles.

"You know, Rick, you're just a hoseman," Donald said. "You don't have the technical expertise of a towerman, a ladderman, or even a rescueman. I feel kind of sorry for you. Just stick to dragging hose, opening and closing nozzles. It requires no knowledge at all. The right jake for the right job, I always say."

"Well," retorted Rick, "as I always say, Donald, stick this Tower up your ass. You jerks look wonderful on TV, trying to position this glorified crane so you'll look pretty on the evening news. Meanwhile, some poor hoseman is laying on his belly on a line in a hallway, knockin' the shit outta the fire."

This particular argument has been going on since a caveman threw a bucket of water on the guy who discovered fire, and will continue until there are no more jakes. The truth is that none of the specialties performed by the various companies at a fire will succeed without the contribution of the others. Without adequate forcible entry and proper ventilation, the efforts of the hosemen may not succeed. Similarly, opening up and providing access may contribute to fire extension unless the hose lines and water can be properly placed in a timely fashion. Jakes respect their counterparts on other companies—but they never admit it.

As a matter of fact, the competition between companies is a major part of the aggressiveness that results in a successful fire attack. First due engine and ladder companies feel disgraced if other units beat them to the scene, and when it happens, the winners always manage to look smug and forgiving. However, one thing is certain, there'll always be a next time, so you can't get too complacent.

When Rick and Donald backed the apparatus into quarters, it was time for lunch so they washed up and joined the other jakes in the mess hall.

"Nice goin', you twerps," said Frank Sheehan from Rescue One. "You two ass-kissers are out front in the cold makin' the rest of us look like goofs."

"Well," said Rick, "you are a goof. We're tryin' to enhance the image of this group and we really have nothing to work with. But we'll keep tryin', right Donald, old pal?"

Donald chuckled as he looked around the room. This kind of banter was endless; it created the clubhouse atmosphere he loved. He now understood the fire department would be altogether different without the characters that comprised its membership. In spite of the constant complaints about how overworked they are and how many responses they make, firefighters in every fire company in the country still spend more time in quarters than on the road, so boredom could be a real problem. But not around here, he reflected.

Look at them. There's Frank Sheehan, known to everyone as "Snot" because of his constantly running nose. He gets pissed off about twice every tour of duty because someone's always riding him about something, but he can't stay mad for long and he's as good an auto mechanic as there is. If he's not in the kitchen or the bunkroom, he's probably under someone's hood in the garage beneath the main floor.

"Dot-head" Doherty—the guy with the mole in the middle of his forehead. He usually starts all the arguments, but he can sing like an angel and entertained us over the P.A. system when we worked Christmas Eve.

"Gap" Keefe has that space between his teeth, a great sense of humor and is a terrific worker at a fire.

"Brows" Brennan, the Cro-Magnon man, who does all the cooking, never smiles and loses at cards. One of a kind.

Steve Tucker drives the Tower like it's a Volkswagen; he can get it anywhere and put it anywhere. Only reason I'm the operator this week is because the lieutenant makes us all take a turn for the experience. But Steve's the best, and when the rest of us complete our periodic turns at the wheel, he's the man.

Mark Palmer—now there's a character. Been on the job thirty years, got that flowing white mustache and hair that make him look like a jake from the last century...but he's still showing me tricks at every fire.

Arthur Hall—aka "Monty" after the host of "Let's Make a Deal." He's always setting up trips to somewhere. Without him we'd never have made it to Disney.

The guys on the other companies too. Captain Hardy, Walter Timmons and Vinnie Sterlings on Rescue 1. Lieutenant Grimes and Jerry Nagle on Engine 10, and also, of course, my pal, Rick.

All different individuals who contribute to the success of the entire group.

But my favorite is Lieutenant Joe Desmond. The guy is a natural leader. Sure, he participates in all the nonsense and pranks that take place in the house, but when he drills us or gives us orders at fires, he's all business. The other stuff is for playtime. Firefighting is what we were hired for and no one understands that fact better than Lieutenant Desmond. Sometimes when a fire's knocked down and he's showing you how it extended or his theory on how it started, it can get a little stale—particularly when you've worked your ass off, which is usually the case when he's in charge. But, if you start to drift away, he'll growl, "Hey, nitwits, pay attention here. I'm trying to keep you alive for those unfortunate women who married you."

The few times Donald had exchanged tours of duty with members on other work groups or been detailed to other firehouses, he had come to realize that the people he worked with are far from unique, even though they think they are. Each group and each house has its own cast of characters with their own nicknames and their own conviction that they're the best in the city. If you don't think so, just look at the various units' T-shirts with their distinctive, individual designs and slogans that have flourished throughout the department, and around the country. Fire buffs, sparks and visitors who stop into firehouses in any district are always provided with the opportunity to return home with shirts proclaiming "The Big House—Huntington Avenue Express", "Broadway", "Grove Hall", "The Hill to the Bury", or a score of other slogans.

While each house has its own salesman, they all get their supply from Mark Palmer. Not only can he get you as many shirts as you need, he has access to some guy in Bangkok who will develop the most fierce looking designs, shoulder patches and symbols you could desire. Mark has established a thriving business as a vendor at various fire expositions in the northeast and along the eastern seaboard. So, if you can't manage to get to Boston to pick up your shirts, if you're a true fire buff, you'll run into him at one of these shows. His modest objective is to have every fire service aficionado in the country proudly displaying a shirt with a dramatic scene of the Boston Tower Unit battling a massive conflagration against all odds. By a strange coincidence, the jakes in the bucket at this disaster have long flowing mustaches and white hair.

As they were leaving the kitchen area, Lieutenant Desmond told Donald to report to his office. "OK, Luft, I'll be right in. I just have to put away some gear." He whistled softly as he strolled down the corridor and into the area set aside for the jakes personal gear storage, washroom and toilets. He opened the door of his spacious locker and started hanging up the freshly pressed work clothes he'd brought from home. As he did so, he spied his notebook on the top shelf. I better make an entry for Boylston Street before I forget.

On the recommendation of Captain Murray and Deputy Simpson, who had retired a few months ago, Donald made an entry in the book for every working fire, multiple alarm or unusual incident to which he responded. They had advised him if he didn't do so right from the beginning, then after a while he wouldn't be able to recall what happened where or when. Good advice, he mused, but I don't think I'll ever forget Boylston Street.

His mouth formed into a faint smile as he walked toward the lieutenant's room. Lieutenant. Nice title. Just like in the Corps. Only thing is, no one on the job here ever calls them that. Everyone calls the commissioner by his title, and you'd better not call deputies, chiefs and captains anything but what they are. But lieutenants? They're called either "Loo" or "Luft." Donald could reason the Loo all right, but Luft? He asked around when he first heard the nickname, but no one seemed to know, including the lieutenants themselves. One jake said he thought the term came along when the World War II vets got on the job back in 1945. A lot of them had served with the British in Europe, and their lowest ranked officers are Leftenants. Donald thought it was a stretch to get to luft from there, but until someone offered a more reasonable explanation, it would work for him.

Donald knocked on the door to the office, swung it open and said,

"Hi, Luft," chuckling as he entered.

"Yeah, Donald, sit down," Desmond said and waved at the wooden spoked captain's chair next to his desk. "How was Disneyworld? Last I saw of you was at the hospital after the fire."

"Disney was super, sir. Everything Monty Hall told us was right. I'm not sure who had a better time, my daughter or my wife and I. One thing I know, it won't be our last trip down there."

"Great, glad you had a good time. How ya feelin'? I thought you might still be kinda beat up from the job we had."

"No, sir. I was pretty stiff for a couple of days, but once I got down in that sunshine and warm water, all the aches and pains disappeared."

"OK, but I want to know how you feel mentally. Anything botherin' you? Do you want to talk to Billy O'Laughlin or the psychologist? I guess I want to know what your reaction is to the fire. You're a new jake and it was quite an experience for you, but it was for the rest of us too."

Donald felt a sense of relief pass through his body. To hear Desmond say the fire was a big deal made him feel much less apprehensive. The fire had occurred shortly before the Disneyworld trip and it happened to be on the day Donald and the rest of his drill class were automatically elevated from rookies—knows as "ffops" for fire fighters on probation—to permanent fire fighters. It was a fifth alarm in a vacant building on Boylston Street and was complicated by the presence of several homeless people, some of whom were above the fire on the upper floors. In the course of the rescue attempts, one victim and two fire fighters were trapped on the fifth floor, and one of the jakes was wedged into a collapsed area of the floor.

With tremendous difficulty, Desmond and his crew, including Donald, eventually managed to reach them. As they were attempting to exit the area, Donald and one of the jakes collapsed while carrying the injured member. Desmond and Gap Keefe managed to hold back the fire with a charged line of hose. When additional assistance arrived, they got everyone out safely, but Donald and the other two jakes were hospitalized.

Donald's stay was brief, his miraculous recovery attributed to a great fear of having to cancel the Disney trip and then facing the penetrating stares of his wife, Gena, and daughter, Nancy, who had just finished packing. The fire was tough, but they would be tougher.

"To tell you the truth, Luft, " Donald answered, "I was kind of shook up the first night I got home from the hospital. I'm really glad to hear you say it was an experience for you guys too. My first thoughts were that maybe this stuff happens all the time, but as I analyzed it in my mind, I guess I knew that's not true." He looked at his lieutenant before he continued. "But you know what impressed me most of all, and took away all my fears?"

"No," said Desmond, "tell me."

"It was the fact that I realized how this job works. You had us do everything humanly possible to get to the victim and those trapped jakes. There was never any thought of giving up. And then as I reviewed the operation in my own mind when I finally got home, I understood that you and Gap would never have left us lying on the floor there. You would have died with us before you would ever abandon us." Donald shook his head. "No, Luft, I don't need any psychologist this time around. Maybe sometime in the future...but for now, I know where I belong. It's right here."

Desmond patted Donald on the shoulder and shook his hand as he said, "Kid, I think you're gonna do just fine. Go write in your notebook."

As Donald sat on the bench in front of his locker, flipping the pages of his journal, he could hear a box striking faintly over the department radio. The first alarm response of the Tower Unit includes most of the fire alarm boxes in Fire District Three whose borders cover most of downtown Boston as well as the Charlestown section of the city. Donald's firehouse is located on the southern edge of the district; consequently, the unit is also dispatched into several boxes in the high value area of the adjoining Fire District Six across the Fort Point Channel in South Boston.

Boxes are struck over both the radio and a wire system to each firehouse where a member on house patrol records them. If any of the companies in the station are assigned to respond on the initial alarm, the jake on watch hits the master control switch on the panel in the patrol desk. This turns on the emergency lights in the building, sounds a continuous whooping alarm and opens the overhead doors. The jake then announces the box number and the location and dashes for his or her company, donning turnout gear and mounting the apparatus.

The Tower also has a number of first alarm assignments to specific high-rise buildings in other districts when a box is struck for an actual fire. The first alarm boxes the unit responds to are in the 1200, 1300, 1400, 1500, 1600, 7100 and 7500 series. So, if Box 1234 is struck, it sounds a series of blows to identify the number. One blow, space, two blows, space, three blows, space, four blows, equals 1234. This series is repeated once. The Fire Alarm dispatcher at the central station then announces the building location of the fire over the radio as follows: "Attention, Box 1 2 3 4 has been struck for a building fire at 300 Commercial Street."

The Tower unit, because it is the only aerial platform in the department, is also dispatched to any working fire or multiple alarm in the entire city. The reason for this response is that if the fire becomes of such proportions as to require the heavy stream attack the unit can deliver from the enclosed platform attached to its nine-five foot height, it is prudent to have it en route in the early stages of a serious fire for proper placement.

The first alarm response to an actual building fire in any section of the city is three engine companies, two ladder companies, one heavy duty rescue company, one district chief and, in the high value area, a safety chief and a deputy chief who is the division commander. When a unit at the scene reports a working fire, this brings an additional engine and truck, plus the Tower, the safety chief and the division commander if they are not already at the scene. A second alarm brings another district chief, two engines, and a truck, so the total number of units at any second alarm is six engines, four trucks, one heavy duty rescue company, one Tower Unit, four chief officers, and auxiliary units that would include an air supply unit, lighting plant, apparatus maintenance unit and a Fire Investigation team.

The Boston Fire Department uses a nine alarm response system, so that orders for additional alarms beyond the second alarm response could eventually result in a total of thirty fire companies and about a hundred-fifty personnel, but fires of this magnitude are infrequent.

The box Donald counted striking as he was about to make his entry was in the 3000 series, so he knew it wasn't a first alarm for the Tower. Donald began making his record of the Boylston Street fire in his notebook. He had a slip of paper with some data he had already gathered, so entered, "2/10/92, Box 1535, 0158 hours. Boylston Street, five alarms. Weather clear, temp. 26 deg. F." Before he could continue, the speaker in the locker room crackled and the jake on patrol announced, "That box they just struck, 3 6 4 8, Fire Alarm says they're gettin' a lot of calls." Donald put his journal back on the shelf, closed his locker and walked over toward the pole hole. He didn't have long to wait. He could hear the district chief in Fire District Eight reporting at the scene: "Car Eight to Fire Alarm." "Go ahead, Car Eight," answered the Fire Alarm operator. "We have a working fire at Box 3648," said the district chief. Donald wrapped his arms and legs around the brass pole and slid towards the main floor. When he landed he dashed towards the Tower Unit, kicking off his shoes, stepping into his boots, putting on his helmet and sliding into his fire coat as he climbed into the driver's side of the apparatus. He could hear a second alarm striking over the tapper as he started the truck. Lieutenant Desmond was standing on the running board, looking back to make certain the other crew members were on the piece. As the officer sat down he said "OK, Donald. It's in District Eight. Get right on the Expressway. Sounds like the rear porches of some three deckers."

Donald turned the unit to the right as they reached Purchase Street from the apron. They moved through the intersection with Congress Street, the green light on the traffic signal clearing the traffic ahead of them. He maneuvered onto the down ramp and into the South Station underpass, picking up speed as the electronic siren wail bounced off the walls of the tunnel.

The overhead rotating and blinking lights also helped to clear a path through the moderate traffic. During rush hour, the Expressway is usually the world's longest parking lot, but fortunately, it was a little early for the suburbanites to start their daily exodus, so the Tower's progress was rapid.

They quickly broke out into the sunshine and moved along the elevated roadway toward the Mattapan-Dorchester districts. The journey would be about six miles, but soon after they climbed to the top of the roadway, they could see a huge cloud of black smoke in the distance to their right. Car 8 ordered a third alarm and reported the fire was extending via rear porches to adjacent three deckers. The chief expanded his evaluation by describing the origin as the first floor rear of enclosed porches of a duplex three decker with extension to both sides of the unit. The fire had now jumped across a narrow alleyway into a building of identical size.

Three deckers are constructed entirely of wood and usually contain a minimum of seventeen rooms, housing three different occupancies. They are also described as "three families" because that was the purpose of their construction when they were built to house the many thousands of immigrants who arrived in Boston in the late nineteenth century. The last triple deckers were built in 1917. Since then most of them have been remodeled many times; consequently, firefighting is usually complicated by dropped ceilings, vertical openings due to the addition of electricity and heating systems, remodeled bathrooms and kitchens, and a variety of other alterations. Some of the structures still retain piping inside the walls that was used for gas lighting fixtures, and occasionally illuminating gas is still retained inside the system.

One positive feature of three deckers, however, is that they were erected at a time when labor and materials were inexpensive, so they were sturdily constructed and seldom collapse unless the fire is overwhelming. They also have thirty or more windows, which permit fire fighters to provide adequate ventilation during operations.

The rear porches are supported with solid beams and matched wood flooring and four foot high pickets around the perimeter. When they are enclosed, they become all-weather sun porches that have been used as living spaces in recent years as property has become more expensive.

Some three deckers also have front porches, but these contain hollow round beam supports that are subject to early failure when fire travels inside the posts.

Duplex three deckers are two units joined together for a total of at least thirty-four rooms. Since the fire had already extended to an adjacent duplex of similar size and construction, the potential for a conflagration was a factor the chief had to consider.

When the division commander arrived, he reported the fire had jumped across the street to 34 Fessenden Street and ordered another box to be struck for that incident. The locations were now 19-21-23 and 34 Fessenden in the Mattapan district.

Lieutenant Desmond directed Donald to take Gallivan Boulevard as they exited the Expressway and kept leaning toward the radio as they approached the fire area, seeking specific orders for his company. Gallivan Boulevard merged with Morton Street and this wide thoroughfare permitted Donald to pass the traffic that was clogging badly as smoke darkened the sky, driven by the high winds blowing it horizontally through the streets. As they approached Norfolk Street, about a dozen blocks along Morton, they could see a chief's aide, waving his light at them. He jumped up beside Desmond and said, "Luft, the deputy wants you to go in the rear, on Mildred Ave. Take a hand line off anyone, run it through the alley and into the one on your right, from the back."

"The one it's extending to now?" Desmond asked.

"Yep. Try to hold it there. The deputy's gettin' more help for all the exposures."

Swinging right into Mildred Avenue, they could see the original building was now fully involved with jakes operating outside streams. The next duplex, the one they were assigned to, had fire showing from half its rear porches and from the top floor windows. Donald heard a sixth alarm striking on the radio as he cautiously moved the apparatus along the street, Desmond urging him as close as possible until they were directly behind the involved structures.

"All right, Donald, here's what I want you to do. Get into position so we can swing the bucket between these two buildings." He pointed at two three deckers with a ten foot wide alley between them. "Don't set the jacks or anything, just get in position. If we cut the fire off before it gets over here, we won't need the piece, but you never know."

He shouted to the rest of the crew, "Get a big line off Engine Twenty-four," he pointed to the fire engine directly in front of the Tower. Desmond dashed down the alley, climbed up on a fence and then came racing back. "Eight lengths," he yelled to his crew who were pulling hose from the back of the pumper. "Donald," he said, "once you get set, help Twenty-four's pump operator hook up. Then grab an axe, rake and Halligan bar and follow the line till you find us."

Donald maneuvered the truck until he thought it would be usable if the fire extended. He climbed up on the turntable and could see beyond the fence. The main fire building was blocked from his vision by the building on his immediate left, but directly ahead of him, he could see a duplex three decker with fire eating through all the porches closest to the original fire and flames spreading into the adjoining one.

Beneath him he could see Gap Keefe with a line of 2 1/2" hose draped over his shoulder and nozzle attached. He was followed by Mark Palmer and Steve Tucker, each with part of the line looped over their shoulders, moving rapidly toward the fence. Lieutenant Desmond had taken a small extension ladder, separated it into two parts and placed one on each side of the fence. He waved the crew forward and they disappeared over the fence, with a jake from another company feeding more line to them.

Donald secured the apparatus, ran over to Twenty-four's pump and the operator waved to him. "Gonna break it right here," he said, indicating two couplings joined together. The jake grabbed the female end while Donald held the male firmly. Twenty-four's member spun the threads until the pieces separated, took his end and connected it to a male outlet next to the pump panel. "OK, I'm all set! Thanks, kid," he said to Donald. "Your officer will call me on the radio when he wants water. You can take off now." Donald could see three other lines, already charged, extending from the pump, as well as the four inch charged feeder line he had passed while driving into position.

As he ran back to the Tower, it struck him just how important that one pump was at this fire. He glanced back at the hydrant on the corner, saw the connected line and quickly figured the four lines would be providing a thousand gallons per minute to help control the fire. That's a big deal.

He grabbed his mask, quickly flipped the cylinder over his head and slid his arms into the shoulder straps, buckling on the waist belt. He gathered the tools Desmond wanted and walked quickly down the alley, clambered over the ladders and followed the flat hose line as it disappeared up a short flight of wooden stairs into the right rear entrance of the three decker directly in front of him. He was being hit with water from overhead and as he looked up, he realized it was coming from a small, lightweight, portable heavy stream appliance operating in the yard to his left. The front shields on the jakes' helmets read "Engine 48". Donald paused to see what they were doing and understood that they were sweeping the small gun back and forth, first hitting the fully involved rear porches of the original fire building and then the one he was going to enter, trying to cut down the radiated heat and prevent extension across the yards.

As soon as Donald entered the doorway, the sound from above was deafening—a combination of shouting voices, breaking glass, doors being forced, and somewhere the pounding of hose streams. He knew his own crew had climbed up the narrow, winding stairway to his immediate left, and he could see the hose was still flat so he trudged upward, following the line and bending lower as the smoke thickened the higher he went.

At the third floor level he could see the splintered door and knew that was one of the sounds he'd heard. He shouted, "Tower company, where are you?" He heard a voice he thought must be Desmond's, although it was muffled by a gas mask facepiece. "In here, Holden. Follow the line." Donald dropped to his knees, straddled the hose, removed his helmet, put on his facepiece, sucked in the fresh air and replaced the headgear. As he did so, the flat line suddenly swelled into a hard circular one. He found himself in a room that must be a kitchen because he bumped into a stove.

He heard air rushing from the nozzle and then the sound of water hitting a solid surface as he collided with a jake kneeling on the floor. Donald shouted, "It's me—Holden." The guy in front of him said, "Good, we need a rake." Donald squirmed past and the lieutenant, who was standing erect said, "OK, kid, stand up and punch into the ceiling directly overhead." Donald pushed the tool, whose head is shaped like a shepherd's hook, as hard as he could into the plaster. It broke through easily and a shower of sparks dropped from the overhead. "Keep goin', keep goin'!" shouted Desmond. "Move towards the back, towards the porches." Donald hooked onto the laths above the plaster and pulled them, three at a time, causing large chunks of the ceiling to crash onto them. Another jake—he thought it was Gap Keefe—was punching holes with the Halligan bar into the ceiling above the wall adjoining the other side of the duplex. The fire was intensifying above them, but Desmond urged them to keep pulling. The stream from their line was driving out into the enclosed porch, hitting large volumes of fire, with Steve Tucker and Mark Palmer swinging the nozzle from side to side.

The heat inside grew more intense and finally Desmond told Donald and Gap to drop to the floor. When they did, the stream was now directed up above them, driving into the burning roof beams overhead. The smoke thickened even more, but it felt somewhat cooler. Desmond said, "Keefe, Holden, Palmer, get in the next room quick and get the ceiling. Take it all the way from side to side." The three jakes half crouched, entered a long hallway leading to the front of the building and turned to their left at the first doorway. They bumped into a large round table and figured it was probably a dining room. Reaching the partition adjoining the kitchen, Donald drove his rake upward again and more sparks dropped onto his arms. Gap retraced his steps, then Donald could hear him yelling, "Yep, it's in here, Luft." Donald kept pulling, moving deeper into the building and still feeling the heat overhead.

Desmond appeared with the line, turned to Gap and said, "Keefe, get on the pipe with Tucker." The officer then crouched down, pressed his radio remote microphone and said, "Tower to Car Eight." He was answered promptly by the district chief. "Chief, we're on the top floor, left side of the second duplex. Fire on the rear porch and at least two rooms heading towards the front. Could use another line and a truck."

Car Eight replied, "OK, it'll be a couple of minutes. There's fire under you on the second floor, but we've got a line in there. Get you help as soon as possible. Keep me informed."

Desmond acknowledged the message, then said, "Gap, take a break. Give your tool to Steve," nodding toward Tucker. "Go down that stairway we came up and see how they're doin' underneath us." He dropped his hand on Donald's shoulder as he said, "Gimme your rake and take the line for a while."

Donald squatted on the floor with both arms wrapped around the hose and one hand on the nozzle control, waiting for orders to open the line. Desmond, Tucker and Palmer worked as a team, opening more and more of the ceiling. When they reached the circular, decorative plaster design centered in the middle of the ceiling, they could see no more fire, but they kept going until they had exposed a couple of more feet of the overhead.

Desmond dropped down beside Donald: "OK, pal, open it up!" Donald slowly pulled back on the lever as they had taught him in drill school, and, with Desmond leaning against him for support, drove the solid stream upward, moving it back and forth, the water hitting the wood and coming back down on them much warmer from the intensity of the fire.

Gap appeared in the doorway and said, "They got it cut off right below us. Got a lot of work left to do there, though." Desmond stood up, shined his light upward and said, "I'm pretty sure we got most of this. Gotta get some windows." He had Donald adjust the nozzle lever to reduce the force of the stream and said, "Keep hitting it. We'll move back in the kitchen in a coupla minutes." The crew moved rapidly toward the front, opening windows as they went, including the outside storm windows, pulling down from the top and up from the bottom.

When Desmond was sure they had cut off the extension of the fire towards the front, he had everyone move the line back through the kitchen and play into the enclosed porch, most of which had been consumed from the intensity of the flames that had spread across and upward from the adjoining building.

Donald could see a stream playing outward from that portion of the structure as well as hear water coming from below. The smoke was now rapidly turning to steam and they were joined by an engine and truck company that had come up from the first floor via the front stairs. "The deputy told us to relieve you, Tower," the officer of the truck company said. "He wants you to take a look at the roof and then report to him in the street."

There was a small scuttle over the rear stairway with a short wooden staircase that could be lowered by a cleated rope to provide access from the interior. The scuttle had been opened by laddermen early in the fire and helped to clear out the smoke as the fire was controlled. The crew ascended to the roof, and the first thing Donald noticed was how much colder it had gotten since they first arrived. Desmond said, "It'll start turning to ice up here as soon as the fire cools down, so be careful."

With the axe, rake and Halligan bar they managed to cut a foot wide trench across the end of the building where it joined the porch and were able to determine that the inside hose stream had managed to hit all of the burning embers. Desmond spent a few minutes showing them how the fire had crossed over from the next building via the rear porch and the common side wall, how insidious it could be, coming through any opening and burning through heavy wooden beams without difficulty. He showed them how the operation had been conducted in the rear, pointing to the portable guns in the yard, the hand lines that had been used for more mobility in knocking down the heavy fire and protecting the buildings on the next street. Donald was interested to see there were even fire companies in the next building adjacent to their own that apparently hadn't been touched by the fire. Desmond explained that they were checking for any possible extension: "You can never be sure till you take a look. The time you get too casual and assume you've cut it all off is when you get a nasty surprise."

Next he took them to the front of the roof where they got a panoramic view that every chief would like to have when he arrived at a fire. They could see aerials raised to four different roofs and lines clogging the street and then extending into buildings on both sides. "Jeez, Luft, how many buildings were involved?" Donald asked.

"Looks like five," was the reply, "but they had to check out several others. With the wind and the flying embers, it can spread a long way." Desmond pointed to a two and a half story dwelling across the street from the building of origin. Donald could see portions of the sloping roof and the attic burned away. Jakes were throwing debris out of the narrow front window. An aerial rested against the pointed peak. "That's the place the fire jumped to. Probably radiated heat. A little longer and this could've been another Bellflower Street fire." Desmond was referring to a famous conflagration in the city three decades earlier in which over thirty of these types of structures on three different streets were wiped out one windy afternoon. The lieutenant explained the same potential is still a factor in certain neighborhoods. "Some of these areas, Donald, they're like lumber yards with people livin' in them, ya know!"

As they were looking downward, the division commander spotted them, waved to Desmond and yelled, "Nice job, Joe. Got you some help as soon as I could. Make up and go home. See ya at the next one."

Desmond touched the brim of his helmet in salute and said out of the corner of his mouth, "We're outta here. Let's go before he finds something else for us."

On Mildred Avenue he showed the crew why he wanted the Tower where Donald placed it. "See, we couldn't reach all the way across to the buildings, but if the fire got away we could elevate up until our gun could sweep about three or four structures. Remember, if we can get enough supply, we can throw a stream about the length of a football field." In the truck he said to Donald, "Put that in your notebook, kid. You always have to be tryin' to anticipate, even though it doesn't always mean a damn thing."

He directed Donald to turn onto Babson Street and then right on Blue Hill Avenue. This divided roadway runs from the Roxbury section of the city, through Dorchester to Mattapan and then into the town of Milton, across the Neponset River. The contrasts between the wealthy suburb and the Boston neighborhoods are significant. Milton has magnificent single family structures lining the parkway, erected a half century ago by upper middle class people who left the city for a more placid life. It's still quiet there in the evening, although nowadays everyone has exotic burglar alarm systems, floodlit yards and roaming private guards to provide them with a sense of well being and security.

The reasons for their concerns are not difficult to understand in today's society. On the Boston side of the river, the nights are substantially less quiet, with the sound of gunfire an every day and every night occurrence. Drugs are the major reason for the turmoil, just as in every other major city in the country. The people living in these three huge Boston neighborhoods would love to have the luxury of the protection their wealthier abutters enjoy, but that's not going to happen. The Boston cops are at least as effective as any other police force in the country, and just like their counterparts elsewhere, there are never enough of them to go around.

Along with all the murders, robberies and other crimes the narcotics trade brings, arson for revenge is another part of the urban plague the residents of these area must endure.

The sun was setting early on this winter afternoon, but as Donald drove along Blue Hill Avenue Desmond said, "Take a look around, Holden. We'll spend a lot more time out this way."

They crossed nearly a hundred intersecting streets along the length of "Blue" as the jakes who work in the area call the major artery. There was every imaginable type of residential and small business structure. Some of the buildings were occupied, some were vacant, and some showed the charred marks of past fires. Building heights ranged from one story blocks of stores to four and five story apartment houses, along with housing projects, schools and churches.

Desmond occasionally pointed down side streets to which they'd responded on multiple alarms, and he grinned as he saw the frown on Donald's face: "Jeez, kid, I'm probably givin' you the impression this is the worst place on earth. Believe me, it isn't. There's plenty of decent folks here who are trying to make good lives for themselves...but it's not easy out here today." He added that many of the minority jakes on the job live in the area, and they and their friends are determined to improve the quality of life. "Just by stayin' they're helpin' because they have good jobs, good incomes. They can fix up their houses, be like anchors in the neighborhood. The city's trying, too," he continued. "They've spent a lot of dough fixin' up the Franklin Park Zoo and the golf course. A dozen years ago, no white people would come out here at all, but now there's a lot of activity here on weekends in the good weather." As they passed through the Grove Hall section of Dorchester, Desmond concluded with, "The city just has to get a handle on crime...of course, so does the rest of the country."

By the time they arrived back in quarters, darkness had fallen and the temperature was dropping even more. Donald spotted his relief, Roscoe Kearns, standing just inside the main floor. He held a garden hose in his hands and motioned Donald to slow down as he was backing in the apparatus. He directed the water stream at the wheels, knocking off the accumulated ice and dirt as the equipment rolled deeper into the house. "Hey, Holden," he yelled up to Donald, a grin creasing his bright black face, "You put any dents in my baby?"

"No way, Roscoe. Was a piece of cake. How come you always told me this was a tough job?"

Donald was delighted he'd made it through the afternoon without whacking anything. It had been his biggest worry until the box struck. He was pleased when he realized he had not thought of it again until now. Not bad, he thought to himself. Not bad at all.

He pulled down his three-quarter length boots, stepped out of them and into the low cut work shoes he'd left on the main floor when responding. He thought back to when he first came on the job and how strange it looked when he arrived in quarters to find the apparatus was out at a fire. All that remained on the main floor were pairs of shoes lining both sides of the space where the fire engines were usually parked, deposited there haphazardly by the jakes when they donned their boots before responding to the alarm. In a way they looked quite funny—just shoes, everywhere; but in another way they looked ominous because the people who left them were in danger somewhere.

Donald shook off the emotion the memory evoked and approached the gear room, passing by the patrol desk enclosure. The jake on patrol was Jeff Stoler, a member of the Tower Company from the oncoming group. Stoler was a husky jake of average height who was in charge of the house fund, as well as being the cook for his work crew. He was also the company clown who did his best to keep the place in turmoil as often as possible. He would take elaborate measures to pull off some practical joke that would usually result in someone getting pissed off at him.

He bent over the public address microphone and announced, "Attention, attention, all members of the dead-ass Rescue Company One. The heroic Tower Company has returned from a disastrous six alarm fire out in the *other division*. You twerps who have been crapped out all afternoon should come down and welcome them back. They have been maintaining the image of this firehouse. Shit, even dry line Engine Ten made it out to the fire. Have you people *no* shame?"

Donald stood at the watch room doorway, waiting to hear the inevitable ring of the intercom phone as someone from upstairs called to reply to this insult. "Towerman Stoler answering," the big man said into the phone. Donald could hear a voice shouting over the line but couldn't decipher the message. Stoler replied, "Fire Fighter Timmons, you oughtta be ashamed using that kind of language to a brother member. Besides, I don't think I could physically accomplish what you're suggesting." He winked at Donald and chuckled as he hung up the phone.

Donald smiled as he entered the locker room. Stoler scores again, he thought. The jakes who worked with the comedian every day were well used to him and accepted his antics philosophically. However, those who saw him on a change of shift were much easier targets. He usually relieved his partner early in the afternoon of his night tour, probably just to irritate those members he didn't see regularly.

While Donald was storing his fire clothes, he heard the speaker once again: "Attention, attention. The following brave Towermen, who just returned from Disneyworld, Fire Fighters Keefe, Tucker, and Holden, report immediately to the patrol desk."

"What now?" Gap wondered.

The answer came promptly: "For the benefit of you members who did not have the opportunity to visit Florida with these four-flushers and remained here protecting the beautiful city of Boston, I have some disquieting information. These pricks haven't paid the house fund since they got back and have been sucking up coffee, peanut butter and jelly and other delicacies at your expense. That is all."

"Never quits, does he," Steve said. "Hear what he did at Mark's house while we were out of town?"

Besides having the T-shirt monopoly, Mark Palmer has a collection of fire service memorabilia in his home that is the envy of every fire buff in the country. He has shoulder patch collections from hundreds of fire departments in the United States as well as from Canada, Mexico, Europe and the Pacific rim. They are mounted in three huge glass frames on all four walls of his basement museum. He also has every type of nozzle, tool and helmet ever issued in the department—many of them liberated without the official knowledge of the leadership. At least one chief of department was startled to see his helmets from the rank of fire fighter through deputy mounted on a special stand when he visited Mark's house for a Christmas party. When he retired he sent Mark his last hat and a note stating, "Might as well complete the set, you crook."

Mark even had an antique fire engine—a hand operated pumper from the nineteenth century—which was his pride and joy. He kept the pumper in a small metal shed in the back yard just off the driveway. He frequently entered it in muster contests throughout New England during the summer months.

At the other side of the yard was a doghouse designed to resemble a Boston firehouse, equipped with a spring-raised overhead door which his dalmatian, Jake, was trained to operate.

"He had a bunch of these guys and their wives over for a Valentine's Day party. You know he loves to show off all his stuff. In his living room he's got a fire alarm box he permanently borrowed that's in working condition." Tucker grinned. "Usually, first time visitors pull the box and it strikes the signal and it's a lot of fun—for a while. Pretty soon though, the noise becomes a pain in the ass and that's the end of it." He shook his head. "Not with our boy Stoler, though. The asshole kept pulling it and pulling it all through the evening, naturally getting everyone pissed off. Finally, his wife—who has got to be a saint to have stayed with the nitwit this long—gave him the stare."

"What's that?" Donald asked.

"Well, when Helen's had enough, she has this look that could penetrate steel and when she aims it at Jeff, he gets as quiet as a mouse. He told me once he can feel it through his back if she's behind him and he immediately shuts up and sits down. So, she gives him the look and things went along OK after that. They all had dinner and were having a few drinks, looking at the hundreds of fire pictures Mark's collected through the years. Of course, any that he's in himself are in a special book. You gotta get over there to realize how often he gets his face in front of a camera. With that goofy mustache of his covered with snots, he looks like a jake from Hollywood central casting. If they'd ever shot that movie *Backdraft* in Boston, he'd've probably got an Oscar."

"Hey, Stevie Boy," Gap said, "will you finish the fuckin' story! My relief's in and I gotta take a shower. What's the fuckin' punch line?"

"Yeah, yeah, OK. Well, Jeff disappears for a few minutes and then, just as everyone's getting ready to go home, he dashes into the living room, pulls the box and the alarm starts sounding again. Naturally, everyone starts yellin' at him, callin' him a stupid bastard, and Helen is warming up the stare, but Stoler screams, 'What's the matter with you jerks? When there's a fire, you pull a box, right? Look out the window!'

"So they do and they see that the metal shed with Mark's pumper's engulfed in smoke and the dalmatian's running in circles because his house was smoking too. Mark almost jumps through the window and everyone runs for the yard, a couple of jakes grabbing the garden hose attached to the rear wall outlet."

"Don't tell me he really set a fire!" Donald pleaded.

"Naw, he's bad but not crazy. He got a couple of those bombs they use to make smoke down at the drill school and set them off. He planned the whole thing as soon as he got the invitation."

"He really is nuts," Donald said. "Bet Mark is still bullshit at him."

"Not really. Stoler tipped him off first. Didn't want him to have a heart attack or something. But one thing he forgot was Helen. I guess that stare is starting to look permanent. The joke was a success but his love life is down the tubes. Gonna cost him big time to get back in the big bed!"

Donald got home just after the six o'clock news had ended and he was peppered with questions about the fire by his daughter Nancy. She wanted to know how many people lost their homes, did any of them get hurt, but most of all, did any fire fighters get injured and was he all right. This was his first shift since his own injury during the Boylston Street fire, and Nancy looked a little haunted as she recalled seeing him in the hospital.

"Well, honey, it was a big fire. But no one got hurt at all. I'm fine and so are all the firemen." He smiled at her and then said, "We don't get banged up all the time. Those pictures make it look worse than it really is, sweetheart." She smiled but didn't look convinced.

Later, after she had finished her homework and he kissed her good-night, he joined Gena on the couch in the living room. He slid his arm around her shoulder and she leaned against his chest. They sat that way for a while, the stereo softly playing one of her favorite CDs, a collection of music box romantic classics that Gena claimed relaxed her completely. Sometimes they make her romantic as well, Donald thought, but tonight doesn't seem to be one of those times. He could feel that she was pretty tense and finally he said, "What's the matter, hon? The music didn't work the magic?"

She looked up at him: "Oh, Donald, I don't know...I don't know."

"Don't know what, Gena?"

"About you and that job," she said, then she started sobbing.

He was startled and squeezed her closer. "Jeez, Gena, I-uh...I love the job. I wouldn't want to do anything else."

"I know that's how you feel, Donald, but it's, it's oh so damned dangerous." She continued. "Nancy feels the same way I do. This afternoon when she got home from school she saw a bulletin about the fire on Channel Four and knew you were working so she started worrying and I wasn't home from work. Mrs. O'Connor told me she said a couple of prayers with her."

Gena worked as a computer analyst for a company in the Back Bay; Mrs. O'Connor, the elderly widow who lived upstairs in their two family house, took care of Nancy after school until one of the parents arrived home. The arrangement usually was wonderful for everyone. Gena's folks lived on the North Shore, some thirty miles from Boston, and Donald's mother and father died when he was very young, so Nancy hadn't much exposure to grandparents. Mrs. O'Connor was a terrific surrogate and the two of them had developed a warm relationship. The house was mortgage free, since Donald had inherited it from his Uncle Frank, so the child-watching chores served as a form of rent. The Holden family's friendship with Mrs. O'Connor had grown over the years, which is an essential factor for occupants of these old multi-story, multiple residences in the heart of the city.

Donald worked the next night and was relieved on house patrol by Gap Keefe at midnight. Instead of going to the bunkroom, however, he stayed in the patrol area and talked with Keefe about his concerns for Gena and Nancy. "I mean, Gap," he said, "I love the job, but I can't stand having them worrying about me. Gena's able to deal with her fears rationally—most of the time—but the poor kid is having a tough time."

Gap, who usually spent more time laughing during his tours of duty than anyone else, swiveled his seat from the desk and looked seriously at Donald: "Yeah, I know whatcha mean. Marion and I went through the same deal when I first came on." He frowned, then continued. You met my two kids down Disney. Well, my boy, little Freddie, thinks I'm Superman or somethin'. But, my girl, Debbie, she useta worry all the time, just like your kid."

"What'd you do about it?"

"Well, if it was up to me I'd a probably done nothin'. But Rachel, she's got all the smarts in the family and she called Billy O'Laughlin."

"You mean the lieutenant with the E.A.P.?" Donald asked.

"Yeah. He not only came to my house and talked to everyone, he even introduced us to his own wife and kids." Gap began to smile. "The guy's got a way about him that I can't explain. It's like talking to a priest or somethin', but not, you know, not exactly. He seems to rationalize the job and life and all kinds of stuff in a way that we all could understand. My daughter loves him and she never even seems to mention the job anymore, except when we're doin' a Christmas party, or Disney or somethin' that's got nothin' to do with fires."

Gap went on to explain that O'Laughlin, like many people in programs like the Boston Fire Department's Employees Assistance Program, had returned from Vietnam with a substance abuse problem and probably would have been just another permanent casualty of that eight year horror show except for his determination to get on the fire department. He realized he was unacceptable unless he got clean. the local AA chapter turned his life around and helped him achieve his goal.

After he was appointed, he served for several years on one of the busiest engine companies in the city. While he loved being an active fire fighter and going to fires, he was troubled by the number of jakes he saw who needed the same kind of help that had saved his life. Eventually, he and another guy with a similar background and similar concerns convinced the leadership of the department to start the Employees Assistance Program. In the years that followed, their program had become one of the finest of its kind in the fire service; in the Boston department, it created an atmosphere in which it was known that immediate help and support were always available for any jake and his or her family.

O'Laughlin was a much sought after speaker around the country and, along with one of his friends in Chicago, had helped to develop programs in several other states.

"Does he miss fire fighting?" asked Donald.

"Sure," replied Gap, "but he accepts it as part of what he thinks he owes the job. Hope he stays where he is for as long as I'm around. Give him a call, Donald. He's always available."

Two

Donald placed the copy of the General Orders on his bureau and opened the door of his closet. He removed his plastic wrapped uniform coat and pants and laid them across the bed. Yep, he thought, the time has sure whisked by since that night.

Just as Gap had predicted, Billy O'Laughlin had performed as advertised. The success of his accomplishments in the following months had made Donald's life much happier. Now, a few years later, not only did his Gena and Nancy accept the hazards of the job as a part of his and their lives, they had developed close relationships with the families of most of the jakes with whom Donald worked. Naturally, they still had their moments—especially whenever something serious took place—but they now had an outlook that helped them to cope. When the strain starts to show, just call Billy O'—like everyone else.

Donald had brought his journal home from work for this special day. The promotion ceremonies were scheduled for noon at headquarters, and he wanted to enter his thoughts later in the day while they were still fresh. He sat on the bed, flipping back though the pages and realized it wouldn't be long before he'd have to start Volume Two. Well, how about today, he thought. A new job and a new book.

He found his entry for the fire on Fessenden Street, which had really been the start of a new approach to the job for himself and his family. Look at the variety of jobs since then! When he saw them all written down, he realized he'd responded to a significant number of fires since that day. Of course, his records didn't include any one alarm incidents that the unit normally responded to because there were hundreds of them annually, and many times they were relatively minor. Also, even some of the extra alarm fires were just listed without much comment because the Tower crew frequently performed axe, rake and overhauling duties. Donald came to realize that these types of chores are what jakes do at every fire, and while they contribute greatly to the learning process, they become quite routine. Funny thing, he reflected, the spectators and the general public are never aware of these extremely arduous duties which result in so many injuries to fire fighters. The just see all those deck guns on the news programs. It was really his own view of firefighting until he came on the job. Now he had a much better understanding of what jakes meant when they said, "It ain't the big ones—it's those one room jobs that kill ya."

He slid his finger down through the various incidents, including working fires, second and third alarms in 1993. He paused at a lengthy entry in April and had no difficulty recalling that major incident: "4/22—Box 1662, 6 alarms, District 5/ Roxbury. 1649 hours. Washington Street. 5 story, brick and wood, vacant, posted building. 3rd floor, rear bedroom, extended through 3rd, 4th 5th and roof. Partial collapse, 5th floor, rear."

Donald smiled as he examined his entry. It made him realize how valuable keeping his personal record was becoming. The notes really did give him instant recall of the event, even though it had happened over three years before. Captain Murray was correct. Write it down...write it down.

This building was once a well known hotel with stores on the first floor. It had been the scene of several fires over the years, and all the jakes in the district were very familiar with it. Some of them knew it enough to hate it.

A posted building is one marked with a white X centered on a red sign. Because of the size of the building, it was marked in several places. These are warnings to fire fighters not to conduct interior operations unless they have information that occupants are inside.

The fire started in the late afternoon, just as Donald's group was finishing its tour of duty; however, he'd agreed to work for Jeff Stoler on the night tour so he was at the scene for most of the night. This situation is referred to as a "long stand" and the incident helped him to understand the term's origin. Fortunately, the weather was moderate with the temperature above freezing, so the accumulation of ice on the building and in the streets was not a factor.

Donald was on patrol when the original alarm, Box 1662, was struck over the system at 1650 hours. The first company at the scene, Engine 3, reported smoke showing and Donald relayed the information over the P.A. system. Within a few minutes the chief of District 5 reporting a working fire and announced the fact that it was a posted building. Donald hit the house alarm and dashed for the apparatus, donning his gear and climbing into the passenger compartment.

All of the night crew had already relieved their partners, so Captain Dan Murray was the officer in charge, with Roscoe Kearns the driver, Nick Deliago and Monty Hall the other jakes besides Donald.

Their response was via the Expressway, exiting at Mass. Ave. En route, Donald could see immense clouds of black smoke showing over the tops of the Boston City and University Hospitals and Nick told him they had been to this location in the past. "Yeah, it's really an enormous, beat up old building, pretty dangerous too," he said. "You hear the chief tell everyone to stay out? Deck gun job." A second alarm was sounding as they passed the City Morgue at Harrison Ave., and Donald could hear the deputy, who had just arrived at the scene, directing the Tower to take position on the Massachusetts Avenue side of the structure. Captain Murray acknowledged the message, and then Donald heard the deputy ordering third and fourth alarms just as they were arriving at the incident.

As soon as Donald stepped down from the cab he could see why they needed so much help. From the fourth floor upward, heavy smoke was pushing out of every window opening and fire was already blowing outward from several windows on the third floor. Many of the windows had been covered over with plywood. While Donald was assisting in setting the jacks, he heard the district chief shout to the captain, "Dan, set up right where you are, but try to peel off the coverings before you use the gun."

Murray turned and said, "Nick, Donald, in the bucket. Take the saw, Halligan and axe." He pointed to Hall and said, "Come on. We'll get some line offa Three," and he indicated the pumper connected to the domestic hydrant at the intersection.

Roscoe Kearns elevated the ladder and bucket with Donald and Nick inside, rotating the unit so it could be lowered into the top floor area but away from the fire lapping out of the third floor. At the first boarded up window, they found out they didn't need the power saw to remove the plywood covering. The nails had deteriorated from oxidation over the years; simply by hooking the adz end of the Halligan and peen of the axe behind the splintered layers they could work their way around rapidly and remove the sheet. They called Roscoe to tell him they were dropping the covering and he told them it was clear below so they let it go.

The window was filthy and badly cracked, but they could see a glow through it. Nick pulled the six foot rake from its holder and swung it though the glass and framework, quickly making a three foot by two foot opening. The jakes could now see the glow was coming from the fire, which was visible in the corridor beyond the open door of the room they had vented. Nick pressed the intercom and shouted, "Roscoe, tell the captain we got plenty of fire on this floor. It's roaring in the hallway. Give us the controls, will ya?"

Kearns transferred the power from the turntable up to the pair in the bucket. They were then able to methodically go from window to window, removing the paneling, breaking the glass and venting the heavy smoke. They could see two ladder trucks, one at the front on Washington Street and one at the end of Mass. Ave., both with their 110 foot aerials raised to the roof. By monitoring the messages over their radio, Donald and Nick learned the roofmen had been ordered to ascend to a point opposite the roof and report the conditions they could observe. The message they gave indicated the fire was not only starting to come through beat up old skylights, it was also showing at some holes cut by jakes at previous incidents in the building.

Deck guns from pumpers in the street were starting to hit the fire beneath them on the third floor. While this caused visibility to deteriorate from the rising smoke the water created, it also protected them as they repeated their wood peeling activities on the fourth floor. When they removed the last one, Captain Murray told them he was bringing them down and Roscoe took over the controls, swung them out away from the building and lowered the aerial into the bed.

When they reached the street, Murray said, "Good job. We have to reposition the piece further across the avenue." He explained that the commissioner and the chief were getting very concerned that a major collapse could occur; they wanted their equipment at a distance where it would be safe from falling walls and debris, but still able to operate effectively on the fire. Fortunately, Mass. Ave. is a wide street with a divided roadway, a real luxury in the city. It was, therefore, possible to get the Tower some forty feet away and, with the ninety-five foot extension of the aerial, still place a powerful high pressure stream along much of the extensive side of the five story building.

Ladder pipes were also placed into operation on each side of them, as well as at the front of the building on Washington Street. Additional deck guns from pumpers were operated at their most advantageous positions. There wasn't the usual urgency to surround the building; it was obvious not much was going to be salvaged from the old structure. Lines could be somewhat carefully placed on the adjacent and adjoining rooftops, and members operating such equipment were relieved peiodically as the evening progressed.

Sometime during the night Donald had completed another period in the bucket, driving the stream from the gun into the heart of the still intense flames. At the street level, Captain Murray, who had been with him this time, took him and Nick on a tour of the fire area. "I want you to get a look at the overall scene," he said. "Ya don't get this kind of chance too often." First, they ascended the stairway of the adjoining building to the left on Washington Street. When they reached the top floor, climbing over several charged big lines on the way up, he brought them into the various areas that butted up against the fire wall dividing the two buildings. In each of the large rooms was an engine company with a line, a ladder company with rakes pulling down large areas of the ceiling, and a district chief directing the operation. As at every fire where there was a lot of overhead work, the truckies were filthy, covered with plaster dust, rat feces, cork insulation and splinters of wood laths. Murray explained that initially the companies had poked through several small openings to see if the fire was crossing over, even though the fire wall was designed to prevent such extension. In this case, as in many others, sure enough the fire had broken through cracks in the ancient brick and cement plaster, igniting the roof boards from underneath.

Once that happened, the chiefs required wide areas of the overhead to be opened up vertically and horizontally so the extension could be contained and to insure that no fire skipped along the beams into other sections.

The floors underneath the top also had to be checked but without the same immediacy as the highest one because the construction features make it less likely that the fire will extend rapidly at those locations.

Donald was looking at the helmet shields in the various rooms. Sure were plenty of companies here. He saw jakes from Engines 14, 37, 33, 42, and yeah, there was 10 from his own house. Truckies were from 4, 26, 18 and 15. He knew more companies were in other sections. Six alarms brings a big crowd, he thought, but when you're busy yourself, you're not even aware of it.

As they headed for the stairway to the roof, a truckie from Ladder 4 yelled, "Hey, Nick! Whynchu pricks give us some relief here! We're pooped. You shitheads just stay outside throwin' water at everything. If ya knew what ya was doin' we'd a been outta here by now."

Nick peered into the room until he could see who was talking, then said, "Well, well, my old friend the Pink Panther." He grabbed Ladder 4's officer by the arm. "Hey, Luft, how come he ain't off injured yet?"

The officer laughed: "Kinda early, Nick. Besides, he's my top man, right Edgar?"

"Definitely, Loo. You ain't got any better," came the reply.

Nick shouted again, "If you want, Edgar dear, I can you a job with T.J. Jensen and C.G. Green. This must be a real big fire 'cause they're out in the street checkin' the seating capacity.

As they moved up the stairway, Donald could hear a voice shouting in exasperation, "Fuck you, Deliago, and fuck them, too."

On the roof Captain Murray was laughing as he said, "Jeez, Nick, you got him again. Think he'd know better by now."

Donald asked what the hell was going on and Nick explained: "That poor bastard. He's really a great kid. I went to drill school with him. We could tell even then how easy it is to get his ass. And his name doesn't help either. Edgar Clouseau. So naturally they call him Inspector and Pink Panther just like Peter Sellers. But to make matters worse, he really is kinda clumsy. Works as hard as anyone but he's always gettin' hit on the head or somethin'. So the name fits pretty good.

"Who are those guys with the initials?" Donald asked.

Nick chuckled: "Those two assholes? They're not here. They'd never be this close to a fire."

"But who are they" Donald demanded.

"Coupla night club inspectors," Captain Murray said. "They only work nights, checkin' exits and overcrowdin' all around the city. Those jobs started way back after the Coconut Grove fire, back in 1942—496 people got killed."

"But what are the initials for, Nick?" Donald asked. "Knowing you, they must be something good."

"Sure! Tit-Job Jensen and Cardboard Giant Green. They're each about six foot-four, but chances are, you'll never meet them—and *never* at a fire."

"How'd they get those jobs?"

"Well, they met the most important qualifications for the positions."

"Which are what?" asked Donald.

"Which are that they reached the right politicians. The thing they really do best is campaign for elections."

"Are they officers or what?"

"Bullshit! No way," said Captain Murray, somewhat vehemently, his face reddening. "You don't get promoted here that way. Strictly Civil Service. Those two wouldn't open a book if you paid them."

On the roof the sound of gasoline powered saws was deafening. Donald peered through the dense smoke and saw jakes bent over, cutting through the roof covering along the fire wall. The trench they were creating was about three feet wide and he could see they were exposing some charred beams, still glowing where the fire had broken through the walls. Other jakes with hose lines were playing down into the original fire building. To the rear, across an alley, more companies were operating portable guns, directing their streams into the flames.

In spite of the massive attack continuing from all accessible sides and the roof, the intensity of the fire didn't appear to be diminishing. "Jeez, Cap," said Donald, "why isn't it going out? Looks like we're pouring gasoline on it."

"I know it. It's kind of frustrating. But that's how it is with an outside attack a lot of times. You can't get the water exactly where you want it. There's so many concealed spaces the streams just can't hit. But you hafta have patience. Eventually stuff will burn through and we'll get it. But it's going to take time in the old joint. Useta be a hotel, you know. Plenty of small rooms, each with four walls. The biggest thing the chiefs are watching for is a collapse. They're keepin' everyone away so no one gets hurt. But if some of it does drop, we'll get it a lot quicker."

Just as he finished speaking, a low but loud rumbling noise began, then was transformed into a ripping, tearing, crashing sound as sparks jumped skyward and smoke poured upward, driving the jakes on the roofs backward, away from the fire.

The rear section of the building, from the third floor through the roof, had dropped into the alleyway and out onto Mass. Ave. Murray immediately called the Tower on the separate channel they used to maintain contact and Roscoe Kearns answered promptly: "Everything's OK, Cap. Soon as we heard the rumble, I pulled the bucket away. Monty and a jake from Three were operating, but they were well clear." Murray told Roscoe that they were returning to the street and the trio descended the stairs, pausing to look down into the fire which was still boiling furiously but seemed much more accessible to the heavy streams now that a large section had burned through and dropped.

Nick and Donald took their turn in the bucket and were able to blast away with much more success than earlier; the ladder pipe streams were also extremely effective. About an hour later, the commissioner started reducing the size of the force at the scene, dismissing those units no longer deemed essential. Murray explained to Donald this would permit the release of the Mutual Aid assistance from the surrounding communities who were presently covering at Boston stations. Six alarms required Brookline, Cambridge, Quincy,

Needham, Newton and Somerville to provide such support for this location. "Of course, if it went up to nine alarms, we'd be getting a lot more help from outside. There's thirteen towns that border on Boston and a bunch more beyond, and they're all in the plan." Donald asked if those departments minded coming into the city. "Naw, the outside jakes love it. Gives them braggin' rights back home. The town governments don't complain much either. They know they get a lot more help from us than we get from them. Shit, we must send places like Chelsea about a hundred companies a year. They're so understaffed, they gotta get help on a working fire. Nope, the plan's OK. Only thing is, they never let the Tower leave town because we're the only one in the city."

"What do those other guys do if they need one?"

"Oh, some of them have their own and they share with each other a lot of times when we're not involved."

The release of so many units did not mean the Tower would be dismissed. Because of its unique capabilities, it was used for several more hours at the scene. The spare Tower, which was older but similar to the first line piece, was also brought to the fire by the Maintenance Division, and between the two units, the operation was reduced to a fire detail procedure in the early morning hours. This meant that fire companies who had not been engaged during the earlier stages were rotated in periodically to keep the streams operating, reduce the area that had to be roped off, and permit limited resumption of traffic so the approaching morning rush hour wouldn't result in gridlocking the district.

They were finally dismissed at 0300 hours, having spent over ten hours at the scene. It had grown somewhat colder during the night, and they were all grateful for the enclosed passenger compartments on the truck which surrounded them with heat that penetrated to their chilled bones.

"Big Job," Donald had noted in his journal, and it sure had been. He continued his review, dropping down to another entry in July, 1993: "7/18—Box 16-1573—2 alarms/ Dist. 4-Back Bay-2201 hours. Boylston Street, 22 story, 1st class—3 room apartment, 15th floor." Sure, this was an incident to remember, a definite keeper.

He had been detailed for a night tour to Engine Company 33 in the Back Bay section of the city. It was pretty exciting just to visit this famous firehouse. He had read about the structure in an architectural guide to Boston; the building was built in 1888 on the site of former wetlands to protect the newly created neighborhood in a rapidly growing city. The book called the firehouse "a classic example of the Romanesque revival influence"—whatever that is. Donald had seen the place many times, with its beautiful arched doorways, multi-colored stone and brick exterior and sharply pitched roof. Its location is just adjacent to the Prudential Center, the Hynes Convention Center, the Sheraton and Hilton Hotel complexes, and numerous high-rise apartment houses. Their immediate response area also includes hundreds of residences ranging from three to six stories in height, many of them with stores and commercial occupancies on the lower floors.

The firehouse was on Boylston Street, bordering Hereford, and during the Boston Marathon its side windows are jammed with visitors watching the runners as they make their final turn towards the finish line just a quarter of a mile away.

It's a densely populated and exciting area of the city; the jakes who are stationed on Engine 33 and Ladder 15 seldom request transfers to other companies. In the spring and summer months, the members can be found in the early evening at the front doorways, viewing with pleasure the constant stream of foot traffic that flows across the apron. Over the years, a few dates have been negotiated with the female students from the numerous college dormitories in the area, and a couple of these have ended in permanent arrangements. The soda machine outside the front entrance is a source of considerable revenue for the house fund, and many of those who stop by to chat with jakes often leave with dark blue T-shirts emblazoned with companies' logos. Yeah, it's a happy place, Donald thought.

About the only complaint the jakes have is the many needless responses they are required to make to malfunctions of alarm systems in the high-rise buildings; however, the number of actual fires they respond to makes up for these constant irritations. They are part of the fire protection in both Districts 4 and 5. These areas comprise the South End, Back Bay and Roxbury sections of the city and are extremely busy. The two fire companies are also frequently dispatched to District 11 in the Allston-Brighton section, which is somewhat isolated from the rest of the city by its distance and limited access, yet is populated with over seventy thousand residents.

Donald's detail was the result of a shortage of personnel on Thirty-three due to a couple of injuries at recent fires and the somewhat heavy summer vacation schedule currently in effect. Vacations in the department commence in late February and are completed on the last day in December. It's something about which the general public is never aware. In non-emergency businesses, including most municipal employees, summer vacations are sacred, an absolute must. Fires, however, don't respect the need for R&R; consequently, neither does the department's vacation policy. An adequate force must be maintained throughout the year; therefore, the number of people excused from duty at any one time is rigidly controlled and enforced.

However, through union negotiations in contracts over the years, every jake is required to receive two weeks off sometime between the beginning of June and the end of September. Since the balance of their entitlements are divided between spring and fall, fewer personnel are available during the summer months. Consequently, details from one company to another are more frequent during this period, and Donald's one tour assignment resulted from the shortage. The Tower unit, rescue companies and the marine units carry a large number of personnel on their rosters because of their stronger staffing requirement, but this also makes them logical targets for details to other companies when overall staffs are depleted.

The division commanders receive daily reports from every district in their commands that list the strength of all companies for the next day and night tours. They subsequently balance the staffing to insure an adequate on-duty force in compliance with the commissioner's guidelines. Any jake detailed for such a tour is notified the day before and takes his/her protective clothing, mask facepiece and Sunlance light home and reports directly to the assignment rather than to the regular station.

Donald parked in the rear yard of the firehouse, grabbed his gear, strolled through the back entrance and walked to the patrol desk at the front of the house. He told the jake on patrol who he was and the guy handed him a piece of chalk, saying, "Put it on the slate, kid. I can't spell worth a shit." Donald wrote *Holden—Tower to 33*. The jake, a guy who looked to be in his fifties, had his feet up on the desk and was leaning back in the swivel chair. He dropped his lanky legs to the floor and peered at what Donald had written, then said, "Holden, huh? You must be Frank's nephew. I useta work with him on Tremont Street."

Donald smiled to himself. His parents had been killed in an accident when he was ten years old; his Uncle Frank had raised him after that. Uncle Frank was a Boston fire fighter, but Donald did not know his uncle was a *famous* Boston jake until he went on the job himself. While Uncle Frank never became an officer, he was considered one of the best in the business. Throughout Donald's first few months on the job, he was constantly meeting people, including the commissioner and other high ranking officers, who had sung Frank's praises. Most of them claimed Frank taught them whatever they knew about fighting fires.

Donald truly appreciated the comments, but they did eventually wear a little thin. Also, he had proven himself enough during his first year and a half on the job that it was rarely mentioned anymore, except on an occasional detail like this one. That was one of the elements of the job he loved: you had to make it on your own, no matter what your background was, no matter what relative was on the job before you. And you had to keep doing it throughout your career.

"I'm Harold Spencer, but they call me 'Scarecrow' on account of I'm so damned skinny. This house has some great cooks, which means there's a lot of fat bastids here. It's supposed to be a good house 'cause it's busy, but that's the shit. They just like to eat, is all."

Spencer said he had been a Ladder 13 truckee when that legendary unit was paired with Engine 22 on Tremont Street. Back in 1981-82, however, massive budget cuts to the department had eliminated several fire companies, including his truck. "No shit, just like that!" he said. "Seems like those headquarters cats got rid of all the good companies."

"How do you like it over here?" Donald asked.

"Sucks. These truckies don't know squat. I been tryin' to teach them for a dozen freakin' years now. No progress." He shook his head. "Back in the old days, we useta call them 'the chimney sweeps' on account of all they ever got was sparks from fireplaces. Thirteen was the first truck in Boston to raise the aerial at fires over three-hundred-sixty-five times in a year. These wimps are complainin' if they do half that much."

He directed Donald to the second floor office of Engine 33 where he knocked on the door and was told to enter. As Donald gave his name and company, the lieutenant, a young, energetic guy with a blond crew cut, held out his hand in greeting. "Glad to meet you. I'm Lieutenant Felix Dober. You did a good job on Boylston Street last winter. You all better now?"

"Oh sure," replied Donald. "I wasn't really hurt much. Just knocked out from the heat. Never went off injured or anything."

Dober asked if he had checked in at the desk and then said, "Who's on patrol? Oh, jeez, the Scarecrow! Bet he gave you a lot of good information about this house, huh? Well, he's wrong, of course, but he'll never change." Dober smiled. "He really is a good jake. Just doesn't think anyone who wasn't with him on Ladder Thirteen can make the grade."

He explained that Spencer was almost sixty, even though he looked younger. "Just about everybody else in this house is twenty years younger. They kinda like him, even with all his bitching. Matter of fact, we got a couple of characters that keep him riled up all the time. You'll meet them later."

Lieutenant Dober gave Donald his assignment for the tour, riding on the left side of the pump. This meant that if they had a fire and if it was on his side of the pump, he would be the nozzle man or pipeman. If the fire was on the right side, then Donald would help the pump operator connect the feeder line and then help to advance the hose into the building. "If we get anything," Dober said, "I'll tell you whether to run a big line or an inch and three quarter."

Donald was assigned a bed in the bunkroom and went into the combination kitchen and mess hall. A few jakes were sitting at the long tables; Donald recalled they were engaged in a lengthy argument about the Red Sox. He chuckled as he remembered how certain one guy was that this was their year to go all the way, to win the World Series, thus reversing the miserable, humiliating, annual failure the team had experienced since 1918.

But in a firehouse this doesn't make a lot of difference. Another argument about another team or on the general decline of western civilization or any other subject is certain to arise.

Donald couldn't remember who was pro and who was con in the Sox discussion, but he had no difficulty in recalling the evening meal. Coley Fleming, the driver of Ladder 15, was the cook and his specialty was baked stuffed haddock. It was at least equal to the fare provided by any of the famous Boston seafood restaurants—and the price was much better.

After dinner some of the jakes went to the recreation room to continue a table tennis series that had been going on for years, but Donald went to the main floor and sat on a bench in front of the house to watch the passing parade of citizens and visitors as they strolled by on the beautiful summer evening. He was joined by Steve Clark, a black guy with greying hair at his temples that belied his youthful appearance. Steve told Donald that he, like Harold Spencer, was also a refugee from Ladder 13: "Scarecrow never forgets. He's still livin' in the past. We been over here a dozen years and believe me, it's a good house with two great companies. But he'll never change." Steve talked about how much he loved the job and how proud he was that one of his sons had been appointed a couple of years before.

They were joined by Lieutenant Tom McLoughlin of Ladder 15,

Walker Blair, another black jake, and Jim Barnes, both from Engine 33. Jim said to Donald, "See this guy? Don't believe anything he says. Know why?" Donald shook his head. "'Cause he's got his name reversed. Who the hell ever heard of that? He really should be Blair Walker, but I think he made the switch so no on knows who the fuck he is. He's an imposter just impersonating a jake."

"Barnes...now there's a name," Walker casually replied. "Someone found his great-grandfather abandoned in a cow barn in Ireland. Know why they deserted him?" Donald again shook his head. "Because he was as ugly as this shithead. Can't say I blame them, can you?"

Donald noticed that while Walker and Barnes were engaged in this banter they were also busily evaluating the potentials of the scores of young women crossing the apron. However, before this pair of Romeos could make any initial contact, the companies were dispatched to an auto fire on the Massachusetts Turnpike.

The access ramp on Newbury Street was just a block away, and as the companies descended onto the toll road, with lights flashing and sirens blaring, traffic came to a complete stop as a result of the fire. It was slow going, but with persistence Walker Blair managed to weave through the bunched vehicles toward the cloud of black smoke a half mile in the distance. The car, when they finally reached the scene, was fully involved with fire belching from both the engine compartment and the interior.

The apparatus stopped about a hundred feet short of the car, and Donald, at the direction of Lieutenant Dober, stretched a couple of lengths of one and three quarter inch line, with Jim Barnes pulling behind him. It was a fairly simple task to hit the fire, first with a solid stream and then with fog; the incident was controlled without difficulty in about twenty minutes. The State Police assumed charge of the area and the companies were dismissed. However, this was just the first response in what became an extremely busy tour of duty.

Even before they got back to quarters they were dispatched to an automatic alarm at the Lenox Hotel on Boylston Street. The routine procedure for these signals requires one engine company, one truck and the chief of the district to respond to the scene. If there is an additional call received for an actual fire, a box is struck and a total of three engines, two trucks, a rescue company, the Tower, and air supply unit, deputy chief, district chief and safety chief are dispatched. Since most of these incidents are the result of malfunctions of the system, boxes are seldom struck; but the two units are still required to use the high-rise procedure established for an actual fire in accordance with the Standard Operating Procedure.

While these nuisance alarms become a constant irritant for jakes stationed in the areas with the most high-rise buildings, company officers and chiefs do not permit a reduction in the required duties. Besides, it's great practice. Consequently, the engine company must take position to anticipate connecting a line into the sprinkler and/or standpipe inlets protruding from the ground floor of the building while the aerial ladder truck is centrally positioned at the front of the structure. The engine company jakes roll a two wheel cart, pre-loaded with three lengths of donut-rolled two and a half inch hose and nozzle into the lobby of the building while their counterparts on the truck bring a power saw, Rabbit tool, axes, rakes, Halligan bar and resuscitator. One of the officers confirms the floor number of the alarm while the other captures the elevators, using the fire fighter's key that every jake carries. All members are required to open the cylinder valves on their masks, thus activating them in the event smoke enters the elevator while they are ascending.

In this case, the alarm was from the ninth floor, so they ascended to the seventh floor, two floors below the reported location of the fire. This two-floors-below policy prevents the possibility of jakes arriving at the fire floor on the elevator, which could be catastrophic. This has happened in a few cases around the country, usually resulting in the death of some unfortunate fire fighters; the two-floor-below requirement is essential. In the event that there is actually a fire, an Upper Command Post will also be established on this floor.

On arrival at the seventh floor, the truck company members walk up the stairway to the fire floor to determine if there actually is a fire while the engine company prepares to connect their hose line to the two and a half inch outlet of the vertical standpipe, one floor below the fire. They make the connection one floor below so that if the fire blows out into the stairway, they will be able to advance and control it rather than being driven downward without the protection of the line.

At the Lenox, on this evening, no fire was present, just a false signal from a smoke detector; once the investigation was completed, they were dismissed and returned to quarters.

During the next couple of hours, they responded to one more of these incidents, plus a one room fire in the South End section of the district. The fire was rapidly controlled by the first due engine and truck, so they were promptly dismissed.

Donald remained on the main floor when they returned to quarters because it seemed obvious that this was going to be one of those nights. He had already learned that sometimes you got into work and didn't do a thing for hours at a time; but once in a while, it seemed as though the companies were on a roll and it was going to be in and out all night. Besides, he was enjoying the constant needling between the two friends, Blair and Barnes. Blair had taken over the patrol desk from the Scarecrow, who wasted no time in retreating upstairs but did offer Donald some advice before he left: "Listen, kid," he said to Donald, "don't hang around those two clowns. All they talk about is dames and neither one of them has much of a track record around here. Lotta talk, no action."

After he left, Jim Barnes said, "How the fuck would that old geezer know? When he ain't doing a watch he's in bed restin' those creakin' bones. One of his old girlfriends walked by here one day and she was a real charmer. Only thing is, she was on Medicaid and just escaped from a nursing home. She kept calling him Spenser 'cause she thinks he's the guy Robert Urich useta play on TV. Poor old woman must've had bad eyes, too."

Blair and Barnes started bragging about their own conquests, but finally were interrupted by the radio warning beep announcing another incident. The Fire Alarm operator directed both companies to respond to an automatic alarm from an apartment house in the Prudential Center complex, which is located within a half block of the firehouse. Walker Blair pushed the master control switch and announced the location over the P.A. system.

As Donald slid into the passenger compartment of the pump, Barnes said, "More bells. We gotta be the champions of the department on these fuckin' things. You guys get many of them on the Tower?"

"Not as many as this," Donald replied as they moved out the doorway. "Sure can get to be a pain in the ass, can't it?"

"Yeah. Some nights I put that damn mask on a dozen times and never use it. But that's the way the big wheels want it." He nodded his head in the direction of the officer riding in the front seat next to Walker Blair.

They arrived quickly and Donald looped his arms though his mask, jumped into the street and with Barnes lowered the cart to the sidewalk and moved towards the address location of the alarm. Getting used to it, he thought—by tomorrow morning I'll be an expert. This time the situation in the lobby was different than on their previous automatic alarm responses. Several tenants were moving towards them anxiously, and one of them screamed, "There's a fire on the sixteenth floor! Lots of smoke up there."

Lieutenant Dober moved rapidly toward the elevators and inserted his key while Lieutenant McLoughlin depressed the button on his remote radio microphone and said, "Ladder Fifteen to Fire Alarm." The operator answered promptly and McLoughlin continued: "Report of a fire on floor sixteen at this location. Strike the box."

They crowded into the first elevator to arrive, and just as they were going to close the doors, the aide to the chief of District Four sprinted into the lobby and pushed into the elevator with them. "The chief got the word," he said. "Let's go." Donald recognized the aide as Vic Williams, whom he'd seen at other fires with his boss, District Chief Bob Macklin.

On the way up, Dober stopped the elevator twice with the emergency button to be certain he was maintaining control. At the fourteenth floor he carefully operated the door open button, and they could see a haze of blue smoke drifting across the overhead lights in the elevator lobby. As Donald grabbed a length of rolled hose, he could hear Vic reporting to the chief, "Light smoke on fourteen. OK here to set up the Upper Command."

Lieutenant McLoughlin, Spencer and Steve Clark from the truck had already disappeared up the nearby enclosed stairway as the hosemen followed them with the gear. When they got to the fifteenth floor, smoke was banking down in the stairway. Dober said, "Connect to the outlet as fast as you can—two lengths—and bring it right up." He sprinted up the staircase behind the chief's aide.

Barnes spun the cap off the standpipe as Donald connected the female end to the male outlet. Dober came bounding down the stairs and said, "We got a good fire in an apartment. Jim, you stay here and fill the line as soon as I tell you. Holden, come with me." As they pulled the hose upward, he said, "Put your facepiece on...it's really juicy." At the floor landing, the smoke was so black that Donald couldn't see anything, but he heard Dober ordering Barnes to open the outlet valve. Donald crawled into the corridor and could hear muffled voices ahead of him. He could also hear water running somewhere and as he worked his way deeper along the hallways, he could feel the wetness striking his helmet. Dober mumbled to him, "Water's coming. Bleed the air out of the pipe." Donald opened the nozzle and could hear the burst of air, followed by a powerful stream of water. He shut it down and kept moving forward, although the charged line was much heavier and more cumbersome.

He finally bumped into someone laying flat on the floor. He wasn't certain who it was but the jake said, "Apartment's fully involved. No sprinklers inside. Doorway's about fifteen feet down on the left."

Donald kept moving, the heat now penetrating the corridor even though a sprinkler head was pounding away, spreading the water upward and sideways. As he approached the doorway, he could see a glow penetrating the smoke and he heard Dober say, "OK, kid, open the pipe. Put it on fog and keep low."

He did as he was told and managed to get to the entrance. When he did, Dober had him set the nozzle to a solid stream and they huddled together, hitting the ceiling inside the apartment and whipping the hose from side to side. Initially, the heat was intense, but as the hundreds of gallons of water penetrated more deeply, the atmosphere became somewhat cooler and they crept forward into the kitchen, which opened up into a dining area and living room. The force of the stream knocked out the windows, and as they moved towards what appeared to be a bedroom, Scarecrow Spencer wriggled past them. "Might be someone here," he said, and he inched his way ahead of them, through the doorway while they kept hitting the overhead to protect him.

When they moved into the room, they could hear other jakes entering behind them and soon another line was operating to kill the fire they had bypassed to follow the ladderman. Donald could hear more glass breaking ahead of him and realized Scarecrow was venting by cleaning out the window. This immediately helped to reduce the heat, and the visibility, while still poor, was improving.

Lieutenant Dober moved towards the bed, which was destroyed, as were all the furnishings, but before he got there, Scarecrow shouted, "Got someone, over here, near the window. Think it's a woman. Yeah, it is."

Vic Williams crawled into the room and Dober told him to notify the chief they had a female victim and needed a body bag. "OK, Luft, I'll notify the deputy. We got a second alarm on this now." The smoke was lifting rapidly now and Donald was able to stand upright as he continued to spray water against the overhead but now with the nozzle half-gated so the stream was greatly reduced.

In a few minutes the apartment was full of jakes, including members of Rescue One who entered the bedroom with the body wrapper and began the process of removing the remains of the woman. Donald helped Scarecrow, Walt Timmons and Snot Sheehan of Rescue One move the body into the wrapper, then they carried it out to the hallway where he relinquished his grip on the bundle and re-entered the apartment.

While Donald reviewed his notes on the incident, he closed his eyes and grimaced as he recalled how the body was almost incinerated from the tremendous heat. So much of the flesh was so badly charred that only the breasts indicated the victim's sex. He shook his head quickly to erase the image from his mind before he returned his eyes to the journal.

Back in quarters he asked Lieutenant Dober about the lack of sprinklers inside the apartment. "Well, those apartments were built before 1975," he said, "when a law was passed mandating sprinklers in all new buildings over seventy feet high." He went on to explain that following the huge fire in the Prudential Tower in 1986, the department prevailed on the state legislature to enact a retroactive law that required all of the pre-1975 buildings to have complete sprinkler systems installed by 1997. "These apartment buildings," Dober continued, "are in the process of putting them in now, and they've completed all the common areas such as corridors, lobbies and stairways. Good thing they did or we'd have gotten murdered trying to make it down that hallway to the apartment doorway. Of course, if the whole place was done, the woman would have survived. But we're getting there."

The companies responded to another automatic alarm that proved to be a malfunction, then to an auto accident and a false alarm from a street box within the next couple of hours after midnight. By this time, everyone except the jake on house patrol was in the kitchen, drinking coffee and waiting for the next run, which they felt was assured, the way the tour was going. Jim Barnes and Walker Blair had decided that Donald had to be a jinx. Walker was saying, "All us brothers got a big golf tournament at Franklin Park today, Holden, and now I'll be so wore out I'll get the shit kicked outta me. You know, we're not like you cheap white dudes on the course with your chickenshit bets. We play for some real money and you are gonna cost me a bundle."

"Fuck him and his golf tournament, you Tower stiff!" bellowed Jim Barnes. "What about me?"

Donald laughed and asked, "What about you, James?"

Barnes began to describe the gorgeous girl he was taking to Martha's Vineyard for his seventy-two hours off duty when he was interrupted by the alarm signal. "Shit!" he shouted. "See what I mean."

As they raced for the brass pole to slide to the apparatus floor, they could hear the message, "Engine Thirty-three, Ladder Fifteen, District

Five, respond to an inside fire, 468 Commonwealth Avenue. We're striking Box 2311."

The units sped along Boylston Street, took a right onto Mass. Ave., then a left onto Commonwealth, crossing over the left side at Charlesgate, advancing into Kenmore Square against traffic, which was sparse at this hour.

Smoke was issuing up a front stairway from a Japanese restaurant located in the basement. An all night video store occupied the first floor, and the store's clerk was on the sidewalk shouting, "I smelled it and called you guys. I rung the fire alarm upstairs, too." A steady stream of occupants, most in nightclothes, moved rapidly down the exit stairway from the apartments.

Dober yelled to Donald, "Big line, down the stairs. Let's go." Donald stepped up on the running board, grabbed the nozzle of the cross-laid two and a half inch attack line and pulled it towards him, dragging several feet behind him. Jim Barnes looped a coupling over his shoulder and followed Donald down the metal stairway. Ahead of them, Scarecrow inserted the Rabbit tool into the door jamb, and when he activated it, the entrance door popped outward, releasing dense, brownish smoke.

As he was donning his mask facepiece, Donald heard Lieutenant McLoughlin shout to Scarecrow to clean out the entire opening, removing both sides of the double hung door and providing a clear wide entrance for the companies. Donald dropped to his knees and as he moved inward, Lieutenant Dober passed to his left in a crouched position, his portable light beam penetrating the smoke. He had his glove off and was feeling the floor. "Cement, but it's kinda warm," he said. "Keep coming."

It had been relatively cool when they entered, but the further they advance the hotter it became. Scarecrow also moved ahead of them as Donald and Barnes kept dragging the line forward. The slight visibility they had enjoyed rapidly degenerated into blackness, and Donald heard Dober's muffled shout, "Charge the line. We got a stairway goin' down." Barnes relayed the message to District 5's aide and it was acknowledged. Donald kept bumping into tables with metal chairs turned upside down on them; he was starting to get disoriented when he bumped into Dober. He could hear the lieutenant speaking into his mike: "Car Five, there's a sub-basement here. The fire has come up the rear stairway and passed us. Must be in the first floor. We're gonna start hitting it here. Let you know," he concluded as the water filled the line. "Holden," he said, "drive the line straight ahead of you into the stairway."

Donald did as he was directed and Dober got beside him and guided him forward. Scarecrow was just ahead, pushing tables and chairs aside to make a clear pathway for the hosemen. Dober next directed Donald to shoot the line directly up the stairs in an attempt to cut off the rapid extension of fire. The stream hit something high overhead and much of the water cascaded down into the lower stairway, drenching cardboard boxes stacked along the rear wall.

Scarecrow shouted, "Luft, the floor don't feel too hot. I don't think there's much fire under us." Donald kept moving the nozzle back and forth, hoping the ladderman was right. He was able to move to the top of the stairs and direct the stream downward since the fire above seemed to have diminished somewhat.

Dober said, "I think it must be a small storeroom or something down there. Keep the line on me—I'm gonna take a look." The lieutenant turned around and faced the stairs so the heat was striking his back and carefully descended, one step at a time, while Donald and Barnes carefully sprayed over his head, the nozzle barely opened.

Scarecrow tapped Barnes on the shoulder and said, "Tell the lieutenant I got the rear exit door open. It's startin' to vent pretty good."

Just as District 5's aide appeared behind them and asked for a report for the chief, Dober shouted up, "Bring the line down. I think we can get it." He told the aide the fire had originated in a storeroom, about fifteen feet square, and involved several cartons of goods. The aide relayed the information and then said, "The fire went up the back stairs to the second floor. We got a second alarm. Lot of smoke up above, but it didn't get in any of the apartments."

The water they had been shooting down enabled them to make it to the bottom of the stairs, and in a few moments they managed to knock down all the remaining fire. Dober sent Barnes back for a smaller hose so the line would be more maneuverable during overhauling operations. He turned to Donald and said, "You're a good jake, Holden. Stayed right with it. Pretty hairy, huh?"

"Hairy! I was scared shitless, Luft," Donald responded. "I felt like running right out the door. If you weren't here maybe I would have."

Dober laughed. "Naw, you wouldn't. But we got a real break here. This building is all cement. If that floor was wood, we'd've never made it to the stairway. Another thing—the rear stairway is all metal. What was burning was a bunch of cartons those goofs had stored everywhere."

When Donald was relieved at the end of the tour, as he was putting his gear into his car, Scarecrow grabbed him by the arm. "Hey, Holden, you're OK," he said. "I think your Uncle Frank would give you an A for last night."

Donald realized the older jake was actually smiling. I didn't think he had it in him, Donald thought. "Well, pal, Uncle Frank would have been proud of you too. If I every get to be as good a ladderman as you are, I will die a happy guy."

"Two multiples in one night," Donald said aloud, softly, as he moved down the list. "That was a first for me."

Three

The next entry brought back much more pleasant memories: "Vacation—Yeah!"

Since his graduation from drill school and his assignment to a permanent group, Donald had developed close relationships with most of the jakes he worked with but especially with his classmate, Rick Foster, and also Fred "Gap" Keefe. While Rick and his wife Sandy were newlyweds and had no children, Gap and Marion Keefe had two. Their son, Freddy, Jr., was twelve, but their daughter, Bethany, was born the same month as Donald and Gena's daughter, Nancy.

During the Disneyworld trip the two young ladies had become close friends, and even though they lived some distance apart, they wrote to each other and made many phone calls—so many that their parents were always complaining about the phone bills.

Gap had a summer place in Meredith, New Hampshire, on the shores of Lake Winnipesaukee, a spacious eight room cottage that his father had bought after his return from World War II. Gap, his brother and sister spend their childhood summers at the idyllic location. Their parents were gone, but the kids continued to share it as their own families grew. Gap invited both Donald and Rick to spend some time with him in August, probably to quiet the continuous nagging of his daughter, Beth. "We got plenty of room," he told them, "and our wives get along great, so come on up."

It was true that the women were good friends. The three couples had developed a ritual of going out for dinner and visiting a club afterwards every two weeks or so. This was not uncommon among jakes. The work schedule that required tours of duty on many weekends and holidays resulted in a certain isolation from their friends who worked regular five day jobs. Consequently, as time passes, jakes and their wives become closer, not only because of the common availability at strange times during the week, but because of the jakes' shared danger, which is an ever present concern for their wives.

Even though Donald and Rick were not yet eligible for vacation, with the simple expedient of swapping two tours of duty with other members of their companies, they were able to combine that time with their regular off duty hours to generate a half dozen days absence—and six days by a beautiful lake in the mountains sounded pretty good.

Nancy was squirming with anticipation as they rode up Interstate 93 to their destination. Actually, Donald and Gena were just as excited because they seldom visited the lakes and mountain regions of New Hampshire. When they were able to escape for a couple of days in the summer, they tended to head south for Cape Cod and the ocean, probably because they lived so close to the ocean themselves. They always intended to visit the gorgeous mountains and enormous lakes in the north country, but they just never got around to doing it. The trip to Gap's cottage was their big chance, and Gena was armed with maps and resort brochures that she studied as they sped past Nashua, Manchester and Concord before exiting towards Laconia, Weirs Beach and into Meredith.

Following Gap's explicit instructions, they were soon driving down a narrow tree lined road, and as they came over a rise they were given their first unobstructed view of the magnificent lake which stretched for thirty miles in length and as much as ten miles in width. They could see scores of islands and inlets and countless boats of every type, from canoes and tiny sailboats to much more substantial craft, both sail and motor powered. Water skiers, jet skiers, and wind surfers were whizzing by in the brisk breeze. The Holdens were mesmerized by the scene.

The even smaller crossroads they passed had numerous rustic name-signs nailed on trees to indicate the locations of various families' cottages. The last one they came to had the same types of signs, but the one on the top had a painting of a fire hat with an inscription beneath it: "Keefe-Tower 1—You light 'em/ We fight 'em." Donald grinned as he turned into the roadway.

As Gap had boasted, the brightly painted cottage was located just off the beach, with a small wooden pier jutting out onto the lake. Gap's daughter, Bethany, squealed with delight as the car pulled into the dirt covered driveway. Nancy bounded out the car door as soon as they stopped and the pair disappeared into the house, chattering away, because, after all, they hadn't talked on the phone for at least two days.

Rick and Sandy, Gap and Marion were gathered in the spacious combination living and dining room, all four sprawled on two ancient overstuffed divans, drinking coffee. When Donald and Gena joined them, it became obvious after a few minutes discussion that the men and women had two different agendas in mind for the week.

The sportsmen were interested in fishing, boating, golf and eating; the ladies wanted to hit all of the tourist attractions. In the end, Gap stood up and said, "All right, here's the A plan: Every morning, we'll jump up and depart for all those wonderful scenic attractions that drags all these tourists up here," he waved at the other two couples. "We'll hit Kancamagus, the Old Man in the Mountain, Conway, Attitash, Mt. Cranmore and the Castle in the Clouds, so you can go back to the inner city you came from and tell all those poverty-stricken neighbors of yours what they're missin'. But, afternoons will be for male bonding. We guys, including Fred Junior will do what we have to do."

Marion interrupted him, "Like what?"

Gap smiled. "Oh, you know. First we're gonna play golf, then we're goin' fishin', then canoeing and some sailing."

"Well, my dear," Marion replied, "that's all very interesting. Now I'm going to give you plan B, which is what we will actually do. First of all, we ladies are on vacation. There will be absolutely no *jumping up* in the morning. If you macho men want to quietly sneak out onto the lake at the crack of dawn, go ahead. We will rise at a more leisurely pace and maybe, just maybe, feed you when you get back, or not, depending on how we feel about it. Then we will determine how the day will be spent. Right girls?"

Plan B was selected by a five to one margin. Neither Rick nor Donald supported Gap's position after they caught the glares from Sandy and Gena.

In reality, everyone ended up satisfied as the week drew to a close. The weather was magnificent, with warm, cloudless days and cool evenings under starry skies. Gap and Marion were perfect hosts and the nightly barbecue at the outdoor grill after busy days was great fun. Gap had the goofiest looking chef's hat and a long white apron, naturally emblazoned with a picture of the Tower Company. He proved to be such a good cook that Rick asked why he never tried it in the firehouse. "Naw, Brows Brennan would kill me. Besides, I do *not* want to listen to all the complaints from a bunch of ungrateful jakes. Can you imagine what Dot-head Doherty would say if I burned the bacon or something? Nope. Brows is the guy. If they give him any shit, he'll just crush 'em."

The final night, they had their own karaoke and while Rick gave a passable impression of Michael Jackson, complete with glove, lipstick and mascara, Nancy and Bethany were the sentimental favorites and eventual winners with their unusual duet of Madonna and Bette Midler—minus the x-rated lyrics, of course.

The two young ladies had a tearful goodbye at the close of the visit but Donald made a stop at a water wonderland before they left the state. This was followed by dinner at the famous Green Ridge Turkey Farm in Nashua and by the time they eventually returned to Massachusetts, Nancy was chattering away about her friends in the neighborhood and how envious she was going to make them with her tales of the trip to the Northland.

Once she had retired for the night back home, her parents snuggled on the living room couch, their embrace growing more intense as they listened to the soft music from the C.D. player. They eventually made their way to the master bedroom, still maintaining their close contact, Gena's feet just barely touching the floor. Their intimacy proved to be as exquisite as any they had experienced in a long time and when it was over, Gena clasped her hands behind her head and stared out the picture window that provided a clear view of the moon reflecting off the ocean some two city blocks to her south. "You know, honey. It was great visiting with our friends. The more I get to know the people you work with and their wives, the more I can truly appreciate the close relationships that develop between jakes and their families."

"I knew you would, Gena," Donald somewhat smugly replied. "It's the way the system works."

"Well, maybe," she replied with a smirk, "but when we're all crowded into a cottage on a lake, the chances of experiencing what we just had are nil." She finished as she turned away from him: "Next time, how about a little less 'All in together, boys' and a little more 'Have a nice day, see you in the morning.'"

Donald chuckled as he closed his eyes. She might be right, he thought as he drifted off to sleep, but these homecomings seem pretty good to me.

The final extra alarm fire of 1993 occurred just after midnight on December 31st and was in District 12, Mattapan. It was a second alarm in a three decker and when they returned to quarters, Donald made his last entry for the year. He counted up the extra alarms he'd responded to and found out it was twenty-five. They involved several fires in three deckers and he realized how many thousands of them there were in the city. He couldn't say they were just routine, because every fire had its own peculiarity. But, he sure knew a lot more about how these structures were laid out, how rapidly they burned and how many of them extended into adjoining buildings. But three deckers weren't the only types of buildings he had been to. There were also many four, five and six story apartment houses, as well as all kinds of commercial properties he had worked in both for routine incidents as well as extra alarms. He also noted that there had been a few serious snow storms, arriving a little earlier than most years. What he didn't realize at the time was that the winter of '93-'94 would break all existing records for snow accumulation. Boston averages forty inches per year, but by the time April arrived, 96.3 inches was the final total. His journal was full of notations about the difficulties this made for access to so many alarms. The cold weather with the extremely low wind chill factors also caused him to understand just what their drill instructors had been driving into the class throughout their weeks of training.

He considered the whole year a great learning experience, including his brush with death back in February. Yeah, but that taught me a lot, too. Death is part of the job and this year he had been to a few fires where civilians died. He had learned to accept the adults without too much difficulty, but the kids had troubled him, just as they troubled every jake.

Lt. Desmond is truly a great teacher. As a result of his insistence on making us all the best possible jakes, I feel I'm becoming a pretty good driver of the Tower, operator of the aerial, the bucket and the water delivery system. I'm doing better with power tools and forcible entry equipment, and I really know quite a bit about pulling ceilings, opening floors and walls. The way the snow keeps coming, I'm pretty sure before this lousy winter is over, I'll have shoveled out every hydrant in our sub-district and be able to find them all blind-folded.

Donald felt he was learning quite a bit about building construction, how fire travels, how to ventilate buildings and how essential it is to put the water at the seat of the fire, whether it is done by hand operated nozzles or massive heavy stream appliances. One of the great advantages of the Tower bucket was the occasional ability to observe, from up high, how frequently water was misdirected by fire companies due to their inability to see the most advantageous area for the placement of powerful streams.

He was becoming much more familiar with the city itself. Boston has sixteen different sections, each with its own name, and, while he hated to admit it, prior to his appointment as a jake, he was totally unfamiliar with several of them. But, that was definitely changing.

His company's extra alarm assignments were much better than any of the travel brochures the chamber of commerce provided for the lucrative tourist trade the city enjoyed. But, then again, the out of towners probably wouldn't be attracted to some of the neighborhoods he was seeing, nor his unscheduled visiting hours.

Donald also watched and tried to understand how Desmond related to his jakes. While the officer had a wonderful sense of humor, when they were gathered together, in the kitchen, mess hall, recreation rooms or elsewhere, he chose to be pretty much an observer rather than an active participant in the horseplay that was almost continuous. When the troops did something particularly outrageous, Donald tried to sneak a glance at Desmond to see his reaction; he was usually rewarded with a glimpse of a tiny smile appearing on the lieutenant's otherwise serious countenance.

The first tour Donald worked in 1994 seemed to confirm that this winter would be memorable. It was snowing once again, the temperature was well below freezing and hydrant snow removal was a certainty as one of their chores for the day. In the mess hall, Dot-head Doherty was holding forth on that very subject as Donald slid onto his favorite bench, leaned his elbows on the long table, and cradled his coffee cup in his hands.

Doherty, sitting a few seats away from his captain, Stan Hardy of Rescue One, was professing his usual, unrequested advice to the officer, while glancing sideways at Brows Brennan of Engine 10. Brows, an easy mark whenever anyone criticized his company, particularly if the spokesman was not a hoseman, was facing away from Dot-head, preparing to crunch into a massive Dunkin Donuts honey-dipped bow-tie. Calorie counting was not Brennan's strong suit. He looked with disdain on the jakes in the house who were trying to watch their diets and were involved in a regular training program in the fully equipped exercise room in back of the house.

"Say, Cap," said Doherty. "Yessss," answered his boss, who could tell by the increase in volume of this character's voice that this would be the start of some kind of a confrontation. "Could you please explain to me, sir, why we rescue jakes have to participate in these ridiculous snow clearing operations? Look at that snow piling up out there." Hardy, who was the senior officer in the station, and therefore the Captain of the House, sighed before he replied. While he never admitted it, he was a strong believer in the clowning that was so prevalent in most fire houses he had served in during his decades on the job. He felt that jakes were exposed to many horrifying incidents and great danger at fires and emergencies, and, when they were in quarters, some of the screwball ideas they came up with were nothing more than a means to avoid deep soul-searching about the frailties of life and its endless perils as well as the evils and miseries they often witnessed in the human persona.

"Well, Fire Fighter Doherty," he answered, "if we don't clear the hydrants, we don't get any water. It's still the best weapon we have to put out fires."

Doherty nodded in agreement, "I fully understand that, mon Capitaine, but it seems like such a waste of rescue personnel." He continued, "As you know, sir, we are highly skilled workers. The only reason our pay isn't double that of those other louts—you know, hosepersons, ladderpersons and Towerpersons, is because of that ridiculous union we belong to, where they believe in all that equality shit."

Donald could see the back of Brows Brennan's neck turning a deep crimson. Dot-head appeared unconcerned as he said, "Our expertise should be guarded and preserved so we will be ready to do what we do best."

"What's that?" asked Hardy.

"Why, sir, you know, bail out everything these undisciplined oafs screw up at every fire."

Brennan spun around, his dark black bushy eyebrow scrunched across his wrinkled forehead. "Lissen, you pimple-headed prick, hosemen are the only important jakes at any fire. The rest of you assholes could stay home, particularly you fuckin' rescue shitheads." He paused and took a deep breath, "Er, not you, Captain. I feel sorry for you when I see what you gotta work with. But, jeez, who puts out the fire? You could throw all those winches, saws and all that other special shit you got at it and they'd melt. You could even throw Dot-head at it." He chuckled as he realized what he had said. "Naw, don't do that. His blubber would turn to whale oil and make the fire worse. We'd hafta use foam on him."

Dot-head appeared outraged and in no time, the two of them were shouting back and forth while the captain and the rest of the jakes in the room continued reading the morning papers, talking about the NFL play-offs currently in progress and dissecting the New England Patriots for their failure to reach the semi-finals again.

When Hardy felt the argument had run its course, he calmly glanced up from the sports section of the *Globe* and said, "Enough! Rescue One—check out those banjos downstairs. We're doin' our sub-district 0900-1100, Engine 10 next, 1100-1300, Tower, 1300-1500. Let's go."

Donald smiled as he heard the order. The first time the captain mentioned "banjos" he had no idea what he meant. He asked Gap Keefe what they were. "Big shovels," Gap replied and explained that when Hardy was a fire fighter, the department had a musical band and two jakes from his company were members of the group. They were constantly being excused for practice and for appearances at parades and concerts. This meant they missed out on doing a lot of house patrol watches, which didn't endear them to the other jakes who had to fill in for them. During their frequent absences, they also missed a lot of fires as well. Hardy's company officer was a grizzled veteran who thought these specialists were a pain in the ass, but the administration at headquarters loved them. Any time the mayor wanted a band to make him look good at some function, he'd call his fire commissioner and thirty jakes with everything from kazoos to french horns would show up. It was at a time before the department was depoliticized and the commissioner was always a civilian.

The long suffering chiefs of department would bite their tongues and comply with the orders. Since the mid-seventies, when the fire commissioner and chief of department jobs were merged and the boss became a uniformed member, the band was on a countdown for elimination. It was done away with one winter day and Hardy's officer cheerfully announced, "O.K. Toodly-toot and rat-a-tat-tat—you can substitute these banjos for those instruments." He handed each of them one of the wide shovels and dispatched them on foot out into the deep snow, adding, "See how good you can strum a tune on those fuckin' hydrants." The name stuck, at least with Hardy, and whenever he announced it was banjo time everyone knew what he meant.

Donald had the noon to 1500 watch in the patrol desk and both Gap Keefe and Brows Brennan were sitting behind him playing their usual cribbage game. One time Donald asked Gap how much longer they were going to continue this obvious mismatch because it had been going on ever since his appointment. Gap replied, "Thirty-two years."

His response was so prompt and positive it startled Donald. "How the hell do you know that, Gap?"

"Easy," was the immediate reply. "You see, Donald, my friend, Brows," he waved his arm towards Brennan, "is basically just a hoseman. He isn't blessed with our intelligence and he has never beaten me."

Brows, who was studying his hand, missed the comment and said, "Huh?"

"I was just explaining to Donald, pal, that we need thirty-two years of service to achieve the maximum retirement benefits. By then I'll have won enough money from you to move my dear wife to Florida. If I'm lucky, I'll find a retired hoseman from Chicago or New

York and we'll live in luxury the rest of our lives."

Donald said, "How about a retired Boston jake?"

Gap shook his head, "Naw. The guys up here know how good I am. They're smart enough to stay away from me."

Brows kept staring at Keefe with a puzzled expression on his face and finally said, "Shut up and deal the fuckin' cards, you toothless bastard."

At 1240 hours Box 319 was struck over the alarm system. Donald turned and thumbed his way through the assignment card box which listed every fire alarm box location in the city and the full nine alarm response listed on each card. As he was pulling up the specific card for the box, the radio crackled, "Box 319, we're receiving calls for a fire on Faulkner Street. Report of people in the building." This was promptly followed by the officer on Ladder Seven reporting fire showing. Donald depressed the mike button on the P.A. system and announced, "Ladder Seven reports fire showing." This alerted the members of the Tower Company of a possible response if extra apparatus were requested. The next message was from the chief of District Seven and reported a "Working Fire." Donald hit the master control switch and announced the box location. He could hear the signal 45-319 striking over the system as he raced toward the truck. Gap was already there, slipping out of his shoes and into his boots. Just as he was getting onto the truck Keefe shouted to Brennan, "Hey Brows, old pal, take Engine 10 out and do our hydrants, will ya?" Donald couldn't hear the response because of the engine noise but Brennan's lips seemed to form the words *fuck you* as the truck roared out the door. As they swung right, they could hear Car Seven ordering a second alarm.

This fire originated in a first floor ceiling of a three decker and extended rapidly upward. The first truck at the scene, Ladder 7, rescued three people from the top floor over a thirty five foot ladder. The Tower jakes carried ground ladders through the snow clogged street and then worked inside pulling ceilings and walls. Snow, snow, snow, he noted.

As Donald glanced down through his notebook, he recalled that there were several multiples throughout the city in the next few weeks, but none of them on his work group. They made plenty of responses to alarms of all kinds but no serious fires. The snow kept piling up, hydrants had to be shoveled out on both day and night tours and it was bitter cold.

He smiled as he remembered the night of the 20-21st. Everyone was in the kitchen sometime after 0200. They had just returned from an investigation of an odor of smoke in a department store at Downtown Crossing. It had been a pain in the ass kind of run because they definitely could smell something burning but couldn't locate it. It seemed to be rubbish of some kind but couldn't be located as the Tower, rescue and ladder company crews spread out and trooped through the several floors of the building without success. Finally, the deputy's aide located a small pile of burning rags outside, in the rear of the structure. The smoke had drifted into a ventilation duct through the exhaust grillwork and worked its way upward.

It was the kind of frequent job that everyone, especially the chief in charge, hates. He knows the place is well sprinklered and he also knows from the odor that it's rubbish—but no one's leaving until we find it. Period.

When they returned to quarters, Brows was in a foul mood, which was not an unusual condition for him. He had been standing outside the front door of the building, a dry hose line stretched at his feet, waiting to see if the line would be run in through the door or into the sprinkler connection if there actually was a serious fire. The temperature was seven degrees and the wind chill minus twenty. He was expressing his view about how incompetent the investigators were, none of them, of course, hosemen. "It took the dog-robber deputy's aide to find a pile of shit burnin'. What a bunch of dummies we got. Another thing. This fuckin' group doesn't do nuthin'. Just rubbish, auto fires, bells and inhalators. I'm askin' the captain to get on his group. They been burnin' the town down and he needs a real jake with him."

Gap replied, "Please, Brows, don't leave me. I can't afford to have you gone. My kids have been eating regular ever since I met you. I'll have to get a moonlight job."

Before Brennan could reply, an alarm started striking over the tapper. It was followed immediately by the familiar message, "Calls being received on Box 2331 for a fire, top floor, at 335 Huntington Avenue, District 5."

Dot-head Doherty shouted, "Hey, Brows, better start suiting up. Sounds like business."

The first company at the scene reported heavy smoke showing, fifth floor. Donald had already slid the pole to the main floor and was looking at the street location book and map of the city since he was driving the unit for this tour of duty. He saw that the building was located only a short distance beyond Symphony Hall where he had taken Gena and Nancy to see the Boston Pops Christmas show a few weeks earlier so he'd have no difficulty getting there if it became an extra alarm fire. Let's see, he mused, tracing the route with his finger, Expressway to Mass. Ave. exit, turn right. Go past Albany, Harrison Ave., Washington, Shawmut Ave., Tremont, St.Botolph, left on Huntington to the fire.

The chief of the district reported people trapped and ordered a second alarm as Donald maneuvered out through the overhead doors. Lieutenant Desmond calmly asked, "Know where we're goin', Donald?" He nodded yes and swung to the right, following the plan he had reviewed moments ago. Desmond never seemed to get excited. He didn't want to distract the driver and would only speak if he had to give an instruction. When they cleared the down ramp onto Mass. Ave., and moved onto the flat surface, the deputy at the scene was ordering a third alarm.

He told Fire Alarm to direct the Tower company to take position adjacent to Ladder 15 on Huntington and attempt to reach occupants on the fifth floor with the bucket. "O.K., Donald," said Desmond, "Piece of cake. Swing into Huntington and I'll get you into position."

True to his word, as the truck got on the avenue, the officer jumped off, raced on foot ahead and placed himself at the next intersection, holding up his arms and stopping two engine companies coming down Gainsborough Street. They would have blocked access to the front of the building for the Tower and he waved Donald towards him, guiding him into the narrow opening next to the already extended aerial of Ladder 15.

By this time, fire was bursting out of some of the fifth floor windows and two aerials were into windows with jakes leading occupants down the ladders. The residents were mostly students at nearby Northeastern University and since they were young, agile and frightened, they came down rapidly.

Donald stopped the truck where Desmond told him, shifted the controls to power take-off and sped to the rear of the unit. He quickly operated the controls to set the four diagonal, downward thrusting, hydraulic support jacks. He transferred the weight of the body onto the supports and raised the truck until the green light lit, indicating that the balance required to elevate the aerial had been achieved.

He pounced on the rungs leading to the turntable, climbed to the platform and grasped the controls on the vertical console. He could see Desmond and Gap sprinting along the horizontal structure of the massive ladder and watched as they dropped into the bucket attached to the last section of the extension. Desmond elevated his glove-covered right thumb and Donald pulled back on the elevation knob smoothly, the bucket and ladder climbing and moving rapidly upright. Desmond spoke to him on the intercom. "O.K. Donald, take a look and then start rotating." Donald had been looking directly upward, making certain there were no wires or other obstructions overhead. Now, he looked to his right and could see heavy smoke and fire increasing on the upper floor. He pulled the rotation control and swung the aerial towards the building. When it was horizontal to the structure, Desmond directed him to commence extending the ladder sections to the proper height and lowering the unit towards the windows. As the bucket dipped into the smoke, Desmond said, "Give it to us, Donald," and he switched the power to them. He could no longer see either the jakes or the bucket and he kept his hand on the control lever, ready to override them if ordered to do so. He could now see smoke appearing on the third and fourth floors underneath Desmond and Gap and he called on the intercom to let them know. "Yeah. O.K., Donald. We know," said Desmond. Jeez, thought Donald, doesn't he ever get excited? A couple of minutes passed with Donald getting more and more nervous but then Desmond called and said tersely, "Pull us out and swing us away fast, Holden." Donald overrode the controls, pulled back first on the elevation control and as he felt the unit respond, activated the left rotation so both operations were performing simultaneously.

The bucket appeared through the smoke and as it continued to swing towards the middle of the street a burst of flame licked towards it but failed to envelop it or the ladder.

He started retracting the ladder extensions and as they seated themselves compactly, he could see that the bucket was now crowded with occupants. He could hear Desmond talking to the deputy on the portable radio. He was requesting ambulances for the victims, reporting that two of them had burns and one was dazed from smoke inhalation.

He then instructed Donald to rotate the ladder to the left and attempt to lower it to the street. Steve Tucker and Howie Rosen, who had been with Donald, jumped to the ground and took position and then guided him down into the narrow area between the rear of the truck and the nearby street car tracks. When they signaled the bucket was close enough to the street, he centered the control knobs and waited. He could see jakes and EMTs from Health and Hospitals reaching upward and the victims being transported towards waiting ambulances.

In a few minutes Desmond waved him towards the ground as Steve appeared on the turntable beside him. "I got it, Donald," said Tucker. This time when Donald saw Desmond he was more animated than he had ever seen him. "Nice job, kid. We got 'em all, and you got us out just in time." He patted Donald on the shoulder. "Now, you and Howie get in the bucket and go knock the shit outta that fire. We got lines coming into the pump. Don't forget your mask. It'll be ripe up there."

Steve Tucker hoisted them upward and released the controls to them when they requested them. They could see some fire on the third and fourth floors but it was confined to one window on each level and didn't appear to be extending. The fifth floor, however, was fully involved and fire was visible above the roof line as well. They commenced operating the powerful nozzle into the windows and were rewarded in a few minutes as the thousand gallon per minute discharge drove into the flames, converting them to dense whitish smoke. The two jakes could see that the fire had extended into the adjoining apartment house to their right and black smoke was showing in some of the fifth floor windows of that location as well. They could also observe that water was spurting out through the window openings, indicating that jakes were in on the floor and driving the fire from the structure. Aerials were extended through the smoke into that building and jakes were ascending with hose lines.

Once the Tower stream had effectively controlled the fire in front of them, they notified Desmond who told them to shut down and stand by. In a few moments he advised them that hose lines were advancing up the front stairway to control the fire in a shaft that had caused extension down into the floors immediately below them. He instructed them to hold the bucket in position because he and Gap were coming up over the aerial.

When all four jakes were crowded together in the small space, Desmond said, "OK, connect the donut roll to the standpipe and we'll get inside." The bucket was equipped with an outlet for a two and a half inch line and a coiled hose with nozzle. As Donald started to step into the room Desmond said, "O.K. boys, remember what they told you in drill school. Feel that floor and make sure it will hold you." He was talking to all of them but Donald appreciated he was really reminding the new guy, Holden, since the other jakes had done this many times. He leaned in and pounded his axe head onto the floor and was pleased to feel the solid response from the wood.

The heavy stream they had operated had effectively killed most of the fire in the room they entered and Gap and Howie reached the doorway to a corridor without much difficulty. While there was a lot of heat in the hallway, a water stream from the stairway to their left could be heard hitting the ceiling over their heads. They were able to determine that the fire was now being controlled throughout the area. Desmond told Donald and Gap to find the stairway to the roof and try to gain access to the penthouse.

They crawled towards the sound of the hose stream and eventually collided with jakes from an engine company. The one operating the nozzle shut it down, pulled off his mask facepiece and said, "Who the fuck are ya?" Gap slipped off his own mask and started laughing. "Brows, my old pal. You saved my life. Did you get a good shot at the fire? Let's see you give me a smile."

When Donald got back to quarters and was making the entry into his journal, he smiled and shook his head. Engine Ten had taken a severe beating working their way up the stairway to the fifth floor but Brennan was in his element and while he would never be a bundle of charm, he was almost civil when they were changing gear back in the firehouse. Gap managed to irritate him by asking him when he was going to move over to the captain's group and the answer was a deeply growled, "I never said that."

That particular fire seemed to shift the balance of fires back to Donald's work group. During the next ten days, they responded to six multiple alarms in various parts of the city. Donald caught Brows Brennan with an actual full smile one day. Won't last long. Seems as though fires move from one group to another. Bulby told us in drill school, if you're on long enough, it all evens out. I think I'm starting to believe him.

Two of the fires were in posted buildings and the Tower used its heavy streams extensively. Desmond continued to amaze Donald. He seemed to know the peculiarities of all of the streets in the various districts they responded to. He usually had a better method of approaching a location than the established routes indicated, and, once they arrived, directed the Tower into the most effective position. But at the many incidents where the unit wasn't required to operate, the officer had an uncanny way of finding what task was the most essential when they arrived. They frequently assisted in opening roofs, doors, cleaning out windows and even occasionally relieving an engine company on a hose line. Many chief officers considered them to be a bonus company, similar to the rescue companies. This was because of their eagerness to perform any task without complaint, but also because they frequently arrived at the critical time of an incident, when just one action would be the key to the control of the fire.

With so many vacant buildings in the city, many of them in hazardous condition, the ability of the Tower to place so much water into the fire at the appropriate angle also allowed the chiefs to gain control of the incident without seriously endangering the operating forces.

One entry Donald made in mid-June didn't result in the Tower unit actually performing any duties but it was certainly unusual enough to require comment. There are extensive construction projects underway in the city, including the digging of a third harbor tunnel from South Boston to East Boston at Logan Airport, the depression of the Central Artery, called "the Big Dig," and a ten mile tunnel out into the Atlantic Ocean. This last project is for the disposal of treated sewage from the city with the objective of contributing to cleaning the waters of Boston Harbor.

A fire in a vertical conveyor belt extended from the bottom of the shaft, 290 feet to the main entrance located on Deer Island. This island, connected by a causeway to the city of Winthrop, is part of Boston and apparatus from both cities respond. There were forty-one workers trapped in the tunnel and the amount of fire venting upward prevented a rescue effort at that point, although hose streams were successfully used to attempt to kill the fire. The workers eventually managed to make their way over four miles to an escape shaft on Long Island, which is also part of the city. Long Island has a hospital for terminal AIDS patients, accommodations for over a thousand homeless people, a lodging house for juvenile offenders and a couple of secret federal programs. The Boston Fire Department has a brigade of four jakes on duty there and they managed to assist the victims to the surface.

The next entry had been the most difficult for Donald to make in his journal. It was for a fire he didn't respond to because his group was off duty. There have been 168 Boston fire fighters killed in the line of duty since the mid-1800s. Unfortunately, jakes who serve on the job for three decades will have to face the fact that a member will be lost from time to time. However, it is easy to become complacent when time passes without such tragedies occurring. The last Boston fire fighter killed in the line of duty was in March of 1986. The several new classes of recruits appointed since that tragic day had never experienced such a loss. That all changed on June 24, 1994.

Donald wrote: "I'm making this entry from official accounts of the incident. 6/24—Box 4113-District 3 (Charlestown), 9 alarms. Charles River Avenue. 0037 hours. 2 story, wood frame, tin-clad, vacant furniture warehouse on wooden pier. Building approximately 600 hundred feet long. The first companies at the scene advanced a line into the first floor under light smoke conditions, attempting to locate the fire, which had originated underneath the pier at the water end of the structure. They had penetrated deeply when conditions deteriorated rapidly and they were ordered to evacuate as extra alarms were sounded. Two members of one engine company were unaccounted for. The officer in charge of Ladder 15, arriving on a multiple alarm response, penetrated with his company into the building in a rescue attempt, under the direction of the officer in charge. They followed the line that the engine company had stretched to the nozzle, which was unattended. At this time, conditions worsened dramatically. The officer was forced to order his company to retreat, pushing them back in the direction they had entered. When they stumbled to safety, they realized he had not accompanied them outside. By this time, the fire increased in such intensity, it was no longer possible to re-enter. The two jakes who had been missing had been located unconscious by other jakes and were safely evacuated.

"They could not be revived but were still breathing and were eventually transported by helicopter to Connecticut where a hyperbaric chamber is located. Both members were unconscious for days, but eventually recovered although their return to duty is unlikely.

"The fire continued to extend, eventually involving the entire pier and building and it was several hours before it could be controlled to a point where an attempt could be made to recover the missing officer. No one really believed he could have survived, but every jake at the scene was hoping for a miracle. It was not to be. He was eventually located, a long distance from where he had been last seen. His air cylinder was empty and he had removed his facepiece when his supply was exhausted. It appeared that he had attempted to break through the tin clad wall but was unable to. Fire Alarm had recorded his last message when he notified them he was trapped and this made it even more difficult for those who were present because it was obvious no further rescue effort was possible."

Donald first heard about the incident on the radio when he awoke on June 24th. His first thought was that he must keep the news from Gena and Nancy, but when he realized this was going to be impossible, he started thinking about the best way to break the news. The media took the dilemma out of his hands. Nancy came running out of her bedroom, where she had put on her TV as soon as she awoke. "Daddy, daddy," she screamed, running into the kitchen. "A fireman is missing and they say he's dead." Gena, her face pale, stood behind her, looking for confirmation from her husband. He nodded, and replied, "Yes, honey, you're right. I just heard it myself but we'd better just watch and listen for more information."

It turned out to be a dreadful day. All of the stations had frequent news breaks to keep the public informed. Their helicopters were constantly circling the scene and it was obvious from the first pictures that no one could survive inside the tremendous inferno. Donald could see the Tower, its monitor nozzle aimed into the heart of the fire, plugging away desperately, along with several ladder pipes, deck guns from land companies, and the fire boats with their massive streams striking the pier and warehouse from the water side.

When conditions finally permitted, a team of jakes gained access to the building and a report was issued stating that the victim's remains had been located. In a sad and traditional action, members of Ladder 15, their faces streaked with tears, carried the officer, Fire Lieutenant Stephen F. Minehan, from the building.

During the long wait, Donald had called Rick Foster about going to the scene because he felt hopeless just waiting at home. Rick said, "Yeah, I feel the same way, but I called Lieutenant Desmond at home and he told me not to go. He said the bridges were closed from intown and it's impossible to get there."

When the body was finally removed, Nancy said, "Daddy, do you know him? What about his family? Does he have any children?"

"Yes, honey. I know him," Donald said. "Everybody knows Stevie Minehan." He went on to explain that this jake was a prominent member of the union and one of his major duties was conducting the annual election of officers that had just taken place a few weeks earlier. "I was in line, waiting to vote and I heard Stevie talking about his vacation. Every year he works extra tours for other officers in the house, saves up his time and takes his wife and four kids to Martha's Vineyard for the month of July. They all love camping and he was so enthusiastic about the trip; some of the jakes in line were kidding him, telling him it was going to rain all month. But he was always so positive and upbeat, he just waved them off."

Donald had been trying to figure out all morning how to console his wife and daughter. Oh, he realized that Billy O'Laughlin and his partners in the EAP would have a lot of advice for anyone who needed it, but he suspected those guys were going to be overwhelmed from this incident, particularly by those jakes who were at the scene. He tried to remember everything he'd heard from others about what happens when a jake gets killed, but he finally settled on some advice he had gotten from his deputy after Donald had returned from a fire where six people had burned to death. It had been Donald's first encounter with having to pick up a little child's lifeless body and it had bothered him quite a bit. The deputy emphasized the fact that the youngster's pain was brief and now it was over and the soul was gone to a better place.

Donald sat between Gena and Nancy, his arms around them both and said, "You know, everything that happened to Stevie today is over, now. And you know where he is honey?" He leaned towards his daughter. "With God, in heaven. I really believe that, don't you? And guess what?" She looked up at him with tear-filled eyes, "What?" He answered, "He died trying to save two other fire fighters. God really has a special place for people like him. I know he's up there right now, watching all his buddies carry him out. I bet he's probably smiling, because he knows he did the best he could and knows the other jakes are safe."

That night, after all of the evening news reports and the constant chatter on the radio talk shows, Nancy eventually dropped off to sleep. She had been holding her father's hand tightly throughout much of the time they were watching. He cradled her in his arms and put her to bed, both he and Gena mentally and physically exhausted from the events of the long day. Gena said, "I know what you told Nancy was designed to comfort her, darling"—she smiled slowly—"but guess what?" He looked at her quizzically. "It worked on me. I've been thinking all day long about the horror of it all. I can just imagine how his wife and kids must be right now. It's terrible. But, you know, I believe you're right. There must be a special place for people like him because of what he did. He surely must be at peace."

The next few days were very difficult for the entire department. Donald went to the wake in uniform as did so many other fire fighters. He was amazed at the composure of Lieutenant Minehan's wife, who thanked each member as they passed through the line. His young son stood close to his mother, wearing his dad's dress hat and shirt and looking so very brave. It was a very touching scene.

The tragic circumstances of the heroic death, combined with the survival of the two trapped jakes captured the attention of the public and enlarged the story so much it gained national attention, and the entire funeral was broadcast live by Boston' three major TV stations.

Donald was on duty the day the services took place and the coverage was spectacular. Approximately 10,000 jakes were in the honor guard. In the United States when a fire fighter is killed in the line of duty, fire fighters from all over the country frequently come to pay tribute to a fallen comrade. This was no exception.

Soon after Donald had reported for duty, the officers brought all of the jakes into the recreation room, where the huge TV was located. Captain Hardy of Rescue One stood at the podium: "OK you guys, house work and inspections are suspended. We'll all watch Stevie. He was a great jake and we'll miss him. But, I just want to tell you a couple of things. Those of you who never ran into this before are probably pretty shook up. That's O.K., we understand. My first experience with losing a brother fire fighter was the Vendome. As everyone knows, we had nine jakes killed that day. Shit, I wanted to run away and never come back. Not only was I scared to death, it was the saddest thing I ever saw." He paused and looked around the room. "But, know what? Believe it or not, time passes and even the worst memories kind of fade into the background. Because life and the job keep going on." He started to speak again and the house alarm sounded. The speaker announced, "Engine Ten and the Tower respond to a building fire," then the message gave the building location and address and as they raced for the pole hole, they could hear Hardy shouting, "That's what I mean. Let's go get it."

The fire turned out to be minor but the message from the captain was clear. You can let this type of tragedy eat into you and end up with an outlook that will stop you from performing the job you have grown to love. If you do, in time you will probably grow to hate it and either quit or live in fear and dread going to work. Or you can accept it, put it behind you and go on. Will it ever happen again? Yes, but isn't life pretty much of a crap shoot anyway? Donald did his best to reason his way through the period, just like most of the jakes on the job did. The next serious fire he went to was a little intimidating, and when it was knocked down, he realized he was looking around the burned out room he was working in, staring at faces, wondering if anyone here could be next. He caught himself and then thought, Yeah, maybe it will be me, but what a send off I'd get—and he smiled.

Donald's most poignant memory of the funeral was the TV picture of the jake, Davie Walsh, who led the honor guard and carried Stevie's helmet, waist high, in both of his hands. The beat up leather head gear, warped and filthy from many fires, was symbolic to Donald of jakes and everything they stand for.

For the next several weeks the group ran into a dry spell as far as extra alarm fires were concerned, but the routine responses continued at the same pace as always. Donald was starting to understand that this was the way it would probably be throughout his career. At first, he'd start getting a little bit apprehensive when he'd complete tour after tour without much happening, but he finally decided that even when nothing big was happening, there was still plenty to learn at the minor incidents. Just watching the way Desmond approached investigations was worthwhile. He never assumed anything was insignificant until it was over. He explained that over the years he had been at locations where a simple odor of smoke developed into a serious fire; and, he freely admitted, he'd been to a few where the guy in charge wasn't paying attention and casually dismissed companies too soon, only to be called back and find a building fully involved. When Donald asked what would happen to someone like that, Desmond replied, "Oh, not much. The fire report is gonna be a nice fairy tale. But, the job knows. It's not a great reputation to develop. Jakes can be pretty cruel at times."

Desmond and Andy Novak, the lieutenant from another group on the company, had been immersed in the books for several months in preparation for the captains' exam, scheduled for November. "As soon as it's over, I'm going to start a study class for all of you guys." He pointed at Donald and Rick Foster: "That includes you two. You'll both be eligible for the next lieutenants' exam in November of '95. I truly believe it takes a year to get ready, so if you're interested, we're getting together right after Thanksgiving."

Gap Keefe said, "Not me, mon Lieutenant. When you make captain, pal, I'm following you wherever you go. I'm the guy's been enhancing your reputation since you got here, and without me along to hold your hand, you'd make us all look bad."

One early Saturday morning in September, a fire in a large three and a half story duplex, wooden dwelling in the Brighton district resulted in the Tower rescuing several occupants in the bucket. They responded via the Mass. Turnpike and the fire was just a few blocks from the Brighton exit. The fact that it was a Saturday meant they encountered very little traffic en route, and as they were directed into the narrow street from the opposite end of the local fire companies, Steve managed to get the unit close enough to extend the aerial over the cab towards the building. The first arriving ladder companies were removing victims over their own ladders so the Tower, with Donald and Gap in the bucket, nosed into the attic where occupants were screaming at two large windows. The fire was extending rapidly upward from the first floor and the situation was quite desperate. Gap was his usual witty self. He held his arms out to one young woman, clutching her bathrobe tightly around her throat and said, "Guinivere, my dear, your chariot awaits you." The poor girl was actually thrust into the bucket by a guy behind her who had no interest in chivalry. He was coming out and that was that. "Rude, rude," said Keefe as he squeezed aside to let more occupants inside. They actually transported five people to the ground; Donald got out onto the main ladder itself to create enough space.

Soon after they descended, the fire extended into the attic and blew out into the street. This gave them an opportunity to swing back upward and attack it with their nozzle. Once they knocked down the heaviest fire, Desmond joined them, instructed them to extend a hose line and the threesome advanced into the large attic area with its sloping roof. Using their masks, they were able to creep forward, hitting the fire and eventually reaching the narrow stairway from the third floor, where they were joined by an engine company advancing upward from the interior. It was the kind of job that gave Donald immense satisfaction, not only because of the timely rescues, but because of their effective attack as well. He was starting to feel that he was making a real contribution not only to the company, but to public safety as well. Jeez, I'd better not express those kind of thoughts out loud, he thought. I'd hate to hear what guys like Gap, Dot-head or Jeff Stoler would do with such do-gooder expressions.

True to his word, Desmond started his study group at the end of November. Andy Novak remained after he had completed his night tour of duty, just to give some moral support to the group of potential students. He said that both he and Desmond felt pretty confident about how they performed in the captains' test, which had been held just two weeks ago. They had set up a program that had taken just about a year, and as a result they didn't find too many surprises in the exam. Novak also told them he had enlisted a few members from his own work group and they would keep each other up to date and abreast of what they were studying.

Donald was pleased to see Jerry Nagle, Derek Burton and his pal Rick, all from Engine 10, gathered around the conference table. Walt Timmons and Vinnie Sterling from Rescue 1 and Steve Tucker, Howie Rosen and Donald completed the group.

Desmond began by telling them that they were going to be required to purchase a number of books and then be prepared to dedicate some time every day to studying. "I don't just mean while you're on duty. As a matter of fact, it is often pretty difficult to put in the time you have to in the firehouse. Too many interruptions. My own method has been to do all of my memorizing work at home and then just try to review what I've learned when I'm in here." He explained that the station was also a good place to exchange information, ask questions of the class and review past exams. But, the bulk of the work must really be accomplished by the individual.

"There are three kinds of jakes who show up for exams. The first type are those who never study a damned thing and think they are smart enough to know the answers. This group includes guys who've been forced to apply by their wives, poor women who can't understand why the genius they married hasn't been promoted. No one in this group will ever make it, but the exam gives them a chance to say hello to jakes they went to drill school with and maybe go out for a few pops afterward. A nice social Saturday.

"The second group, and this is the largest, are jakes who try to study hard but end up constantly making excuses to themselves as to why they couldn't put the time in today, but will do it for sure tomorrow. These guys won't make it either and if they don't admit to themselves that they didn't put the time in, they figure they got screwed and someone must have bagged the exam.

"The last group—and I hope all of you are in it—are those who make up their minds in the beginning that they are setting aside a part of their lives for a period of time, to concentrate on this highly competitive endeavor. Naw, it doesn't mean you neglect your family or the job; it just means you use the time that would usually be *your* time. Just think about that. Are you really busy all the time in here, or at home? I don't know about any of you, but at home, I'm a pretty early riser. I set up my regimen so that I get up at five and study for a couple of hours before coming to work. If I'm off duty in the day, I may go for four hours or more, depending on what I'm trying to accomplish. It's really just a habit you have to develop. But, you know the best part of it?" When they asked what that was, he replied, "You know exactly when the exam will take place. You can set that date in your head and any time you get discouraged, just flip that calendar over to next November."

He said that both he and Novak, when they exited from the exam, felt the same way.

"What was that, Luft?" asked Vinnie Sterling.

"We were cautiously optimistic and mentally exhausted, but we knew one thing for sure—*No* studying tomorrow and what a relief it is."

Novak told them that while it wasn't an easy job to study, it was much better than it had been in the past. He explained that when his father had been a captain many years ago, the hardest part was trying to guess what to study. Students would be constantly trying to find out the kinds of questions that were being asked in the most recent promotional tests around the state. Nothing was ever published to indicate which of the many available texts would be used in developing the questions. Many poor guys would spend months concentrating on stuff that would never be included.

But, he explained, since the mid-eighties the department had developed a much closer relationship with the State Department of Personnel, which conducted the examinations.

He tossed a Special Order on the desk. "Nowadays, the department provides the state with the type of material they believe is essential to produce the most effective fire officers. They are most certain to include our Standard Operating Procedures, our Rules and Regulations and our Progressive Discipline Guidelines, because they are all used constantly on the job." He continued, "But, and I think this is the best thing they've accomplished, you don't have to learn every item in every book for each exam. They have it divided up pretty well so that what you learn to become a lieutenant is limited in scope and the same applies for captain, district chief and deputy. You're not wasting a lot of time on material that will not be applicable to you in your job."

Desmond said, "We made copies of what you need before you start. We can tell you where to pick up the books you need. It'll probably cost you about a hundred bucks for everything, but you won't have to get them all at once if you're a little short right now."

He gave them a couple of weeks to pick up the various texts other than the department materials they already had. Everyone on the job had been issued SOPs, Rules and Regs, and Discipline Guidelines, but naturally, some of those in the room had already lost theirs or had no idea where they were. Desmond had a connection at headquarters who would provide them the latest department issues.

He told them that classes would be held every afternoon they worked and each evening they would review what they had been doing. He wished them luck and asked for questions.

Steve Tucker said he didn't really know if he wanted to be an officer. He asked both of the lieutenants what they thought about their jobs. "Well," Desmond said, "I guess I felt the same as you when I started thinking about it. I know I was pretty uncertain if I could even handle being in charge of other jakes. But, the more I learned about fire fighting, the more I felt I had something to contribute." He smiled, "That's why I'm always yapping at you jerks to pay attention at fires. This is a pretty simple business we're in, provided you do try to learn at every fire. Oh, I'm not saying you or me or anyone will ever know everything, because it is a business of surprises, too. When you finally get pensioned, you still won't know everything, but you'll sure know a lot if you've been trying to learn."

He said that at every fire, there were just two primary objectives: saving lives and saving property. How do you do this? If you're on an engine company, your role is to try to knock the fire down as quickly as possible, and if you're on a truck or a rescue company, you are trying to evacuate those in danger, ventilate and open up so the engine company can achieve their objective as quickly as possible.

Novak added that he found that when you're in charge, success breeds success: "I don't mean you won't screw up sometimes, but, like Joe said, if you've been paying attention and you get enough experience, you'll do all right."

Desmond said, "One other thing. Remember, we've all gotta be here about thirty years. Now if any of you are good in math, give this a little thought. A lieutenant makes 23% more than a fire fighter. Each other grade gets an additional 15%. That's a lot of dough per year, per decade and per three decades. When you finally retire, you're eligible for 80%. Just what do you want it to be 80% of? See you tomorrow night."

After the officers left, the students read over the types of books they would need. The list was extensive and included the names of the publishers and how they could be purchased. Rick was shaking his head, "Cripes, Donald, look at all this crap. How we gonna learn everything in a year?"

"I don't know, but that math he just mentioned is going to make me give it a big try." He gazed at the list, "But, look. Desmond's right. There's only eight chapters of the rules listed for lieutenants, and not all of the SOPs are on there."

"Yeah, but look at the other stuff. *Fire Stream Practices, Hazardous Materials First Responders, Fire Department Company Officer, Fire Inspection and Code Enforcement, Massachusetts General Laws, Building Construction for the Fire Service, Engine and Truck Company Fireground Operations, Boston Fire Department*

Incident Command System."

"I know," Donald replied, "But even those books have certain chapters listed. And the General Laws, too. C'mon, pal, let's give it a try. If it gets too tough, we can quit."

Vinnie Sterling said he didn't think he'd do it. He'd come into the session just to see what was involved. "I'll tell you the truth. I love being a jake, I love the Rescue Company. And I love this house. Nope, this—this is the way I want to go." Derek Burton, the young black jake who kept pretty much to himself, said, "How would you feel if any of us end up becoming your boss, Vinnie?"

Sterling smiled, "Well, kid, first of all you have to go do it. It's not easy as Desmond and Novak told us. But I've had a lot of bosses on this job. I can't tell you I loved them all." He chuckled. "As a matter of fact, I could tell you a few that I thought were real dumbbells. But...I respected the fact they had earned what they got and I know it's available to me. If I don't choose to take advantage of it, that's my fault. I can live with whoever they send me, but I hope the one we got right now sticks around for a long time." He was referring to Captain Hardy who they all believed was as good as they come.

That evening, Donald told Gena about the day and how he was going to join the class. "But, you know, honey, I'm really not as certain or as confident as I told Rick. Lieutenant Desmond makes it look easy, but I know I've still got plenty to learn. He amazes me at every fire we go to. He's not that old, but sometimes I think he's been going to fires forever." With some insight she never thought she possessed, Gena said, "Remember when you started, um, two and a half years ago? You told me then you were so scared because you didn't think you knew what you were doing. Do you still feel the same way?" He started to reply and she held up her hand. "You know, Donald, both Nancy and I enjoy listening to you talk about the job and how much you love it. But, what I really notice the most is how you tell about the things you do when you're at work. Maybe you don't think you are learning anything but you're constantly mentioning something we never heard before. Did you ever think you'd be able to drive that monstrous truck you have? How about the different parts of the city you've been to now? And the fires—the ones where you were involved in rescues, or you and your crew did something important to control the fire. Or even those sad cases where you had people killed and you had to pick them up. To me, that's learning the job. That's experience and you're getting it." She smiled and said, "If you don't take the exam, maybe Nancy and I will, because we're learning too."

The next evening, as they began reviewing the opening session, Jeff Stoler, who was working for someone on the group, and Dot-head Doherty wandered into the conference room. Desmond glanced up at them and asked, "You fellas want to join the class?" He raised his eyebrows in amazement.

"Naw," replied Stoler, "we just wanna see how you're gonna try to teach these dummies. Ain't we got enough goof balls in the officers' corps already? You even got Holden the Hero in here. He's too brave to be a Lufty." Ever since Donald had been involved in the rescue of two jakes in the Boylston Street fire, Stoler had christened him with the moniker *Hero*.

"Men," Desmond said to the class. "These two are definitely in that first group I described to you yesterday. When you see them the day of the exam, keep away from them. They'll poison your intellect."

Later, Donald stopped by the officer's room to ask Lieutenant Desmond a question about one of the text books. Desmond answered his query and then said, "You know, Donald, those two characters, Doherty and Stoler—I would never, ever, admit it, but they're the type of guys that make this job work. Neither of them will ever open a book and they'll make fun of everyone who does. But, they will work their asses off throughout their careers and without them, there'd be no fire department. If you become an officer, always remember this: the Boston Fire Department has three hundred and fifty officers, including lieutenants, captains and chiefs. There are twelve hundred fire fighters. So, the greatest percentage of them will never get promoted. Some will try and never make it, but many of them are perfectly content with their job. And thank God they are. If they don't work as hard as the job requires them to do, we'll fail in our mission. So, respect them and treat them like the good people they are and if you do, you'll enjoy being an officer as much as I do."

The students spent a week obtaining the necessary material and the sessions started in earnest early in December. Since Desmond considered the SOPs to be the most essential material—not only for the exam, but for knowledge of fire fighting procedures—he had them concentrate on them initially. Donald and Rick had read some of them before in drill school, so they looked like superstars for a couple of sessions. The other jakes in the class hadn't a clue about any of the SOPs because they had been out of drill school too long; many procedures had been updated and changed, and like most jakes on the job, these guys really hadn't been interested. The average non-student learns what is required of him at a fire and does it to the best of his ability. Seeing operations laid out in precise, methodical and boring detail is not likely to instill motivation. But, let any jakes think they've got a good shot at getting a line into the seat of a good fire, or the chance to save someone's life, watch out—they'll go right by you.

The group settled into a routine just as Desmond had described it to them, and it soon became a part of their day and evening grind. The work, of course, didn't stop. As the year drew to a close, the work group became quite busy, responding to four extra alarm fires in as many shifts.

On December 31st, Donald was on patrol at 0700 hours. They were just completing a fairly busy night with an extra alarm fire in Roxbury before mid-night and four responses after midnight including an auto accident, dumpster fire and two accidental alarms in high-rise buildings. Donald was looking forward to New Year's Eve. The three couples—Donald and Gena, Rick and Sandy Foster, and Gap and Marion Keefe, were planning a festive time. They were going to dinner first, then maybe enjoy a few of the First Night events downtown before heading back to Rick's condo in Southie to watch the big ball drop at Times Square. Sandy had completely redecorated his once Spartan bachelor apartment, and she was anxious to show their home to their friends.

The public phone rang and Donald answered. It was a member of Engine 10. He was due into work in an hour but one of his kids was sick and had to go to the hospital. Donald volunteered to stand by for him and told him to take his time. He notified the company officer, Lieutenant Grimes, and then called Gena to tell her he'd be late. Since it was Saturday, she wasn't working and she and Nancy had nothing more vital than hair stylist's appointments, which were within walking distance.

At 0755 hours Box 5127 was struck for a fire in the Brighton district and Donald dispatched Rescue One, which responded to all boxes struck in the division.

No sooner had they cleared the apron than the captain of the first truck at the scene, Ladder 14, reported people trapped and struck a second alarm. Donald dispatched the deputy and the Tower and listened anxiously for more information, looking carefully at the running card to see if Engine 10 had an assignment. The instructions listed the company to cover another station on a third alarm. He didn't have long to wait; the district chief ordered a third alarm within a few minutes.

Donald announced they were to cover in Brighton and, if it became a fourth alarm, they were to respond directly to the fire.

They sped through the South Station underpass, then exited onto the Mass. Pike, and immediately they could see clouds of black smoke in the distance. Grimes was telling the driver, Bobby Hartman, that the fire was only a couple of blocks from the Turnpike exit and he knew an easy access route if they were dispatched. Edgar Street and Phil Morrison were seated with Donald in the passenger compartment. They had just arrived for duty on the day tour and Donald hadn't worked with any of them before, except for the officer, who was on the same shift as he.

The smoke was thick and heavy as they swung onto Cambridge Street, and Donald heard Grimes say, "Slow down a bit Bobby, I think they'll be asking for more help." He didn't want to drive a couple of miles to their covering assignment and then have to come back. They were creeping along, trying to see over the buildings on their left. Sparks and brands were flying into the sky and a message was transmitted, "Strike fourth alarm, Box 5127." Donald grabbed the straps of his mask and slipped them onto his shoulders, the other two jakes doing the same. He could hear Grimes laughing: "See, Bobby," he said to the driver, "even I'm right once in a while."

He directed Hartman to turn into Linden Street and then onto Ashford, speeding to the location of the fire on Pratt Street. Most of the units already at the scene had arrived at the opposite end of the street so Engine 10 was able to secure a hydrant not far from the intersection. The district chief's aide was happy to see them. "Boy, Luft, I've been trying to get someone over this side but the traffic's all fucked up." He told the officer the chief wanted a big line stretched into an adjacent building. "We got one line on the first floor, but we need one for upstairs and the attic."

Three separate fires had been set in the first floor of an enormous, two and one half story duplex wood frame dwelling occupied by college students. Although many of them were on vacation between semesters, some were still in the building. The accelerants used to set the building ablaze had caused such a rapid spread of intense fire that not only were both sides of the duplex fully involved, the adjacent building, separated by a narrow alley, had also been ignited throughout the two floors and the attic. Jakes from the ladder companies and the Tower were engaged in rescuing occupants over ground ladders; consequently, the building Engine 10 was assigned to had not been properly vented when they arrived.

Grimes turned and yelled, "Big line. Holden, it's your side."

Donald jumped to the street, moved up to the cross lay, grabbed the nozzle, looped it over his shoulder. He moved rapidly towards the building, with the two and a half inch hose dragging behind him. Edgar Street stopped to assist Hartman in connecting the feeder line into the pump. Phil Morrison was back at the hydrant, over a hundred feet away, where they had looped the huge water supply carrier hose before moving the apparatus towards their destination.

Donald sped up the four wooden steps leading to a porch and the front entrance of the dwelling. Grimes was several feet back, dragging a portion of the line to provide Donald with the slack he needed to continue forward. A charged line was already inside and Donald could hear the water striking inside the first floor. The visibility was poor but he stumbled into the inside stairway leading upward. Grimes told him to pause where he was and the officer disappeared into the first floor, following the operating hose line. He was back momentarily, and said, "O.K. Engine Forty-two's line is doing good on this floor. We're going up. Get your facepiece on—the roof's not open yet."

Donald moved forward; his visibility was poor as he mounted each step and he could feel the temperature rising as he approached the turn to the second floor landing. Suddenly, he saw a bright glow directly ahead of him and he mumbled the information to Grimes. "O.K., kid. I'll get the line filled." The officer placed the remote mike of his radio onto his facepiece and said, "Engine Ten, fill the big line." Bobby Hartman must have been waiting for the order because Donald could immediately hear air rushing through the open nozzle as he heard the prompt reply, "On the way."

The water burst forth and he drove it right into the brightness, the force of the hundreds of gallons under high pressure, darkening the flames as the volume of smoke increased significantly. "Try movin' ahead, Donald," Grimes voice mouthed into his right ear. The officer was kind of leaning on him, influencing his forward motion. He flattened his body on the hallway landing and kept moving the pipe from side to side. Now, they were inside a room and as the stream went to the left, they could hear glass breaking and crashing as it was blown from the window sashes by the solid, circular force of the water.

They could hear another engine company dragging a line somewhere down below and Edgar Street appeared beside them. "Engine Fourteen's on the way up, Luft. They got a big line." Grimes immediately tapped Donald on the shoulder and said, "Shut it down and back out. We're goin' up the top." The three of them muscled the line out of the room, along the hallway and stopped at a front room that was burning, but not with the same intensity as the one they had just knocked down. Grimes directed the officer of Fourteen into the rear room, told him they were moving up and then had Donald swish the line around the front room, quickly killing the fire they could see.

Phil Morrison joined them in the hallway and Grimes said, "Phil, we're gonna try to make the attic. Stay in the hall and if Fourteen can't hold the fire under us, let me know right away."

Donald crept up the narrow steps on his knees, the black, ominous smoke, heated by the lack of overhead ventilation, enveloping him. "Open the pipe, Holden," Grimes shouted in his ear. He could feel the officer's hands pressing on his shoulder blades. "Put it on a straight stream and shoot it right up over your head." Donald twisted the control valve and created the more narrow, solid and concentrated delivery of the water. He could hear it hitting the interior of the pitched roof covering and kept rotating it to provide the best distribution.

Morrison grabbed Edgar's leg and yelled, "Fourteen's officer says there's a couple of people missin'. They ain't on this floor. Must be in the attic." Street relayed the message and Grimes said, "OK, Donald, try to climb through the opening." Morrison also passed the word that the fire below them was being contained, which was a relief to the three jakes moving forward.

In spite of the delivery of the powerful stream from the nozzle, the heat was still intense as Donald elevated his head through the opening and above the floor level. He asked Grimes to grab the pipe and then wriggled his way onto the flat surface. He became partially entangled in debris but managed to push through it. Apparently a false ceiling had been installed and it had now collapsed, creating piles of fiberboard tiles and their twisted, metal supports.

It was difficult advancing through the heat and obstacles but Donald suddenly heard pounding somewhere overhead. In a matter of seconds, the smoke and heat lessened slightly. He kept going and was joined by Grimes, who said, "Start feeling around everywhere." A cracking noise now joined the pounding and the area became much more liveable as a significant opening appeared near the ridge line, drawing up huge quantities of the products of combustion.

Donald made it to his knees and made better progress into the area. His gloved hand feeling ahead of him, touched something he knew had to be a human figure lying on the floor. "Got someone, Luft." At first his arm automatically recoiled but he willed himself to feel the unmoving figure. "It's a woman, I think," he said as his hands moved over the chest area. Grimes shut down the nozzle and got on the radio, requesting flexi-cots. These are body bags, but the old name is used because it's not always understood by people monitoring fire department radio communications. The less known term lets the officer in charge know a victim has been located without actually saying the words over the system. As the visibility improved and the heat dissipated, it was now possible to rise to a crouch. Grimes and Edgar moved past Donald, and Street soon shouted, "In the bed, Luft. This one's a woman too." The roof opening was now a couple of feet square and as Donald looked upward, he could see the cherub-like face of Jeff Stoler looking down at him. "Hey, Hero Holden," shouted the voluble Towerman, "I'm showin' you how we open a roof on this group. Those stiffs you work with only know how to make pin holes."

Donald didn't reply because he was looking at the badly burned victim, the face unrecognizable and the clenched fists and arms badly charred.

In a matter of moments, members of the rescue company climbed into the room and soon had the two women, who were later identified as students, enveloped in the heavy plastic coverings. They transported them down the front stairways to the street.

These were the only two victims at the fire, the department having rescued many others from the adjacent dwellings. But even though the jakes were euphoric about the number who had been saved, the deaths of the young women diminished the cheerful atmosphere.

Because they had responded on the fourth alarm, Engine 10 was dismissed soon after the fire was under control and by the time they were backing into the firehouse, Donald could see the jake he had stood by for, standing in the doorway with his fire gear waiting for the pumper to come to a stop. He thanked Donald for taking his place and reported that his child had been admitted for observation. "Tough job, huh Donald?"

"Yeah. Kind of sad," Donald replied. "But, we got a great shot at the fire." He really didn't want to concentrate on the thought of the victims.

As he emerged from the shower, Jeff Stoler and Mark Palmer were just entering, their faces and necks filthy with a ring of soot ending at the top of their turnout coat line. Stoler was his usual outrageous self: "Hey, Hero, I hope you learned somethin' today. We laid that bucket right through a back yard from the next street and saved you clowns' asses in that attic. If you were working with Desmond and them other lightweights, you'd have never stayed there. You'd've been backin' down the stairs to the street, right Mark?" He turned to his partner for support.

Palmer rolled his eyes: "Of course, Fatso. If we didn't chop those holes, you'd have probably fell through with the weight of that, er, magnificent body of yours."

Stoler sputtered and started to reply but Donald said, "You know Jeff, you look like one of those guys who used to lead the minstrel shows years ago. The contrast of that black face with the sickly white blubber under it would get a big laugh anywhere—Mr. Interlocutor." Donald ran from the room as he could hear Palmer laughing and Jeff screaming. He had to admit, though, that they had really done a terrific job of maneuvering the Tower into the proper spot to let them get the roof open. Maybe Ten would have had to retreat. It sure was tough trying to make that floor. He remembered how in drill school the instructors would set a fire on the top floor of the fire building, send groups of recruits inside and then, just as it got unbearable, open the roof scuttle. It was a practical and dramatic demonstration of effective proper overhead ventilation and today was like a perfect field test to confirm the lesson.

The New Year's Eve party proved to be a great success. Barrett's Restaurant in Charlestown was festively decorated for the season, and their menu was sprinkled with their famous seafood chowders, fish, lamb and beef. They stopped in Quincy Marketplace to see some of the First Night revelry and the beautiful ice sculptures carved by some of Boston's best chefs. Back at Rick and Sandy's home, after the mandatory tour of the unit by the ladies, the celebration continued. At midnight, as the ball dropped in Times Square, Donald wrapped his arms around Gena and held her tightly before he kissed her with a fervor that startled and pleased her. He had been struck with an almost overwhelming sadness as he realized the two tragic victims would never see 1995. He wondered what the year would bring to him.

As spring gradually approached, Donald realized—much to his surprise—that the winter had been almost gentle, at least compared to the one before it. The 1993-94 season had produced a record high snowfall of ninety-six inches, over fifty inches more than the average for Boston. By contrast, 1994-95 was slightly less than fifteen inches, twenty-five inches less than the average. Oh, to be a weather forecaster in New England, he thought, as he marked the figures in his journal on the first day of spring.

The much more favorable weather conditions didn't mean there were no serious fires, only fighting them was much less complicated.

The hydrants were free and easily accessible and the banjos didn't get any strumming.

Donald had responded to thirty extra alarm fires in 1994, and the new year looked like it too would be busy.

His studying activities consumed quite a bit of his time, both on and off duty. He found that his best time for attempting to commit to memory much of the extensive material was at home during the day while Gena was at work and Nancy was at school. Once he understood that these hours didn't detract much from his duties and pleasures as a husband and father, it became relatively simple to develop a habit. He knew he was getting on to the right track when he began to feel guilty if he didn't put in the time he felt he should.

It also became intriguing to him that the department had put in a major effort to develop practical and effective Standard Operating Procedures dealing with any possible activity of the membership, however minute or seemingly inconsequential, but primarily with fire fighting. There are both tactical and strategic instructions as well as different procedures for different occupancies and types of construction, ranging from dwellings to the monstrous high rise buildings. What pleased him most of all was that, as a result of the fires he had been too, he was able to understand the logic of most of the instructions and assignments. However, he also appreciated the preface to each set of procedures that emphasized they were merely guidelines and the officer in charge of a unit or the incident had the authority to alter activities to adapt to the unusual or changing conditions encountered at a fire.

Donald breathed a sigh of relief at that sentence because he had already seen instances where the ability to be flexible was the key to what they accomplished. Yeah, he reflected, Desmond was not only a great teacher, but an innovative leader who tried to anticipate situations that could develop during operations. During the times Donald was assigned to drive the Tower, he would concentrate on following the route he had mapped out in his head to reach the location of fires in other districts. Frequently, as they neared the area of the incident, Desmond, who remained silent most of the time so as not to interfere with the operator's concentration, would tap him on the shoulder and give him directions that would put them in the most advantageous spot for effective use of the unit. He would be listening closely to the radio, trying to determine the extent of the fire they were going to and what was the most logic assumption to make regarding where they would be most needed on arrival. Naturally, sometimes he'd be wrong, because the descriptions on the air would not describe accurately what was happening, but Desmond's percentage was a lot more positive than negative.

When he was wrong, he'd have the same slight smile he had when he had made the appropriate call. When Donald asked the officer about it, Desmond just shrugged his shoulders and said, "Holden, nobody really knows everything about this crazy business. When you're involved in the type of guessing game I use, you gotta accept the fact you'll make the incorrect choice of options sometimes. But, that's also what's good about the business. If we can't get the truck where we want it at a particular operation, we still are not out of the ball game. There's always lines to be advanced, ladders to be raised and portable gear to be moved and used, so we are always gonna make a contribution." He laughed and added, "But, there's nothing I like better than making the right call and having us be the key to knocking down the fire."

The study sessions in work were not as intense for Donald as his solitary efforts at home. Still, he enjoyed them even when he didn't learn anything he hadn't already covered. Desmond usually had a quiz for them, and those who didn't have the answers were required to find them and read them so they would be current with the rest of the students by the time the study period was completed.

Donald was impressed with the fact that there was no fooling around in the study room. Desmond saw to that right from the beginning. That didn't stop the repartee once they were all in the kitchen. Nor did it stop Dot-head Doherty and Gap Keefe from giving the students unwanted advice. Dot-head always had the latest rumor about changes in the exam procedures, battlefield commissions and the lack of intelligence of some of those enrolled in the class, while Gap would dig out some rule or regulation they hadn't covered yet, commit it to memory and quote it at the appropriate time. They set up Donald nicely during lunch one day. Dot-head said, "Hey, Gap old pal, I'm on patrol this morning and I'm doing what every good jake does."

"What's that, Fire Fighter Doherty?"

"Why studying the Rules and Regulations, of course, what else!"

Keefe smiled, his grin showing the huge space between his upper teeth. "That's very good. Do you have any questions?"

"Yes, I do. There's this rule says, 'No animal except one cat shall be permitted or kept in quarters.' Is that correct, Fire fighter Keefe?"

Donald lifted his head to pay attention. He hadn't seen that in his edition.

"Well, it's almost correct," answered Gap. "The complete rule reads, 'No animal except one cat, OR, one U.S. Marine, shall be permitted or kept in quarters." Before Donald could shout his objections, Keefe continued: "And it makes sense. Just look around this room and tell me the truth—wouldn't you rather have a nice little kitty cat than any one of those jar heads we got in this house?"

Donald started to sputter, trying to produce an appropriate reply, but the house alarm sounded and they were dispatched to a report of a fire in one of the two forty story apartment houses located on the waterfront, about a quarter of a mile from their quarters on the opposite side of the Expressway. Steve Tucker drove the truck on the tunnel-surface crossover at Congress Street, swung left on Atlantic Avenue, past the Boston Harbor Hotel and turned onto East India Row. Heavy smoke was showing on an upper floor of one of the concrete apartment Towers. Engine 10 had arrived just before them and Lieutenant Grimes was reporting that fact on the main radio channel. Fire Alarm established Channel Two as the fireground frequency. Desmond stepped from the piece and directed the members to bring the high rise equipment. Donald grabbed the Halligan bar and an axe, while Gap dragged off the resuscitator and Howie Rosen got the forcible entry hydraulic Rabbit tool. They all had donned their breathing apparatus and sped into the small lobby, opening the supply valves on their high pressure air cylinders. Before he stepped inside, Donald looked directly overhead and could see the smoke was permeated with tongues of flame blowing out into the crisp winter atmosphere. Engine 10's crew was just ahead of them, wheeling in their two wheel cart, piled high with donut rolled lengths of 2 and 1/2 inch yellow hose.

Desmond inserted the fire fighter's elevator key into the lock and turned it, bringing the two elevators to the lobby. Through Desmond's radio, Donald could hear Deputy Chief Franklin ordering a second alarm. Some occupants were crowding into the lobby and Lieutenant Grimes directed them into the first floor of the adjacent building where they'd be warmer and also would not be interfering with the operation.

As the elevator doors opened, a group of four middle-aged people stumbled into the lobby, coughing and gasping. District Chief Kinsella of District Three had just arrived and he asked them where they came from. They shouted they had been on the thirty-ninth floor and their apartments were filled with smoke. They had pressed the elevator button and when it arrived, crowded into it and pushed the first floor button. They passed right through the fire floor, which was the thirty-sixth, in spite of the signs they had glanced at for years advising them to use the stairs in case of fire. Fortunately, they all made it to safety although they had inhaled substantial smoke during their descent. Members of Rescue One led them outside as Engine 10 and the Tower unit crews, along with Chief Kinsella and the deputy's aide entered the elevator. Desmond punched the button for the thirty-fourth floor, in compliance with the SOP requiring a destination two floors below the reported fire floor.

At the twentieth floor, he made a stop to insure they had proper control of the elevator and they then resumed the ascent. Deputy Franklin contacted Kinsella and said they had a report of occupants still in apartments on floor thirty-seven and possibly on the top floor as well. When the elevator stopped, a slight haze permeated the floor area and Kinsella said, "O.K., I'm establishing the Upper Command post right here." He then directed Ten to connect to the standpipe on the next floor above. "Tower," he shouted to Desmond, "try to get an entrance into the fire floor for Ten and then get up above the fire." It was almost an unnecessary order because Desmond knew what they had to do, just as Grimes did.

Desmond, Donald, Gap and Howie Rosen walked briskly up the stairs, passing Jerry Nagle, Rick Foster and Derek Burton who were at the standpipe, unrolling their hose and starting to make their connection.

At the fire floor, the door to the corridor was closed and dense brown smoke was oozing out into the stairway through the door jambs. Desmond pulled off his glove and slid his hand along the steel surface. "Warm, but not too bad," he said. He felt the knob and it was a little hotter. "I'm gonna ease it open a little. Lean against me," he said to Gap. "If it has a lot of pressure, I'll slam it shut." He carefully twisted the knob, pushed against the door and then cracked it open towards himself, almost gently. Quantities of smoke escaped outward but he managed to close the opening without difficulty. "OK," he said, "Howie, stay here and tell Grimes there's not too much pressure yet. Open the door when he tells you, after he gets his water."

He motioned Donald and Gap to follow him. "We have to get into the rooms above. Remember, if it gets too tough, each one of these units has an outside patio." He explained that if any occupants were still there, that's probably where they'd go to escape the smoke and it's where the jakes could go as well if they became trapped. The SOPS Donald was learning made it clear that at high-rise fires no one was to go above the fire floor, unless people were trapped, because of the great danger these fires presented, and this was the case at this incident.

As the jakes approached the thirty-seventh floor on the stairway, the smoke became thicker and Desmond told them to put on their facepieces. The fresh air from the cylinder felt good, thought Donald. At the landing, Desmond said, "O.K. Open this door slowly, like I did down below. Shouldn't be any fire up here, but you never know." Donald felt the door, just as he had seen the officer do a few moments before; he couldn't feel any abnormal heat. As he swung the door slowly outward, smoke vented into the stairway but without too much intensity. The three of them entered in a crouched position and came to an apartment door. It was locked and Donald pounded on it, hoping there'd be a reply from inside. There was none, so he inserted the adz of the Halligan between the frame and the jamb, above the knob, whacked it with the heel of his gloved hand and then pulled back on the straight, steel shaft. The door popped inward easily and they made their way inside. The visibility was extremely poor but they determined from the furnishings that they bumped into, they were in a living room. As Donald made his way into a dining area, he thought he could hear someone yelling. He continued to advance and bumped into a sliding door, which apparently led to the porch. He pulled it back and almost knocked down a woman who was huddled on the concrete deck, whimpering and coughing. "Ma'am, you're OK. We're here now, ma'am!" was all he could think to say. It was enough—as he bent closer to her, pulling off his mask, she grabbed him in a stranglehold and he almost fell on top of her. Desmond appeared at the opening and said, "Holden, stay with her. I can hear water hitting the fire. She should be all right here. But, if you gotta get out, you know where the stairway is." He indicated he and Gap were continuing the search and he faded back into the smoke. Donald pushed the door until it was almost closed, allowing smoke to continue venting outward but leaving a fairly sheltered place for himself and the victim. He wished he had a radio to try to find out what was happening. However, within a few minutes, the sliding door opened again and Dot-head Doherty, his face covered with his mask, stepped out to join them. "Hey, Hero, at it again, huh?" he said. As he started to speak again, a solid stream of water burst out directly underneath their perch and Donald breathed a sigh of relief. Ten's line had made it through the burning apartment below them and they appeared to be bringing the fire under control.

They explained to the woman that she was safe now and they would stay with her until she could be brought down to the lobby. She immediately wanted to make them coffee or give them a drink or dinner or anything. She was hysterical with joy. "I thought I was dead," she said. "I was trying to pray and all I could think of was Steve McQueen in the *Towering Inferno*." She giggled and said to Donald, "When you opened that door and grabbed me, I thought, 'This man looks better than Steve ever did.'"

Eventually, the smoke cleared enough so Donald could escort her over to the stairway and down to the Upper Command Post. He learned that one apartment on the thirty-sixth floor had been almost entirely destroyed; fortunately, the occupants weren't home at the time of the fire and no one was killed.

Desmond and Gap had gotten two people on the thirty-eighth. Rescue One, Ladder 1 and 24 had completed the search on the top two floors and brought four people up onto the roof as the most expedient safe area.

Engine 8 had joined Engine 10 with another big line on the fire floor and both Engines 4 and 50 had stretched lines into the area where Donald was but neither line proved necessary.

The press had a field day interviewing those who were rescued; the elderly woman Donald had removed had another stranglehold on him in the lobby, squealing about how he had saved her life.

The fire commissioner was at the scene and he was surrounded by reporters from both the print and electronic media. Donald heard him patiently answering the non-stop questions. He made a point of emphasizing that automatic sprinklers would have stopped this fire with only minor damage. In answering the question why the building didn't have sprinklers, he carefully explained that under the retroactive law they would have such protection within the next two years. He concluded his remarks by saying, "Until then, we hope everyone in these buildings will make themselves aware of how they should escape in case of emergency. However, if they can't get out, these fire fighters, who saved so many today, will make every possible attempt to do it again."

Back in quarters, the jakes got their equipment back in service and filed into the mess hall, gratefully savoring the coffee that was always available. Rick Foster said to Grimes, "Hey, Luft, I was listening to the boss talking about sprinklers to the reporters. I thought all these big buildings had them anyway."

Grimes answered, "Yeah, well, when you students finish studying the laws with Lieutenant Desmond, you'll know all that stuff."

At the next study session they attended, Desmond distributed a copy of the sprinkler law, telling them not to commit it to memory now because they'd be spending time on the fire laws at a future date.

In spite of the reduction in the amount of snow this season, it didn't mean there weren't some bitterly cold nights. Early in February, a second alarm shortly after 0200 in the Roxbury district with the temperature in the single digits and the wind chill at -26 was as typical as hundreds of other fires like it in the past. A vacant three decker, rear porches fully involved and extending into all floors caused the chief officers to shift to an outside attack. Desmond, with his usual foresight, had directed the placement of the Tower so it came down a small intersecting street. The deputy at the scene was delighted to see the unit positioned to utilize its heavy stream appliance from the bucket by simply rotating under some power cables and extending at an angle of thirty degrees. This enabled them to drive the powerful stream directly into the second and third floors, effectively blackening down the intense fire. Donald, who was operating the controls in the bucket while Gap directed the nozzle, was pleased with his ability to maneuver the aerial into the most advantageous position to let the water do its work effectively. By the time they were ordered to shut down, the front of the building was completely coated with ice that was thickening considerably while they watched. It was a very satisfactory performance, and when they were leaving, the deputy tipped his hat towards Desmond and said, "Joe, you can come to any of my fires, anytime."

As was their usual practice on the way back to quarters, they stopped at a Dunkin' Donuts and the most bedraggled looking and ice covered jake in the crew went in and ordered two dozen doughnuts, forlornly trying to fumble for his wallet. Invariably, the night manager would come out from the bakery and refuse payment. Donald no longer shook his head at this charade; jakes will be jakes and a bargain is a bargain. And I'm one of them.

At 0135 on another cold night in the middle of the month, they responded to a fourth alarm in a group of four story brick and wood apartments on Warren Street in the Brighton district. This heavily populated area often would go for several weeks without much action and then seemed to explode with a number of extra alarm fires and this was one of those periods. Whenever a fire got a good start, it invariably extended to adjoining buildings and the high population density often resulted in fatalities. At this fire, great ladder work by the first alarm companies managed to get everyone out, but while they were concentrating on this essential effort, the fire extended from the third floor of one building to the fourth floor and roof, and then into the adjoining occupancies on each side.

The Tower Unit followed a big line into one of the involved exposures and, as the engine company drove the fire towards the rear, Desmond had the crew pulling ceilings quickly to prevent advancement of the fire towards the front of the building. As soon as he was satisfied they had opened a large enough area with their rakes, the engine company drove their stream upward, effectively controlling the extension.

Desmond had them move up to the top floor where another hose line was just arriving from the stairway and they performed the same duties, pulling, pulling, pulling until all of the charred and glowing wood was completely exposed.

Once he was confident the fire couldn't get any further, Desmond, who had been pulling as much as anyone, told them to take a break. They all sat right on the debris-covered floor, completely covered with plaster dust and chunks of insulation. Even the lieutenant was breathing deeply and shrugging his shoulders to ward off the aches that accompanied such vigorous overhead work.

Dot-head Doherty appeared in the doorway of the room, Walt Timmons and Captain Hardy just behind him. They were also filthy and Doherty shook his head and said, "Jeez, Cap, get a look at this. That damned Tower crew is fuckin' off as usual. They give the whole house a bad name."

Gap, his breathing restored to normal said, "Say Dot, since you didn't do shit at this fire, would you get us four coffees. One cream, no sugar, one black and two regular. Get some napkins too. We'll have to look neat for the interviews out front."

As Hardy and Desmond walked over to the front windows to look down at the mass of ice covered hose in the street and the position of the three aerials that had been extended to the fire buildings, their crews were chattering away, insulting each company's performance. Hardy said, "Joe, they never change, do they?"

Desmond smiled: "Nope, Cap, and we better hope they never do. Thank God jakes never learned about political correctness or human rights or whatever. We'd be getting sued for harassment at every fire." He looked back at the group, and said, "D'ya think this building is a Smoking or Non-smoking area?"

Hardy burst out laughing, "I don't know, but don't give Doherty any ideas. He'll put in a grievance that I'm neglecting his health."

February continued to be a busy month with another multiple

alarm for the group. This one occurred in the Dorchester section of District Eight shortly after 1900 hours on the 27th, an evening when the temperature was again in the teens. The fire started in a mattress of a bedroom on the first floor of a six family three decker. The fire had gained great headway because of delayed notification to the department, and when the first companies reported at the scene, it had already extended into both sides of the three story wood frame structure and was jumping across a narrow alley into the right side of an identical adjacent building.

The Tower crew hand-carried a forty foot extension ladder and threw it to the roof of the exposed building. Gap and Donald made their way over the aluminum rungs, bringing a power saw and an axe with them. First, they removed a scuttle cover, which drew a lot of smoke out of the building. Then, with Donald standing behind him, his hand leaning on Keefe's back, Gap started the saw and rapidly made four large cuts, completing a square, directly over the fire which was engulfing two rooms at the front of the structure. After Gap shut down the saw, Donald stepped forward and pounded the severed wood with his axe, splintering it and driving it downward. The fire spewed upward as they stepped back in retreat. Both jakes leaned over the edge of the roof and could see charged lines stretched up the stairway of the building they were working. Donald lay flat on the tar and gravel surface, held his axe in one hand, swung it out towards the street and let it drop through the already blackened large, middle window. As it crashed through, flames leaped outward. He crawled to his left and performed the same activity on the offset side window and then repeated it again on the opposite panes of glass. As he was completing the task, he heard a gushing noise beneath him and a spray of water swept out into the street. An engine company crew had made it to the top floor and they were now hitting their stream into the ceiling below Donald and Gap, breaking it up into minute particles and effectively killing the fire.

The two Tower jakes managed to drop down onto the top floor of the rear porch and soon joined Desmond and the rest of the company in their most frequent task—pulling, pulling, pulling plastered ceilings.

Back in quarters, as they were trying to rinse the quantities of dirt from their fire clothes, Desmond said, "Don't spend too much time on that gear. The new stuff's arriving in the morning." He was referring to the new bunker gear the department was issuing to everyone in the fire fighting force. Jakes in Boston have been wearing rubber coats since before the turn of the century, along with three-quarter length rubber boots, leather fire helmet and gloves. Of course, over the years, many changes have occurred so that the coat, still smooth surfaced on the exterior, is lined with nomex and other fire resistive materials to protect the wearer. Jakes, who wore chambray shirts and dungaree pants for many years, had been issued fire resistive uniform work shirts and trousers for well over a decade.

It had been a fairly satisfactory combination. In the late 1970s, however, the National Aeronautics and Space Administration (NASA), the National Fire Administration (NFA), and the International Association of Fire Fighters (IAFF) formed a committee composed of users, manufacturers and scientists to try to develop more effective personal protective equipment. NASA and the fire fighters had already succeeded in developing a much better breathing system and that dramatic success encouraged them to make a similar effort in the area of individual protective outer clothing. The program, plagued with underfunding, dragged on through the '80s, with many discouraging attempts and a few notable successes, the major ones being the development of a rechargeable ninety minute flashlight, chest mounted on fire fighters' turn out gear and much more effective hand and wrist protection against cuts and burns.

By the middle of the decade, however, many departments were changing the outer gear to a combination of fire resistive coats, bunker pants and short boots that terminated under the knee. While the new gear offered better overall protection, it didn't receive unanimous and immediate acceptance. It restricted movement somewhat and it caused the user to be overheated much more rapidly, sometimes resulting in dehydration.

Boston, which had initiated the breathing apparatus program, and was the first department in the country to adopt the commercially produced breathing system when it became available, was slow to adopt the changes. Department members served on the national committee and once the new equipment appeared on the market, field tests began, but the same fire companies that had been so enthusiastic with the masks tests rejected protective gear from each manufacturer, citing how impractical the equipment was when used at fires as opposed to laboratory tests. In time they did find some acceptable gear, but when they finally were as satisfied as they were ever going to be, the city budget wouldn't support the funds necessary to equip the entire department. So, the field tests continued for a few years and by 1994, a new drill class was issued the chosen ensemble. As a result of the continuing use of the test gear at fires in the interim, several changes had been made, and the department safety committee believed the equipment would now suit the needs of the fire fighters.

When Donald was relieved by his partner, Jeff Stoler, in the morning he decided to remain in quarters and await the arrival of the gear. Gena was working, Nancy was at school and he had some free time. Of course, as he lounged in the mess hall, he was entertained by Stoler and his rapier wit. Today his target was Frank O'Neill, otherwise known as Ball-buster O'Neill, usually shortened to Buster. O'Neill had his own reputation to protect; he was noted for his own insights into the flaws in other jakes' characters and earned his nickname from his brutal frankness when someone made a mistake. He had been yapping away at Ramon Rafael Romero, or "Triple R" as he was called. Romero had just returned from injured leave caused by three broken fingers, received when a frozen halyard on a ground ladder broke as he and two other Tower jakes were removing it from a window at the conclusion of a fire. Unfortunately, Ramon had put one hand on a rung rather than the accepted method of holding the ladder with the hand cupped around the spars. When the extension ladder slid downward, he couldn't get his entire hand removed in time and the ice-crusted rung cracked the last joints of the fingers.

Buster was now ragging Triple R unmercifully: "They should call you Triple F from now on. Frozen Fuckin' Fingers, you dumb-dumb." Romero laughed. He was so glad to be back, even O'Neill couldn't upset him. Triple R had been born in Puerto Rico, came to the mainland when he was a grown man, primarily to try to get work. He managed to get a job at a major shoe distributor in Roxbury and was trying to save enough to bring his young wife and daughter to the states. But, the cost of living in Boston, along with what he had to send back home, didn't allow him to make much progress in reaching his objective. At a meeting of an Hispanic association, a Boston fire fighter, himself a native of St. Thomas in the Virgin Islands, talked about the fire department, the court order that gave preference to minorities and passed out applications for the next competitive examination.

The department also held instructional classes and Ramon spent many hours studying the material he had been provided. He not only passed the exam, he managed to finish high on the minority list; within a year of first hearing about the job, he was appointed. It was love at first sight for him, and he couldn't believe the pay, especially for performing a job he enjoyed so much. When he completed drill school, he managed to get a nice apartment in the Dorchester district and his wife and child finally joined him.

In the ensuing years, the family expanded by two more girls and the Romeros now had managed to purchase a small single house in Roslindale. While Ramon didn't like the cold weather very much, he noticed that even the jakes from the Boston area weren't crazy about it—when they were working. Of course, several of them played that crazy ice hockey game and went skiing whenever they could. Not Ramon. In the winter, when it was cold, if he wasn't working, he stayed inside. That's why he was so happy to be back to work. He loved his family very much, but after months of being cooped up with four females, he was delighted to listen to the Ball-buster trying to break his chops.

"Buster," my friend, "I've really missed you. I'm sorry about your condition."

O'Neill looked puzzled: "What condition?" he said.

Ramon smiled as he said, "Why Jeff Stoler told me you put on twenty pounds while I was away, and you sure look it. He says they call you Quadruple B now."

"For what?" sputtered O'Neill.

Stoler shouted from across the room, "Blubber Belly Ball Breaker, you fat shit."

O'Neill, always sensitive about his weight, said, "Lissen, Romero, I been real good to you since you came here. I told you before, don't pay any attention to that dork Stoler. When you been up here long enough, you'll understand some of the best jakes add a coupla pounds in the winter so we can stay outside all night and do our job."

O'Neill was assigned to the Haz-Mat truck, and the chances of him being outside at a fire of any kind for long periods were remote. Stoler, his piercing voice grating on everyone's nerves, screamed, "What a scenario. O'Neill outside and actually working. Let me picture it." He paused and closed his eyes, "Naw. Triple R, if you do thirty years here, you ain't gonna see that happen."

Buster gave the only reply he could think of, "Fuck you."

Box 1653 was struck over the alarm system and the house gong shut off the argument as Rescue One was dispatched. Fire Alarm announced that the signal was for the report of an explosion at the University Hospital on Harrison Avenue in the South End district. Donald slid the pole and went to his gear locker. Before he could open the door, the department Lighting Plant, stationed in Engine 3's quarters, reported at the scene and ordered a second alarm struck. The Lighting Plant is manned by one fire fighter but department rules emphasize that the first member at the scene of an incident has the same authority as the highest ranked member and may take any action deemed necessary until relieved by a superior officer.

Captain Dan Murray was the officer in charge of the Tower and Donald asked permission to respond to the fire. Murray nodded and Donald crowded into the passenger compartment. Roscoe Kearns was driving, Nick Deliago, Mark Palmer and the irrepressible Stoler comprised the rest of the crew.

The truck sped out the door and Stoler, busily adjusting his gear, looked over at Donald seated opposite him: "Hey, Hero," Stoler began, "tryin' to suck up to the captain? Don't even try. Me, Roscoe, Nick and Mark got the boss all locked up." Donald started to laugh but the radio crackled as the chief of District Four ordered a third alarm struck, followed by the deputy of the division ordering a fourth. All of this within four minutes. The smiles stopped. This was serious business.

The University Hospital is one of several in the city. It is associated with Boston University and is world renowned for its cardiac surgeons as well as the Evans Clinic. The clinic is located in an adjoining twelve story building, most of which is devoted to hospital affiliated doctors' offices; this buiding forms an L shaped complex, leading from the main hospital and fronting on Harrison Avenue. The Evans Clinic treats hundreds of patients daily with day surgery as well as non-invasive procedures. The rear of the garage has an enormous Boston Edison vault located on the third floor. Inside the vault is a powerful transformer. A tremendous explosion occurred at 0847, blowing off the doors of the vault, causing extensive structural damage in the garage and forcing huge quantities of dense black smoke into the crowded doctor's building. Eventually, six alarms were struck to get enough assistance to evacuate the scores of patients, doctors and nurses scattered throughout the twelve floors.

The fire itself was rapidly contained by the first alarm engine companies but the other responders, including the Tower, trudged up the stairways, already crowded with mobile people who wasted no time in racing down to the street. Captain Murray led the company up to their assignment on the tenth floor; when they reached the destination, a handful of nurses were visible through the heavy haze. Each one had a patient in a wheelchair and they had oxygen masks strapped on their charges and were trying to keep them calm. The sight of the fire fighters brought broad smiles to the faces of the women and the elderly people they were protecting.

The Tower and another ladder company worked together in evacuating the floor, carrying the patients down to a lower floor where they could be crossed over into the main hospital building. The temperature outside was in the low thirties with freezing rain, so an effort was made to keep as many of the sick victims as possible inside.

Donald and Nick were assigned to search the floor, open those windows that dropped inward and make certain everyone was accounted for. At first the smoke was bad enough at the furthest end of the corridor to require them to wear their masks, but before they finished their chores, it became more livable. The fire was being brought under control and the two jakes' success in providing some ventilation improved conditions throughout the rooms and corridors.

After they finished, they dropped down a couple of more floors where the company was now operating. The remaining patients were able to be held in place because the haze had been substantially reduced, and the radio messages reported the success of attack being conducted inside the garage. The first thing Donald saw was Jeff Stoler, his fire hat removed and a doctor's stethoscope dangling from his neck. He was advising a very pretty young nurse, "Ma'am, I am a fully qualified EMT of the Boston Fire Department. You must follow my instructions, because you have inhaled poisonous and noxious smoke and fumes."

The girl was playing her role for the still frightened group of senior citizen men and women gathered in the reception area. "Yes sir," she replied, "are you something like a doctor?"

Jeff modestly replied, "Well, not exactly, but I'm in the same business. You know saving lives?" She asked what he wanted her to do and he said, "Well, after I carry you to safety, I'll have to do a follow up. Give me your name, address and phone number and report to my office this evening." He gave her the name of a well known singles bar in the Quincy Market complex.

A lady, sitting in her wheelchair, raised her voice and said, "Miss Tracey, don't you pay no attention to him."

The nurse laughed, "Why, what do you know about fire fighters, Mrs. Kelly?"

The woman frowned before she said, "When I was a little girl in St. Brigid's school, every time the fire engines went by, the nun used to make us all pray for those wonderful fire fighters who were going to a fire. And you know, I still pray for them even now 'cause I can't break the habit. But...I married one of them and I can tell you, after a while I didn't spend much time prayin' for him. He was chasin' every skirt in town." She shook her head. "And that one you're talkin' to, sounds just like him. Keep away from him, honey. He's about as much like a doctor as my dear departed."

Stoler looked shocked: "Mrs. Kelly, my dear, how could you? I didn't say I was a doctor. Actually, I'm more like a priest. Want me to hear your confession, case we don't get out alive?"

Donald smiled to himself. All of these folks who were so frightened a few minutes earlier, were now relaxed and laughing at the byplay. Captain Murray was leaning against a door jamb, his legs crossed, reporting on his radio that they were going to keep the occupants where they were. Why not, thought Donald, they're having a better time here than they would outside. He had to admit that Stoler, with all his nonsense, sure knew how to prevent any panic.

Partial elevator service was restored some time later, and before they were to be transported to the lobby, Stoler addressed the group: "Now listen, my students, when you get downstairs, the TV cameras will be everywhere. All of you ladies, check your make-up; we want you to make us proud." They were giggling and following his advice. "Now, when they ask if you were in great danger, tell them you certainly were. But you were never frightened because you knew you were with Jeff Stoler of the Tower. They'll understand. Those reporters and cameramen all know I'm the best fire fighter in this city."

When they returned to quarters, the new protective gear had arrived. Donald's first reactions were much the same as everyone else: Glad they stayed with black as the basic color. Those white and yellow stripes look nice and clean. Wonder how long that will last? There were a number of convenient pockets to accommodate gloves and other equipment. The knee-length boots seemed to make a pretty good combination with the bunker pants pulled down over them. Suspenders supported the pants and the turnout coat ended below the hips. A clip was fastened in position to hold the personal light. Zippers and snaps were provided to make a sealed, watertight closure.

Donald took his issue, attached his light and his PASS device before storing the gear in his locker. Well, he thought, something different. Jakes—including himself—will first criticize the new stuff, blaming the commissioner and everyone else they could think of for the decision. This will include the fire companies that did most of the field tests, the safety committee and the union. And why not? Jakes are not that much different than anyone else; they hate change—especially if they've been satisfied with what they've been using. Glad they didn't attempt to change the fire hat, thought Donald. They'd have had a revolt. "Leather forever" was almost like part of the constitution in a lot of old eastern cities and towns.

After every jake has had his say about how bad the new gear is, once they realize it's not going away, they'll make it work. And sometime in the future, when they think no one's looking, they may even admit it's pretty good—never as good as what was taken away from them, but...well, not too shabby. If the leadership of the department is lucky, some other new change to castigate will come over the horizon and the bunker gear will drop into obscurity.

The PASS device is a good indication of evolution. The department started using these emergency devices back in the eighties. They were issued as a result of a donation from Boston University, whose president, Dr. John Silber, was so impressed with the department's performance at a major fire in one of the campus buildings that he wanted to make a significant gesture of appreciation that would also contribute to fire fighters' safety. This compact signalling unit is designed so that a fire fighter who is in trouble can activate it and produce an almost ear-shattering pulsating sound at 105 decibels. In the event the fire fighter is unconscious or unable to reach the activation switch, lack of movement will cause a motion detector to operate the PASS in about a half a minute.

The initial units were early in the developmental phase; they were plagued by malfunctions and false activations. Consequently, over a period of time their use was almost discontinued. Of course, the purpose of the device presents a motivational problem for the users. In the course of their careers, most fire fighters are almost never trapped in a manner that they can't escape. So, it may be years before anyone in an entire department membership is required to use the device. As time passes, they can become a nuisance because of their maintenance requirements, and most jakes figure they personally will never have to use them. That other guy will, but not me. Besides, no one's used it yet, right?

The death of Lieutenant Minehan in June, 1994, reactivated interest in the units. Not that it would have saved his life. The extreme conditions when he was lost wouldn't have permitted a rescue attempt even had they known where he was. However, two major private companies, in a magnanimous gesture, re-equipped the entire membership. The new units were much less accident prone, although it was soon discovered that if the PASS was securely fastened to a turnout coat, such as the personal lights are, lack of movement would often produce a false alarm. It was kind of funny at first because whenever a jake's device went off and he wasn't in trouble, jakes like Jeff Stoler or Gap Keefe would immediately shout, "Move you lazy, prick. Start using that fuckin'axe." It soon became known as the "fuck-off finder". However, as usually happens with any new equipment, some jake will figure out how to improve it. Consequently, the PASS devices now dangle from an O ring attached to the fire coat so it is always moving slightly, preventing false activation but capable of working as designed when someone is completely immobile. Of course, like everything used in this strange business, it's not perfect. The noise it produces will certainly notify others that someone is trapped, but it will not provide precise directions to the victim. Also, if the jake is conscious and unable to reach the deactivation switch, the noise will drive him nuts.

An excellent example of how the units could have helped locate a fire fighter promptly occurred in the early '80s in Boston. The partial collapse of a commercial building in the Back Bay district during a fire caused the deaths of a fire lieutenant and a fire fighter. The building was in deplorable condition following the massive structural failure. Jakes, desperately picking through the rubble, were in great danger should a secondary collapse occur. The lieutenant's body was located almost immediately. However, fire fighters had to search for three hours to find the second victim who was some distance from his officer. It was obvious from the condition of the fire fighter's body that he must have died instantly from the force of the blow of the descending floors and stairways; however, until he was found there was always a chance, a possibility that he might be alive, unconscious and trapped, but alive. Until this was determined after the three hour search succeeded, many other jakes were exposed to great danger throughout the lengthy period. If PASS devices existed at that time, the victim would probably have been located promptly, thus safeguarding all of the searchers from potential injury or death. This fact was stressed to Donald and his drill class during their training and he was pleased to see the new and more effective devices when they were issued.

The almost snowless winter continued into March, and while it didn't result in any reduction in fires, when they did occur all the winter problems of ice and snow were not usually factors. It made Donald realize how much more difficult it is when access, not only into streets, but to all sides of a fire building are hampered by the elements. After trying to hand-carry ground ladders through clogged alleyways to ladder the rear of a fire building, or drag lines through huge drifts of snow, he'd take clear streets anytime. Prior to his appointment he agreed with Gena and Nancy about how wonderful it is when there's a white Christmas, with the sleigh bells, holiday cheer and warm, friendly atmosphere it produces. After the winter of 1993-94, snow to Donald, like most jakes in the north, became a lot of shit. Let the family watch it pile up on TV in some other part of the country if they want to enjoy the romance of those memorable and heartwarming scenes.

On March 13th, Donald was detailed to Engine 10 to cover Jerry Nagle who had received a ten stitch laceration at a fire two weeks earlier and was currently on injured leave. At 0341 hours an alarm was struck for a one story block of stores in the Brighton district. Donald was on patrol, talking to Derek Burton, who was about to relieve him on watch. They had just returned from extinguishing two rubbish-filled dumpsters in the rear of a six story building on Water Street. Someone always seemed to be touching off the contents of these large steel containers in the downtown and Back Bay districts. Occasionally, when not promptly detected, the fires would extend into a building and result in major fires. This time, however, the cops had spotted the fire and Ten had knocked it down before it could penetrate into the adjoining structure. Donald was remarking to Derek how effective the company had been in killing the fire. Because of the lack of snow, Brows Brennan, who was driving, was able to maneuver the pumper into the alley and immediately activated the preconnected 1000 GPM monitor gun, mounted on the deck of the apparatus, thus giving it the name "deck gun." Donald and Derek had swept the powerful stream above the fire and along the rear wall of the exposed, multi-storied building to prevent inward advancement and then directed the stream downward, flooding the dumpsters.

The young, black fire fighter, who had befriended Donald when he was first appointed, said, "Yeah, we got that gun joined right into the pump and a 750 gallon tank. Knocks the shit out of those rubbish fires and also a lot of auto fires when they're fully involved. I was here before we got this kind of gear, and it was always a pain in the ass. Now, shit, we can fill up the whole fuckin' container in about two minutes. Saves running long lines and cuts down a lot of overhauling, too. Hey, Donald, by the time we get pensioned, we'll probably just push a button and a computer will make the fire go out." Box 514 struck just as Derek finished speaking. Donald hit the house alarm, announced the intersecting streets location, and dispatched Rescue One as part of the first alarm response.

As the large van sped out the doorway, the voice from Fire Alarm announced, "Box 514 was struck for dumpster fires, rear of 170 Harvard Avenue." When Engine 41 arrived from their station a couple of blocks away, the officer reported smoke showing from the basement and first floor of the building. Derek jumped up, thumbed through the assignment cards and said, "No computers yet, Donald. Sounds like those dumpsters got inside."

He determined that the Tower responded to the incident if it became either a working fire or a multiple alarm, with Engine Ten covering Engine 41. When the chief of District Eleven reported at the scene, he confirmed it was a building fire and ordered a second alarm to be struck, six minutes after the first alarm.

Donald hit the house alarm once again, announced the assignments for the deputy of the division and the two fire companies and raced to his gear, stepping into his boots, set upright on the main floor, adjacent to the pump, pulled up his overlapped bunker pants, looped his suspenders over his shoulders and shrugged into his fire coat as he entered the passenger compartment along with Derek and Rick Foster. Lieutenant Grimes slid into the front seat and Brows Brennan jammed his foot on the accelerator, trying to beat the Tower out through the overhead doors. Derek and Rick laughed as they heard Grimes shouting, "Brows, for cripes sake, let the Tower go. They're goin' right to the fire. We're only covering." Brows frowned and answered, "Lissen, Luft, I got fire pains. This is gonna be a third, sure as shit."

As they entered the Mass. Turnpike, the quickest route to Brighton from their quarters, Donald thought, "This is getting to be routine. Been out here a lot lately. Always come back worn out. Lot of difficult fires in this district." He almost grinned as he reflected, "I'm starting to sound like I've been on forever." Whenever he read the papers and they were quoting a fire fighter at some disaster, they always described the spokesperson as a "veteran fire fighter." He remembered his friend from drill school, Peter Justice. Boy, could he talk! Justice was a short, muscular jake with rapidly thinning hair that resulted in his classmates dubbing him "Cueball" over his voluble objections. While they'd been on the job for less than three years, at a recent fire a TV reporter grabbed Justice as he was exiting the building and after Peter finished filling the guy up with a lot of fantasies about what he personally had accomplished at the incident, the camera swung back to the reporter who said, "That was veteran fire fighter, Peter Justice, Engine Company Twenty-Two, who just saved the lives of three people in this building." The reporter went on to say how he was "constantly *amazed* at what these brave people do, day in and day out." Naturally, Donald and about a hundred other jakes were on the line asking for "Amazing Justice." By the time Donald made his call, the jake on patrol had had enough: "Listen, Holden, why don't you go fuck yourself. But before you do, come here and take this asshole back to your own company. This nitwit hasn't shut up since he got appointed here and both of my ears are perforated."

Shortly before they exited the turnpike, Deputy Chief Franklin of Division One ordered a third alarm and Donald forgot all about his friend.

They passed quickly through the toll booth, turned right on Cambridge Street, and as they approached Harvard Avenue, the radio sputtered, "C-Six to Fire Alarm." The operator answered and Deputy Franklin said, "Have an engine company come in from Brighton Avenue, drop a big line and report to me at the front of 164 Harvard Ave." The operator came on and said, "Fire Alarm to Engine Ten, respond to the fire." He then repeated the division commander's instructions. The fire had extended from a row of dumpsters in the rear of number 168-170 Harvard Avenue. This was a small sized department store in the middle of an entire block of one story buildings, all interconnected, with no fire walls subdividing the cellars, first floors and roofs. A total of ten different businesses occupied the complex. The fire had gained great headway before it was discovered and now it was extending rapidly in both directions.

The pump stopped just after crossing Brighton Avenue. Brows and Derek commenced connecting into the hydrant assist valve of an engine company already using the available fire hydrant. Lieutenant Grimes ordered Donald and Rick to stretch a two and a half inch line up Harvard Avenue towards the fire.

Black smoke, punctuated by sparks and flames, rolled across the street, driven by a strong wind and the pressure of the combustion. When they reached the front of the building, Grimes was partially obscured by the smoke. "O.K. Ten," he said, "we're gonna try to stop it in the cellar of this joint," and he pointed at a one story attached structure, about twenty-five feet wide, occupied by a realty company. Donald could see three jakes busily cleaning out the plate glass storefront windows and removing the entrance doors as brown smoke oozed out and made the fire fighters difficult to identify. He dragged the line forward, just behind Rick, who had the nozzle draped over his shoulder. As they got closer, they could see Lieutenant Desmond, Gap

Keefe and Howie Rosen doing the ventilation work.

Desmond said to Grimes, "The cellar stairs are in the back. Trapdoor. We got it open." He then told Ten's officer, "Lookit. I'll have a guy right behind you. This fire is really moving. I'm gonna open the ceilings overhead. If the fire's up there and we can't hold it, I'll tell you to get out." Desmond also said the rear doorway to the alley was boarded up and they'd be working to get it open as a second way out.

Ten's crew donned their masks and crawled in deeper, Grimes feeling the floor with one bared hand, trying to determine if the fire was directly beneath them yet.

As Rick groped ahead, he was able to identify the uncovered hatchway that led to a flight of wooden stairs providing access to the basement. He told Grimes he could feel some heat and the officer ordered the big line to be charged with water, prior to their descent. When the water arrived, swelling the hose, Grimes directed Rick to partially open the line and adjust it to a fine water spray. Foster then squatted and wormed his way down the several steps until both feet were firmly planted on the cement floor; Donald and the lieutenant backed down the stairs as the heat vented upward past them and were soon hunched down beside Rick. The nozzle was fully opened and the thousands of particles of water under force drove the heat away from them. Grimes next had the nozzle set for a solid stream and then all three of them swung the line back and forth, striking the ceiling and directing the water from the front to the rear of the area continuously. Donald could feel heat hitting the back of his neck and ears even though he was lying almost prone, his head and shoulders grinding into Rick's lower back.

It seemed like a very long time, but was probably only a couple of minutes when the heat began to feel as if it were dissipating, but Grimes had them keep the nozzle fully open. When he had Rick and Donald exchange positions and Donald grasped the nozzle and handle, he could feel the power of the fifty pound pressure driving through the circular opening in the metal pipe. The noise as the force hit the overhead was deafening but also produced a comforting feeling under the dangerous conditions.

Gap Keefe crawled across the floor, tapped Grimes on the leg and said, "Luft, Lieutenant Desmond says the fire's in the first floor ceiling but we already got an engine company hitting it with a line. It's O.K. so far." Grimes nodded and had Donald shut down the line. The four jakes, using their personal lights, managed to crawl over to the wall separating this basement from the next occupancy. It was a combination wooden and plaster partition and had burned through at the point where it joined the ceiling.

Equipped with a Halligan bar, Gap punched upward and hooked onto the ceiling laths above the plaster. When he ripped downward, large chunks plummeted to the floor, exposing the fire as it traveled horizontally through the bays between the floor joists. The more he pulled, the more the fire curled towards them. Grimes had him open an area about six feet square before he directed Donald to reopen the nozzle. The officer told him to aim the stream to cut off any further extension towards the next exposed occupancy, which so far, had not become involved.

A few minutes later, Desmond and Rosen clambered down the stairs, reporting they had managed to stop the fire in the first floor overhead. They had brought an axe and rake with them and the group was soon busily stripping the entire ceiling, allowing the water to hit all of the fire remaining. They also dismantled much of the partition into the still burning adjoining cellar. This placed them in position to effectively attack the fire on that side and the still intense fire was gradually reduced to hot, wet steam.

Eventually, the chief of the district and Deputy Franklin climbed down to their location. Franklin said, "I knew we put the right jakes in the best location." He smiled as he patted Grimes on the shoulder. Grimes asked him how far the fire had traveled. "Seven stores. There's this place, a hair salon, Chinese restaurant, a cleaners, the department store and a couple of others." However, both he and the district chief were very pleased with the operation.

Without the aggressive attack from both sides, as many as a dozen firms could have been out of business. They both knew cellar fires are the most difficult and hazardous types of fires in buildings. Unless in the early stages of the fire you succeed in getting down to the lower levels, it is usually prudent to abandon the interior attacks. Once in a while the use of cellar pipes through holes cut in the first floor is effective, but, more often than not, stored materials obstruct them and prevent them from controlling the main body of the fire and the operating force may be in great danger from a partial collapse.

Fortunately, in this case, Ten's line managed to contain the horizontal extension in one area, while other engine companies had similar successes in the other direction. The ladder companies, in conjunction with Rescue One, managed to produce effective ventilation openings in the roofs above the fire before the area became unsafe.

This action drew much of the fire upward so companies could open the ceilings inside on the first floors and utilize hose streams most advantageously.

Chief Franklin had Ten relieved by another company. When they got to the street, it was a sheet of ice. The temperature was near zero. Donald hadn't given the cold a thought until this moment. "I guess when you're busy you forget about the cold," he thought. He joined a line of jakes getting coffee from the Red Cross, Salvation Army and Boston Sparks Association canteen wagons. Up ahead, he could hear a sharply piercing voice, that could only belong to Cueball Justice, berating the people in front of him. "C'mon you assholes. Make way for Fighting Twenty-two. We put this fuckin' fire out for ya. It takes South End jakes to cover your asses every time."

A huge, black truckie from Ladder 14, a Brighton company, reached back and pulled Justice forward by his collar, almost off his feet, and hissed into his face, "Lissen, you little snot, you don't never cover my ass, boy." He shook the little redhead vigorously.

Cueball, who adapted to any situation admirably and quickly, said, "Not you, Dwayne, my old pal! I meant all those stiffs from Ladder Eleven."

Dwayne dropped him carefully to his feet and said thoughtfully, "Well, O.K. I think you might be right about some of those mothers."

Donald chuckled. Cueball had kept everyone entertained throughout the months of drill school, and even though he was frequently threatened, he always managed to talk himself out of trouble before someone squashed him.

The next night tour they worked they were back in Brighton once again, this time to a fifth alarm that originated in the cellar of a three story wooden building on Western Avenue. The first floor was a pizza shop with occupied dwellings overhead. Although it was early in the evening, a delayed alarm permitted the fire to gain such great headway that it extended throughout this building and into two others on Waverly Street. The vinyl siding on the exterior of the structures prevented adequate venting through the original wooden exterior walls. Consequently, extremely heavy smoke conditions required extensive use of breathing apparatus. An additional supply of high pressure air cylinders was provided by the Air Supply Unit at the scene.

The Tower company, along with jakes from six ladder company crews, performed heavy duty axe, rake and overhauling activities throughout all of the structures. By the time they were finished, Donald had used three of the thirty minute cylinders. When they were finally relieved, they all sat on the sidewalk curb, exhausted. Even Desmond looked weary. "That's it boys. Time for the Gatorade."

Since the arrival of the new turnout gear, the department was sending supplies of the refreshing drink to extra alarm fires to try to prevent dehydration from the excessive overheating, which was becoming a fact of life at long term operations. Oh well, at least we're warm, thought Donald as he guzzled the tangy liquid. But, as he wiped his brow, he considered the possibility that maybe cold wasn't too bad after all.

Spring finally arrived, and although the winter of 1994-95 was exceptionally gentle, with a minimum of snow accumulation and very few severely cold nights, it's always much better when the possibility of ice covered ladders, frozen hydrants and hose has disappeared for several months. The study group was now well organized and the amount of material they were absorbing under Desmond's direction was growing significantly. Those members of the three fire companies that were not interested in the books generally left the students to their own devices during the afternoon sessions. Not completely, of course. With jakes like Gap and Dot-head on duty, you couldn't expect not to be interrupted occasionally.

When either one of them was on house patrol, insignificant announcements would grow in importance and be given extra emphasis, just to create a distraction. "Could I have your attention, please," the speaker system would blast out the amplified tones. "The Fire Alarm office has just informed me that high pressure fire hydrant number three-zero-eight is temporarily out of service. I repeat...The Fire Alarm office has just...."

Desmond would grind his teeth as the message came again, this time even louder. He would reach for the house intercom phone, press the button for the patrol desk and shout, "Doherty, shut the fuck up. Nobody knows where that fuckin' hydrant is anyway. We're in the middle of a test."

Doherty replied, "Jeez, Luft, you chewed me out last week for not telling you Pearl Street was closed. I'm just tryin' to do my duty the best I possibly can for you, sir."

Desmond would sputter and tell him there's a big difference between their major access artery to the financial district being blocked and one hydrant out of thirteen thousand being defective. Donald and Rick snickered at the exchange because Desmond rarely became irritated by this kind of horseplay.

On this day, however, he was having the class take an examination that had been given a couple of years earlier. This was great practice for the students to become accustomed to the examination atmosphere; it was also a great opportunity to teach them that while they already had made very good progress, there was still a long way to go, based on the questions they couldn't answer.

About a half hour later, the speaker crackled again: "Attention, attention. This is Fire Fighter Keefe, Tower Company. I am assuming house patrol from Fire Fighter Doherty, Rescue Company One. All major and minor access routes for the companies are open and in service. All fire hydrants, except high pressure number three-zero-eight, are functioning properly."

Before Desmond could reach the phone, Rick Foster grabbed it. When Keefe answered, Rick said, "Gap, you and Dot-head are a couple of Code eight-nineties." He slammed the receiver down and laughed. "That'll keep them quiet, Luft. They'll spend the rest of the day tryin' to figure out what they are."

"Well, what the hell are they?" Desmond asked.

Rick waved a pamphlet over his head, exclaiming, "Why, Lieutenant, what kind of a teacher are you?" The paper he held was the latest National BFIRS identification numbers for various incident types. It started at Code 110 to identify fires in buildings and contents, or contents only and then ran the gamut of every possible kind of occurrence that the fire service intelligentia could image, concluding with Code 990, identified as "other conditions not listed above," some one hundred and thirty-five items further down the list.

The officer shook his head: "Foster, they never ask that shit in the exams. Don't waste your time on it. What the fuck is that eight-ninety, anyway?"

Rick smiled. "It says, 'Natural Disasters not listed above.' Pretty appropriate for those two clowns, don't ya think?"

As April drew to a close, a fire in Boston City Hall created a lot of headlines. This structure, completed in 1968, is located in the heart of the downtown Government Center, next to the JFK Federal Building and diagonally across the street from the Saltonstall State Office Building. A huge brick plaza extends from the main entrance to the nine story building, out to Cambridge street with a subway entrance piercing the otherwise unbroken surface. This concrete seat of city government was erected following an international architectural contest. The winner produced an edifice that is praised in some circles and vigorously condemned in others, which is probably appropriate for any location where politics is the major game.

At least the mayor has a nice office on the sixth floor with a marvelous panoramic view of Faneuil Hall and Quincy Market and even a piece of Boston Harbor, just beyond the elevated Central Artery.

At 1620 hours on April 28th, Box 12-1259 was struck for a fire in the electrical switch gear room in the sub-basement. Because of the numerous, unprotected vertical openings and large areas of unuseable space incorporated into the award-winning design, tremendous quantities of dense, black smoke vented upward from the intense fire. Smoke entered all floors and offices, but was particularly concentrated from the sixth through the ninth floor areas.

Since this incident took place just eleven days after the horrendous bomb explosion in Oklahoma City, which took the lives of one hundred and sixty eight people, panic was a major consideration for the responding forces. The department was immediately aware of the cause of the fire, but knew it was essential to get as many jakes as possible up through the interior, not only to rescue the occupants, but to assure them that no bomb had exploded. The unusual architectural design hampered the proper placement of sufficient aerial ladders to assist in the removal of large numbers of occupants via the narrow windows.

While Steve Tucker and Howie Rosen elevated the Tower as high as it could reach, Lieutenant Desmond, Donald, Gap Keefe and Mark Palmer headed for the main stairway. The officer, always anticipating, had each member carry an extra thirty minute air cylinder along with their tools.

The stairway was jammed with panicky city employees and other citizens, staggering and stumbling towards the main lobby and escape to the plaza.

Desmond could hear Deputy Franklin ordering additional ladder companies and striking additional alarms over his portable radio. The lieutenant shouted to the evacuees, "O.K. folks, calm down now. You're gonna be O.K. This is an electrical fire, and we'll have it under control shortly." He had Gap and Donald guide the first evacuees through the smoke and out to safety with the others grabbing hands and following rapidly outside to the fresh air.

As the descent became more orderly, the jakes worked upward on the stairs, speaking calmly and pointing the people in the right direction. At the sixth floor level, it became necessary to don their mask facepieces and they began finding confused and anxious victims, some crouching, some gasping and laying prone on the floor.

Desmond reported the deteriorating conditions to the district and deputy chiefs and he was informed that several fire companies were on their way to all of the upper floors. The extra help proved to be essential. While the fire in the sub-basement was rapidly contained, the heavy smoke and the hundreds of trapped occupants created an enormously difficult and lengthy evacuation.

The Tower company crew shared their air supply with numerous occupants as they led them down to floors where the fumes and smoke were not as thick or pungent. Once again, Desmond's foresight was a contributing factor to their success. When their low pressure alarm signals began operating, they changed to the full cylinders he had stashed on the sixth floor and continued the evacuation.

By the time the building had been cleared, fifty victims had been transported to various hospitals, including seven jakes and ten cops.

Of course, the press had a field day. After the spectacular video footage that continued for a couple of days, the questions came one on top of the other. Who designed that joint? How often are fire drills held? Why hasn't the city complied with the high-rise sprinkler laws? Doesn't anyone care about city workers? (This query was from the municipal unions currently negotiating contracts.) Who's in charge here?

Desmond suggested it was a good time to watch how clever politicians were in diverting attention away from themselves whenever there was blame to be placed. "Watch and see what happens, though. The stories will peter out in a week or so and everything will return to normal—all fucked up."

Donald said, "But what about that sprinkler law, Lieutenant? Don't they have to comply?"

The officer answered, "Sure. But just like everyone else they don't wanna spend the money. The private companies will eventually all comply, but the feds, state and city people will find all kinds of ways to get exemptions. That's show business, kiddo."

May slipped into June and as the last day of school and the first day of summer vacation approached, Donald's daughter, Nancy, grew more excited. She and Gap's daughter, Bethany, had become close friends. Not that they saw each other too frequently, but their telephone conversations were endless. Circumstances had prevented a repeat of their initial visit to the Keefe family's summer retreat at Lake Winnipesaukee, and this year Donald's summer vacation was scheduled late in September. However, that wasn't going to stop Nancy. After days of nagging, Donald and Gena had finally agreed that she could spend two weeks in late August with Bethany and Gap and Marion in Meredith, New Hampshire. It would keep her there through Labor Day, but since school would start immediately afterward, she had to promise to have everything completed before she went away.

Her shopping for school essentials in mid-August would cut into her time at the South Boston Yacht Club, where the junior sailing program kept her busy all summer, but she swore she'd do everything required. After all, two weeks away from the folks when you're going on twelve is worth any kind of sacrifices.

On June 10th, Donald was detailed for a night tour to Engine Company 3, District 4 in the South End. Desmond told him the day before that he needn't arrive until 1800 hours because he would be the fourth fire fighter assigned to the company for the shift. Since the day tour only had three jakes on duty, he wouldn't actually be relieving anyone.

The Tower had an extra member on duty that night, so the division deputy made the assignment to balance the company and district strengths.

Donald decided to stop by Engine Twenty-two's quarters in the same district and visit Cueball Justice so he left home at his usual time. Since their graduation from drill school three years earlier, Cueball had become a fixture on his company, just as he knew he would. Pete Justice could out talk and out shout anyone in the school and he continued his vocal tirades at his permanent assignment. While he managed to irritate most of the jakes he worked with, they also grew to like him. They did what all jakes have to do—they adjusted. They knew he was fiercely loyal to the company and its members, thus spreading his outrageous opinions to the rest of the district.

The one sensitivity Pete had was about his thinning red locks of hair. One of his classmates had nicknamed him "Cueball"; however, so far his company hadn't picked up on it. He swore Donald to secrecy and the oath hadn't been violated yet. Still, whenever Justice started denigrating his good friend, Donald would just say, "Oh, by the way, Cue...er I mean, Peter..." and Cueball would immeiately cease his verbal attack.

Donald parked on the apron of the one story Tremont Street station and walked through one of the apparatus doorways which were open because of the mild weather. He could hear Cueball's voice coming over the P.A. system from the patrol desk: "Attention, attention, ladies in quarters. Watch your language." A moment passed and another announcement pierced the air: "Cancel that last message. No ladies in quarters, just a jake from the Tower company. They all look like dames."

Donald walked into the patrol desk area, shook his fist and said, "You're getting pretty close to the limit there...what's your name...oh ya, Peter!"

Justice laughed and draped his arm over Donald's shoulder, "My old pal," he bellowed, "you have a wonderful sense of humor."

The pair sat chatting for a while, discussing fires they had been to, together and separately. Jakes from the night tour arrived and relieved their partners. Donald had been detailed to this house before and had worked with some of the crew. The captain, Dave Tilden, a middle-aged black officer, entered and Cueball promptly announced, "Attention, attention, my favorite officer in the world is in quarters. Lieutenant Cummings, go home, you're relieved."

Tilden shook his head and said to Donald, "Hey, Holden, how ya doin'? Notice how grey my hair's getting from this yapper?" As each member passed by, Cueball had something to announce.

"Attention. Rags Crossen and Buddy Sawtelle have arrived. They have passed the breathilizer test. Bad Ankles Brosnahan and Fish Head O'Farrel, you are properly relieved."

Donald chuckled as he asked, "Where the hell do you come up with those names, Ace?"

Justice replied, "Why it's easy. Look at Crosson's clothes. He got picked up as one of the homeless one very cold night last winter. The cops were gonna take him to a shelter 'til he showed them his badge." He went on to explain how he had given Brosnahan his title when he transferred in from another house. The poor guy had broken both of his heels when he slid the pole with wet hands and struck the floor too hard while responding to a fire. They never completely healed properly and he had a decided limp. He really didn't want to retire so he came to this house where there are no poles.

"But what about his ankles?"

"Nothing, you dope. Bad Heels is just a lousy nickname, is all. Don't you know nothing?"

He had christened O'Farrell after the poor guy had made a chowder one night for an evening meal and Cueball found an eye floating among the other ingredients in his bowl. When Justice finally announced "Donkey Dick Dukas in quarters!" Donald had had enough. He stood up and said, "That's it, pal. You're full of shit. See you at the big one."

As he was getting in his car he heard, "Hero Holden, pride of the

Tower company and United States Marine Corps is leaving quarters."

Donald was still smiling as turned from Tremont Street into West Newton, en route to Engine 3. When he approached the intersection of Shawmut Avenue, where West became East Newton, he could see a blue haze passing across the sun. He slowed the car and eased into the left side curb. A full city block of five story brick and wood apartments fills the right side of the block, terminating at the intersection with Washington Street. Over the years, many serious fires have occurred in these buildings and a lot of jakes have been injured while fighting them. In the late '60s, two members were trapped on the top floor while attempting to rescue the occupants. They were both eventually located and removed to safety, but their injuries ended their fire fighting careers.

Directly across from the buildings is Blackstone Park, which, while presently quite peaceful, has been the site of many civil disturbances, riots and demonstrations. Now it's more popular for the purchase of a little crack, a little horse and a lot of grass. The rear of the buildings are all empty lots, the locations of similar structures long since destroyed by fire. Donald got out of the car and could now see that the haze had grown darker and that it was definetly smoke, increasing in volume as it pushed from the fourth and fifth floors of a building, the second last one from the Washington Street end of the block. He quickly popped the trunk of his car, reached in and grabbed his gloves, fire hat and coat, his personal light and PASS device bouncing off his chest as he pulled the coat flaps together.

Donald jogged rapidly down the street, spying a fire alarm box diagonally across the intersection on Washington Street. He could also see the involved building had a red, fire department sign with a white X prominently displayed over the front door. This identified the structure as being unsafe for interior fire fighting operations. Outside, in front of the abandoned building, Donald saw a young, dark-skinned, Hispanic youth. He looked about ten years old and was weeping, his chest heaving up and down as he tried to catch his breath.

"Blanca and Ciro," he screamed when he saw Donald, "my brothers, in there," pointing upward.

Donald grabbed the boy's shoulders: "OK, what's your name?"

"Gallegos. Please save them!" the boy pleaded.

"I will, but you have to help. You know about pulling a fire box, Gallegos?" The boy nodded. Donald pointed across the street. "Go pull it, right now." The boy started running as Donald sprinted up the long flight of brick stairs, activating the PASS as he pushed open the slightly ajar, boarded up entrance door. Just before he stepped inside, he looked up and could see flames spurting out of some of the fourth floor windows. The hall foyer was clogged with dense, brown smoke.

He ascended rapidly, stomping on the wooden steps to the second floor, where he paused briefly and shouted, "Blanca! Ciro! Where are you?" He thought he heard a child's voice answer somewhere up above, but he couldn't be sure.

Stay calm, stay calm, he muttered, and crept cautiously up to the third floor through the now thickening smoke. Donald pushed open a door and could see the front room engulfed in fire. He shouted again, but there was no answer from inside. Pulling the door shut, he hesitated in the hallway. They have to be up above. Shit. Here I go, above the fire. "Ciro, Blanca, where are you?" he repeated. This time he heard a louder reply and thought the sound came from the top floor.

The wooden treads leading upward were deeply scorched from a previous fire and were tilted downward to the left, away from the fire wall on the right side. Realizing the stairs were not solidly supported, and remembering Desmond's advice, Donald tried to keep his weight towards the wall.

The fourth floor hallway was totally obscured by thick smoke and he had to crawl to gain access to the next flight; exposed nail heads pierced both of his knees as he progressed over charred floorboards. He was having difficulty breathing and wished he had a mask. By taking short, shallow breaths he summoned enough strength to shout the two names once again. The faint reply he heard, spurred him up to the top floor.

A small form lay huddled on the landing and fire was roaring out of the transoms above two closed doorways. Donald pulled the almost motionless figure to his chest. He now had better visibility. About ten feet above his head, a broken skylight was momentarily drawing the smoke and heat upward and away from him. He could see there was no one else in the hallway and the closed doors indicated the other boy wasn't here. Moving as quickly as possible, he sped down the way he had come, the extra weight of the youngster producing a cracking noise on some of the steps. As he exited the building, he could see a crowd gathered on the sidewalk. He raced down the outside stairs and thrust the young victim at a tall black man.

He took several deep breaths and started back into the fire building. Now, Donald could hear fire apparatus sirens and horns sounding somewhere in the distance. He shouted to the crowd, "Tell the firemen there's a kid still inside and I'm gonna get him."

Up again. This time he knew where he had to try to go. On the first trip, he'd seen no one on the third floor and the fifth had the closed doors, so he had to try the fourth. On the third floor, the door he had pulled closed earlier was now showing fire at the top panels and the brown paint was blistering throughout its length.

Up, up, up he went, realizing he would only have a brief period to try to locate the kid. From the fourth floor hallway, he could see the door to the front room was partially open. Creeping forward, he nudged it open fully and managed to crawl about five feet past the threshold. Donald recoiled in horror. To his left, towards the front of the building, he spotted a body, but he knew immediately he was too late; fire had already eaten into the flesh and the lifeless form was already charring badly.

Then Donald was struck a tremendous blow on his head and shoulders, and, as he was losing consciousness, he could feel himself dropping and tumbling downward.

A large section of the burning roof had collapsed into the fifth floor. The previous fires had so weakened the structural supports that they couldn't support the added weight. Consequently, the fourth and fifth floors split and plunged to the third level, the entire mass coming to rest and piling up on the somewhat stronger third floor, which had not been previously damaged. Donald and the young victim were buried somewhere inside the jumble of flooring, laths, plaster, roof boards, tar and brick.

The plunging roof had pushed much of the rear wall into the rear alleyway, although about half of the bricks remained starkly intact, unsupported and hovering over the collapsed area. All of the front wall had been forced outward down to the level of the mounds of debris on the third floor, but was intact from there to the foundation.

Both Engine 22 and Engine 3 arrived at the same time in response to Box 1652 and the calls that were being received for the fire. Captain Tilden grabbed the radio mike and transmitted, "Engine Twenty-two to Fire Alarm. Orders of Captain Tilden, Engine Twenty-two strike second alarm Box 1652." He added that there was heavy fire showing from 37 East Newton and that there had been a partial collapse of the building.

Tilden waved Engine 3 towards the rear of the group of apartments and that company turned on Washington Street, dropping their feeder line at a hydrant on Rutland Street as they moved into position for a heavy stream operation.

Some of the people in front of the building had been struck by debris and although none of them appeared to be seriously injured, they were all dazed. Piles of bricks littered the sidewalk and gutter of the street and a mass of rubble made the long front stairway impassable.

The man still clutched the young boy in his arms as he staggered across the street into Blackstone Park. When Tilden saw him, he called for several ambulances, as his company commenced operating their pre-connected deck gun, directing the solid stream into the heavy fire. At this point the tall black screamed to Tilden, "There's a fireman inside that place, lookin' for another kid."

Tilden was momentarily stunned: "Are you sure?" he asked, hoping the man would correct his statement. "Did you see him?"

"Yessir, I seen him. He got this kid, then he went back inside."

District Chief Macklin was just arriving and when Tilden gave him the information, he ordered a third alarm and directed both engine companies to shut down their heavy streams and change to hand lines with combination nozzles. He had to try to control the fire, but he wanted to avoid any further structural collapse that could occur from the solid streams' incessant pounding.

Macklin had other engine companies run hand lines front and rear with the same types of streams. He instructed all of them to avoid striking the dangling sections of the rear wall with the streams, which would certainly have pushed it inward and down onto the debris below.

Deputy Chief Jackie Franklin arrived and assumed command. Aerial ladders were raised to the adjoining exposed structures on both sides and he kept a space clear for the placement of the Tower in Blackstone Park, directly opposite the collapse. The one positive effect of the building failure was that much of the fire was smothered by the debris, making it much easier to gain control, although many combustibles were still burning and smouldering inside the twisted structural materials.

When the Tower was elevated, rotated and extended towards the top of the compressed structural failure, Desmond promptly sent Gap down the ladder. Keefe saluted the deputy and said, "Sir, we can hear a PASS device operating somewhere underneath us.". The Tower officer didn't want the information relayed throughout the communication system, which was constantly monitored by the media and by every fire buff in the Metropolitan area and much of New England. However, the information confirmed that a jake was somewhere inside the pile. Of course, the sound didn't tell them whether he was alive and it didn't provide a pinpoint location, but it was performing the way it was designed to operate.

The commissioner arrived and assumed command. He immediately ordered the reserve Tower unit to be brought to the scene by the Motor Squad. The department only has one suppression company permanently equipped with a Tower, but does maintain an older, identically equipped apparatus in reserve. While the unit is superior to regular ladder trucks in many respects, it has a longer wheel base, wider stabilizer jacks and a higher travel height than the traditional 110 foot aerials. The narrow streets that comprise much of the city of Boston necessitate the use of the more maneuverable regular ladder trucks for ordinary response assignments.

The additional unit was sited at the rear of the collapse and was extended through the open space created by the section of the rear wall that had fallen. This made it possible to commence digging out the debris from two stable platforms. Small hose lines from the buckets were used to try to extinguish the still smouldering embers and cool down the hot bricks and the glowing wooden beams and laths comprising much of the massive jumble.

Both heavy duty Rescue companies were positioned to be able to use their power winches, and the department wrecker with its more powerful capabilities was also made available. The commissioner requested the head of the Inspectional Services Department to take the action necessary to bring a commercial crane to the fire.

While all of these activities were being initiated, jakes were already manually digging into the debris. The PASS was still operating somewhere below them but they were quite certain it was several feet away. Members were placed on each adjoining rooftop with battery operated loud hailer megaphones. Their instructions were to constantly watch the rear wall for any movement, no matter how insignificant, and to shout warnings to the work force below if they witnessed anything to indicate an imminent collapse. This danger continued throughout the rescue operation and was a constant source of worry to the leadership, as well as those working down through the rubble.

Donald awakened gradually. At first he believed he was home in bed and dreaming he was working in some kind of noisy factory. The 105 decibel sound of the PASS was so loud, it actually hurt his ears. However, it helped to revive him completely and he realized he was really in trouble.

His mouth was clogged with plaster dust, he thought his nose was bleeding and there was something wrong with his left arm. His vision was bleary, but he could see his hand directly in front of his face; however, it was turned at a curious angle, as if it belonged to someone else. He tried to wiggle the fingers but nothing moved. His right arm was pressed against his lower chest and he had more success moving

By twisting his forearm back and forth, he managed to get his hand to a point where he could deactivate the PASS switch. He wanted the noise stopped so he could think, but then he realized he'd have to turn it back on so someone would know he was here. He knew for a fact that the department was at the scene because he heard them coming—and besides, they always show up anyway, don't they? They'd better. He almost smiled at the thought, but cut it off when he realized the building had collapsed and he was trapped. Yeah, and what if it collapses even more. He reasoned that whatever was directly above him had created something of a pocket around his head, neck and shoulders and he hoped it would continue to do so. While he was trying to figure out what he could do, the image of the little kid appeared in his mind forcefully. The kid must be here somewhere too, he thought. Realistically, though, Donald was pretty certain the boy was probably dead from the fire, but, he wasn't certain.

Up above, Desmond and his crew along with Captain Hardy and members of Rescue One were systematically removing debris. A procedure was being established to transport the materials to the street and rear yard for disposal. When the noise from the PASS stopped, everyone momentarily froze. Dot-head Doherty, his arms cradling sections of broken wooden beams, yelled, "Shit, it stopped." His face fell in dejection. But Desmond, always evaluating possibilities, said, "Hey, maybe he's conscious now and shut it off. Fuckin' noise'd drive anyone nuts. Keep digging."

Out front in the street, the commissioner had just received a positive report from Chiefs Franklin and Macklin. They, along with the safety chief, had voluntarily entered the basement of the building via the ground floor level under the main outside entrance flight of stairs. They worked their way up to the first floor and were able to determine that the ceiling, while spalled and cracked, was still intact without any sags or visible broken beams. The previous fires had apparently done the most structural damage to the upper floors. This did not insure that an additional failure couldn't occur at any time, but it did make them feel more confident.

The work force on top of the debris had to be confined to a small number of jakes to keep the added weight to a minimum as well as to limit the number of members exposed to great danger. Those working had short life lines attached to their belts from both buckets of the aerial Towers as a means of trying to secure them if another drop occurred either above or below them.

When Desmond's crew was replaced with fresh workers, they climbed down to the street. Pete Justice grabbed the officer by the arm. "Luft, Luft, do they know who's in there?" The usually upbeat young jake was ghostly pale and his hands were shaking. Desmond shook his head and Cueball started sniffling, trying to hold back tears. "I...I think it's Donald Holden."

Desmond was startled and said, "What...what? Why the fuck do you think that?"

"That's his car parked right there. He just left Twenty-two before the box was struck. He was on his way to Three."

Desmond raced over to the commissioner and quietly told him what he had learned. The boss nodded grimly. It really didn't change anything for him. A missing jake is terrible, no matter who it is; but now it became imperative that no identity be given to the media until the family was notified. He summoned his public relations officer and the chief chaplain of the department to his side. It was obvious to him that word of the identity would spread rapidly throughout the operating force at the scene, but he hoped his own good relationship with the press, which he had worked to develop and maintain during his tenure, would restrict any premature broadcast. Hell, I still think he's alive anyway, and maybe it's someone else. Nope, no confirmation of anything would be given.

The chaplain was briefed and departed with a district chief, prepared to make a notification, good or bad, to Donald's family, when the search was completed.

Since a member of his command was involved, Desmond allowed his crew just a brief rest and then requested they be allowed back up on top. Deputy Franklin looked at the officer with Gap, Howie Rosen and Mark Palmer, crowded close behind him, and nodded his assent.

Donald had kept pushing his right arm upward and was just inches away from the light switch. But, he decided he'd first turn the PASS back on. If it worked, they'd realize he had activated it manually and was alive.

Up above, Desmond was having similar thoughts. He started shouting, "Donald Holden! Turn on your PASS!" He kept bellowing the phrase and soon the other jakes were yelling with him.

While he couldn't make out what was being said, Donald could hear voices and his spirits rose immediately. He moved the switch and the noise, while it was horrendous, made him understand he had established communications. Now, if I can just keep calm and get that light on. He inched the fingers back along his bunker coat. When his index digit touched the top of the light casing, he worked it over the horizontal protrusion and pulled. The light was on! It couldn't throw its penetrating beam anywhere because it was surrounded by debris—but Donald could see it and knew he was doing something else to help himself. It was comforting. He shut off the PASS again because of the tremendous pulsation.

Up above, Vinnie Sterling of Rescue One suddenly exclaimed, "Cap, Cap, I can see a light!" It was glowing effectively and appeared to be several feet below and to the left of their position. The crew increased their speed, now feverishly heaving bricks, laths, plaster and chunks of wood into the two buckets. Justice, who had pleaded with Desmond to accompany the Tower jakes, suddenly screamed, "Red, red! I can see red. I can see his fire hat!" What he meant was that the top of Donald's fire helmet, painted red to identify ladder and Tower jakes was now visible, although covered with plaster dust.

Captain Hardy took command. His expertise as a rescue company officer now became essential to insure the effort would not endanger the victim nor add to his injuries. He spoke in measured tones, his voice actually having a calming effect on the excited jakes.

Piece by piece the remaining debris was gently lifted, exposing Donald's head and shoulders. He felt a cupped hand circling under his chin, and through his dust caked eyes, his blurred vision focused on the anxious face of Peter Justice, whose helmet shield had the numbers 22 inscribed on it. Donald managed to open his mouth, spit out a glob of plaster and said, "Hey, Cueball, you tryin' to be a hero now, huh?" His classmate burst into tears of relief.

Hardy continued to maintain control of the operation, with Chief Macklin standing nearby as he'd done since completing his examination of the structure's stability. He was available for advice but wise enough not to interfere as long as the operation progressed satisfactorily.

After several moments, Donald was stabilized with a neck brace and a backboard, carefully lifted and placed horizontally across the top of the Tower bucket. He vaguely remembered a huge cheer sounding as the aerial device lowered its cargo to the street. He was quickly transferred to a waiting ambulance and apparently passed in and out of consciousness because he had little memory of the trip.

His injuries consisted of a concussion, a broken left arm and four fractured ribs on his left side. The fire helmet, while badly damaged, had limited the head injury, just as it was designed to do.

Based on information Donald had provided, the search continued for young Ciro and it was soon discovered that he was within a dozen feet of Donald's location. However, it was obvious the lad was beyond help. The slight figure, badly charred from the intensity of the fire, was placed in a body bag and transported to the street. As soon as this recovery was completed, the work force was rapidly evacuated, awaiting the arrival of the commercial crane which was en route from a nearby construction project. Their first duty would be to eliminate the danger from the remaining rear wall. Once that had been accomplished, the fire department and the city's structural engineers could make an unhurried examination of the structure. There was no longer any need for speed or to endanger any jakes.

Gena and Nancy were walking down L Street. They were returning from the corner variety store, their arms filled with groceries. Nancy was chatting excitedly about the end of the school year in another week and she was counting the days until her August visit with the Keefes. As they turned the corner into Marine Road, Gena spotted a dark red fire department car parked in front of her house. Nothing registered with her until she recognized Father McGrath, the chief chaplain, emerging from the driver's side, dressed in a black, soot covered turnout coat.

His familiar smile was absent and this usually cheerful cleric said softly, "Gena, Nancy, Donald is at City Hospital." As Gena gasped, he quickly added, "But he's all right. He just saved a young boy who was trapped in a fire. Donald has some injuries, but believe me, he's O.K."

In a short period of time, they were transported to the South End and to the huge medical facility that encompasses the area bounded by Mass. Ave, Harrison Ave, East Concord and Albany Streets. As the chaplain escorted them through the entrance and the passage to the Emergency Room, they passed several fire fighters all in turnout gear who respectfully moved aside to let them through.

Just outside a closed door, the commissioner, two chief officers and Lieutenant Desmond were gathered. "He's going to be fine, Gena.

I want you to know he is responsible for saving a little boy who would surely be gone now if it wasn't for your Donald," said the grime covered boss of the department.

Gena was grateful for this kindly man's words, but she wished he'd step aside. She and Nancy burst into the room where two doctors and three nurses were crowded around the bed. Donald had an IV thrust into his right hand but even so, he managed to elevate his fingers and waggle them. They could see his eyes were bright as they gleamed with recognition of his two women. While his face was reasonably clear of dirt, his ears, neck and the hand they could see were filthy. They managed to hug his legs and tell him they loved him before they were gently escorted outside.

For the next two hours, they sat in the cafeteria with the chaplain and Lieutenant Billy O'Laughlin of the EAP, whom they knew very well as a result of Donald's previous injuries two years earlier. A number of jakes stopped by and spoke briefly. All of them were so dirty, they looked like they'd been made-up for a movie. The greasy, sooty ears and necks were almost a trademark. Gena recognized Desmond and, of course, their close friend, Rick Foster, and several of the others looked vaguely familiar but her thoughts remained concentrated on her husband.

Finally, the department hospital representative, wearing his dress uniform, escorted them to the elevators and to the ICU area. They were taken to a private visitors room, where one of the doctors they had seen earlier was waiting for them. He explained the nature of Donald's injuries and was very optimistic about his eventual complete recovery. "He's going to have quite a headache for a few days, and his ribs will be sore for a while, but we've managed to have great success in er, manipulating his arm." He went on to say that Donald was still asleep from anesthesia but was resting comfortably and they could certainly go in and see him.

When the doctor left, Nancy said to Paul Flaherty, the hospital rep, "What's manipulate mean? It sounds awful."

Flaherty grinned. "Aw, it's just the way they talk around here, Nancy. It just means they did a good job of fixing his arm and they think it'll come out fine." He continued, "I'm almost like an interpreter here, Nancy. Anything you wanna know, ask me. C'mon, now, let's go see your dad."

Inside the room, with its subdued lighting and battery of machines, each of them with digitized readings blinking constantly, they could see Donald. He was snoring gently, an oxygen feed clipped to his nostrils. And he was immaculate—all of the grime had been washed away.

His left arm was elevated and encased in a massive cast. All Gena could think of was that he looked like a little boy, sleeping without a care in the world. Nancy started crying and her mother was soon sobbing uncontrollably as they stood beside the bed, their hands resting on his right arm, which was the only part of his upper torso that was exposed. The portly black nurse left them alone for a few minutes and then stepped forward, her arms encircling them both from the rear. "All right, ladies. There's nothing like a good cry at a time like this. C'mon, now, sit over here," and she indicated chairs arranged behind them. "Stay as long as you want. I'll just be messing around with a few things for a while." She busily started adjusting the IV bottles, checking the machines and moving professionally around, taking care of her patient.

The mother and daughter waited patiently, and in about an hour Donald opened his eyes and spotted the pair of them huddled nearby. They didn't realize he was awake until he said, "Hi, girls. What's new?" They were both on their feet instantly, crying and smiling at the same time. He winced as they tried to hug and kiss him together. And God, what a headache! And it hurts like hell to breathe. But they couldn't see his grimace and by the time they stepped back, he managed a smile.

"What a way to wake up. The two best lookin' girls in the world here to visit me. How about a little smile, ladies?" This caused them to cry all the more, but they soon calmed down, and, following the nurse's advice, limited their talk to his condition, not even mentioning the fire or the ordeal he had been through. After a short time, he lost track of what they were saying, his medication causing him to doze until he eventually dropped into a deep sleep.

Donald stayed in the ICU for two days and then he was moved to a private room where he remained for ten days. His headache lasted for half of his stay, but except for his still aching ribs, a condition that would last for weeks to come, he was feeling very well.

Gena and Nancy were frequent visitors and his daughter became expert at waiting on him, mimicking the duties of the nurses whom she loved because of the way they took care of her dad. Thank God the hospital limited the number of visitors and the hours they could come in because jakes came by constantly. The nurse on duty gave them each a few minutes and then swept them out, insisting the patient was "going down for tests." When she said that to Cueball, who showed up almost every day, he said, "Hey lady, this guy gets more tests than the astronauts. You gonna make him into the six million dollar man or what?"

The on duty hospital rep visited Donald twice a day, bringing him the papers, books, magazines and anything else he wanted. They always managed to bring a gift for Nancy as well. Her job included taking care of the flowers and plants that were everywhere.

The papers fully covered the fire and Donald's actions in saving Blanca, but he was saddened as he watched the film clip of Ciro's funeral. Each night during his stay, late at night, when the room was quiet, he would review the fire in his mind. He sometimes became frustrated as he thought about the young boy, but he always came to the same conclusion. The kid didn't have a chance and was probably dead when Donald entered the building. He would pretty much convince himself that was the case, but then a different scenario would momentarily nag at his consciousness until he could push it away.

One night during his stay, he heard a commotion and groggily opened his eyes to see his room rapidly filling up with jakes. There had to be a dozen of them, and they were all filthy. He spotted Desmond, Gap, Captain Hardy, Vinnie Sterling and Walter Timmons, among others. They were returning from a multiple alarm in the Back Bay. When they had entered the hospital, the security guard wanted to know what they were there for, but Captain Hardy, in his authoritarian style, ordered that they be immediately taken to the floor where Donald was located. He garbled something about a haz-mat investigation, and the poor guard, who hadn't heard any alarms, saluted and led them to the elevators.

Gap and Dot-head were on their worst possible behavior and soon had Donald gasping with pain from laughter as one used a stethoscope to check his breathing while the other pantomimed giving him a rectal temperature check. After a few moments, a stern-faced, middle-aged nurse, who bore an amazing likeness to Mrs. Doubtfire, burst into the room. She paused, crossed her arms and in a much more military manner than even Hardy possessed said, "Who's in charge of this rabble?" When Harding sheepishly raised his hand she said, "Take yourself and these other nitwits out of here immediately or you'll all be in another business in the morning."

Dot-head tried to charm her with his best "God, you're beautiful, ma'am" line but she was implacable. "I don't care what you do to this goof," she waved her hand at Donald, "he's as bad as the rest of you. But I have some real sick patients in here and you are disturbing them.

Now get out!" They exited the room, the floor and the building faster than they would have come in if there had been a real emergency.

One visitor Donald was always pleased to see was Billy O'Laughlin. He knew that his objective was to help him mentally through the ordeal he had experienced, although Donald surprised himself that he didn't experience any nightmares or flashbacks to what he'd gone through. He felt that the incident was a once in a lifetime event and since Billy talked a lot about the job and how fate affected whatever happened it wasn't difficult to push aside the horrors of the fire and the collapse. Actually, he was pleased he had been able to save at least one of the poor kids who'd been trapped. And the fact that he had actually been able to see the body of the one who died before the floors crumbled was somewhat comforting. It helped him understand that nothing he could have done would have saved the boy and he knew that whatever pain the youngster had suffered, it was already over when Donald spotted the lifeless figure.

He also reflected on the advice his old boss, Deputy Chief Simpson, had given him after Donald's first multiple fatality fire during his rookie year on the job. The deputy, who had since retired, emphasized that if your faith taught you that all humans have a soul, once the body has expired, the real person has gone to a better place and what is left is just the remains that were the victim's dwelling place on earth.

Donald spoke at length about these views to Billy O'Laughlin and came to realize that this officer, wise beyond his years or educational background, was a great listener. He would sit for as long as necessary, and as long as Donald wanted to talk, occasionally nodding or making a comment that would result in an expansion or pertinent digression of the discussion. Gena was frequently present during these sessions and not only did she learn an awful lot about her husband, she gained an even greater appreciation of fire fighters and was able to penetrate the mystique that motivates them to face the dangers they do to accomplish their goals.

But O'Laughlin didn't just sit stoically during his visits. He had a wonderful sense of humor and a keen eye for the bizarre behavior of some of the characters that serve in the department. Gena was convulsed with laughter as she heard him describe the activities he had witnessed during a recent visit to the firehouse on Columbus Avenue in the South End, the home of Engine 7, Ladder 17 and the chief of District Four. Billy was there to see how one of his clients was doing. In the course of a year, he had a number of jakes who required his service. In addition to the stresses that everyone faces in today's high pressure society, fire fighters also constantly witness tragedies to which the general populace is never exposed. Death, sickness and injury along with the destruction of property are parts of the business and not every jake comes through these experiences mentally unscathed.

Those who are strong enough are able to healthily rationalize many calamitous events throughout their careers. Others are not so fortunate. Alcohol and other substance abuses are no strangers to the job. Billy O'Laughlin and his team are unlikely to be deactivated for lack of work in the foreseeable future. What keeps him and his partners motivated is their occasional spectacular successes and their ability to help a jake restore his dignity and effectiveness to the job and his family.

The visits are also a form of therapy for the EAP personnel. They will see the members who are most troubled, but they'll also get to experience the clubhouse atmosphere of the firehouses, which they forfeited when they accepted their difficult assignment.

When Billy entered the kitchen of the South End house, a serious discussion was going on. Those not really interested in the merits of the conversation, tried to keep it going, just so the officers wouldn't make them commence housework, which today included washing the windows, a chore they all despised. Paul Moishe was proudly displaying the nicotine patch he was wearing, fixed to his bicep. He was describing how effective it was working for him. He had now gone for almost two weeks without a cigarette, and while he was just a little bit jumpy, he was going to make it—and that was that.

Diagonally across from Paul sat Beefy Higgins. He was a frequent visitor to the house whenever he was on duty. Higgins had served on Engine 7 for over two decades and was now one of the department hospital representatives. His primary duty was responding to any hospital in the city whenever a fire fighter was injured at a fire. The purpose of his response was to insure that the member received immediate treatment in the overcrowded emergency rooms that seemed to be the norm in all of the major medical facilities. The department reasoned that since its members were injured while serving the public, they should receive priority treatment when hurt as a result of their efforts.

The fire fighters selected to serve as hospital reps must be over fifty years of age and must have at least twenty years of active duty on a fire company in order to be eligible. However, and this is most important, they must have a pleasant and enthusiastic personality that allows them to develop friendships with all of the hospital personnel they encounter. The hospital rep is also equipped with a list of all of the top specialists in every field to insure that members receive the best treatment available. The fire fighters' local makes certain that quite a bit of good cheer is distributed during the holiday season to the hospitals' key staff members to maintain the close relationships that ease the way when a member is brought in for treatment.

Whenever a member is admitted, such as Donald, the hospital rep brings the daily papers and will provide transport for family members when required. Every jake knows that he is also the guy to call whenever they need advice or assistance for any members of their family. He's the man and Beefy really enjoys his job.

He listened with what appeared to be great concentration to Moishe's technical description of the nicotine patch, then he left for his rounds of the hospitals. He returned at lunch time, removed his jacket and once again sat opposite Paul Moishe, who was gobbling down a huge submarine sandwich, his appetite having grown since he got off the cigarettes. As he glanced up at Beefy, his eyes widened. Strapped with surgical tape to the massive bicep of the hospital rep was a pork chop. "What the hell is that?" the startled jake asked.

"New diet," said Beefy. "I told one of the nutrition specialists at the Mass. General about your patch. I thought it was a lot of nonsense, but no, she said you're on the right track. As a matter of fact, now they're using the procedure for diets." He pointed to his arm, "You see, just like your patch, the pork is goin' through my pores and into my blood stream. I figure I should lose about a ton in a month or so."

Moishe shook his head in disbelief and said, "You're fulla shit. That's impossible."

"Oh, yeah. Well listen, my friend, the way you're chompin' down the chow since you got that stupid patch, you better slap a pizza on the other arm or you'll look like the Goddamn Goodyear Blimp."

Donald chuckled at Billy's story; he wished he could have been there when it had happened, and this wish made him realize how much he wanted to continue to be a part of this crazy business.

Each day during his hospitalization a stack of mail from well wishers within and outside of the department arrived. His daughter, Nancy, who came each evening with Gena, loved to act as secretary, opening and reading each one. One letter, however, she started to read and then stopped, her eyes filling with tears. She handed it to her mother who glanced through it and passed it over to Donald. It was from the mother of the three young boys who had been involved in the fire.

Donald was quite touched by the fact that although she had great difficulty in using and writing the proper English phrases, she took the time and trouble to write to him. Her sincerity was obvious. She expressed her deep gratitude to Donald for the great danger he faced in saving one of her sons and for his courageous attempt to save the boy who had died. She hoped he was recovering from his injuries and she prayed for him every day. She said she would do so for the rest of her life. In closing, she said that Ciro was now with his father, who had died in a construction accident two years ago. She would ask them both to also pray for Donald because she believed they were both angels in heaven.

Donald could see Nancy was sobbing deeply as he finished reading and he held out his good arm and enveloped her shoulders as she laid her head on his chest. "Honey, don't cry," he said softly. "I know that poor woman is right. Just think—those two folks will be watching out for me forever. Everyone else should be that lucky."

When Donald was discharged, Beefy Higgins was working and he drove him home in the department car. While he was as solicitous as required, collecting all the flowers, cards and belongings of his patient, he seemed to be in a grouchy mood. As they settled into the car, he said to Donald, "Look, Holden, I know you're on the Tower so you must know this Jeff Stoler asshole, right?"

"Well, sure," said Donald, "he's on the captain's group."

"Well, I just caught that scumbag givin' me the shaft." He went on to explain that he often visited the big house on Purchase Street because it was such a beautiful place. It was the newest firehouse in the department and since it occupied the two lower floors of a thirty story office building, it was equipped with the finest facilities. The best kitchen, best mess hall, best bunkroom, showers, exercise equipment, recreation room—and most important of all to Beefy, the nicest toilets in the entire department.

Since Beefy kept a methodical schedule, he liked to stop by Purchase Street in mid-morning, the daily papers under his arm, and answer the call of nature in one of the luxurious stalls. He'd spend a half hour or so, reading and relaxing, one of the true simple pleasures of life. Lately, however, whenever the captain's group was working in the house, it seemed he'd no sooner drop his trousers, his belt buckle striking the floor, than an announcement would come over the Fire Alarm radio: "Attention, C-11, call the medical examiner's office immediately." Beefy would groan, pull up his pants and go find a department phone.

Naturally, no one at the medical examiner's office was looking for him. The first week he figured it was just an honest mistake. The second week, the same thing, although this time he was directed to call the chief of operations. Another false alarm. He was a little suspicious, but just figured it was another screw up. When he was directed to call the fire commissioner the next time, and that was a fake, he had had enough.

So today he went through his regular routine, but this time, he pulled off his belt, clanged the buckle against the tile floor and raced out of the room, just as Stoler started playing the tape he had recorded over a period of several months as he patiently listened to Fire Alarm while on patrol. Every time they called C-11, Stoler recorded it until he got just what he wanted. Needless to say, when he saw the monstrous hospital rep bearing down on him like a rhino seeking revenge, he dove for the pole hole, slid to the main floor and disappeared down into the underground garage.

"But," Beefy explained to Donald, "I'll get him yet. Wait 'til he shows up at the hospital with some phony injury. I know every doctor and nurse in this town. I'll have to figure out what's the worst thing I can do to him. Right now, castration is leading the list."

Donald expressed his sympathy to Higgins, but he had great difficulty not bursting into laughter. Stoler was a beaut, all right. Imagine the trouble he would go to for a practical joke. Yeah, castration was one option, but how about a little laxative in the soup, Donald thought. See how quick Stoler's buckle strikes the floor. Right about then'd be a good time to hit the house gong. The possibilities are endless. Maybe he'd make a list for Beefy.

Four

The department car moved along Day Boulevard which borders Dorchester Bay, a road that Donald frequently traveled, but today, somehow the scenery looked especially beautiful. Although it had only been a little over a week, it seemed like he'd been away for a much longer period of time. The bay was clogged with tiny sailboats, no doubt the junior members of the yacht club engaging in their initial summertime races that were a main feature of the program, now that school was ended. The beaches were also crowded as the temperatures crept into the eighties. "It's great to be coming home," he said to the hospital rep who was dropping him off.

While his ribs stilled ached and probably would for some time, his arm cast had been changed to one that gave him much more freedom of movement. Oh, his muscles were sore and he got tired quite easily, but, hey, ain't it swell to be alive.

When he arrived at his house, Gena and Nancy were waiting, just inside the chain link fence. The well kept two family home never looked better. They led him up the short flight of stairs, in through the entry to the living room. In the center of the floor was a large and handsome leather reclining chair, placed just opposite his TV set. He looked at his daughter and his wife: "O.K. girls, what's this?" They both grinned slyly. The chair was something Donald frequently talked about when the three of them were in the living room together. He really said it as a joke to get sympathy from Nancy. "Yeah," he would say, "when your poor old dad has fought his last fire and is ready for the trash heap, I'm gonna get me one of those beautiful recliners with the foot rest and everything. Then I can just sit here and dream about my gorgeous daughter, Nancy, and my grandchildren, which I'm sure will look just like her and will love their grandpop."

"Daddy," she said, "We didn't want to wait 'til you're all wrinkled up. And besides, I may not ever have any children. I might become a fire fighter, just like you." Whoa, Donald thought, Billy

O'Laughlin must be working overtime on my daughter. A while ago she wanted me to quit, now she wants to join me. If I ever had any thoughts about leaving, I guess they're gone now.

The doctors had advised Donald to remain indoors resting and relaxing for the next week and he was very glad to comply. He seemed to tire quite easily, which he reasoned was probably both physical and mental forms of fatigue. So, each morning, after Gena went to work and Nancy headed for the South Boston Yacht Club, he eased into his marvelous chair, read all the newspapers, and answered the telephone which was on a small table next to him. And he got plenty of calls, from jakes in the fire house as well as many of his classmates from drill school. When he got too tired, he'd simply pull the plug on the phone and lay back, luxuriating on his comfortable perch.

He had only a few visitors because the word not to bother him was out in the job. But, Rick Foster stopped by frequently to bring him all the latest firehouse gossip and keep him laughing with the outrageous activities of some of the jakes he worked with. One day, however, Rick showed up with Lieutenant Desmond and Monty Hall. They were there on two different missions. First, Desmond, after inquiring about his condition said, "OK, Donald, now here's the deal. That exam is still coming up in November and that Civil Service Commission doesn't give a rat's ass about the fact that you got hurt. If you don't take this exam, you've got another two year wait." He went on to explain that he thought Donald was one of his best students, but it was easy to get away from the books if you're out injured. "It's too bad you got hurt, but, you should probably look at it as a message."

Donald laughed and sputtered, "What the hell kind of a message is that, Luft? It's a good idea to get hit on the head with a building, or what?"

Desmond smiled, "Well, not exactly. But, what do you want to do? Sit in that nice, new recliner staring at Regis, Kathy Lee and Rosie O'Donnell, or do you want to do something productive."

They worked out an agreement that Rick would keep him abreast of whatever they were covering in the class and Desmond would come by every couple of weeks to give him an exam and make sure he was progressing at least as much as the other jakes in the class. When they finished, Donald turned to Monty, "O.K. pal, what's your scheme? I know you're not here about any books."

"Certainly not, my friend. I have come on a mission of comfort and rehabilitation. All of this nonsense about studying and all that shit is fine, I guess, but I want to restore you to your peak of perfection through a fortuitous and monumental event that is transpiring in a couple of months." He continued, "I suppose this officer is correct, although earning one of those shit-house plungers," he pointed at the single silver bugle on the device of Desmond's dress hat that indicated his rank, "has never been my forte."

Donald could not help but recall that two silver bugles indicated a captain, two gold ones a district chief, three gold ones a deputy, four the assistant chief, and five for the commissioner-chief of department. It was a stretch of the imagination to compare these dignified insignia to a plumber's rubber helper, but jakes—especially someone like Monty—could do it easily...as long as they weren't officers themselves.

"But, and this is most important, after you've followed his advice for the next several weeks, I believe you should step back, take a break and attend the thirteenth biennial John P. Redmond Symposium of the International Association of Fire Fighters, an organization in which you are a member in good standing."

"Rick," said Donald, "do you have any idea what the fuck this snake-oil salesman is talking about?"

Foster answered, "Of course I do, but let him finish. He kind of drags it out, but hey, that's part of his charm, don't ya think?"

Hall went into a long explanation of how the I.A.F.F. had started these meetings back in 1971. At the time, it seemed as though every major city was going to be consumed by fire. Beginning with the Watts riots back in 1965, civil disturbances, which often escalated into full blown attacks on the establishment, spread throughout the country. The assassinations of Martin Luther King Jr. and Robert Kennedy in 1968 resulted in an intensification of these problems; fire fighters became the targets of scorn and abuse for several years to come. Urban renewal, which jakes always called "urban arson", was also in full swing. Many cities in an attempt to modernize their communities created situations where arson for profit became a way of life. Fire departments, particularly in the major cities, went through a two decade period that, hopefully, will never be repeated. Many thousands of buildings were destroyed, and for those jakes who were veterans of the military, it seemed somewhat like combat during the wars, but with two different enemies—fire and some of their fellow citizens.

The Redmond Symposium grew out of the International's great concern with the health and safety of its membership. Nobody was really examining what was happening to fire fighters as a result of what they were experiencing; also, the equipment that was being used was inadequate for the tasks. Such items as breathing apparatus, turnout gear, fire apparatus and other tools and equipment were not being improved at a pace commensurate with the expanding needs of the service, and the death and injury rates of fire fighters were at all time highs.

That first meeting was held at Notre Dame University in South Bend, Indiana. It brought together, for the first time, many doctors, scientists and leaders of the fire service to discuss the problems of the fire service and to make recommendations for the future. The delegates were, in general, union members from all of the locals with an emphasis on those jakes primarily interested in safety in their departments. These members were of every rank and their contribution to the success of the venture was the major reason for its continuation through the years. By 1995, there was no doubt about the enormous progress that had been realized as a result of that initial effort, and the meetings, held every two years, were eagerly anticipated by those who were chosen to represent their locals.

When Monty finished his lengthy discourse, Donald said, "Nice going, Ace. Sounds terrific. But, what the hell are you telling me all this stuff for? When did I ever become an expert on safety? And come to think about it, when did you? I thought you were going to get me a cottage on Martha's Vineyard or something. Frankly, why should I really care about this symposium, Mr. Hall?"

Monty smiled like the Cheshire Cat: "Because, my friend, your leader here, Fire Lieutenant Desmond, is going as one of the union safety representatives, and your friend, Fire Fighter Foster, is going as an interested observer, and so, I might add, am I."

"Rick," Donald said, with a shake of his head, "I don't get it. What caused you to develop this devotion to health and safety? You never got many A's in drill school."

Monty looked at Donald with disgust and exclaimed, "Holden, if I may. What's Tony Bennett's best song?"

Donald grabbed his head with both hands and thought, I must be missing something, but answered, "I dunno. My favorite's 'I Left My Heart in San Francisco,' but I'm no expert."

Hall cheered, "Exactly right. And, my friend, that is where the symposium is being held this year. Not only that, but your favorite travel agent has set up an itinerary for some of his close personal friends to make this trip." During the next half hour, Rick, Monty and Lieutenant Desmond explained what they had in mind. First of all, Rick explained, they got the idea because they remembered that the trip would take place at the same time that Nancy was scheduled to go up to New Hampshire with Gap Keefe and his family in late August. Second, Rick's wife, Sandy, had the duty of briefing Gena with the details so it would come as no surprise to her. Third, Monty, who always seemed to have a connection somewhere, had an uncle who was an executive with the Hilton Hotel chain. Subject to everyone's approval, they were getting upgraded rooms at the San Francisco Hilton throughout the symposium and, as a bonus, another few nights at the Reno Hilton a couple of hundred miles east in the Sierra Nevadas. Monty even would arrange for rental cars to take them to Nevada, naturally with his uncle's discounts and they would even be able to fly home from Reno on Labor Day.

Donald's head was spinning. "Wait a minute, wait a minute. How much do you think I can absorb in one day?" He looked at Desmond: "Geez, Luft, I'm surprised at you. What about our studies? What about the exam?"

Desmond looked a little bit sheepish, which was unusual for him. "Er, I know Donald, I know what you're thinking. I told you in the beginning, everyone has to go all out and forget everything else when we're studying. I truly believe that is the only way. But, I have given this a lot of thought and I believe if you and Rick really go all out for the next couple of months, the break shouldn't hurt you that much. In fact, it may be beneficial. I think you could really learn a lot at the Redmond to help you in the future. I think we all will. I've taken a look at the programs they've developed so far and believe me, it sounds terrific." He opened the notebook he had brought with him. "They have guys from Oklahoma City, Pittsburgh, New York and Memphis, all going to speak on the tragedies they had during the year. Also, presentations on minimum staffing, NFPA safety standards, OSHA and a lot of other issues we should be interested in for the future."

After they left, Donald's mind was in a whirl. Monty and Desmond left him a lot of material to read, but, he was exhausted. Boy, he thought as he started to doze off, with friends like those, I'll be either dead or as healthy as a horse by the fall.

That evening, after Nancy had gone to bed, he hesitantly brought up the subject to Gena, whom he had joined on the couch, the scene of the start of many satisfactory amorous adventures in the past. Donald, a true romantic, whose mind still automatically jumped to thoughts of sensual fantasies with this woman he loved so deeply, knew that his aching ribs and clumsy cast, plus his wife's sensible concern for his injuries, would preclude any fumbling attempts he made at intimacy. So he mentioned the symposium and was quite surprised when she smiled and grabbed his good arm. Hm, Sandy must have done a good selling job. "Oh, Donald, I'd love it. I've always wanted to visit San Francisco." He knew it was all decided long before they talked to him because she spoke at length about how Nancy would be well cared for and how they'd have her all ready for school and several other items that demonstrated she had given it considerable thought long before this dumb husband broached the subject.

The visit from his friends on this day set the pattern for Donald's recovery period. Shortly after Desmond had talked to him, Rick began bringing the latest lessons the group was covering in the firehouse. While Donald still tired easily for a couple of weeks, he was pleased to find he hadn't lost interest in the material he'd been studying prior to his injuries. He actually developed a regimen whereby he would awaken early in the morning and hit the books for the next few hours, the time of day when he was most alert. Gena and Nancy quickly became accustomed to his routine; they'd just speak briefly to him from the doorway of his den prior to their departures for work, in the case of his wife, and the yacht club for Nancy.

After completing his studying, he'd eat a brunch of some sort and, when the weather was good, take a walk. At first, he couldn't go more than a half a mile before his calves would start to ache, and of course, the ever present pain in his rib cage kept reminding him that it was going to be a while before he would recover completely. The break in his arm didn't bother him much, particularly after the cast was reduced to a more manageable size.

When he first started his walking routine, one of his biggest problems was meeting so many people from the neighborhood who wanted to find out how he was doing and to congratulate him on his act of bravery. Eventually, though, he managed to maintain a brisk solitary pace, waving cheerfully to many people with a stride readily understood by all veteran walkers to indicate "I'd like to stop and chat, but I'm on a tight schedule."

The route of choice for everyone living in the district, as well as scores of others attracted to the scenic waterfront, was along the boulevard and past the four yacht clubs with their hundreds of motorized boats and sailing craft anchored in the bay. It continued past the public landing and then out onto the causeway which curved to the left, anchoring itself on Castle Island. Actually, the island was a misnomer because a road had been connected to it early in the century, but the combination of this road, the island and the causeway, created a salt water lagoon that could be adjusted to compensate for tidal fluctuations. This enclosure, completed in the mid-1950s, provided all day bathing during the summer months because the water level was constantly maintained at the mid-point of the beaches. By the time Donald completed the entire circumnavigation, he had traveled over three miles, which helped to restore his strength rapidly.

One afternoon about five weeks after the incident, Donald was strolling along Castle Island, dividing his gaze between the harbor, where three Canadian warships were transiting the channel, and Logan International Airport, where a Boeing 767 was swiftly rising from runway Four R, its nose piercing the brisk southwest breeze. He hardly glanced at the huge granite fort that occupied all of the elevated portions of the island. It had been there all his life and for a couple of centuries before he arrived, so it failed to interest him much except on Independence Day when its ramparts were manned by minutemen who exchanged cannonade salutes with the *U.S.S.Constitution* as it was towed past in the annual celebration of the nation's birthday. To his right, just at the water's edge, he passed the neighborhood's impressive monument to seventeen servicemen of South Boston who died in the Korean War. The site was carefully maintained with a plot of grass and flowers and with two flagpoles, one flying the national colors and the other the flag designed for the missing members of the Vietnam War.

He heard a voice shout, "Hey, Donald, got time for an old pensioned jake?" Seated on the bench he was passing to his left was retired Deputy Chief Billy Simpson. Donald stopped, his mouth agape, and eagerly grasped the outstretched hand on the man who, more than anyone else, had influenced Donald and his classmates in drill school. The deputy, the most senior chief on the job at the time, had been temporarily detailed to the Training Division while recovering from injuries received at a major pier fire. Throughout the ten week course he had not only spoken to the new members frequently in class, but had made himself constantly available for individual problems that so many people experienced while trying to adapt to this unique job.

Following graduation, Donald and Rick were fortunate enough to be stationed in the same firehouse as the deputy and had the benefit of responding to fires with this man. He seemed to know more about fire fighting than anyone, and had the unusual gift and the patience to share his knowledge, not only with the newest members, but with everyone who worked under his command.

When Simpson's first question was about Donald's arm, Donald simply stated he had been injured at a fire in the South End. He knew immediately that the chief had no knowledge of the fire nor of its consequence. Simpson then told Donald that he and his wife had just returned yesterday from a six week visit to Ireland, something close to a pilgrimage for retired Southie people whose ancestors had arrived here at the close of the nineteenth century.

At the deputy's urging, Donald explained, as best and as modestly as he could, what had transpired on East Newton Street that day in June. When he finished, Simpson rubbed his chin thoughtfully and then asked a series of questions to determine, as tactfully as possible, what effect this momentous event had on Donald and what his prognosis was for the future of his career, both mentally and physically.

After he'd asked his final question, the chief leaned back and said, "Well, Donald, there's no question in my mind about the bravery you exhibited in what you did. You were confronted with a situation that most jakes will never experience and, you know something? No one who wasn't there knows how they would have performed themselves. I believe many jakes would have made an attempt, but, once you reached a point on that day where you had to go past and then above the fire to try to save those boys, you were taking an action above and beyond the call of duty.

"What that means in the most simple terms is that you were knowingly placing the lives of those kids above your own. You were doing what the department wishes every member would do. You, my friend, now know what your response would be. I congratulate you." He reached out and grasped Donald's hand once, this time shaking it more vigorously with both of his.

Simpson smiled broadly when Donald told him he was continuing his studies. "That just proves to me even more strongly the type of jake you're becoming. I'm certain you're analyzing and then filing away all of your practical experiences so far on the job. If you continue to do that and continue your studies, I'm sure that you'll eventually be promoted. " He then expressed his deep admiration for Lieutenant Desmond and his performance as a leader. "You may not be aware of it yet, Donald, but that first officer you have when you're appointed can have a tremendous effect on your outlook for the rest of your career. You're lucky to have landed on his group."

Donald smiled as he rose to go, "Yeah, well, I guess I can't argue with that, Chief, but that deputy we had wasn't that bad either."

In the ensuing weeks, Donald figured out Simpson's schedule and kept "accidentally" meeting the chief at the same spot. He found him to be a fountain of knowledge, not only about fire fighting and the job in general, but also about the thought processes essential to becoming a leader. Through all of the discussions ran the thread of the genuine affection the chief displayed for the people in the fire service in general, and those he had served with in particular.

Donald was amazed at how familiar the chief was with much of the horseplay that took place in quarters, even though he seemed to assume a posture of innocence with some of the nonsense people like Dothead, Gap, Brows and others were constantly producing.

"Donald, you've already experienced more than your share of tragedy during your short time on the job. That's part of the business and it'll be part of the business throughout your career. I never really got upset as a company officer with what jakes did in the house—within reason. Oh, I was always tough on guys who were unfit for duty, and I made that clear, wherever I was stationed. Just being noisy or playing harmless tricks on each other certainly never bothered me. Actually, it was the funniest job I ever had. Most of the time I would go home laughing. But I always realized and remembered the next run we had, these people could experience some hideous event and would be expected to perform their duties efficiently, in spite of the horrors they'd be required to witness. That hell-raising in quarters, I just viewed as a form of relieving tension." He explained that if it ever became too serious, he would put a stop to it. "I never allowed fighting or other serious disruptions. I always figured I may not be able to keep them from getting injured or killed at a fire, but, jeez, I should be able to keep them safe in quarters."

He related a few funny experiences he'd had in the past, going back over forty years, and Donald grew to understand that jakes really didn't change that much no matter what era you examine. It must be the type of person the job attracts—I'm glad I'm one of them.

One day during their conversation Donald casually mentioned that he was going to the union symposium at the end of August, and Deputy Simpson laughed and said, "No kidding? So am I." He explained he had been requested to present a paper on minimum staffing for safety at the conference and he was looking forward to it himself. It wouldn't be his first appearance at this event because his own local had asked him to attend some of the others in the past as part of the safety committee.

He spoke eagerly about how much he felt the International had accomplished with these meetings and he was pleased the current leadership at the national level had the same concerns as their predecessors for the health and welfare of the membership.

"My wife is coming this time. She usually doesn't, but we have some old friends from Frisco that we haven't seen for a long time. Well, Donald, maybe we'll get together out there. The Boston local brings about ten members from the safety committee, and we always set aside one evening together."

He mentioned that his friend not only served in the San Francisco Fire Department, they had first met as shipmates when they served in the Pacific during World War II. "San Francisco is almost identical to Boston in area, population and the size of its fire and police departments. There are some amazing similarities. They're on the ocean, so are we. We have plenty of hills, so do they, but theirs are steeper. My friend, Fred, retired as a deputy just about the same time I did. He's got a son on the job out there. Funny, we're always writing about how we'll get together, but never do. Now we've got no excuses. Should be a great trip."

Up until now Donald had been pampered by his buddy, Rick Foster, who not only brought him the study material, but his paycheck and all the latest gossip from the house as well. Now he decided to alter the direction of his training route at least one day a week and walk in town to the firehouse. Since the South Boston district bordered the financial center of the city, it was just about a three mile distance from his home and it passed through an area he never tired of seeing.

After passing the Edison plant on Summer Street, the piers at the long closed Boston Army Base and Navy Yard came into view. The city-owned property had a massive ten story edifice adjoining the docks, now fully occupied with hundreds of businesses, many of them related to shipping. The docks occasionally had several ocean going vessels alongside, and, at least once a week in season, brightly decorated cruise ships, either discharging or boarding passengers for their pleasure cruises to Bermuda or the Caribbean.

After passing this area, the scenery included many huge buildings, formerly occupied as warehouses for the nation's wool trade, but long since converted to ten story office buildings. The sounds of business activity where thousands of employees spent their work week always impressed Donald as a thriving part of a major community. As he crossed over the bridge into the main part of the city, the giant post office annex loomed on his left, followed by the South Station train and bus terminal just ahead of it and the high-rise Federal Reserve building rising thirty stories, across the street.

The intersection of Summer Street and Atlantic Avenue was filled with a mass of humanity exiting the terminal from the commuter trains and advancing sluggishly up the slight rise of elevation that funnelled them to their places of employment. A couple of hundred thousand came to business this way every work day and produced a large portion of the temporary population increase the public safety agencies were charged with protecting, along with their equally large counterparts arriving at the North Station on the opposite side of downtown, or by various types of motor vehicles via the expressways. The crowd would be just as huge in the late afternoon—although their pace would be much more rapid as they headed out of the city towards their suburban digs.

Donald experienced a slight tremor of excitement as he approached the firehouse along Purchase Street. It had now been almost two months since he had been in to work. Actually, other than visits to the department medical examiner at fire headquarters, as the rules required injured personnel to do, his only connection with the department was through Rick and other jakes who either visited him at home or called to check him out.

One of his most faithful contacts was Cueball Justice. His poor drill class buddy had been badly shaken by the East Newton Street fire when he thought Donald was dead. When he first stopped by at the Holden house, Donald was alarmed at his condition. No wise cracking, no superior attitude, just a very pale and nervous little man. He sat glumly as Donald tried to infuse the old spirit into him, without success. When he realized how depression was eating away at his friend, Donald made a discrete phone call to Lieutenant O'Laughlin, and within a matter of weeks, Justice seemed to be returning to his abrasive but cheerful persona.

Just yesterday, Donald chuckled in remembrance as he reached for the entrance door at the firehouse, Cueball had said as he was ending his visit, "Hey, Hero, how much longer you gonna fake those scratches? The rest of us are working our asses off night and day while you limp around in the sunshine. Knock it off and give us a break, will ya?"

At the patrol desk, Jerry Nagle of Engine 10 was on patrol. He reached out and shook Donald's hand in welcome and announced over the PA system, "Holden's here. How much does he owe on the house fund?" Donald greeted the brief message with glee. All of the well meaning, but eventually irritating sympathy he had received when he was first hurt, was over. He felt like he was back in the ballgame, which really meant no more special treatment. This was proven when he arrived upstairs where Gap Keefe was engaged in a spirited conversation with Derek Burton over the current winning streak of the '95 edition of the Red Sox. Burton loved the team, and particularly Moe Vaughn, the huge first baseman who was frequently mentioned as a MVP candidate. "Now listen, Derek, you're becoming too emotionally involved with those stiffs. How old are you anyway? You haven't even lived long enough to appreciate the tradition of those nitwits' annual collapses."

The slender black jake, his voice rising, replied, "Lissen, gap mouth, I'm a lot older than you think. But, I'm tellin' you, these guys are goin' all the way, and my boy, Moe, will lead the way." He paused, glanced at Donald and said, "Hey, man, good to see ya." He then continued his tirade, citing the pitching records of the staff and the brilliance of the managerial leadership. Steve Tucker, the driver of the Tower unit, added his views, followed by comments from any number of jakes seated at the three long tables, their white coffee mugs cupped in their hands. The din was growing louder and louder.

Finally, Stan Hardy, the captain of Rescue One, slapped his palm on the table, the noise sounding almost like a gunshot. All the voices stopped at once. The officer calmly said, "House work begins immediately. The final decision on who won this stupid argument will be announced in early October. Let's have some action on those brooms and mops."

It became a delightful morning for Donald. He stayed in the kitchen with the officers after the troops disappeared to accomplish their various tasks and had a friendly discussion with the captain, Lieutenants Desmond and Grimes as well as Deputy Chief Franklin. He had been either called or visited by all of them since the fire so he just updated them on his condition and the subject, to his relief, was dropped.

He listened closely as they discussed a second alarm the group had worked during their last night shift. It was an apartment fire on the fourth floor of a ten story housing project in the South End. The Tower and first alarm ladder companies had managed to evacuate a dozen occupants over ladders from the floors above the fire and led several others down the smoke filled stairways. Chief Franklin smiled and said, "But, you know, Donald, fires in that district are never simple." He explained that just as he was assuming everything was progressing successfully, an occupant came running out the front door and shouted, "They's robbin' my stuff up there. You gotta stop them," and he pounded his fists on the deputy's chest. "I tried to calm him down and find out who was doing what." It seems that while the department was methodically doing its job of evacuating everyone and knocking down the fire, a few of the occupants were going through opened apartments and stealing whatever they could get their hands on. It took the efforts of a squad of police, along with the security force of the building to straighten things out. But, the chief, instead of being interviewed by the media about the bravery of his force, was kept busy fending off questions about the lack of control the department had exhibited in securing the building during their efforts. "Donald," he concluded, "I know you're doing a lot of studying, along with Joe and his class, so just remember—it isn't all written down in books. The various SOPs and Incident Command Systems make everything look pretty precise. But the human element has escaped capture by the computer bytes." After listening to this discussion, Donald decided it might be prudent to enhance his journal entries to include other factors related not just to strategy and tactics, but to the people involved in the incidents and what effect their behavior could have on the outcome of an operation. They're not stamped out by machines.

Before Donald left for home, Desmond invited him into the company office. "I'm really glad you and Rick are going to the symposium. It'll be great. You'll learn a lot at the various sessions, but even more important, you'll get to talk to jakes from everywhere. It's a meeting where you'll find out, first of all, that we're not the only department on earth. Sometimes, when you're so focused on the job in your own town, you tend to forget that plenty of other jakes are facing the same dangers you are all over the country and up in Canada." He continued, "Get to talk to a lot of them. I think you'll learn, as I did years ago, that we all think pretty much alike on so many things. I believe the job shapes the way you approach, not only the work itself, but life as well. You'll come home feeling you're a member of a much bigger fraternity than you imagined. And, you'll meet some funny guys. Oh, their accents will be different, but the same brand of humor exists throughout the fire service. You'll also meet guys who can tell even bigger lies than our own heroes—although with jakes like Dothead, Stoler and a few others, that may be hard to believe."

Donald strode homeward at an even brisker pace, glad that Rick had come up with the idea to make the trip. This would be his and Gena's first trip across the country since their honeymoon in Hawaii years ago. The romantic possibilities of the trip entered Donald's mind for the first time, and he was whistling as he strode up the front stairs of his home.

Five

In spite of his anticipation of the West Coast trip, Donald resolved that he wouldn't let it distract him from his study program. The exam was coming in November and if he wasted his time thinking of other things, there'd be no time to catch up later. Success, however, breeds success, and each time he learned a particularly difficult lesson, it encouraged him to keep going. He discovered that memory can be expanded and developed by constant use. He developed a method of trying to learn something new and difficult early in the day and then, after lunch, reviewing something he had already committed to memory previously. While this made the hours he spent with the books more numerous than they'd been when he started, he understood that it was essential as the scope of what he was absorbing continued to widen.

Each week he set aside the afternoon when he knew Desmond's group was on duty and went to the firehouse to participate with the class of students. He was pleased to discover that the time he was putting in at home was proving very valuable. Now when Desmond gave a test that Civil Service had previously used, Donald was able to answer most of the questions because of his familiarity with the material. However, the sheer volume of what had to be covered was finally making him fully understand why it required a year of preparation to have any chance of success. He now understood that those jakes who thought they could take a couple of months and expect to do well enough to get a job were just kidding themselves. You just had to grind it out and keep your concentration on the objective.

At the end of July, the doctor who had set his arm removed the cast and set up a thrice weekly therapy program to rebuild the strength he had lost during the period. Between these sessions and the books, Donald had no trouble with boredom, and, at times was grateful when Sunday arrived. On the advice of Desmond, he took one day a week off from everything and found this break from the routine renewed his interest each Monday. On each of these days off he took Gena and Nancy someplace special because he understood they needed a change as much as he did. They traveled to York Beach, Maine, Canobie Lake Park in New Hampshire, and to Nantucket and Provincetown in their own state. Nancy was thrilled to spend so much time with her folks, knowing of course that she'd be back with her own friends at the yacht club on Monday. She also felt it was helping to pass the time until she'd be leaving for her two week stay with Bethany Keefe up at Winnipesaukee. She had a huge red circle around the date, August 19th, on the kitchen calendar just in case anyone forgot.

When that Saturday arrived, she was up before anyone else, packed and ready to go long before her parents had breakfast and packed their overnight bags. "Jeez, honey," Donald said as they were getting in the car, "you must be dying to get away from dear old mom and dad! Aren't you going to miss us at all?"

"Get real, pop," said the precocious pre-teen, "I've had a great time with you mature adults for the last few weeks, but this is my time. Beth and I haven't been together for a long time and now's our chance. Besides, Freddie is getting handsomer and handsomer." Donald made a face. Gap's son was almost seventeen. Oh my God, she's going on twelve. He shook his head. Ah, what a thrill to be parents of a young girl in the 1990s. This caused him to chuckle. Bet fathers have been saying that since the dark ages.

When he and Gena were riding home, enmeshed in the Sunday night return traffic from the resort area, they reflected on what a great weekend it had been. Donald's arm had recovered sufficiently to allow him to swim in the sparkling lake and Gap had taken him fishing. Although they caught a couple of scrawny looking trout, nobody was in the mood for living like real outdoorsmen. Nope. A dinner of steaks cooked on the gas powered grill, baked potatoes and corn on the cob, bought from a nearby farmer's stand was as close to roughing it as they wanted to get.

Before starting home, Sunday afternoon, they had another cookout, this time with hot dogs, hamburgers and potato salad, and after one more dip in the lake, it was time to go. Gena sniffled as she squeezed her daughter, but Nancy, while hugging her mother tightly, was winking at Beth over her shoulder. Donald caught the interplay between the two girls and it made him feel old. It seemed only a short time ago that his daughter was hugging his knees, and now she was charging relentlessly into womanhood. Time marches on. Shit.

The following Sunday morning the four couples met at Logan

Airport for their early morning departure. The women quickly became reacquainted and soon Emma Desmond, Joanie Hall, Sandy Foster and Gena were seated together in the Dunkin' Donut shop near the Delta ticket counter. The men gathered outside, marveling at how quickly jakes' wives gravitated together. They agreed the ladies were probably pretty sick of listening to their fire stories.

Their flight departed on time at 7:30 A.M. and soon the 757 was speeding non-stop to Salt Lake City, where they would make a connection for California. The cloud cover prevented much cross-country sightseeing, but the excitement of the trip, plus the breakfast service, followed by a movie, helped prevent boredom during the four hour leg of their journey.

Coming over the mountains on the approach to the airport, the skies had cleared and the Great Salt Lake was clearly visible as well as some peaks that even this late in the summer still retained snowcaps. The landing was smooth and the Boston couples were soon strolling through one terminal, then crossing over to another and boarding an identical plane for the remainder of their trip westward.

The skies remained clear during this flight; they had great views of the Sierra Nevada Mountains as they crossed over them just south of Lake Tahoe before dropping downward towards the Pacific coast. The plane continued westward over the ocean and circled for the approach to the airport. The pilot advised the passengers not to be alarmed if they observed another aircraft flying adjacent to them at the same height. He explained that the two runways they were using were side by side and, just as he said, another airliner appeared directly across from them. Both craft glided downward and touched the runways effortlessly and then rolled along their separate ways towards their assigned gates.

The four couples retrieved their luggage and soon were en route in two taxis to the city via the Bayshore Freeway. They could see a range of hills off to their left, the city of South San Francisco, its name emblazoned on the dominant hillside to their right, and, just beyond the community, the famous Candlestick Park.

The Holdens and the Fosters were riding together and none of them could hold back their excitement as they got closer to the famous city by the bay. Gena was the first to spot the pointed Interstate Bank Building which had become a landmark for the town, almost as famous as the Golden Gate and Bay Bridges, the latter span clearly visible to their right as they approached downtown.

Shortly after exiting the freeway they traveled up Taylor Street, turned onto O'Farrell and pulled up at the entrance to the Hilton. They were greeted warmly by the doorman and bellmen and found their way down the steps and to the registration desk across the beautiful lobby. Following Monty's explicit instructions, they did not enter the line of guests checking in at the main counter. When he arrived a few minutes behind them, he went to a separate desk and they could see him talking animatedly to the concierge. He called the group over and in just a few minutes, they had filled out the registration forms, received their card keys and walked to a bank of elevators that took them rapidly to the twentieth floor.

Their rooms were standard size and quite beautiful, but they soon discovered they were on one of the VIP floors, which featured an on duty concierge and a lounge that served complimentary cocktails in the afternoon as well as a breakfast buffet each morning. Good old Monty. He seemed even more at home in the hotel than he did in the firehouse back home. A born confidence man, thought Donald—and am I glad I know him.

Since they were now on Pacific Daylight Time, it was three hours earlier than it was back in Boston. They should have been tired, but the excitement of the trip had them at a point where nobody wanted to just relax. The Holdens and Fosters wanted to start sightseeing immediately, while Desmond had to go to a meeting of Boston delegates and Monty was taking care of signing them up for the conference. The two couples set out down the street, hiking towards Union Square.

The first thing they noticed was how much cooler it was than back home. The sky was bright blue, the temperature was in the sixties and a soft breeze from the bay made it quite exhilarating. This climatic condition continued throughout their stay, with cool days and chilly evenings. Fortunately, Monty had briefed them on what to expect and they had brought sweaters and light jackets which were quite appropriate. They smiled when they saw many tourists shivering in shorts and sport shirts. No doubt their travel agents were not as wise as Mr. Hall. It took just a few minutes to reach Union Square, which looked like a small oasis surrounded by high-rise hotels and department stores. The palm trees were somewhat startling because of the cool weather. The Easterners thought it was too cool to support such tropical growths, although they were much shorter than what they had seen in warmer climates.

Powell Street was thronged with people and the clang of the cable cars added to the din. It didn't take much coaxing to stroll down to

Market Street and join the long line of folks waiting to board these fabled and unique transports. The two women managed to get outward facing seats and the husbands gallantly stood on the running boards in the accepted manner. Up the hill, the cable pulled the crowded car, past the fabled St. Francis and Sir Francis Drake hotels, and then directly up the enormous hill, leveling off near Chinatown, swinging over to Mason and working its way downward to Columbus Avenue and Taylor Street.

Along the way, both Donald and Rick noticed how close together the buildings were to each other, many of them rising to four or five stories. However, they could also see that most of them had well kept exterior fire escapes with dry fire department standpipes and connections rising upwards to the roof. "How'd ya like to have them back home?" asked Donald. "Yeah. They musta learned a lot when they rebuilt this place after that earthquake," said his friend. "And none of these buildings touch each other." Donald looked closely and could see a tiny space, sometimes not more than an inch or two, separating each structure from its neighbors. "Hm, that must have something to do with earthquakes, too. Pretty clever. Gives an extra wall as a fire-stop too."

Before they could continue the discussion, Gena pulled their arms and pointed. The car was now descending towards the bay and they had a clear view of the blue water. "Alcatraz," she said. "It's sitting so close to the shore." She had always envisioned it somewhere far off but there it was, rising ominously from the sea.

When they exited the cable car, it was just a short walk to the heart of Fisherman'sWharf. They passed many shops along the way, some with all kinds of souvenirs and others with clerks hawking every kind of fish, shrimp and other seafood. The smell reminded them somewhat of the Boston Fish Pier but on a much larger scale. Sandy Foster was armed with a camera and the group posed under the famous sign, shaped like a boat wheel, with the name, identifying the wharf printed in bold letters around the face of it. A young Asian man posed them somewhat professionally and then they reciprocated as he lined up his family for a group shot.

The rest of the afternoon sped by. They took a cruise on the bay on one of the famous Red Fleet craft and were delighted to actually go under the Golden Gate Bridge and gaze upward at it. Even on such a clear day, there were thin banks of fog drifting by the spires on the brisk wind. The bay was quite rough, with three foot waves but nobody seemed to mind; they were enchanted by the scenery. While the two bridges were at opposite ends of the huge bay, the skyline of San Francisco was the dominant view. The high-rise buildings and hundreds of apartment houses and other residences really did seem to climb on top of each other as they marched toward the peaks that dominated the city. When they returned to the wharf, they walked eastward to Pier 39 where they were fascinated by the hundreds of seals that had appropriated the adjacent yachting slips and talked to each other incessantly in their hoarse barking voices.

Pier 39 had hundreds of shops, each one beckoning to the ladies; fortunately, everyone had to admit they were feeling fatigued, and they prudently turned away. Gena and Sandy vowed they'd be back here tomorrow while their heroes were attending those meetings.

A police officer directed them along Jefferson to Hyde, where they could join the queue for the cable car back to downtown. The line was quite long and just in front of them were two couples, about their own age. The men had jackets with patches identifying them as jakes from Hartford, Connecticut and they soon were talking like old friends from back home, meeting in a far off country. It was this group's first trip out west and they had arrived a day early. By the time they had completed their return trip, the women were already developing a plan for the following day. The men were discussing the symposium and were looking forward to the massive reception scheduled for this evening.

The reception proved to be the start of a marvelous week for all of the attendees, and there were over a thousand of them present at the symposium. They were entertained by the Irish Pipers Band of San Francisco and there were buffets set up at several stations around the Continental Ballroom that featured many types of food specialties from the area.

By ten o'clock the four Boston couples were exhausted. The time lag was catching up to them. They repaired to the lounge on the roof of the hotel, sipped nightcap cocktails as they gazed fondly at the city lights rising up the hills and then descended to their rooms. Donald had no idea what transpired behind the closed doors of his friends, nor was he much interested, but he had envisioned several exotic scenarios for himself and his beloved in this city where you could almost taste the aphrodisiac impulses the setting generated.

He quickly disrobed and climbed into bed, yawning expectantly while Gena completed her preparatory ablutions in the bathroom. The next thing he knew, the sun was shining in the windows and his eyes popped open. At first he didn't know where the hell he was, but when he figured it out, he groaned. The heroic jake had collapsed at the crucial moment, proving once again, how reality defeats fantasy.

He stumbled into the bathroom, glancing at his watch and saw it was already after seven. Boy, that jet lag really was a fact of life. Gena had been turned away from him when he arose, so he quietly returned to the bedroom, determined not to disturb her. But, as he approached the windows to try to shut out the light, he heard her say, "Hey, marine, you gonna leave without sayin' goodbye!" She raised the covers seductively and he could just catch a glimpse of her uncovered form before she let them drop.

The first session opening ceremonies were scheduled to begin at 0830 hours, and, they did, but you couldn't prove it by fire fighter Holden, who raced into the Grand Ballroom a little after nine. The lights were dimmed and Senator Barbara Boxer of California was addressing the sea of humanity jammed into the hall. Donald assumed she must have been great, but all he could really think about during her presentation was Gena. How the hell did he ever meet anyone like her? After fifteen years of marriage, you'd think things in bed would be settled down into a somewhat routine operation, but she still kept him intrigued. In spite of her parochial school education and religious devotion, she still managed to be not only inventive, but downright sensual in her earthy approach to their lovemaking. Yes, he thought contentedly, she's a keeper all right, and I'm a lucky guy. Now, what the hell is this meeting about?

The balance of the early morning consisted of welcoming addresses by the mayor, the chief of the San Francisco department and other local dignitaries, reaching a climax with addresses by General President Alfred Whitehead and Secretary Treasurer Vincent Bollon. It was particularly interesting to Donald to see the leaders of the International Union. He had seen their names several times and read their columns in the newsletters, but to actually hear them in person made him understand how enormous the organization is and how important it is to be a part of this membership of over 200,000 fire fighters.

After all of these introductory speeches were completed, the real work of the conference began. It started with the dramatic presentation of Assistant Chief Jon Hansen. He was very familiar to everyone in the audience as a result of his spokesperson duties for the Oklahoma City Fire Department during the massive rescue effort following the bombing of the Murrah Federal Building on April 19th. Donald took many notes about the technical aspects of the recovery operation, including the valiant work of the sixteen search and rescue teams from other fire departments that participated in the days following those first desperate hours. For Donald, however, the most lasting impression of this incident was how much more difficult it became after that first day when it was more obvious as time went by that no more occupants would be recovered alive. It clearly demonstrated to him how fire fighters have to persevere, to hang in there and keep working until the job is completed, no matter how frustrating the circumstances become. You just can't pack up and go home until the job is done. Desmond was always emphasizing this phase of the job, particularly when the Tower was operating at long duration fires in the winter after it became obvious their efforts weren't very successful.

There were presentations that were extremely disquieting the next morning. These were reports by chief officers from four major cities about incidents involving fire fighter fatalities. While Donald appreciated the honesty of these senior officers in discussing the tragic tactical and strategic errors that contributed in part to the deaths of their members, it brought home quite forcefully that the fire service is still a long way from having the knowledge essential to eliminate such tragedies. Once again, Donald thought of Desmond and how important his constant emphasis on safety and learning at each incident is to their survival. Donald realized—perhaps for the first time—that there's more to becoming a leader than simply trying to outstudy and outperform everyone else in an exam and get a higher paying job. The four departments had conducted in depth critiques that enumerated the changes which had to be made to attempt to prevent such losses in the future and Donald could see that each of these officers had been deeply affected by the incidents. It made him more determined than ever to pay attention at every fire, keep his notes more diligently and always try to return to quarters with more knowledge, no matter how insignificant it seemed at the time.

The afternoon sessions were divided into workshops on various subjects and it became difficult to cover them all. Rick and Donald split up so that each would cover two and then exchange information. Donald was really pleased that Rick was just as impressed as he was and was much more serious than normal.

Donald enjoyed two panel discussions in particular. Not that some of the others weren't at least as interesting but because two of his favorites were active participants. Retired Deputy Billy Simpson discussed staffing for safety. His logic for the number of personnel required to conduct effective and efficient operations was obviously based on his own observations after four decades of fire fighting. The other presentation was on "Staying Alive—Wellness and Employee Assistance Programs". Billy O'Laughlin was one of the panelists and Donald could really relate personally to how important and effective this relatively new approach to health was to jakes.

In spite of all of this day time dedication, the nights were something else. At first, Donald was quite concerned that Gena would be bored trying to keep amused while he was diligently attending the sessions. He needn't have worried, however. The ladies were having a great time without them. It was obvious they had fallen under the charms of Baghdad by the Sea, as the travel agents described the beautiful city. With the advice of the SFFD local's wives, they had taken guided tours that encompassed everything from Golden Gate Park to the Cable Car Museum and had also managed to traipse through the magnificent department stores and, of course, Pier 39's inviting shops. They even visited Alcatraz. The men started feeling neglected. They were determined they were going to spend at least one day doing something special, but, in the meantime, there were certainly no evening sessions.

On the advice of local jakes the group dined one night at Harry Denton's in the Harbor Court Hotel. They were seated at picture windows facing the Embarcardero and the bay, where scores of sailboats passed by, many of them obviously engaged in a race. As the sun set, the Oakland Bay Bridge, just to their right and so close it seemed within reach, was illuminated with thousands of lights, adding to the enchantment.

As they were finishing dinner, they could hear a rock band begin playing out in the lounge, and, spurred on by the drinks they had consumed with their meal, the eight friends were soon on the dance floor, jammed into the crowd, many of whom, no doubt, were jakes. Monty and Joanie Hall were country western freaks and after a discussion with the band and the passage of a couple of bills, the music changed in the next set. Monty had no qualms about grabbing the mike and in a short time his Boston accent was directing the crowd in a somewhat stumbling imitation of the "Wild Horse Saloon" show on The Nashville Network. Donald, attempting to match the beat with Gena, shook his head in amazement at the uninhibited brashness of their tour director. Joanie told him later that her husband had a lot of experience in stirring up a crowd: "You should see him on the cruises he books. He gets senior citizens up out of wheel chairs into Conga lines."

Later they worked their way along the waterfront until their collective feet started to ache, then the group moved inland to the financial district. On the advice of a police officer they went into the Bank of America building and ascended in the high speed elevator to the Carnelian Room at the top of the skyscraper. The view was spectacular. The topography of not only the city, but the entire bay area left them in awe. Their waiter pointed out Oakland, Richmond and Berkeley across the water as well as the Golden Gate Bridge and Marin County, to their left, off in the distance.

What was most revealing the first evening to Rick and Donald was how relaxed Joe Desmond was. He really had a wonderful sense of humor, something that wasn't so obvious in work, not only because of his duties, but also because the group of crazy jakes with whom they worked left little room for this officer to let his hair down. His wife, Emma, a full-figured, short, grayish-blonde haired woman, was truly hilarious. She had a quick wit and had no qualms about chastising her mate whenever he started to get officious. At one point, as he tried knowledgeably to point out some well known landmarks, she crossed her blue eyes, grimaced and said, "Hey, general, slip off that podium. You're not on duty tonight. Besides, we ladies know more about this town than you students ever will." Desmond drew himself up to his full height, pointed his finger at her, just as he sometimes did when he was giving orders at a fire, and meekly said, "Yes, ma'am," sinking sheepishly into his chair, but obviously enjoying the put-down immensely.

The group's final day in the city was the most memorable. The men skipped the remainder of the program, with a surprising lack of guilt. They had attended the sessions they thought were most beneficial to them and were anxious to see as much as they could of the area before they departed. The ladies knew exactly what they wanted to do and they advised their mates to wear their walking shoes. They maneuvered the men along the sidewalks down to Market and Powell Streets, not to board the cable cars this time, but to watch the street musicians entertaining the throngs gathered there.

From there, the women strode purposefully along Market to Grant Avenue. Rick groaned as he saw them turn left and stride up the hill, significantly higher than those back home. Their objective was Chinatown, and after passing through the archway entrance, it was easy to imagine they were actually in the far east. Although many other tourists were in the crowd, most of the people were Chinese, and there were scores of shops displaying goods out on the sidewalks, as well as markets, jewelry stores and restaurants. At the peak of the grade, they stopped to catch their breath and entered a charming cafe featuring exotic teas and fortune cookies. Naturally, Monty was soon engaged in a conversation with the owner, and through a combination of English and Chinese phrases, managed to extract the information that the family had relatives who owned a similar cafe on Tyler Street in Boston's Chinatown, which is somewhat smaller but provides the same atmosphere of being in the Orient.

By the time the Bostonians departed, Monty and the owner were bowing with their hands clasped together. As they started to head down the opposite side of the avenue, Donald said, "Hey Monty, what are you doin', trying to set up a tour?" Hall grinned: "You never know, my friend. I really like this town; it fascinates me. And if an expert like me enjoys himself here, can you imagine what those dumbbells back home would pay to get here? After, of course, I use my charm and wit to draw up a tour." He rubbed his hands together. "I'll have half of them coming here just to see where their relatives did time on the Rock."

When they reached Broadway and crossed over to Columbus Avenue, the area changed dramatically. They were in North Beach and for the next several blocks the shops and restaurants were now all Italian. It further emphasized to Donald how cosmopolitan the city is, a quality that is as much a part of its charm as the visual beauty.

When they approached Washington Square, the tiny park had a group of elderly Chinese men and women doing Tai Chi exercises that require the use of both mental and physical senses designed to maintain health and serenity. The park also had a memorial to volunteer fire fighters, the figures sculpted in darkened bronze.

Across the street was the beautiful St. Peter and Paul's church, and the women insisted on a brief visit. The interior was almost like a cathedral in Rome and the motif was definitely Italian. Gena insisted that she and Donald light candles in thanksgiving for his survival at the East Newton Street fire, and also for the repose of the soul of Ciro, the little boy who had been lost.

The remainder of their foot journey was down hill towards the bay and the ladies purposefully strode to the ferry slips, and soon had their spouses boarding the substantial craft that took them through the choppy seas across to Tiburon, stopping en route at Angel Island where many bicyclists disembarked to explore the hilly, forested terrain.

By mid-afternoon, the group was back in San Francisco seated at a table in the Buena Vista restaurant, famous for its purported invention of Irish coffee—although the Bostonians couldn't believe it took a guy from the West Coast to think of adding whiskey to caffeine. Hell, back home they'd add booze to anything from breakfast cereal to omelettes without giving it a second thought. However, the crowd jammed into the place certified its popularity and no one complained about the drinks. They were delicious.

They returned to the downtown area via cable car and in the lobby of the hotel were informed that the entire Boston contingent was going out to dinner that evening and they were all invited to join the group. It turned out to be a fitting finale to their stay. Deputy Simpson had arranged through his SFFD friend of many years to get a reservation for all twenty of them at the Washington Square Bar and Grill. This famous bistro, called the "Washbag" by the locals, set up an enormous table through the middle of the main dining room. The friendly atmosphere was reminiscent of the neighborhood Farragut House back home. Donald marveled at the fact that all of these people, including himself, were gathered together some three thousand miles from where they lived as a direct result of their membership in the fire service.

He listened with amusement as Gena described their outing to some of the other women. After they had arrived in Tiburon, Monty slipped into a travel agency and soon they had a guide with a mini-bus, who escorted them to all of the shops, then over to Sausilito where they lunched at a restaurant that not only offered a magnificent view of San Francisco and the bay, but had a startling number of sailing craft gliding past its picture windows.

From there, they were taken across the Golden Gate Bridge and back to the city, passing through neighborhoods where the minimum price of a dwelling was in the million dollar range. Donald hadn't seen his wife so animated since their honeymoon. She was having a marvelous time, and he could see the source of his daughter Nancy's enthusiastic personality.

On Labor Day, on the last leg of their plane trip back home, he looked at her seated beside him. She was fast asleep, her head resting on a pillow that leaned against the window of the jet. When he looked outside, he could see many stars in the heavens and occasionally, thousands of lights on the ground below, indicating a major city. Gena was exhausted, as were Donald and all of their friends. After leaving San Francisco, they had traveled in two rental cars northeastward via Route 80, across the state and up into the Sierra Nevadas where they ultimately came to Reno, and as arranged by Monty, stayed at the Reno

Hilton for the next few days.

The massive hotel, with over two thousand rooms was unlike anything they had ever seen anywhere. It was so self-contained, with restaurants, showrooms, swimming pools, bowling alleys and every other conceivable type of entertainment, in addition to its enormous casino, they were almost overwhelmed. At first Donald and Gena thought they'd never leave the building, there was so much to do. They soon learned, however, that there was much more to the area they just had to explore. They visited many casinos downtown as well as in the neighboring community of Sparks, and it looked as though they would be arriving home in Boston penniless. Donald was trying to defeat the blackjack dealers, without much success, but when he teamed up with Rick at the dice table, he recovered most of his losses, much to his surprise and delight. Apparently, Rick had learned the game from an expert on the lower decks of the aircraft carrier he served on during the Gulf War; Donald just kept following his lead. When his friend finished his turn with the dice, tossed a couple of chips to the stickmen and gathered up the stack in front of him, Donald was quick to do the same and discovered they had each come out winners.

He went looking for Gena and found her standing near a row of quarter slot machines, clutching a huge panda doll, almost as tall as herself and looking around anxiously, no doubt for her husband. She smiled when she spotted him and shouted, "Donald, I hit for three giant pandas and a man gave me this," she shook the stuffed toy at him. "That's great, dear, but what the hell are we gonna do with it? We'll never get it on the plane." She nodded: "I know it. I'm going to give it to the first little kid I see." Then she grinned and said, "But look at what else the man gave me!" and she waved five crisp one hundred dollar bills at Donald. Dinner at the top of the Flamingo Hilton that evening was on the Holdens.

During the next few days, they traveled southward, up to Lake Tahoe, circling around the deep blue water through the snow-capped mountains lined with giant pine trees. They also visited Carson City, the capital of the state and Virginia City, which offered spectacular views of Reno far below it. Each of these communities had their own casinos, designed to reflect the unique scenic vistas they presented, but never losing sight of the objective—to remove the money from the visitors as painlessly as possible.

As the pilot announced that they were starting their approach into the Boston area, Donald tried to analyze everything that had transpired during the trip. It would certainly be memorable for all the enjoyment they had with their friends and how they had all gotten to know each other so much better in the relaxed atmosphere; but, nagging at the back of his mind were the disturbing thoughts he had about the disastrous fires that had been described so eloquently during the symposium. There were so many things to learn about this unusual business; Donald was even more determined to concentrate on the job more in the future. He also felt he was ready to return to work and hoped the department medical examiner would restore him to full duty soon.

Their reunion with Nancy took place the next day, when she was delivered safely home by the Keefe family. While she politely listened as her parents talked about their journey, she was far more interested in outlining her own fantastic voyage. It was obvious she had a great visit with her friends and, while she was thrilled with the gifts the folks had chosen so carefully for her in San Francisco and Nevada, those far off places could never compare to Winnipesaukee.

In any event, she was back in school on Wednesday, Gena went back to work and Donald reported to Headquarters. While he would have gone back to work that day, the doctor told him to take another two weeks. He reluctantly admitted that the time would help him to develop a little more strength in his arm and the dull ache in his ribs should be lessened even more. The time also let him get out his books and study program and review everything he had learned so far. He was pleased with how well he had retained so many items, but understood that it was quite easy to lose the competitive edge if too much time elapsed between study sessions. He spent four hours each morning in his room, pouring over the text books and committing to memory much of the material Lieutenant Desmond had Rick deliver to him. Afternoons, he would walk for miles, usually along the seashore, but occasionally into the downtown and Back Bay districts. He found his visit out west had made him much more interested in architecture and how it varied in different sections of the country. He also tried to imagine fire problems that could develop primarily because of the way his city had evolved over the past three-hundred-fifty years and how much of a role such things as topography and wind speeds could affect operations. Sometimes he'd feel himself flushing with embarrassment as he realized that he was starting to think like a chief or something and here he was still a fire fighter. Then he'd look down an alley, lined with five and six story buildings and try to visualize how he would place a ladder truck or get a line of hose into position, and his imagination would take over again.

One afternoon he returned to his usual route along the beach and out to Castle Island. He was hoping he'd meet Deputy Simpson at his favorite spot and, sure enough, he could see the familiar figure, binoculars raised to his eyes, staring down the harbor towards Deer Island Light, where a huge vessel was negotiating the narrows leading into the main shipping channel. There seemed to be an extraordinary number of tugboats guiding the ship westward, and Simpson seemed completely absorbed by the scene.

When Donald spoke to him, he lowered the glasses and smiled. "How are you, pal? Got back from the coast OK, I see." He commented about the wonderful evening they all had together in Washington Square and how much he and his wife had enjoyed themselves there and throughout their stay.

When Donald asked him about the ship that was making its way up the harbor, Simpson said, "Yeah, well, that tanker is one of the biggest in the world. It comes from Algeria and it's carrying liquefied natural gas, or LNG. Know anything about that, Donald?" Holden replied that he'd been reading about the dangers associated with the gas, but didn't know they brought it here by ship. Simpson explained that this part of the northeast had to obtain all of its fuels from elsewhere. No oil wells or other fossil fuels around here. Oil and gasoline come by sea and natural gas is piped into the area, underground from Texas, Louisiana and Canada. "The natural gas we get via pipeline isn't sufficient to answer our needs for cooking, heating and industrial use, so it is supplemented with LNG, which is compatible with our regular supplies." Donald asked how dangerous it is, being shipped in like it is. "Well, like any other hazardous product, the greatest danger is complacency. When they first started bringing in this tanker, all shipping in the harbor was halted until it reached its berth over in the city of Everett." He pointed down towards the inner bay. "But over a period of time, nothing much has gone wrong, so the restrictions have been lessened little by little. I just hope we never have a serious incident with it because it could develop into a major disaster."

"But, never mind that, Donald, tell me, what did you learn at the symposium? Did you find it interesting?"

Donald nodded: "Absolutely, I found it interesting, Deputy, but I think it scared me too."

Simpson frowned at the response and asked, "In what way?"

"Well, some of those fires those chiefs described, I, er, I was surprised at some of the things that happened that didn't seem to be right."

Simpson smiled and nodded his head as he said, "Glad to hear you say that. It means you were paying attention. I hope that all the jakes who went there got the same message." He spent the next hour talking with Donald about his own major concerns for the future of the fire service, and it proved to be a most revealing conversation for the young student.

Simpson talked about the tragic fires presented at the conference and why they resulted in such grim losses of life. "It seems to me that some of the people setting policies have kind of lost sight of the whole objective of fire fighting. Every procedure established to control a fire must be as simple as possible. Why? Because the fires will add all the complications needed to test the fire fighting forces. The department should never be guilty of adding its own complexities to the situation." He explained that some of the incident command systems that had been evolving during the past decade actually were attempting to have fire fighters remember a number of procedures really unnecessary to the primary objective. "If the leadership really understood this business, they would realize that the average fire fighter is kind of scared whenever he arrives at a serious fire, it might make a difference in their thought processes."

Donald said, "I'm not sure I know what you mean, Deputy."

Simpson nodded: "Yeah, well maybe I'm not sure myself. But, I know, that even at the last fire I went to, just before I retired, I was, maybe not frightened, but apprehensive about the fire and how we'd do controlling it." He continued, "You see, I have always understood, going back to when I first came on, that it is pretty tough to concentrate on a number of things at one time, and this is particularly true if you're excited or scared when you're trying to accomplish a specific task. Now," he paused to try to choose the right phrases, "if your department has developed a system that requires you to think of several items under pressure, it's more than likely that the average guy will screw up most of them." He shook his head as he mentioned how, in the interest of probably trying to professionalize the job more, systems even changed commonplace terminology. "One department changed the term floor to division, while another changed it to levels. Now, that may seem like a small thing, but a jake running a line really wants to know where you expect him to operate. If you tell him to take it to sub-division three or level five, chances are he'll get confused. If you send him to exposure D, he'll probably go to the wrong place. Why? Because you've complicated his thought processes at a time when he just wants to concentrate on a single, major objective. I never had much trouble placing lines when I said, 'Engine 1, take a big line up the front stairway to the fourth floor.' Or 'Ladder 1, get the roof of the building on the left and check for extension.'" Simpson said he had attended a conference during his last year where a presentation given by a nationally recognized expert on fire fighting was entitled "Back to Basics."

Simpson had many disagreements with what this towering figure described as basics, but his question, which was never really answered, was "Why did you leave the basics to begin with?"

He turned to Donald and grabbed him by the arm, "Donald, so far our department hasn't become too enamored of these computer oriented methods of controlling fires. I think the reason is because there are still enough fires in this town to continue producing experienced jakes from the top to the bottom. When you have personnel who've been to a lot of fires, they understand that simplicity in the operating procedures is essential to success. If you have good, basic first alarm response duties, they can be expanded into any type of major incident without much confusion."

He described how the present rule requiring the first engine and truck to take the front of the fire building, the second engine and truck to take the rear, when accessible, or unless otherwise directed by the officer in command, was a time tested procedure that eliminated unnecessary commands. This automatic assignment helped to relieve the chief of issuing directives and allowed him to make the assumption that these objectives were being accomplished in the initial stages. The rules also allowed officers in charge of companies to deviate from these assignments, when confronted with unusual situations, as long as they notified the officer in command. "Honest to God, Donald, I've seen incident command systems where they almost have a conference before anyone gets their assignments. All I can think of is that they don't have the type of construction we have, where immediate action is essential—or if they do, they must be destroying a lot of property." He smiled, "They seem to be setting up systems that would be able to handle any major disaster, such as the World Trade Center, with the snap of the fingers, but would probably screw up a mattress fire in the South End. If they just paid attention to experienced chiefs, they'd be a lot better off. I read the report of the chief in charge of the World Trade Center bomb explosion and he made a most significant statement in his summary. He said that radio communications were very poor throughout the incident. He attributed the success of the operation, in the number of lives the department saved and the ability to gain control of the fire, to the fire fighting experience of the individual fire companies and the individual fire chiefs who operated so effectively on their own, concentrating on the objective and using their heads as they always do at much less newsworthy events.

"You know, kid, many people make the assumption that the chief standing in front of a fire building knows everything that's going on at the incident. Nothing could be further from the reality of the situation. Don't misunderstand me. He may be the most experienced guy in the country, but he's not a magician. He bases all of his decisions on a few factors."

Donald, thirsting for these secrets, asked, "What are they, Chief?"

"Well, first of all, his own experience. The more buildings he's stood in front of, the more he realizes how much he is the captive of information he must receive from others. Oh, he might be able to determine how the fire is progressing from what he can actually see, but his vision is limited by his position and the visibility within his periphery. Probably the most important jake at the scene is his aide, if he has one, and many fire departments have eliminated this position in the interest of reducing costs. It's a pretty foolish economy because that guy is the only person at the fire whose only duty is to get information for his boss." Simpson paused and looked at his young friend with a searching stare: "You know, pal, I think I'm running off too much at the mouth. Maybe I should shut up."

Donald shook his head vigorously in disagreement as he said, "Chief, I've got no where else I have to be. This is the most revealing talk I've ever had about the job. If you don't mind, I wish you'd just keep going." He could see that Simpson was pleased with his answer and he listened intently as the deputy explained that while company officers were a source of much of the information the chief used in making his evaluations at a fire, they sometimes became distracted in their efforts to get their companies into position to advance on the fire, ventilate, perform search and rescue duties. In other words, they had multiple concerns at the scene. The aide was the key to determining where the fire was, how it was extending and also to nagging the officers for information and verbal reports to the chief. "If you noticed, at all those fires described at the symposium, the officer in charge never had good communications. Sometimes their command systems restricted the ability of the fire companies to let them know what was transpiring and sometimes it was just a lack of knowledge about the basics of the business by the officers in command. Why? I don't know. I met all kinds of chiefs during my career. Most of them were pretty competent and did a good job most of the time. I hope that includes myself, although I can think of a few fires where they'd have been better off if I stayed home. But, I did meet a few—thank God not too many—whose primary objective was to become a chief, wear a gold badge and they'd become automatic geniuses." He laughed out loud, "We had one guy, when I first came on, who we called 'Cement.' He knew that was his nickname, but he figured it was because he was so strong and stern looking while he was commanding a fire, but it was really because he was so dumb. He looked magnificent standing in front of the building, but he never said shit. We had great company officers who knew what they had to do and did it. Cement Head was his full nickname and it really fit him to a tea. But," the deputy concluded, "he sure looked great in uniform. The best boss I ever had looked like a rag picker when he got dressed up, but boy, what a jake he was."

Simpson stood up. "O.K., Donald, that's enough for today. You probably think I'm getting a little senile and have an axe to grind. But, believe me, I don't. I'm just hoping enough people with practical experience continue to rise to the top in most fire departments. If that happens, the service itself will overcome those who, while well meaning in their attempts to intellectualize fire fighters, sometimes increase the dangers to those they are trying to make look smarter. Class dismissed! I'll see ya later, Donald."

Donald's head was in a whirl as he sped along the causeway, heading home. He wanted to get home so he could write down Chief Simpson's views before they slipped away. Actually, he was thrilled that Simpson had expressed his views so openly. It answered many of the questions Donald had had at the symposium, but didn't know how to approach the speakers. Oh, he and the other Boston jakes had had discussions with fire fighters from plenty of other departments who had similar concerns. That was somewhat reassuring, since many of them were chiefs and officers as well as fire fighters back in their own communities, and the fact that they were apprehensive about the future of the fire service should indicate that they would fight for the best possible leadership.

And, those presenters of the disastrous fires were also men of great courage who were not afraid to publicly criticize themselves and their own departments in the interest of the greater, common good. Yep, Donald thought as he trotted up his front stairs, there's a lot more to this business than I figured when I came on, but, so far, anyway, I think I've been with the right teachers. Time will tell.

Six

Donald returned to work at the end of September. He was thrilled to be getting back. He was a little apprehensive as he pulled into the garage under the firehouse and lugged his gear up the stairs and into the locker room. He hadn't had any nightmares about the collapse and his injuries, but that didn't mean he never thought about the fire. Actually, he had reviewed his own actions many times and was convinced he had done what he had to do and was glad he had done so. A couple of times he shivered as he imagined how he would have felt if he had not tried to get in the building and attempt to rescue those kids. Boy, would that be difficult to live with. It was much better to live with the aches and pains in his body, but not in his memory.

His first tour was almost like a reunion, but thankfully, it was not an ego building event. As he stepped into the kitchen, Dot-head Doherty was the first one to spot him. "Hey, Hero, glad you're back. You got the twelve to three watch. We been coverin' for you too long. These poor slobs are exhausted from doin' your work at fires," he waved his arm at the Tower crew.

"Yeah," said his pal, Gap Keefe, "you really milked it. A coupla lumps and you're gone for the summer." He shook his head in disgust. "My very good friend, Brows," he nodded towards Brennan, "got a foot long gash trying to dig you outta that job on Newton Street and never went off duty. Just slapped a blowout patch on his arm and went right back to work. Right, pal?"

Brennan looked up, his usual scowl in place and said, "Holden, you owe your house fund. Get it up or you're not in on the meal tomorrow night."

"Great to be back, guys!" Donald laughed.

After the house work was completed, Desmond assembled all of the students in the study room. Donald was pleased to see that Rick Foster, Derek Burton, Steve Tucker, Jerry Nagle and Howie Rosen were still in the class. There had been no dropouts while he was on injured leave. He was also glad to find out in the course of the class that he hadn't lost any ground while he was away. Actually, his methodical system that required four hours every morning at home had given him an advantage over the others because he had done it every day for months, except for the symposium break. The exam was only six weeks away and the sessions now consumed much of the working day tours, with reviews of what had been covered each evening they were on duty. The only response they had during that first tour was to an auto fire a few blocks from quarters. The sound of the house alarm and the familiar duties of sliding the pole, donning turnout gear and responding sent a thrill through Donald's body, some of it anxious anticipation but mostly joy at being back in business. At the scene, while he was busily pulling apart the rear seat of the fully involved vehicle, District Chief Kinsella tapped him on the shoulder and when he looked up, the chief was smiling: "Glad to see you back, Holden. You did a super job. Made the district look good." Donald was thrilled. Kinsella wasn't noted for lavishing praise on anyone, although he really fit Simpson's description of what an effective chief officer should be. He operated with intelligence and experience and consequently developed great confidence and loyalty from the fire companies under his command.

The next night really seemed like old times. Brows cooked scores of meatballs in his famous sauce and enough pasta to satisfy Dot-head and even Jeff Stoler, who was working for someone on the group. Of course, they had a run in the middle of dinner and when they returned, Stoler complained that the meatballs were charred. This caused an uproar, especially when he said how much better the meals were on his own group. When the shouting got too loud, Captain Hardy of Rescue One cleared his throat meaningfully and the voices quieted down. "Stoler," he said, "you are just a temporary guest on this group. You could never make it here as a regular. If you don't shut up right now, I have a case of brass polish and a half dozen poles that need shining." Stoler bowed humbly from the waist and said, "You know, Captain, sir, one thing I always admired about you is that you're not a mean or vicious leader. However, I understand your concern for these poor unfortunates you've been stuck with. Therefore, sir, my lips are sealed." He turned his thumb and forefinger against his mouth, then made a waving motion with his arm. "And, I've thrown away the key." Even Hardy grinned at the irrepressible jake.

At 0259 hours Donald was on patrol when Box 7251 was struck. Fire Alarm reported that the alarm was sounded for a fire in vacant buildings on Locust Street in the South Boston district, and Rescue 1 was dispatched. Engine 39 reported heavy fire showing from a duplex three decker and Donald announced this report over the loud speaker system because the deputy and the Tower would respond if there was a call for more assistance. It wasn't long in coming. The district chief reported a working fire and Donald hit the house alarm. As the signal 45-7251 was striking over the alarm system, Donald announced the location and jogged across to the Tower, stepping into his hitch, pulling up his bunker gear trousers, looping the suspenders over his shoulders and shrugging into his fire coat. As he entered the rear door and sat on the jump seat, he marveled at how automatic his actions were, even after such a long absence. Creatures of habit, he thought as the huge truck maneuvered out the door under the guidance of Steve Tucker.

The route to the incident was via the South Station Tunnel of the central artery, heading south towards the Andrew Square section of the district. The fire was plainly visible in the clear night sky. Heavy smoke was blowing out towards the harbor, but it was punctuated with bright flames extending up into the sky. The Tower unit moved down the exit ramp, crossed over to Dorchester Ave, turned right and sped toward Locust Street. A cluster of flashing red, white and blue lights directly ahead of them indicated that much of the emergency response equipment couldn't be properly placed on the narrow street. Desmond told the crew to bring a variety of hand tools as he jogged up the avenue seeking the deputy or his aide. By the time Donald and the other members reached the intersection their officer said, "O.K., we're assigned to the adjoining structure. He pointed down towards the buildings and it was obvious no one was operating inside the three decker of origin. The fire was pouring out of every window in spite of the numerous hand lines and deck guns driving high pressure streams of water into the flames. The attached structure had heavy smoke rolling out of each floor, but fire fighters were outlined on the roof, their personal lights casting luminous beams into the night's darkness. Other laddermen were extending ground ladders to windows and dropping the tips of the aluminum extensions through top floor windows, expediting ventilation in conjunction with those opening scuttles and chopping holes on the roof.

Desmond led his company up the wooden flight of stairs to the front entrance. A dry two and a half inch line was already stretched up the inside stairway and the crew moved rapidly upward through the light smoke which became much heavier as they turned onto the second floor landing and approached the top floor. The officer didn't have to tell them to don their facepieces, the conditions made it obvious they couldn't penetrate any higher without them. Engine 21's members were lying prone in the hallway at the entrance to the front living room. Desmond was able to identify the officer, Vic Molten and was told they had just ordered the line filled. "Joe, there's plenty of fire in all of the ceilings," the officer said, his voice muffled by his mask. "I told the chief we need another line for the rear and he said it's coming. See if you guys can get us an opening, will ya?" Desmond tapped Donald and Howie Rosen on the shoulders and said, "Crawl right over these guys and open it up." They wormed their way over the prostrate jakes, through the doorway and into the large room. In the middle of the ceiling was a three foot diameter decorative floral plaster insert. Flames were visibly licking out through the cracks in the overhead. Desmond squatted beside them and said, "Wait'll they give us the word on the water and then get as big a hole as you can." The heat was increasing as they crouched in the heavy smoke. It seemed forever before someone from Twenty-one yelled, "Got it." Donald and Howie stood up cautiously and drove the top of their rakes into the ceiling, both of them hooking onto the circular fixture and pulling down together. A huge piece of the ceiling, much more than they anticipated, dropped all at once, much of it hitting them forcefully on their leather helmets and driving them to their knees. Donald could feel Desmond pulling on the bottom of his turnout coat, pulling him back toward the doorway. Although he was a trifle groggy, he could hear the powerful stream of water driving into the overhead, soaking him, but also reassuring him that they were being protected. He had a frightening thought that this was the start of another collapse, like Newton Street, but as he fell through the opening into the hallway, he reasoned that this was not the roof coming in, just part of the ceiling, wooden lath and plaster covering attached to the beams. Actually, the section's quick drop hastened the control of the fire as the stream was able to strike much of the area rapidly. Within a few minutes, Donald and Howie were back inside, working together, methodically pulling and exposing the beams right over to the division wall separating this structure from the fully involved dwelling next door. Desmond and Steve Tucker had reached the front windows and were cleaning out the remaining glass and frames, improving the ventilation and creating large openings for access or exit. It was obvious that Engine 21 could handle the remainder of the fire in the room, so Desmond had them work back towards the rear of the building where another engine company with a big line was operating in the kitchen and rear bedroom areas. Another ladder company was also working in the area, and between the two units, it wasn't long before the fire was contained on this floor. They could hear rakes pounding into the plaster beneath them and were aware that they were being properly protected from below. Desmond had them remove several more windows, and shortly afterwards they were able to dispense with their facepieces and take a break.

Donald, his arm and ribs aching from his exertions, sat against a wall, his booted legs extended in front of him. He slowly realized that his hands were shaking and a chill passed through his body. Now that he was no longer concentrating on the job, he had a flashback to the collapse and had to choke back a nauseous feeling. In a few minutes he heard Desmond's voice: "Holden, come out on the porch." He sprang up and moved down the rear hallway to the outside piazza and saw his officer leaning against the wooden railing.

"You want me, Luft?" he asked.

"Well, I just wanted to see how you feel. You look a little peaked. Thinking about the South End fire?"

Donald started to deny it but then realized he couldn't fool this perceptive man. "Yeah. But listen, I'm O.K., really. It's just that when that ceiling dropped, I thought everything was gonna come down."

Desmond grinned, "So did I, Donald. I got caught in a partial collapse once years ago, and whenever I hear that rumbling noise, it scares the shit outta me. They had to dig me out too, but I made it...and so did you. I'm betting you and I had our share already. I feel sorry for all those stiffs who haven't experienced it yet.

Donald laughed out loud: "Luft, I don't know whether you're right or not, but I know I like your style."

They were joined by Howie and the three of them watched as the fire next door was pummeled into a mass of wreckage and steam by the outside streams. The chief of the district passed through the area, surveying the progress that had been made and directed Desmond to report with his crew to Deputy Chief Franklin outside at the front of the fire building. He dismissed them and they soon were passing through Edward Everett Square, stopping naturally at Dunkin' Donuts to pick up a slew of pastries that they knew the manager would give sympathetically to those sad looking, filthy jakes, who always seemed to brighten considerably when they found out they weren't paying, again.

As they were backing into quarters, Howie Rosen waved the bag of goodies at Brennan who was on patrol. "Too bad you guys from Ten didn't make it, Brows, old chum. We can only share with the Rescue and the deputy, 'cause they worked their asses off."

Brennan was glowering and he started to say, "Yeah, well fuck you, Rosen," but before he could finish an alarm started striking over the tapper. It was Box 1865 and Fire Alarm immediately reported many calls were being received for 1165 Dorchester Avenue, a location about twenty-five blocks further along the avenue from where they'd just been. The chief of District 7 reported a working fire just after the message and the Tower unit, which hadn't been turned off yet, prepared to respond to the fire. Howie turned to Brows and said, "Here, Mr. Lucky, we gotta go save the rest of the city!" as he tossed the doughnuts to the still fuming Brennan, then slid into the jump seat just as the truck started rolling.

The route was much the same as the one they'd travelled only a couple of hours earlier, but this time, before they had even reached the next exit, the chief had struck a second, third and fourth alarm. While the previous fire was somewhat visible from the Expressway, this one left no doubt about its location. A broad expanse of the now cloudy sky reflected a deep glow with black smoke rolling across much of the district.

This location, since it is across Massachusetts Avene, is in Division 2, because Mass. Ave. is the dividing line between the two fire sectors, each under the command of a deputy chief, division commander. The boss on that side, Arthur Driscoll, had been recently assigned to the post, having completed a tour of duty in the Personnel Division, following his promotion to deputy a year earlier. While Donald hadn't met him yet, he had heard Desmond and the others talk quite enthusiastically about him. The word was that he had spent his whole career in busy assignments in Roxbury and North Dorchester and while he understood when he made deputy that his lack of seniority would doom him, in his words, to duty at the Pentagon for an indeterminate stay, he couldn't wait to get back in the field. Through a couple of unexpected retirements, his tour at headquarters was shorter than he expected; he was probably the most cheerful rookie deputy the department had seen in quite a while.

As they were approaching the intersection of Columbia Road and Dorchester Avenue they could hear his voice on the radio: "Fire Alarm, we have a duplex three decker, fully involved and starting to collapse. Notify all companies to prepare for heavy stream operations." He then gave a series of orders that by their content made everyone aware that he knew which direction every unit was approaching from and where he wanted them to position themselves. The fire had jumped to four other buildings, two on each side of the asphalt shingled structures of origin, and was threatening to extend across the wide avenue, already melting street lights and exterior signs on commercial properties.

Driscoll's aide was waiting for the Tower unit and had kept a pathway open for the truck to a position angled across from the main body of fire. He told them the deputy had already assigned two engine companies to stretch big lines into the Tower's pump and he wanted them to elevate as rapidly as possible and sweep as much of the area as they could encompass with their combination nozzle.

While Donald was placing the jack pads on the side closest to the fire, he could feel the heat striking the back of his neck. He positioned the aluminum plates, climbed up the back of the truck and raced along the ladder to the bucket, joined by Desmond as Steve Tucker elevated them into position. Fortunately, some water was already hitting the fire from the ground level so the flames couldn't reach across the street to them. Tucker turned over control to the bucket and Donald rotated them towards the fire buildings. The intercom crackled with Steve advising them that they had water and could commence operating on the fire.

They opened the manually controlled nozzle and soon were swinging the powerful stream, shaped into a narrow cone, back and forth, left and right, across the rooftops and upper floors of as many of the buildings as they could reach. They had a spectacular view of the entire scene. Several hand lines, deck guns and ladder pipes were functioning efficiently in a comparatively short period of time. As they succeeded in cutting off any further extension, Desmond said, "Well, Donald. This is a little different, huh?" He nodded and the officer continued, "You know what really excites me at a job like this, kid?" Donald shook his head. "When I first came on, all of our equipment was junk, real shit. You could never have done this kind of a job so effectively. In those days, nothing worked and the stuff was pretty impractical. The last decade's been great though. Now we got preconnected deck guns, large feeders, lightweight hose and a lot of other gear that's makes us about ten times as efficient. Someone's been paying attention and it really shows. Look at Brows Brennan down there. He's a happy man." Donald could see the usually grim hoseman seated on the deck of his pump, driving his high pressure stream into the heart of the fire in one of the adjacent buildings.

Donald was staring down from the bucket into the duplex three deckers where the fire had originated when suddenly, the flames, which had appeared to be under control, burst forth again, and as he started to swing the nozzle back towards the center of the buildings, he had a phenomenal view of the remainder of the roof pitching inward, the top of the front walls being pulled towards the direction of the structural failure while the bottom kicked outward across the sidewalk. The jumble of burning material disappeared temporarily into a mass of sparks and dense black smoke. It was a startling sight that momentarily caused him to think of the force created by the weight of the falling materials and what could have happened to him on Newton Street. He shuddered briefly, but Desmond, perceiving the look of horror on Donald's face, shouted, "Sweep that stream right across those sparks. Gotta try to stop them from settin' roof fires all over the district." Donald concentrated on complying with the instructions and the effort brought him right back to the present.

After the dramatic collapse, the fire's intensity seemed to diminish, and when he asked the officer about it Desmond said, "Yeah, well, long as no one gets hurt, it's usually the best thing that can happen. A lot of the fire that we couldn't hit inside the buildings is now much better exposed to our heavy streams. We'll get outta here a lot sooner than if they stayed upright."

The lieutenant's evaluation was prophetic; the fire was rapidly brought under control. In the adjacent buildings, now that the rapid extension was containted, engine companies were able to advance hand lines throughout the interiors of those occupancies still structurally intact.

Now that the smoke was turning to steam, Donald had a wonderful view of the sun just peeping over the Southeast Expressway on a clear, cool October day. For some reason, he felt elated, not only at their success in contributing to the control of the fire, but, just being alive. "This is a great job," he said softly to himself. He rotated the turntable with the onboard hydraulic controls and gradually lowered the massive aluminum ladder and bucket downward toward the body of the apparatus before releasing the power to Steve Tucker at the pedestal controls, who then eased the unit into its solid bed.

Donald cheerfully descended to the street, realising he hadn't been required to wait very long before getting right back in business. Two multiples on his second tour convinced him that he'd have no difficulty with the shadows created by his entrapment on Newton Street. Nope, just move along and don't look back except to draw from whatever his experiences were teaching him.

As he scribbled furiously in his notebook after they returned to quarters, he made note of the fact that most of the material in those wooden buildings had been pulled into the heart of the fire when the roof came down because of the way they had been joined together with so many nails and joists when they had been erected about a hundred years earlier. He also made a note of how in the Newton Street collapse the floors had plunged downward, but the brick exterior walls had mostly been pushed and fallen outward into the street and rear yard because of the way they had been built, probably during the same era. Who knows? Maybe that's what saved his life.

Donald thought it was worth mentioning to Desmond, so he brought it up at the study session during their next day tour. The lieutenant said, "I'm glad you brought that up. There is an old theory in this business that wooden walls fall in and brick walls fall out." He went on to say that it is generally true and for the reasons Donald had mentioned. "But, I want all of you to pay attention to what I'm going to say. *Generally* is a nice word, but it leaves a helluva lot of room for error. That building that's about to fall down may not be aware of the theory and may just decide to do whatever it wants when it collapses." He smiled. "I've seen them go both ways. So my advice to all of you is, if it looks like a fire is gonna produce a collapse, get as far back from it as you can."

As an example, he cited a fire he had been at during a bitter cold night in the mid-'80s: "We had about seven fully involved three deckers in Southie. Cripes, was it cold. There were a bunch of fire fighters from the Dublin Fire Brigade in town and they were all at this scene, freezing their asses off. They said afterwards, it was the coldest any of them had ever been. The temperature was below zero Fahrenheit and none of them had ever seen it below freezing back home.

"The fire was so intense that the boss had everyone move back across the street from the involved structures, assuming that there would be some kind of a collapse. When there was, the wooden walls plunged *outward* to the street, not inward, as is generally expected. Unfortunately, the weight of the buildings knocked over an old elm tree and it fell across the street, landing on two jakes. It killed one of them and badly injured the other. It was a terrible loss and, like so many other fires, it demonstrated how much fate plays a part in our lives. That old tree trunk whipped right past me and a dozen other guys, including the boss. Why did it pick out Eddie Connolly instead of us? I don't know—anymore than I know why those walls didn't fall in as expected. So, just keep alert, boys, and if you hear any strange noises, don't be afraid to run. No matter how fast you go, I'll probably be ahead of you." He laughed. "It's amazing what you can do when you're scared. I worked with a guy when I first came on. They used to call him Gimpy Garfield. He was forever complaining about his left knee, which he said was loaded with shrapnel from Nam. His limping seemed to get worse around Christmas every year and he'd try to get off injured for the holidays. But, our captain was too smart for him. He'd always assign him a paid detail between Christmas and New Years. You can't take an off duty assignment watchin' Santa Claus at Filene's if you're off injured. Gimpy was too cheap to skip the good pay day, so he'd remain on duty." Desmond hesitated, then said, "This story is getting too long...let's get back to the books."

Rick Foster said, "Yeah, but wait a minute, Luft. What's the punch line? You can't leave us hangin' with this character?"

"Oh, all right. We had nine alarms in a six story factory over on A Street one night and at some point, the building next door, which wasn't really that badly involved, was hit by a large section of the fire building and the upper floors started coming down. Did we run! But way out in front of everyone was Gimpy, not a trace of his limp in his stride. From then on he was known as Gazelle Garfield."

"Er, pardon me, Lieutenant, sir," said the usually quiet Derek Burton, "I think you're full of shit, sir."

Desmond burst out laughing, and as he bent over the table, his chest heaving, he swept his gaze across at all of them and said, "Well, maybe I am and maybe I'm not, but I think you get the point. Back to work."

The rest of the month was fairly quiet, although the company responded to three working fires in the Charlestown, Brighton and Roxbury districts. While none of these incidents were spectacular, Donald and his partners pulled quite a few ceilings and opened a couple of floors and roofs. He felt he was continuing to absorb more knowledge about the business from a practical point of view. He now looked around with much keener interest to try to determine how the fire started, but more importantly, how and why it extended. He was occasionally puzzled by the way that buildings, apparently of the same design, were so much different in the way their structural supports had been fastened. Desmond told him that back in the nineteenth century, the strength of the three deckers was not determined by any sophisticated computer designed blueprints, but by how much help was available and how cheap a bucket of nails was. "The foremen, who earned their jobs by being tougher than the rest of the immigrants, were determined that they wouldn't be blamed for any failures, so they kept those carpenters pounding away until they were satisfied the joints were strong enough. That's great for us nowadays, but every now and then, you run into a place that's falling apart when you get inside. That's when you gotta watch it. Sometimes, I think, usually pay day, those workers had a couple of extra brews during the lunch break and they might have forgotten an occasional stud or beam. I try to imagine every place was built on the off days and it makes me kinda conservative."

The week before the exam Desmond didn't try to teach them anything new. He conducted a complete review of every item they had covered during the past year. His theory was that if you hadn't learned everything by then, it was probably too late. Oh, if someone thought he came up with some kind of divine guidance or was into astrology or palm reading, he probably should check out whatever the spirit world inspired him to study, but otherwise, just hang in there with what you already know.

"Finally," he said at their last session, "since the exam's on Saturday, my opinion is, don't study anything on Friday. I always take a walk into the city, go to a movie—one that doesn't require any serious concentration and has a happy ending. Friday night I take my wife out to eat, lay off the booze, come home and try to get some sleep."

He advised them to make sure they got to the site of the exam, which was Brighton High School, well in advance of the scheduled starting time. "Have about a half a dozen number two pencils, and in the classroom, make sure you get a desk with a smooth surface—no gouges or love messages scratched into it—and pay complete attention to the instructions of the monitor. And finally, one other thought." He paused, looked out at them, smiled and said, "Whatever else happens, stay cool, because if you fuck up everything and fail miserably, you still get to come back here Sunday and go to work. We got the best job and the best companies anywhere and we'll still love ya. Now, go get'em!"

Friday evening, Donald, Gena and Nancy arrived at the Farragut House for dinner at six. He'd followed his lieutenant's advice and seen some mindless comedy during the afternoon, and did feel pretty relaxed. The atmosphere in this popular neighborhood restaurant left little room for thinking about tomorrow. The main argument was about the New England Patriots and whether or not Bill Parcells would get them into the playoffs again. There were so many experts seated at the square bar and others in the booths and tables surrounding it that

Donald never gave the exam a thought. Actually, the bar had as many characters as any firehouse, and like their uniformed counterparts, they were just as positive about the absolute correctness of their opinions. The patrons also discussed at length the desire of the Patriots' ownership and some of the state politicians to build a new stadium for these heroes of the gridiron—who currently played in Foxboro, a town some thirty miles south of Boston. Unfortunately, the site these disingenuous, non-resident, alleged movers and shakers most frequently promoted was located in the South Boston district. The consensus that evening was that even if those stiffs ever won the Super Bowl—they ain't gettin' in our town. None of the money people seemed to realize the already monstrous commuter traffic the community experienced every single day because of its close location to downtown. But heck, why should they care? They all lived in Lincoln or Dover or Weston or any of those other hayseed communities the Yankees grabbed when they got off the Mayflower and never let go.

As Donald settled his bill with Frannie, the middle-aged waitress who usually took no position on the world problems that were settled here every day, she said, "You know, folks, these guys usually don't know nothin'. But, for once I agree with them. If we don't want somethin', we'll fight. Lookit the battle we put up on forced school busing. Now, twenty odd years later, even the nitwit judge who forced it on us understands how stupid that decision was. But, they never got our town away from us and neither will these stadium dopes."

As they walked home and entered their house, Donald realized what good advice Desmond had given them. He had almost forgotten about the exam as he pondered the sometimes hilarious discussions and debates that had taken place around them during dinner.

However, the next morning he awoke early, and as he tried to think about what kind of questions would be asked, he panicked because he couldn't remember a damn thing. His wife and daughter were so solicitous of him that he had to get out of the house. He kissed them both quickly, nodded as they said how great he was going to do, jumped into his car and sped towards Castle Island, parking in the large circular lot and almost running to the walkway that circles the fort, then striding briskly around the half mile route. He lost count of how many times he covered the distance, but by the time he headed back to his car, he felt calm and relaxed. The sea always seemed to have this effect on him and he enjoyed the roar of the jets as the daily flow of hundreds of commercial airliners started their everyday routes to all parts of the world, lifting off from Logan Airport, just across the main ship channel.

This feeling remained with him throughout the day. He kept remembering Desmond's final admonition about the fact they'd all still be working no matter what happened and it served him well. He didn't even get upset, like some guys did, when they discovered guys like Jeff Stoler, Dot-head Doherty, Scabs Shaughnessey, Cueball Justice, who never opened a book after drill school, and a host of other characters showed up to take the test. Desmond had warned his students about these clowns, explaining, "They're just there to kill a nice Saturday in November. None of them know shit, but they told their wives they're all gonna get promoted and become chiefs." Derek Burton, who was pretty serious about everything, said, "But, Luft, can they really do good in the test?" "Not a fuckin' chance, Derek. When the marks come out, they'll all flunk and then tell their brides how they got jocked by the system. Just keep away from them."

As he was approaching the entrance to the school, Donald waved off Stoler who was telling everyone he knew that he had a copy of the test. "I'm gonna top the list, Holden, my heroic friend. What kind of a Lufty do you think I'll make?" Donald brushed by him and said, "Well, Jeff, my friend, a guy once told me that an asshole's an asshole no matter what kind of a device he has on his uniform. If the hat fits wear it."

Once inside the test room, all the chatter stopped. The monitor, a Boston school teacher hired by the State Department of Personnel Administration to conduct the exam, made it clear what the ground rules were: "No talking, nothing on the desk except pencils and the material I give you. No one leaves the room. If you must go to the rest room, it had better be an emergency. I'll send a police officer with you if it happens, but I'd prefer it doesn't. Do you understand?" You could hear a pin drop after this stern, middle-aged woman finished her presentation.

After filling out the required forms and finally, receiving the test questions, they were ordered to begin. It was almost a relief to Donald as he turned over the sheets of thick white paper. When he looked at the first question, he breathed a sigh of relief. He knew the answer. Desmond had advised them that if they didn't know the answer to a question, don't spend too much time with it. Just move along to the next one—but make certain you don't forget to come back to it.

The multiple choice answers required the participants to select the one they believed was correct and then fill in one of the four or five squares that corresponded with their answer. Desmond had told them that the three hour time limit was more than enough if they just kept moving. "Don't get caught up in letting an unknown question bother you. Hardly anyone ever gets them all correct. Just concentrate and then move along." He also told them that if they finished early, not to rush out of the room. "You'll see some guys looking smug and strolling out confidently in about an hour and a half. Usually, when the marks come out, they're in the shit. Play your own game, not theirs."

When Donald finally laid down his pencil and glanced up at the clock, the teacher was announcing, "You have fifteen minutes remaining. When I tell you to stop, do so immediately. Anyone who continues will be disqualified." Donald breathed a sigh of relief. He had managed to complete the entire test well within the allotted time and had been able to go over each answer to insure it was marked the way he wanted it to be. He felt the test had been hard but very fair, with a great concentration on Standard Operating Procedures, Progressive Discipline Guidelines, Fire Ground Procedures, Hydraulics and duties related to fire officers.

While he wasn't too sure about four of his answers—and couldn't wait to check them out in his books—overall he felt quite confident. The feeling and fear he had early in the morning about not being able to remember a thing disappeared as soon as he answered that first question. Hanging around outside were Stoler and his counterparts, all of whom had left shortly after looking at the list of questions. "Hey, Hero, how about that? They gave us a screwin'. Me and Dot-head spelled our names wrong and from there on, it was kinda downhill. We'll be back in two years, though."

All of Desmond's study class met at the Venetian Garden restaurant in the Dorchester district. While it was several miles from Brighton, they had all agreed to go there because the lieutenant told them it was a good luck charm for him and his friends when they had studied in the past. It was almost a guarantee you'd get made if you all had a beer there after the test and none of them were about to tempt fate.

Donald was pleased that they all felt they had done about as well as they could. Although they couldn't remember all of the questions or even all of their answers, they were pleased they had put in the time and decided unanimously that it wasn't wasted. Donald was thrilled to discover that of the four questions he was nervous about, he had gotten two of them right. Now, if he was correct in all the ones he thought he was, he should be all right. Desmond had told them not to worry about compiling a list of the questions. "By the next tour you work after the exam, those experts who know everything, or think they do, will have a list all printed. And they'll know every answer—at least until they get their marks."

At home Gena and Nancy were waiting anxiously for his report, and when they heard him whistling as he got out of the car, they both burst into smiles. Of course, they had agreed during the day that no matter what the outcome was, they'd be upbeat and cheerful no matter what Donald said had taken place. Actually, they had taken a bus into the city and visited the Arch Street Shrine, attending mass and lighting candles while Donald was taking the test. Gena remembered from her school days how her favorite teacher, Sister Eulalia always emphasized that if you had faith, no matter what failure befell you, it would work out for the best. While they were lunching in Quincy Market, she explained this philosophy to her daughter because Gena could see she was getting more nervous as the day progressed. Nancy, wise beyond her years, replied, "Sounds like a great theory, Mom, if you're a loser, but isn't it OK for us to celebrate if dad aces this test?"

After a quiet dinner, Nancy appeared in the dining room with a chocolate frosted yellow cake, Donald's favorite, which she had baked for the occasion. She had decorated it with white lettering that read, "Donald Holden, B.F.D., Always Number One at Home."

Later, when his daughter had gone to her room, Donald was watching the late news when he heard the tinkling of glass. He looked up and saw Gena framed in the doorway to the living room. She had two snifters of brandy, which only momentarily grabbed his attention because his gaze jumped to the peach colored lounging pajamas he had picked up at Victoria's Secret for her last birthday. He had wondered what had happened to this rather sensual outfit, which he had agonized over when the young saleswoman had enthusiastically elevated it on its hanger, to demonstrate its sensual qualities to him. He remembered blushing furiously, nodding rapidly and saying, "Yeah, OK, lady, I got the message. Just wrap it nice, will ya?"

When he awoke on Sunday morning, he had a slight headache due to the second round of the powerful drink, but he had no difficulty in recalling with deep pleasure how his gorgeous wife had responded to his passion into the early morning hours. As he gazed over at her, sleeping face up, one arm lying horizontally across her bedcovers and her breathing so gentle, he chuckled as he thought about how acrobatic she had been just a few hours ago. Amazing. But, something was nagging at him. He knew he should be doing something right now, but he couldn't for the life of him, remember what it was. Suddenly, it came to him. He should be up studying. Have to do those four hours. But as he started to throw the covers aside, he thought of another of Desmond's maxims on their last day of studying: "If you think you had a real bad day, look at the bright side of it—when you get up Sunday morning, you won't have to open those Goddamn books. It's all over 'til the next time, so forget about it. You did what you set out to do and now it's time to relax."

Donald sank back onto his pillow, took another look at Gena who had now shifted into a much more enticing position, with a lot more flesh exposed and a slight smile on her lips. "To hell with the books," he murmured as he rolled towards this temptress. If she had looked this way the night before the exam, he'd have never made it to the starting gate.

Seven

When they reported for duty, a list of the questions had been generated and copies were in the mess hall, proving once again that Desmond was right. The copying machine in the deputy's office had to be reloaded with so many jakes interested in what they couldn't remember had been asked. After the house work was completed, Desmond gathered all of his class in the study room and they spent the remainder of the morning going over each question. In general, they were all quite pleased with the results, although everyone of them felt like kicking themselves for some of the questions they now knew they had gotten wrong. Howie Rosen summed it up best when he said, "How the fuck could I forget that stupid SOP from the fire duty section? That's what we do at every fuckin' fire we go to. What an asshole!" Each of the others, Donald included, could nod in agreement. While he remained pretty quiet throughout the meeting, he grew more confident as the discussion continued. It was now pretty obvious that unless he made an error somewhere he could only find two incorrect answers. Each of the others had at least three, and a couple had even more. Well, he thought, this isn't the time to do any bragging, but, boy, I now know I got out of my studying what I put into it. Desmond sure knew what we had to do and he gave us every opportunity to succeed. The guys who get him when he makes captain don't know how lucky they are. Actually, Desmond had done quite well in the captain's exam that had taken place just about a year ago, and while he didn't top the list, he was certain of being promoted within the next year because of scheduled mandatory retirements of several older chiefs and company commanders. The computer printouts that listed everyone's age and date of appointment, and which were squirreled away by every student, made it clear that now that all of the World War II vets were gone, the Korean War crew was in its final stages of extinction due to the sixty-five year limit, which would ease out those who hadn't already been removed from the rolls. Such changes were constant due to deaths, injuries or simple voluntary superannuation when the minimum thirty-two years of service and fifty-five years of age were reached.

A week or so after the exam the talk gradually faded; everyone had dissected the questions and retreated into their individual evaluations about how they had done and what their standing would be when the marks were received in sixty days, and the concentration shifted to the job, sports and what the most popular toys were as Christmas rapidly approached. This year, though, another unpopular factor had to be entered into the equation: snow. The 1993-94 winter had produced record breaking snows with a total accumulation of over ninety-six inches for the season, over fifty more than is normal in the city. By contrast, 1994-95 had been a piece of cake with only a comparative dusting of fifteen inches for the winter. Just as everyone was starting to feel complacent and that the bad year had been a fluke, the white stuff was already clogging the streets well before January. Although nobody knew it at the time, by the end of April over a hundred inches would be recorded, further destroying the already shaky credibility of the meteorological pundits who had been speaking of global heating after the mild conditions of the previous season.

By mid-December, the companies had already been out shoveling hydrants a couple of times, and in the neighborhoods the broken beach chairs, trash cans, milk cases and orange construction cones were already in place, marking the parking places of citizens who had been lucky enough to be parked in front of their garageless houses when the first major snowstorm arrived. The inviolable rule was still in effect: if you shovel out the space to get your car out, you mark it with your personal piece of memorabilia and no one will try to appropriate it. Of course, once in a while some free spirit or recent yuppie import will ignore the custom, but the mysterious deflation of a couple of tires usually effectively emphasized the rules.

Donald was wise enough to use the family car as little as possible during such periods. Both he and Gena could get to work with minimal difficulty by using the fairly efficient public transportation system, and since Nancy was transported to Boston Latin School by the city, they could actually survive quite well without a car when conditions were severe. Donald and Gena had been thrilled when Nancy had been selected for this prestigious school as a result of the competitive exam she had taken the previous year. It is the oldest public school in the country, with a curriculum that results in a high percentage of college scholarships for those completing the six years of study. While the school system has been effectively destroyed since forced busing began over twenty years ago, the three exam schools in the city have managed to maintain their high standards in spite of the federal courts involvement.

Several of Nancy's friends who had not been successful in the exam had moved out of the city to the suburbs. One of the primary reasons for this ongoing exodus through the years is that parents are unable to afford the tuition in the parochial schools and must seek a better public school system elsewhere. Except for those in the exam schools, the other students are subjected to substandard education with little hope of achieving the superior instruction their counterparts receive. Donald pondered these inequities while he was on patrol after midnight. He had been out with the company checking hydrants earlier in the evening, and while the temperature was well below freezing, the city's plows had not destroyed the shoveling the day crews had done so they weren't out very long.

When Box 228 was struck just before 0300, Donald smiled after it had been transmitted because the Fire Alarm operator announced that it was struck for a school fire in Roxbury. Maybe I have ESP or something, he thought. Think about the schools and one comes in. He looked up the location and when the address was announced on Hulbert Street, he was able to pinpoint it on the huge map hung outside the patrol desk.

While he was looking at the framed diagram of the entire city, the officer on Engine 14 reported, "Fire showing, St. Joseph's school." Donald moved rapidly towards the P.A. mike to pass this information on to the companies in the house. Before he could reach it however, the officer reported a working fire. Donald depressed the master switch which illuminated the house lights, sounded the alarm and opened the automatic doors. Before he could mention the location, the lieutenant at the scene ordered a second alarm, reporting the fire was extending rapidly in the ancient three story brick and wood parochial school with a mansard roof.

Donald was driving the Tower this week and Desmond, sliding into the seat in the cab opposite him, said, "Know where we're goin', pal?"

"All set, Luft. Expressway to Melnea Cass, to Harrison Ave to Warren Street. OK?"

The lieutenant nodded and said, "You got it, Donald." As the truck moved down the ramp to the central artery, Desmond said, "Boy, now that you took that exam, you know everything. Even the right routes."

The humor disappeared as they heard the chief of District 5 order a third alarm and they concentrated on listening for instructions over the radio. They raced across the city and as they crossed onto Warren Street, Desmond counted side streets, finally saying, "Next right, onto Regent Street." Donald swung wide and made a right hand turn into the narrower thoroughfare. They were able to see heavy black smoke and sparks over the rooftops of several buildings as they maneuvered closer to the location. It became obvious they would be unable to properly situate the Tower near the fire building because so much apparatus was clogging the route, but a chief's aide standing at Hulbert Street told them the deputy wanted a fifty foot ground ladder raised at the rear of the school. They could see one aerial in front of the building, probably Ladder 4, and another at the intersection, its ladder positioned to reach the roof further back on the side of the structure. Donald could see lights moving on the roof, indicating jakes were attempting overhead ventilation. Desmond gathered the crew together and jogged down the street until he spotted the deputy at the front of the school talking animatedly into his radio remote mike. When he spotted the Tower officer he said, "Joe, get a ground ladder up to the mansard in the rear and open it up. We got enough lines but need more ventilation." The crew removed a three section fifty from one of the trucks whose crews were already committed and made their way through a snow-clogged alley that adjoined the small school yard. At the rear, the footing was poor but the five jakes managed to wrestle the heavy aluminum extension upright. Donald grasped the halyard rope and pulled it rapidly, hand over hand as Desmond counted the number of clicks made by the ladder pawls until he felt it was high enough. As usual, he was right and they lowered the tip towards the building until it came to rest just below the roof, nudging the gutter and resting against the slates in the old style construction. Heavy smoke was pouring out the windows, on the lower floors, but they could see it curling ominously above, obscuring the ladder they had just erected.

They could also hear hose lines pounding against the walls and ceilings on the first floor and knew that the inside attack was progressing, but it was essential to get an opening overhead to allow deeper penetration. Donald sprang up the ladder, his axe secured through his waist belt. When he neared the top, he put his left leg through one rung, bent his knee and hooked his booted foot over the top of a lower cross member. Once he felt he was properly locked in, he took his axe and, using the pointed peen of the head, pounded the slate surfaces, cracking them easily and shouting to the members below to protect themselves from the falling debris. He was also able to break through the wooden roof boards underneath with a half dozen sharp blows. When a hole opened, smoke under high pressure enveloped him, but he was able to rear back and keep chopping. He managed to make a significant vent, about two feet square, and as he was completing the task, Desmond ordered him to descend so Howie Rosen could take his place. Shortly after, Steve Tucker appeared with a K-12 saw and within a short period of time, the Tower crew managed to create a large opening, contributing effectively to the other openings on the roof. The results of all of these efforts enabled not only the initial hose lines to advance, but others, from multiple alarm engine companies to gain access to the second floor, where ladder and Rescue Company jakes were able to open floors and walls in the exposed classrooms and cut off further extension.

Desmond had the crew retrieve some long rakes from the truck and they were soon able to join the operating force on the inside, pulling ceilings in the administrative offices, which had been effectively destroyed by the intensity of the fire. Eventually, the tall, black, acting chief of the district, tapped Desmond on the shoulder and told him to make up and report out to the deputy. Desmond smiled at his friend, who had been stationed with the lieutenant several years before. "First multiple as a chief, huh, Herb?"

"Yeah, Joe." The chief's white teeth flashed through the dark skin. "Glad it's over. What a sweat job. I figured I'd really fuck up and they'd put me in the back of the bus." They both laughed out loud and Desmond said, "You did great. Now all those Catholics can come back to school again. You Baptists are all heart. Nice goin'."

Out front Deputy Driscoll and the fire commissioner were conversing as Desmond reported for instructions. They both looked pretty content. Why not, thought the junior officer. So many school fires turned out to be impossible tasks, with total destruction the end result, that a good stop like this one obviously was a relief.

The commissioner, who seemed to know just about all of the sixteen hundred jakes under his command, said, "Nice job, Joe. I appreciate your efforts. You guys always make me look smarter than I really am."

Desmond smiled: "I don't know about that, boss, but we'll keep at it."

As he turned to go, he was startled when the commissioner said, "Glad to see you up there on the captains' list. Good luck. Hope it won't be long."

Desmond was pretty excited as he followed his crew—the fifty foot ladder now returned to its company—down the slush filled street towards the truck. Boy, he doesn't miss much, does he?

On the way back to quarters, they waited patiently outside the donut shop while Gap Keefe was inside, doing his poor, bedraggled, frozen fire fighter routine, Donald mentioned to Lieutenant Desmond how he had been thinking about the schools when the alarm came in. Desmond said, "Yeah. It's a shame, the way things have turned out. There's Herb Sheffield, gonna be a chief pretty soon. Forced busing was supposed to help minorities get a better education. He loves the city, but now he's out in Braintree, outta the neighborhood he loved and grew up in, just so his kids can get a good education. Kinda ironic, isn't it?" He explained that his friend had come on the job about twenty years earlier and really loved it. He was constantly trying to motivate other black fire fighters to study and advance and his own successes were an excellent example of what everyone could do if they worked at it. "I have no doubt old Herb may be running this whole outfit some day. And if he is, he'll do great."

Donald was off duty on Christmas Eve, but scheduled for the day tour the next morning. He took his wife and daughter to Midnight Mass at St. Brigid's Church. Although the church was only eight blocks from their home, it was bitter cold and another major snowfall had added a foot more to the piles and mounds still laying around from the recent storms. As they were bundling up to leave their house, the weatherman announced that even though winter had officially started only three days earlier, the city had already accumulated fifty-five inches for the season. The Holden family wasted no time in trudging as rapidly as possible up the middle of the streets, which were free of vehicular traffic but crowded with other parishioners following with the neighborhood tradition.

As soon as they stomped their booted feet and passed through the main entrance, they were greeted with a blast of warm air and the sounds of the choir singing carols to the music of the deep-throated organ. They squeezed into a half occupied pew and knelt in prayer, and Donald felt a sense of peace that continued throughout the service. He couldn't concentrate on the pastor's homily because he was reviewing everything that had transpired since this time last year and the train of thought kept him occupied until it was time to receive Holy Communion. He first focused on the collapse, and while he was grateful for his survival, he reflected deeply on the death of the young boy and said a silent prayer for him and his surviving family. He also thought about many of the other fires he had been to, smiled as he remembered the trip out west and of course, the lieutenant's exam and all the effort that preceded it as well as his satisfaction with his performance during the test. Finally, he glanced at Gena and Nancy and said a special prayer of thanks for his good fortune in being with both of them, and how lucky he was to have them. If fate had dealt a different hand, he'd have never made it out of that fire and maybe he'd be looking down from up above instead of up from here. Maybe someone really is watching over me, he thought.

Christmas morning, he arrived at work at 0700. He had agreed to relieve Roscoe Kearns, the driver, early. Roscoe was waiting outside, a wide smile splitting his black face. He had three little kids and the youngest one was just learning about Santa. "Thanks, Donald, I'll make home easy before they get up. Merry Christmas. Besides, I'll be glad to get away from that asshole, Stoler."

Donald nodded his head in understanding: "He acting up again?"

"Again?" replied Kearns incredulously as he slid into his car which had been warming up on the front apron. "You mean *still*. That glom never stops. Have a quiet day, and Merry Christmas again, Donald!" He slammed the door and sped off towards the entrance to the central artery. As he stepped into the building, Donald understood immediately what his partner meant. Stoler's voice was croaking "Silent Night" over the public address system. While he was tone deaf anyway, he seemed to make an even greater effort to sing as badly and as noisily as possible. The house phone was buzzing loudly, no doubt from someone upstairs trying to get him to shut up, but he ignored it. He switched to a medley of "Rudolph the Red-Nosed Reindeer", "Jingle Bells" and "Santa Claus is Coming to Town" as Donald, his hands over his ears, sprinted up the stairway and into the locker room. Ramon Romero, Chris Redden and Kimo Griffiths were seated in front of their lockers, all looking despondent. "Hi folks, Merry Christmas," he greeted them.

"That shithead is drivin' us nuts," said Redden. "You'd think the officers would shut him up, but the deputy and the captain think he's funny."

Triple R said in his accented English, "We had nine runs, including six alarms in Brighton. We got back about an hour ago and since this prick has the last watch, he's gonna make sure none of us get back in the sack. I know what I'd like to give him for Christmas."

Kimo Griffiths said, "What? If it works, I'll help pay for it."

"Two free visits to that Doctor Kavorkian. I bet even that expert couldn't kill him on the first try."

When the song ended, the irrepressible fat man announced, "Good morning, officers, good morning, fire fighters. It is a gorgeous day. The temperature is six degrees. I'm so thrilled to be associated with such a magnificent group of personnel, especially my favorites, Deputy Chief Farley and Fire Captain Murray. Merry Christmas to you all. Have a nice day."

After Donald changed his clothes, he went into the kitchen where the chief and the captain were just finishing their coffee. "Merry Christmas, Deputy. Merry Christmas, Captain," Donald said as he walked into the room.

Captain Murray was smiling. "Thanks, Donald, same to you and the family. We got three days off, away from Pavarotti downstairs. Be nice if he got permanent laryngitis, wouldn't it?" While both of these officers ran a pretty tight ship, they tolerated Stoler and his nonsense. Donald had once asked his own lieutenant why the captain was so benign when it came to handling this particular jake. Desmond laughed and replied, "Well, he keeps that character around for laughs." He explained that while the guy was sometimes overbearing, he was good for morale. Nobody would argue that he wasn't a good jake. At fires, he never stopped working—or talking either. He drove the other fire companies at the scene nuts, insulting them constantly and bragging about his own unit.

"Every once in a while Murray gets irritated. When he does, he gives Stoler the details out to other companies for a couple of weeks and that quiets him down for a spell. But, he gets over it soon and is right back yapping again. When you become an officer, Donald, just keep in mind, it takes all kinds to make a good company. Stoler and guys like him are all a piece of the pie."

The incident from which the companies had returned had involved two, three story brick and wood condominiums in the Brighton district. The fire had originated in the basement of one of them and extended rapidly to the third floor, where it extended swiftly into the adjoining structure. About fifteen residents had been rescued over ground ladders by the ladder companies first at the scene. The deputy explained they had been very fortunate to get them all, particularly with the snow and ice filling the alleys almost waist high. "Yeah, everyone lived but its not gonna be much of a Christmas for about forty people."

Donald spent most of the morning cleaning all the gear used at the multiple alarm as well as the apparatus itself; so by the time he finished, most of the jakes were in the recreation room watching the noontime news which had dramatic videos of the night's activities, not only in Brighton but at an earlier extra alarm response to Hyde Park. No wonder the troops were pissed off at Stoler, thought Donald, they were exhausted—which probably made him even happier to irritate them. He looked across the room to where Gap Keefe and Dot-head were playing their own favorite game of nagging at Brows Brennan just for practice. They were explaining to him what a great job his company, Engine 10, had done the night before. They attributed the successes to the crew working on the tour. "Yeah," Keefe said, "If that was ever today, they'd probably have lost the whole block."

Brows frowned. "Hey, what the fuck you talkin' about?"

Dot-head jumped right in: "Well, Hilbert, my friend," he said, using Brennan's despised given name, "we hate to bring it up, but those jakes working last night are just a bit more intelligent than this crew you're stuck with."

Donald headed for the kitchen and could hear Brows' voice explode as the argument deteriorated into a shouting match. He could hear Brennan's shrill scream, "And don't call me Hilbert, you fuckin' wart-head!" as he walked rapidly down the corridor. Hm, Donald thought, Desmond is right. I should start adding a section about these clowns I work with to my notes on fires.

Fortunately, the day tour was mercifully quiet and by the time he was relieved, he was anxious to get home. Nancy had sworn she wouldn't open her gifts until he arrived and she had called twice during the day to find out when he was coming. It proved to be a delightful evening. From the time he stepped in the door and smelled the roasting turkey until he crawled into bed at midnight, it just seemed to be a continuation of the joy he had felt in church during Midnight Mass. Oh, he and Gena had reduced their own gifts to essential clothing and other necessities, but that was so they could finance the computer their daughter hadn't been expecting. She'd frequently mentioned how competent she was becoming with such equipment in school, but having her own unit was more than she had dreamed about. As he was dozing off he reflected about how jakes adjusted their home lives to accommodate the demands of the job. Now that he'd been on for nearly four years, it just seemed natural that he would be away from home on many occasions when the rest of the population would be at home. But, he had to agree, it wasn't that bad. Tomorrow, when all those folks started hitting the expressways to begin their work week, he'd be taking up the slack for a seventy-two hour stretch. Maybe start fooling around with that IBM. If he didn't, Gena, who used one constantly at her own job, and Nancy would be talking a language he'd never be able to understand. Besides, he had to keep his mind occupied now that there was no more studying to do. Those marks should be coming along in just a few more weeks. Keep your fingers crossed.

    The last fire of the year involved three large offices on the fourth floor of a five story first class office building in the financial district on Broad Street, just a couple of blocks from the fire house. Due to a delayed notification in the unsprinklered structure, flames and dense smoke were rolling out of several windows on the fire floor. Donald was detailed to Engine 10 for the night tour of duty. As they stopped to connect to a high pressure hydrant, Donald noticed how quiet it seemed, other than the noise of the apparatus and the voices of the jakes. The area was deserted and the old fashioned yellowish street lights created a surrealistic image with shadows creeping across the piles of snow, which apparently were going to remain for the entire winter. The half million people enjoying the annual First Night celebration didn't tend to cruise down to this part of downtown. He looped a fold of the two and a half inch line of hose over his shoulder and moved rapidly towards the front stairs, trying to keep up with Brows who advanced up the wide stairway, the attached nozzle hanging over his shoulder. Donald was followed by Lieutenant Grimes who shouted, "Brows, take your time. There's plenty of fire up there. It won't get away from you." Brennan had a reputation for wanting to beat everyone anyway and since the insult from Gap and Doherty the other day, Donald knew the most difficult job they would face at this fire was trying to hold him back. He could hear the powerful jake growling, "C'mon, c'mon, Holden, light up on that line," as they circled upward. At the third floor level, the smoke, which had been fairly light, became much thicker. The pressure of the fire was moving the unburned gases in all directions, filling the corridors and stairway. Since the roof hadn't been opened yet, the rising heat and smoke were bouncing off the still intact skylights and being forced downward, enveloping the fire fighters. Grimes told them to don their mask facepieces and this enabled them to continue up to a point just below the landing on the fourth floor. The officer ordered them to pull up additional hose, enough slack to allow them to reach the involved area, and he ordered the water to be started, transmitting into his remote mike by laying it against the plastic visor of his facepiece. Gap Keefe wriggled up beside Donald. He was equipped with a Halligan bar as well as a hydraulic door opener. He lay beside Brows, waiting patiently for the sound of the air escaping from the nozzle as the high pressure water pushed it out. When Brows mumbled it was coming, Grimes shouted, "OK, Gap, open it and drop down." The thick, wooden door opened outward and Gap inserted the adz of the rigid steel bar between the edge and the frame. He was going to attempt to pop it towards him, but if that failed, he would then use the more sophisticated Rabbit tool, which exerted thousands of pounds of energy. It proved to be unnecessary as the door sprung outward with Gap jumping back into the stairway as intense heat burst towards them. Brows was ready and opened the nozzle slowly until the solid, straight stream drove upward through the inch and an eighth opening. With Donald leaning firmly against his legs, the aggressive fire fighter started worming his way into the large area. The water striking the ceiling broke up into a heavy spray, pushing back the flames and also dropping on the engine company members, drenching them thoroughly. At first the water was hot, but as Brows kept swinging the pipe back and forth as he moved ahead, the temperature of the droplets was reduced. Grimes, just behind Donald, kept up a steady chatter, his muffled voice croaking, "Keep it goin', Brows. Doin' great. Back and forth, back and forth. You're eatin' it up, baby. Knockin' the shit outta it." It's true, Donald thought.

While the heat reflecting off the solidly constructed fire proof walls was significant, the powerful hose line delivering almost three hundred gallons of water per minute was having a tremendous effect as it groped towards the seat of the fire. They could hear glass breaking everywhere as the jakes from the Tower who had reached the roof vented the skylights and created other openings above the fire. Meanwhile, the truckies from Ladder 24 were venting the fire floor and the top floor as well from the outside, gaining access from their extended hundred-ten foot aerial.

Donald asked Brows a couple of times if he wanted a relief on the nozzle but all he got was a gruff grunt in reply. He looked at the lieutenant and could see Grimes grinning inside his facepiece. "He's still pisssed at those guys from Christmas Day, Donald. Leave him alone and just keep leaning on him." Actually, within a few minutes, jakes from Engine 4 advanced into the floor with another big line, but their chances of getting by Brennan were nil. They concentrated on hitting all the areas he had driven through so that no re-ignition could occur, swinging their line forcefully around the area, even cleaning out glass from those windows still intact with the force of the water.

When Brows finally pushed the handle of the nozzle systematically forward, cutting off the flow, it was obvious the fire was knocked down. The area was quite large, involving the administrative offices of three of the executives. With a less aggressive attack, the fire would have probably extended outward and upward. If it had overlapped out the windows, it might even have gained entrance to the floor above and caused a huge loss. But it never got the chance once Brows got his line filled. He finally relinquished the nozzle when an inch and three quarter attachment was made to increase the maneuverability of the line and reduce the flow for overhauling purposes. As he sat contentedly on the floor, his back against the wall and his booted legs extended in front of him comfortably, Gap and Dot-head were busily stripping panels from the dropped ceiling searching for any further extension. When they neared Engine Ten's location, Doherty was shaking his head as he hooked his rake onto the framework overhead. "Boy, what a fuck-up. Engine Four is really pissed. Eddie Sasso told me they'd knocked this down in about two seconds but they couldn't get by that drag ass outfit, Engine Ten. Where's Hilbert?" When they heard the growl behind them, the two antagonistic jakes made a less than heroic dash for the stairway as Brows sprang to his feet. Desmond, who hadn't been aware of the original banter a few days earlier, appeared startled and shouted, "Hey, where're you nitwits goin?'" But, Grimes, chuckling uncontrollably, said, "Don't worry, Joe. It's O.K. They'll just get what they deserve. By, the way, Happy New Year." They had missed the Times Square festivities by this response. 1996 was getting a good start.

The next day they were working, Desmond called a meeting of the students in the study room. It was a few weeks after they had taken the test and it was still well over a month before the marks were due to be mailed so they were a bit puzzled about the reason for the group's assembly. Desmond said, "Well, I think each of you showed a lot of determination throughout the past year. No matter how you finish in the test, it's obvious you're interested in the job and also that you are determined to learn as much as you can to improve your knowledge and understanding about how to perform your duties. Actually, as far as fire fighting is concerned, you are gaining constant knowledge because in this town, we do as much work as anyone anywhere. And, as you already know, fires and how they are handled don't change very dramatically. There hasn't been any miracle equipment developed nor are there any eggheads who can snap their fingers and make the flames disappear. It still requires practical experience—the more the better—common sense and a lot of bull work and I don't see much change in the near future. I think they'd have to tear down this whole city and start all over to reduce the fire problem that's existed since the last century. But, that doesn't mean other aspects of our job aren't changing pretty dramatically. Just look at the number of Haz-Mat responses we're getting. When I came on we just washed everything down the sewers and forgot about it. Sometimes I think that still isn't too bad an idea, but with the environmentalists in complete control, that ain't gonna happen.

"The other phase of our business that has changed so much is our performance at medical emergencies. And this, I must say, is a very positive change. I can't tell you how many people we watched die because we were not knowledgeable enough and didn't have the right equipment less than two decades ago. As you know, now every engine company is trained and equipped with defibrillators and much improved resuscitation equipment. There have been some dramatic life saving incidents recently, and our record will continue to improve."

The lieutenant went on to discuss the city's history in this type of service. The Health and Hospitals department was independent of the fire department and had qualified personnel, many of them paramedics, who operated several full time ambulances, supplemented by private medical services, covering a couple of hundred thousand annual responses. When a call for such assistance was initiated, the nearest fire company and an ambulance were dispatched to the scene. Since the fire department has thirty three engine companies strategically dispersed throughout the city, one of them was usually first at the scene and would initiate immediate treatment until the Health and Hospital personnel arrived and assumed control, thus relieving the fire company and making it available for fire duty.

"This has worked out OK," Desmond continued, "but there is a growing trend around the country to merge these two groups. As a matter of fact, in many communities the fire department has been performing this service for many years. And it makes sense. I am quite certain it will be the case here in Boston in the next decade. Oh, all kinds of problems have to be resolved first, including the fact that jakes and H & H EMTs have never gotten along very well. But an objective observer would easily recognize how much more practical the merge would be."

He started laughing: "Boy, am I getting long-winded. That wasn't my intention. But, since all of you have gotten used to setting aside time to study, I want you to consider signing up for EMT training. It's a four month course that requires you to take two classes a week." He spotted Rick grabbing his head and rocking from side to side. "Yeah, I know it Foster. You think I'm just breaking your balls. Not really. But if I'm right and the two departments are joined together, and if you guys get promoted, which I think you will in time, you'll be better equipped to do the job and teach your own people." The group asked several questions; most of them were hesitant to make a firm commitment. Desmond concluded the session by saying, "Look. I'm not looking for an answer today. It's up to you individually. Just give it some thought and any of you that are interested, let me know and I'll get you signed up."

Later, in the mess hall, when they were discussing the program, they were overheard by Dot-head, Gap and Jeff Stoler, who had relieved his partner early for the night tour. It didn't take long for the three of them to join the conversation. "Excuse me, Foster," said Jeff, "will you be able to cure stuff like herpes? I've had this little itch, nuthin' serious, you understand, since I served my country in the Gulf."

Rick grinned: "How'd you contact that, Ace? There were no ladies available over there. You sure you're heterosexual?" Stoler looked pained and outraged. "Sand fleas, you pervert. I was in the army, not the navy. No one ever knew what you swabbies were doin' on those floating palaces. Those bunks looked too close together to guarantee abstinence."

"Now that I think of it," said Rick, "you guys were living with camels and sheep. Some of them must have looked more attractive than your comrades in arms, male and female." The students and nonstudents were soon screaming back and forth at each other. Donald shook his head. At least this new subject gave them something different to fight about. The Super Bowl was coming up and the Patriots had finished with only six wins along with ten losses, so the jakes didn't care who won that contest. The Bruins and Celtics were playing lousy, and spring training for the Red Sox was still a long way off, so why not dissect the department, the EMT program and anything else to keep the constant arguments going?

During the next day tour they worked, Donald, Rick, Captain Hardy and Vinnie Sterling were doing their exercises in the gym shortly after lunch time. Between his long absence following his injuries and then the time devoted to studying as the exam approached, Donald had been unable to use the treadmills, stairmasters, stationary bikes and lifting paraphernalia in the fully equipped exercise room.

Not only did it feel good to work out with the other gym-rats, as Dot-head described the jakes who conscientiously performed their routines, but he was also pleased that he could complete his routine without undue aches and pains in his ribs and his arm. He had broken a sweat and was jogging comfortably on the tread when he heard Engine 7 and Ladder 17 being dispatched to a report of an outside fire in Chinatown. While this was a routine response that occurred several times daily, within a couple of minutes, Box 1433 was transmitted over the radio and tapper system. The jakes in the gym had brought their turnout gear with them and Donald made a swipe across his sweat soaked face with a towel, jumped into his hitch, pulling the suspenders over his shoulders as he moved rapidly to the sliding pole and followed Captain Hardy, wrapping his arms and legs around the shiny, brass circular stanchion and dropping swiftly towards the main floor. He squeezed his legs tightly to control the drop so he landed softly on the rubber safety pad at the bottom and trotted over to the Tower, donning his fire hat and coat as he stepped into the jump seat. Just in the few seconds it took to cross the main floor to the apparatus, the cold wind chilled him. The temperature was in the lower teens with a wind chill reported well below zero.

The officer on Engine 7 reported that the outside fire to which they had been dispatched was actually an inside fire located in a Chinese restaurant on Tyler Street. As the Tower proceeded along the surface artery, which passed over the South Station Tunnel, clouds of black smoke were pushing upward and were clearly visible above rooftops of the commercial buildings which lined the route. They passed under the Chinese archway, entering onto Beach Street in an effort to position the truck for possible use at the fire. However, it became immediately obvious that they wouldn't be able to get in position without extensive maneuvering because of a line of cars on the narrow thoroughfare that were at a standstill because of the fire. Lieutenant Desmond ordered Steve Tucker and a detailed jake from another company to stay with the unit and keep trying to move up to Tyler Street. The street at the front of the fire building was already partially occupied by a ladder truck. The apparatus was not directly opposite the building because extremely heavy smoke was enveloping all floors of the three and a half story brick and wood structure. The street is so narrow, that if the fire blows outward horizontally, the truck and its crew could be in a dangerous position. So, they wisely stopped at the adjoining structure, set their jacks and rotated the aerial at an angle in order to attempt overhead ventilation. Desmond, Howie Rosen, Gap

Keefe and Donald extracted a thirty-five foot ladder from the bed of the Tower and strode briskly along the street, passing by a pumper whose crew had already stretched a big line and was advancing toward the front of the building. Deputy Franklin was in command position in the street and shouted, "Tower! Start cleaning it out. High as you can reach." The jakes understood he was looking for quick overhead ventilation. Desmond didn't even have to speak. Gap steered the butt of the ladder to the ground, placed both of his feet on the bottom rung and reached forward, grasping a higher cross member with both hands. As the others picked up the opposite end and pushed it upright, Gap's weight anchored the base solidly to the ground and the ladder reached perpendicular. Donald grasped the rope halyard while the others rotated the ladder to face the building. He then pulled hand over hand, listening to the pawls clicking on the rungs. He didn't look up because pieces of glass were striking the top of his helmet. He knew Desmond, who had stepped back to the middle of the street would tell him when his exertions brought the ladder to its appropriate height. Sure enough, the lieutenant shouted, "Lock it there." Donald pulled until he heard one more click and then eased off on the halyard until it slackened, listening for the sound of the hooks dropping into position, confirming the extension was now safely secured in place. Donald moved to the front of the ladder, which allowed him to face the fire building and, on the lieutenant's orders, he and Howie lowered the top of the ladder towards a third floor window, which was barely visible through the dirty brown smoke. The pressure developed by the burning products of combustion was driving the unburned gases out of every opening and even through the ancient brickwork. As the tip of the ladder crashed through the upper pane of glass, the smoke poured outward even more forcefully and they continued lifting and dropping the ladder, splintering the wooden sashes and smashing through the lower pane as well, creating a significant opening and releasing some of the pressure. The jakes then rapidly rolled the ladder over to the next window and then the next, performing the same operation. While this work was transpiring, other ladder companies were performing similar activities on the other floors. The aerial of the first due truck was carefully lowered onto the ridge pole of the roof to attempt venting at that point. But, the fire was too intense and started appearing through the heavy smoke on each floor. The engine company that had commenced operating at the front entrance was forced to retreat and, soon, it became clear that outside streams would be necessary until the fire could be knocked down. Desmond had the members assist in dragging lines down the street so engine companies could operate hand lines, portable and deck guns. Because of the plentiful supply of high pressure fire hydrants in the downtown area, the building and its exposures were soon surrounded with effective fire streams. Naturally, the intense cold created hazardous footing and covered the buildings, apparatus, hose, and, of course, the jakes themselves with ice. The rapid attack was successful in killing much of the visible fire and soon the deputy ordered most of the outside lines shut down.

In the meantime, Steve Tucker had managed to maneuver the Tower to a position where it could be elevated and extended to a position so it could be effectively utilized for operations on the upper floor. He had patiently cajoled pump operators who were not engaged in providing water supplies from their units because of the use of the high pressure outlets to move their vehicles and let the aerial truck work its way down the street so it could be used efficiently. Desmond was pleased to see where it was positioned and said to the others, "That Steve is a real con artist. If there's anyway to get that piece anywhere, just give him time. He could talk a dog off a meat wagon."

The deputy and the chief of District Four, along with their individual aides and Captain Hardy from the Rescue Company were emerging from the fire building, and the bosses smiled when they saw the favorable location of the Tower. Both of these conscientious leaders were just completing an interior inspection prior to allowing engine companies to change to an interior attack. Desmond said to Donald, "These guys are good. They really understand this business. Whenever we use outside streams, any experienced boss knows that those heavy streams really exert tremendous force on the structural members of the building. They've just gone through the floors and if they saw anything they don't like, we won't even get inside." Apparently the chiefs were satisfied that the building was still sound and no vital supports had been severely damaged. Eventually hand lines were advanced, including one from the Tower bucket into the attic. The fire had started in the kitchen of the restaurant and extended via the grease flue to all floors, the attic and the roof. Apparently, the required chemical protection in the vent above the commercial stove had malfunctioned, allowing the fire to extend rapidly. Before they were dismissed, Desmond took them on a tour of the kitchen and explained how most restaurant stoves were vented promptly through flues that went horizontally by the most direct route outside the structure and then extended vertically to a point above the roof line, terminating with a hooded and vented metal cover. "That type of installation is designed so that a fire such as this one, if the extinguishing system malfunctioned, while it would look spectacular, wouldn't damage the interior of the building. It's much easier when they comply with the law, but I suppose if everyone did what they're supposed to, we'd be outta business."

Donald made copious notes about the incident. He was particularly impressed with the thoroughness of both Deputy Franklin and Chief Macklin in trying to determine the safety of the building. They had actually endangered themselves in an effort to protect the membership. Desmond had explained they took Captain Hardy because he probably had more knowledge of building construction than anyone else at the scene. He was constantly studying books on structural engineering and had taken several courses on the subject over the years. "You see," Desmond had concluded, "Stan Hardy will never be a chief because he doesn't want to be, but he knows as much about this business as anyone." He laughed gleefully as he finished: "And Franklin, Macklin and the rest of the bosses know it and aren't too proud to ask his advice. That's another reason Franklin came here when Billy Simpson left. He'll probably stay here 'til he retires, too. Just like our old boss did." During the next two weeks there were several serious incidents in the city when Donald's group was on duty. The responses throughout the period were severely complicated by the tremendous snowfalls and extremely low temperatures. A fire in a four story brick apartment house in the Hyde Park district at 0954 hours one morning probably would have been confined to the room of origin if the first alarm companies could have arrived as promptly as usual. However, the fourteen inches of snow that had fallen during the night had made the approaches to the location very difficult. Consequently, the usual three or four minute response time was doubled, and the district chief immediately ordered a second alarm when he arrived. The apparatus couldn't get close to the building because of the stalled cars, buried in snow, so long stretches of hose became essential.

By the time the Tower crew arrived from downtown, the fire had extended into two other apartments. The crew was directed to help drag big lines from the pumpers and the increased personnel at the scene was the most essential factor in helping the engine companies get their lines in position and ultimately gain control of the fire.

The following night tour was much worse. The temperature was even lower than the previous day, and the city was being battered by a severe northeast snowstorm with a wind averaging thirty miles per hour. A fire in the Mattapan district at 2028 hours involved both sides of a duplex three story occupied dwelling with extension to all floors and the roof. The incident required three alarms because of the delayed arrival and rapid extension. The Tower crew first raised ground ladders in deep snow at the rear of the building, then advanced a big line via one of them onto a second floor porch and then into a rear hallway, moving it through the kitchen and into a bedroom where the wide brown stains in the ceiling made it clear the fire was moving rapidly towards them through the concealed overhead space. Gap and Donald huddled on the floor waiting for the water Desmond had requested in the line they were holding. Due to very heavy radio traffic, the message didn't get through at first, and before the water came, a large section of the plaster dropped. The fire blew downward towards them but the lieutenant, who had been anticipating such extension, was standing upright beside them, protected by the wall to the right of the door opening. He had been leaning forward, his gloved left hand on the knob and as soon as he heard the thunder of the dropping laths and plaster, he grabbed the knob and pulled the door as much as he could, almost closing off the opening. The wait seemed interminable but, finally, the sound of air rushing through the opened pipe reassured them that the high pressure water was on its way. When it came, they pushed back the wooden door and eagerly drove the solid stream into the overhead, methodically sweeping the nozzle back and forth. As the fire darkened, the visibility was reduced to zero. But, Gap and Donald could hear Desmond's voice clearly speaking to Howie and Steve, directing them to start pulling the kitchen ceiling. It passed through Donald's consciousness as he and Gap started advancing forward that technology had improved even in his short time on the job. The officer had an experimental new facepiece on his breathing apparatus with a new speaking diaphragm that made his voice much more understandable than the muffled growling they usually had to try to interpret.

The openings the jakes made in the kitchen with their rakes revealed laths and beams that were relatively clean and so far untouched by the flames. This allowed Donald and Gap to continue their progress towards the front of the dwelling. They were able to knock down the fire in the next bedroom and then move into the front living room where they were joined by a third alarm engine company crew who were entering a window over a ground ladder that had been raised from the street. With the large number of jakes the third alarm had summoned to the scene, once the delayed lines were in position and operating, the fire—even though it involved some thirty rooms in the hundred year old structure—was rapidly knocked down. Laddermen were relieved of their rakes and axes by hosemen as their biceps cramped from pulling, pulling, pulling overhead in the bitter cold.

When the company was dismissed by the commissioner, himself encased in ice from the wind driven snow and water spray, the Tower crew joined the long line of jakes queued for hot coffee at the canteens operated by the Red Cross, Salvation Army and Boston Sparks Association.

Donald was shivering conspicuously, wondering if it wouldn't be better to just get on the apparatus and turn up the heater, when he heard a familiar voice shouting from somewhere behind him, "All right, step aside, you country jakes. We gotta get back in the city and protect the poor downtrodden folks. We can't keep comin' out here savin' your asses." It had to be Cueball Justice. Who else would have the gall to challenge anyone on such a night? Actually, Donald was pleased to hear his old drill school buddy back in his outrageous form. The little redhead had been badly shaken by the Newton Street collapse, especially when he realized his friend Holden was buried in the debris and probably dead. Donald was hoping the wisecracking shrimp didn't spot him, but just as he reached up to the counter to grab the steaming cardboard coffee container, he cringed as he heard, "Why even Hero Holden hadda come out here. He coulda been pickin' tourists outta hotel windows in that bucket downtown. But, naw, he's out here lookin' at cows and sheep and bailing you stiffs out." Donald slunk away, up the street towards the Tower. He knew how to quiet Justice down. Donald was amazed that the drill school moniker "Cueball" hadn't become more widespread, knowing how jakes love to tell stories and antagonize each other; but, after almost four years the members of Engine 22 called him either Pete or more often, Yapper. If Donald wanted to quiet him down, he'd simply say, "Oh, by the way, Cue..." Then he'd pause. Justice would get the message and clam up immediately. But tonight Donald just kept moving away and swung up into the enclosed jump seat, grateful that the heater was functioning properly.

The next night tour involved an unusual incident that required a second alarm response, even though the fire damage was minimal. Engine Company 33 was returning from another alarm near 2300 hours. They discovered a fire alarm street box in the Back Bay spewing flames. When they stopped, they noticed a strong odor of illuminating gas. It was caused by the rupture of an underground six inch gas main.

The officer in command ordered a box struck as it became obvious that the highly flammable gas was entering several buildings in the densely populated area. He started an evacuation procedure of the nearest occupancies. As the district chief and other fire companies arrived, they commenced entering many other buildings and discovered most of them were also contaminated with the hazardous fumes. Eventually a second alarm was ordered and the Tower unit was part of the response. Not only were numerous apartment buildings involved in the crises, student dormitories of both Simmons and Wheelock colleges also had to be emptied. Because of the intense cold, MBTA buses and several ambulances were requested to the scene to offer protection to the evacuees.

Desmond and his crew were assigned to a five story apartment house. The officer separated the members: he and Steve Tucker proceeding to the basement to kill the gas, electrical and heating systems before they created a source of ignition; the other members spread throughout the building, opening windows to provide ventilation and shutting off pilot lights in the gas stoves, whose flames were just barely glowing because of the loss of pressure but were still hot enough to cause ignition if the concentration of gas and oxygen reached the explosive range.

The gas company's emergency crews responded fairly promptly, considering the snow and weather conditions, and they managed to locate the rupture rapidly. As soon as they sealed it off, the deputy, who had kept the entire response at the scene, had the firefighters close the windows as the fumes cleared to prevent water pipes from freezing. When the second alarm companies were leaving, the boss was making arrangements to have heaters and electrical systems restored so the occupants could return. It was a very interesting, educational incident as far as Donald was concerned; he entered everything he could think of in his journal, pausing as he thought once again that the job isn't all just running lines and pulling ceilings. The potential for catastrophe was certainly a factor in that area, but the chiefs seemed to make all the right moves to protect the occupants and mitigate the dangers.

The next night was also different. The January thaw, which was totally unpredictable because some winters it came and some it didn't, showed up on the twelfth, and it included torrential rains that combined with the above freezing temperatures to result in hundreds of flooded basements, leaking roofs, downed power lines and associated problems throughout the city. Shortly after the tour began, a box was struck for an electrical transformer fire in the garage of a twenty-one story apartment house occupied by handicapped and elderly people. Water from the rains and melting snow caused the short circuit which ignited the transformer and its lubricants. Heavy smoke spread throughout the huge structure, trapping hundreds of occupants above the fire. When the district chief realized the extent of the ventilation problems, even though he knew he could confine the fire, he ordered extra alarms to be struck. Eventually a third alarm response was required to get enough personnel on the upper floors. The Tower crew was sent up one of the stairways to the fifteenth floor, joining other companies in getting to the frightened occupants. The stairway was fairly smoky, not really enough to require the jakes to don their masks but far too severe to bring down the type of folks living in the many units. Fortunately, each apartment had a small external balcony, so it wasn't too difficult to move people outside, which many of them had done on their own. There had been a fourth alarm in the building a half a dozen years earlier and they used their experiences from that incident to help them get to safety. Donald had to laugh at one tiny woman, who had to be in her eighties, seated on her patio in her winter fur coat. She was smoking a cigarette and nursing a pre-dinner cocktail. "Hi, honey," she said, "I knew you fire fighters would be right along. You're not the one that got me last time, are you? No...no, you're not. You're even better looking! Wanna drink?" He declined gracefully, explaining he had to go help other people who were much more frightened than she was. "Sure," she said, "that's 'cause they don't know you Boston fire fighters like I do. Keep in touch, sonny. See you next time."

The most serious fire of the seemingly endless month occurred on January 16th. It took place soon after Donald arrived at the station. He knew he was detailed to Rescue One for the day tour and he relieved Snot Sheehan shortly before 0730. Sheehan was a real character. Due to a permanent sinus condition, he was constantly sniffing. Snot liked Donald because he was one of the few jakes who called him by his Christian name. In spite of his constant snorting, he was a terrific jake and like many members attracted to the rescue company, was happiest when he was working on some type of machinery. He could operate any of the complicated tools carried by the unit and could easily be conned into fixing anyone's car. "Hi, Francis, my friend, you are properly relieved!" Sheehan glowed with pleasure. "Thanks, Holden. It's always good to get outta here early and away from that asshole Stoler." Unfortunately, he was overheard by the group comedian who was nearby in the patrol desk. He immediately picked up the house mike and announced, "Hero Holden is present and accounted for. Snot Sheehan is dismissed—thank God." Sheehan started to growl but he was interrupted by the tone signal from Fire Alarm. "Attention, Engine Ten and Tower Company. Respond to a building fire, 48-50 Congress Street. Striking Box 1282, Water and Congress Streets. Fire Alarm at 0734 hours." Donald raced for his gear locker because he understood that the striking of a box following the still alarm meant Rescue One and the deputy would also respond.

When he entered the back of the rescue company van, Vinnie Sterling grabbed his arm as he was about to don his breathing apparatus back pack. "Use the one hour mask, pal. High rise." Donald nodded; he'd forgotten that rescue companies were required to use the sixty minute cylinders whenever they responded to any type of fire in a high-rise building. Most of the thousands of annual responses to these larger structures were relatively minor incidents, usually malfunctions of alarm systems, so the theory of the Standard Operating Procedures, was that the first alarm companies could utilize the regular thirty minute unit, which was adequate and effective for most building fires. However, just in case there was a serious structural fire, the rescue companies donned the larger and heavier unit as a precautionary and protective measure for the rest of the initial operating force. If the incident became a second or greater alarm, all responding extra units used the one hour masks.

The truck roared up Pearl Street, which extended diagonally from Purchase Street across High and Franklin Streets, terminating at Milk Street near Congress. The fire building was on the right hand side of Congress, just beyond the intersection. While en route, messages were broadcast by Fire Alarm reporting a serious fire on the fifth floor towards the rear of the block-deep, ten story structure, with several occupants cut off above the fire floor.

When they were alighting from the vehicle, District Chief Kinsella shouted to Captain Hardy, "Use the stairs, Exchange Place, Stan. We got a water problem and you have to get up above. Lot of people on the top floors." The five member crew jogged past the main entrance which was clogged with jakes attempting to gain entrance and people rushing to the street. From the fifth floor upward, heavy black smoke was belching towards the sky, obscuring much of the face of the building. Donald had the impression that the Tower was turning into the alley to the right of the building and he could see Ladder 24 maneuvering into position on the main thoroughfare. He could hear alarms sounding from the mobile radios on the apparatus, realizing extra help was being summoned, but he directed his concentration to following Hardy and Sterling as they entered the wide doors on the street bordering the building on the left side.

For some strange reason, he noticed the cornerstone with its Roman numerals and as he crossed the small lobby and trudged resolutely up the wide marble stairway, he was converting the Ds, Cs, Xs, and Is into 1894. Hm, didn't know they built them this high a hundred and two years ago. The voices coming over Captain Hardy's portable radio indicated a desperate situation. Engine 10 was reporting they had connected to the standpipe on the fourth floor with their two and a half inch line and there was no water. Deputy Franklin was ordering a third and fourth alarm and reporting many occupants at windows on the upper floors. He requested additional ladder trucks to respond via Kilby Street in the rear and to be prepared to evacuate occupants over aerials. The smoke, which had been only a haze as they reached the fourth floor level, thickened considerably and the officer motioned the order to slip on their facepieces. They didn't need any urging because it became difficult to even make out each others' figures at the fifth floor landing. Hardy's voice directed them to grab onto each others waist straps to maintain contact while they ascended past the floor they knew was the location of the fire. Along with the noises of breaking glass, Donald thought he could hear voices shrieking somewhere up above and as they kept determinately rising, step by step, the sounds grew louder and more desperate. They could also feel the heat increasing as it vented up the stairway. This was pretty disquieting because they knew there was a delay in getting a line on the fire and it had to be growing in intensity as it fed on every combustible in the involved offices.

At the sixth floor level, the entrance door was locked. Hardy used his speaking diaphragm on the facepiece and told the crew to keep going up. He didn't have time to share his thoughts with them, but he reasoned that since it was still over an hour before the regular business day commenced, perhaps the floors with locked entrances had no occupants yet. At least he hoped so. The seventh floor was the same but half way up to the next elevation, a semi-conscious victim was lying prone on the stairs. Vinnie and Donald grabbed him and, with Hardy waving them on, kept going up. The eighth floor door was gaping open and they stumbled into the flat surface of the floor, tripping and almost dropping the sagging form. The smoke wasn't quite so intense in on the floor since the vertical stairway vented much of it up to higher levels. They managed to wrestle the male figure over to a window, and Dot-head Doherty wedged his Halligan bar under the lower sill of a large window, prying it upward and then muscling it open. He reached upward and pulled the upper sash half way down, allowing large volumes of smoke to escape. Walt Timmons entered the room. He was carrying a small resuscitator, which was his tool assignment on high-rise responses. He and Dot-head started working on the victim immediately. Captain Hardy was at the window, waving his light and talking through his remote mike. He was telling the officer in command that they had a victim at this location and needed an aerial raised to the floor in case the fire extended. He also reported he could hear other victims on the top two floors and was proceeding there with part of his crew. He recommend more companies be sent up for rescue purposes and was assured they were already en route. Donald and Vinnie followed him. They re-entered the stairway and moved upward, the smoke, once again, extremely dense. On the ninth floor, Donald entered first and as he moved across the floor in a crouch, bumping into desks and feeling computer terminals and monitors with his gloved hands, he thought he heard sobbing. Working his way towards the sound, he got to an area where the visibility was somewhat better. Huddled on their knees, near an opened window were two middle-aged men, dressed in business suits. Both of them were weeping openly, grasping the window sill with one hand and each others' fingers with the other. Donald pulled off his facepiece and said, "Fire department. We'll get you outta here." They turned around and were startled and seemed to be almost more frightened by the helmeted figure coming through the smoke. One of them started choking and Donald grasped his facepiece, pushed it into the victim's face and shouted, "Breathe, breathe. You're going to be OK." Vinnie Sterling did the same with the other man, and as they calmed down, he said, "Oh, God, we thought we were dead. We don't want to die in a fire. Thank you, thank you." Hardy reported this additional find, and since they seemed to be breathing all right now, he told Vinnie to remain with them. He requested another ladder to this position but was uncertain if this floor was within the maximum reach of the hundred and ten foot ladders. "Donald, you come with me. Vinnie stay with these folks. They have lines operating on the fire now and it sounds like they might have it cut off. We're going up top. We'll get the roof open if we can. If you get in trouble, try to get them up there." Donald and Hardy moved up the stairs, passed the opened door on the tenth floor and continued up a short flight. The heat was intense and there was no visibility as the ascending products of combustion gathered at the highest point. They managed to feel a solid metal door, and, thankfully, had no difficulty in swinging it open. The pressure of the escaping gases seemed to try to propel them onto the roof, but they managed to slip back down the stairs and stagger into the top floor.

By this time, Donald was gasping for a greater volume of air from his mask and, the pressure demand system managed to stay with his requirements. He was grateful for the one hour cylinder, in spite of its weight, because he was certain he would have exhausted the smaller pressure vessel by this time with his constant exertions and having shared his supply with one of the victims. Now, though, he could hear a woman's voice shouting frantically. He moved rapidly across the floor and this time found a woman, probably in her sixties, seated in a wheeled secretary's chair, leaning on the window sill and trying to inhale fresh air from the three inch opening she had created by raising the heavy sash as high as she could. He put one arm around her and pushed upward on the frame, raising it up a couple of feet. She stared at him intently and said, "Jesus Christ, sonny, where the fuck have you been? I've been hollerin' forever up here and I'm scared shitless. That asshole Mr. Tomkins was supposed to be in early for some big meeting and he never showed. Next time, he can go fuck himself or get another secretary."

Donald mumbled, "Yes ma'm. Er, I'm here now. I'll stay with you, don't worry."

"Don't worry? What're you fuckin' crazy? This place is burning down. Aren't you frightened?"

He couldn't help chuckling. "Well, I was ma'am until I found you. Now I think you'll take care of me and we'll be safe." Captain Hardy appeared beside them and he was accompanied by a short, stocky black man, dressed in grey shirt and pants. He was part of the maintenance crew. He had seen the smoke seeping out of the group of offices in suite 545. He called in the alarm and then, knowing some people were already in the building, he raced up the stairs, shouting for them to get out. But, at some point, the smoke became so intense on the stairways that he couldn't get back down and was trapped on the top floor. Now he was grasping Hardy's facepiece with both hands and inhaling fresh air thankfully. Eventually, another fire company joined them in their location. The structure, which is over two hundred feet long and seventy-five feet wide, required a seven alarm response to get enough personnel to reach all of the areas via the many stairways leading upward. About seventy-five occupants were removed, some over ladders, some in the bucket of the Tower and many more down the stairways. Some areas directly above the fire, such as where the rescue company was assigned, were extremely dangerous because of the intensity of the fire and its generation of tremendous volumes of smoke and heat. Other areas, more remote from the point of origin, were less difficult and somewhat easier to evacuate.

When Donald reached the street with his lady friend, she was whisked into an ambulance and, her face covered with an oxygen mask, was ready for transport. But, she grabbed the EMT by the arm and, pulling off the facepiece, whispered to him. He opened the door and shouted to Donald, "Hey, Rescue One. C'mere for a minute, will ya? Lady wants to talk to you."

Donald leaned in the rear entrance and she smiled demurely. "I want to thank you, young man. Your assistance was invaluable to me. And, I might add, you are a perfect gentleman. Your decorum is exceptional. I'll be certain to remember you in my daily prayers." As he backed away, shaking his head in wonderment, he looked into her smoke-blackened face and saw one blue eye wink craftily and a slight grin appeared on her pale lips.

The company had been assigned to work on the overhauling duties up on the fire floor, so Donald joined the other members in the area. The fire had extended from the group of offices up into the ceiling and traveled some distance down the hallway before being cut off. Donald was puzzled to see many fused sprinkler heads, but no water coming from the openings created when the solder melted from the heat of the fire. The pipes were now dangling and twisted as the intensity of the fire reached them.

It didn't take long to find out the problem. Apparently, the building's owner had delayed complying with the retroactive laws and eventually had the sprinklers installed, but never had the piping connected so that both the sprinklers and the standpipes had no water in them and no means of supplementing the supply from the street.

No one was aware of this failure until the fire. Engine Ten did what the SOP required, taking three rolls of big line to the fourth floor and stretching up to the fire floor before finding out there was no water supply. This delay allowed the fire to grow and hand lines had to be stretched from the street up the stairways and even over ladders. This time consuming process further endangered the occupants and fire fighters on the upper floors, but eventually, with the powerful forces brought to the scene, they were able to cut off the fire and overwhelm it. Fortunately, no one died in the fire, but it was apparent that lawsuits and court appearances would be plentiful.

Hardy was a lot like Desmond as an officer. He took his crew on a tour of the building before they left the scene. Donald was impressed with the amount of heat still in the offices and corridors in spite of all the water that had been used. Engine companies with hose lines reduced in size were still swishing the streams back and forth, cooling off the structural supports and furnishings affected by the radiated heat. Down in the street, he had them walk around the outside. Eight aerial devices were elevated on the four sides of the commercial building and Donald was pleased to see how they had managed to maneuver the compact trucks into the alley and the narrow streets.

Back in quarters, after they had changed their cylinders and cleaned all the gear, the three companies gathered in the mess hall. The din was almost unbearable. Jeff Stoler from the night crew had responded to the fire. He and Dot-head Doherty rarely worked the same shift because the officers understood that the pair made enough noise when alone. Now the place was in total turmoil. They were both arguing about who had made the most dramatic rescues and who should get any medals. Stoler bellowed, "Listen, you disfigured pimple head, you are full of shit. If you rescued anyone, it was probably someone from the basement. Probably a guy who was just takin' a nap." He puffed up his chest. "On the other hand, everything I did was captured by those ace videomen from all the channels. There I was, ninety-five feet in the air, scooping cleaning ladies to safety with both hands. I think I'm getting an award from their union."

Doherty replied, "You're nothin' but a fuckin' showboat. An outside jake. Did you have your makeup on for the cameras, you fat fuck?" He continued, "Me and my crew, includin' our witness from that bucket of shit," he nodded towards Donald, "were crawlin' up above the fire, inside, gettin' people who were dying. I personally got two guys who already made out their wills and were reciting their last confessions. Those two empty suits would've died of fright if I hadn't got them. Right, Holden?" Donald tried to slink out of the room but couldn't so he nodded reluctantly.

Stoler grimaced and complained, "Nice goin', Hero, you fuckin' traitor. Whyncha get a transfer to that ice cream truck?"

When Donald got out his notebook, he filled a couple of pages with his notes and impressions of the job. God, that heat in a high rise is really intense. And, it's so much easier to get disoriented in such a big building. You have to keep remembering how you got to where you are and how you might have to get out. And when you get above the reach of the aerials, you've eliminated one potential escape route.

But, how about the adjustment the chief in charge has to make when he realizes the extinguishing system designed to protect the building has failed. Yeah, he has to keep cool and adapt the operation to fit the existing conditions. As he closed the book and replaced it in the locker, he recalled what Deputy Simpson had told him during one of their talks at Castle Island. At the time he wasn't sure if the chief was just condescending or not when he said, "Donald, you just have to keep going to fires to learn this crazy business. And when you finally retire like I did, you realize you still didn't learn it all. Just keep going and paying attention." Now that he was absorbing these lessons from the constant fire duty, he understood Chief Simpson meant what he said. But I bet there wasn't too much he missed along the way, Donald thought with a smile.

Eight

Following the high-rise fire on Congress Street, the department went through a few weeks when it seemed as though all of the fire prevention programs were finally taking effect. There were very few serious incidents throughout the rest of January and during the beginning of February, even though the bitter cold and seemingly endless snowstorms continued unabated. Meteorologists on TV and articles in the newspapers started showing snow levels to compare with the record inches produced during the 1994-95 winter. They seemed delighted that there was a chance new heights and depths would be reached. But, as Jeff Stoler said, "Those assholes don't have to shovel hydrants or drag hose through it. Why shouldn't they be happy? The position of that freakin' jet stream they always show ya on those maps, even a two year old could make the forecasts they're bragging about. If they have to make one of those close calls, they'll fuck it up for sure. If they were in charge of the fires we go to, this town would be a pile of charred wood and ashes when they got done with it." Jeff was considered a rather harsh critic, but Donald attributed it to his itchiness when he wasn't getting enough work. He was much more pleasant when the city was in chaos and he could yell at jakes on all the other companies at whatever incident they were working.

The quiet period gave Donald time to concentrate on the EMT classes he was attending that had begun again following several weather related cancellations. Sometimes they were held at Memorial Hall in Fire Headquarters and sometimes at one of the local hospitals. The instructors varied but included paramedics from the fire department and the Health and Hospitals Department, and doctors and nurses from numerous hospitals throughout the city. Each class lasted four hours and what impressed Donald the most about the program was how much more effective first aid and life saving methods were currently when compared to his somewhat primitive education the Marines gave him during the Gulf War just five years earlier. He was amazed at the successes that were possible in keeping victims alive who most certainly would have died in the not too distant past.

The instructors concentrated heavily on CPR and the use of oxygen, spinal immobilization, splinting and various types of shock treatment for severe trauma. It became increasingly clear to see why over a hundred hours of classroom and hands on instruction were essential to prepare the students for the written and practical tests required to gain the EMT certificate. They were even required to spend several hours as observers at hospital emergency rooms; one of the evenings Donald visited an ER proved to be quite an experience. He was assigned to the Boston City Hospital on a Saturday night, and it more than lived up to its reputation as one of the busiest emergency units in the country. By the time it finally quieted down around 0300, he was weary from wheeling in stretchers of accident victims, shootings, criminal assaults, pregnancies and even a couple of jakes who received lacerations at a building fire. His own opinion of doctors and nurses following his various injuries at fires was at a pretty high level to begin with, but this night increased his admiration and respect. Particularly impressive was how calm they seemed to be even under the worst circumstances, unlike the actors in the TV dramas. He could see that—like the most experienced jakes—they divorced their own personal feelings from whatever horror they were witnessing in order to concentrate on doing their job in the most professional manner possible.

It had been almost a month since the high-rise fire when Donald reported to work on Sunday night during the second week of February. It seemed that the quiet spell had been broken, at least on the other groups. The previous three days had seen a number of working fires and multiples in various sections of the city, and Stoler, whom Donald was relieving, was upstairs, near his locker, totally nude, a towel draped over his shoulder. His face, ears, and neck were filthy, his eyes were bloodshot and he was whistling cheerfully as he headed for the shower. "Hey Hero," he shouted when he saw Donald, "the drought is over. We just went over and showed those East Boston jakes how to knock down a coupla three deckers. I don't know what they'd do without us."

Donald smiled: "Really, Jeff? I'm not sure I should relieve you. I'm a little nervous realizing you won't be around to help us tonight."

Stoler nodded. "Yeah, you're right, Holden, my friend, but even a super jake like me needs a little R and R."

"Well, O.K. But please don't overeat tonight," Donald said sincerely. "That, ahem, chest you have is sagging just a bit. I kinda thought you were a visiting Sumo wrestler when I first saw you."

Stoler inhaled deeply and marched toward the shower room, growling, "You jarheads don't even recognize muscle when you see it. Don't break our streak. Get some work tonight, will ya?"

The early part of the evening produced a cluster of incidents in the downtown area that required a variety of responses. Malfunctions of alarm systems, auto fires, two accidents on the icy Expressway and a one room fire in an apartment house in the North End. It was shortly after midnight before the radio and tapper seemed to quiet down. Donald set his night hitch and crawled into his unused bed after finishing his watch at the patrol desk at 0400 hours. Just as he started to doze off comfortably, he heard the tone system sound and the voice from the Fire Alarm operator announced, "Attention, Engine 10, Tower Company and District Four, respond to a building fire, inside, sixth floor, number 13-15 Oxford Street. We are striking Box 1433. Fire Alarm at 0434 hours."

He sat up as the lights came on and the house alarm sounded, swung his legs into his boots, stood up and pulled the trousers of his bunker gear up around his waist, looping the suspenders over his shoulders as he jogged towards the pole hole. Steve Tucker preceded him and wrapped his arms and legs around the brass pole, disappearing from view as he descended towards the main floor. Donald looked down, waited until it was clear below and then performed the same evolution, squeezing his arms and legs to cushion his landing on the mat encircling the pole on the cement floor.

Ten was out the door more quickly than the Tower, and because there was no traffic at this time of the morning, both units stayed on the surface streets rather than descend into the tunnel that traversed under the downtown arteries. As they crossed Summer Street, heavy smoke punctuated by sparks was visible in the sky over the rooftops of several buildings in the congested Chinatown section of District Four. Fire Alarm reported fire in apartment 602 on the top floor.

Lieutenant Grimes' voice came over the radio speaker: "Engine 10 to Fire Alarm." The operator answered promptly, "Go ahead, Engine 10." Grimes said, "Reporting heavy fire showing, top floor, occupants at windows. This is a working fire, orders of Lieutenant Grimes." The Fire Alarm operator responded just as the Tower was making the turn: "Lieutenant Grimes, Engine 10, reports Box 1433 is a Working Fire, Fire Alarm at 0439 hours. Operator K." On requests for extra assistance such as this, the operator recorded the name of the member giving the order and his or her identification number.

Donald was looking forward and could see the building easily by the amount of fire blowing outward from the windows as he descended to the ground. Since he was assigned as open up man on this tour, he grabbed the portable Rabbit tool, hydraulic door opener, and a Halligan bar, and ran towards the front entrance, while the rest of the crew started setting the Tower to elevate it. He saw Lieutenant Grimes disappear into the lobby and he shouted for him to wait. The high rise SOP required the first due company to capture all the elevators with the fire fighters' key and Donald didn't want to be left behind when the engine company departed for the upper floors. He could hear the voice of Lieutenant Desmond on the Tower ordering a second alarm as he crowded into the small passenger elevator with Grimes, Rick Foster and Derek Burton. The two fire fighters were holding the handle of the two-wheeled high-rise cart. It had three-fifty foot lengths of two and a half inch hose coiled into doughnut rolls with an inch and an eighth nozzle laid across the top of the pile, along with spanner wrenches, rope hose fasteners and a hose clamp.

Just as they were about to close the doors and ascend, District Chief Macklin's aide, Vic Williams, jumped into the elevator. His job in the SOP is to take control of the elevator and operate it throughout the fire. Upon the arrival of the deputy, who is part of the first alarm high-rise response, the district chief goes to a position two floors below the fire, sets up the upper command post and directs the fire attack.

When the elevator stopped at the fourth floor, the automatic system maintained the doors in a closed position until they were opened by Lieutenant Grimes pushing the door open button. This was also a safeguard and part of the high-rise law, so, if the fire fighters arrived at a floor involved in fire, the door could be either quickly closed or just not opened and a rapid descent to a safer level could be accomplished. In this case, however, just a light haze was drifting past the overhead lights, and Donald quickly headed for the stairway at the end of the corridor, leading upward. While the smoke became somewhat heavier as he climbed up the narrow stairway, it still didn't seem too bad. He pointed out the standpipe and its outlets in the corner near the outside wall to Rick at the fifth floor level and then turned upward towards the fire floor.

He could hear the clang below him and knew that Engine 10's crew was removing the cap from the two and a half inch outlet that extended from the vertical, six inch riser pipe and would then attach the female end of their high rise hose to the male outlet.

At the sixth floor, he could see smoke curling out from under the door entering into the corridor. He could also hear voices, but they seemed to be coming from the lower levels of the stairway and he knew they were speaking excitedly in what he assumed was Chinese. There was no sound from inside the hallway. He was hoping those were people who had already escaped from the fire floor and slammed the door behind them.

The first thing he did was to feel the door cautiously, removing his glove and touching the metal gingerly with his palm. Just warm, particularly on the upper part. As he reached for the doorknob, after putting the glove back on, he noticed a stream of water coming under the door. And, he thought he could hear water cascading somewhere inside.

Grimes appeared on the step just below him and Donald said, "Hey Luft, I think I can hear water running. Any sprinklers in this joint?" Grimes shook his head, saying, "I'm not sure, Donald. The line's just behind me and we're gonna fill it now. Soon as I get water, ease it open slowly and get your facepiece on."

Rick spoke from a few steps below: "Got it now, Luft. We're set." Donald could see the swollen big line humped in a loop. He knew from experience, the long length, now filled with water, was stretched along the lower stairway and woven into the corridor below, providing enough footage to traverse the stairway upward and along the corridor of the fire floor to provide an effective attack.

He twisted the knob and the unlocked door opened easily and immediately smoke gushed out and enveloped them. He dropped to his knees and crawled onto the surface of the corridor. He could immediately feel a water spray striking him and, relaxed imperceptibly. "Sprinklers, Luft. I can feel them." Grimes replied, "Yeah, great, kid, but move slowly. They may only be in the hallways."

He's probably right, Donald thought. Many apartment houses were erected with sprinklers only in the common areas, the living spaces remaining unprotected. This was particularly true where the structure didn't reach the minimum of seventy feet in height that required complete automatic protection. But, the constant flow of water under pressure continued from overhead as he moved down the passageway. He passed a few entrance doors to apartments on both sides. All of them were open and he could readily determine there was no fire in them. One of them was fully lighted and he paused to see if he could determine whether there was a sprinkler head visible inside. There wasn't.

"Luft, I can't see a sprinkler in the apartment." He kept going and suddenly he could feel a definite increase in heat near the floor, even though the water spray continued. He had traveled about fifty feet and knew he was nearing the middle of the structure, which appeared to be the location of the fire he had seen from the street. The visibility, in spite of the overhead lights, was deteriorating significantly. He came to a door that was opened just a couple of inches and could just barely see dense brownish smoke curling outward along its vertical length. He touched his gloved hand to the external surface and knew they had reached the apartment of origin. "This one, Luft," he growled through his mask. "Red hot inside."

Grimes, crawling just behind him, said, "Move up with the pipe, Rick!" to Foster who was just behind him with the charged line. "Holden, when I tell you, push the door in and move back this way. Don't go beyond the door." Donald lay almost flat and when Grimes tapped him on the shoulder, he crouched on his knees and pushed with his right hand against the door. It swung inward easily, but, in spite of the sprinkler head distributing water on to them from the ceiling of the hallway, intense heat pushed the crew down flat. Donald moved to the opposite wall as Rick opened the nozzle fully and drove the stream at an angle towards the upper wall and ceiling just inside the door, hoping to cause an effective distribution of the stream and permitting the advance of the line. Donald could no longer see a thing but he crept behind Derek Burton and grasped the fully charged hose. In just a couple of minutes, he could hear Grimes mumbling, "More line, more line, we're starting to make it." Donald pulled on the line and could feel it going forward. He followed along on his knees but leaning against the form of Burton which was wriggling into the apartment.

Once inside, Donald knew they were making progress as he could hear the pounding of the stream striking the overhead, but already several feet deeper than he was. He moved past what seemed to be a smouldering couch and living room chair. It was quite dark, because the lights were out, but exterior lights from the street allowed some visibility.

By now, another line was entering the apartment from the corridor and he felt confident they'd gain control rapidly. Ten's line disappeared into a bedroom to the left and Donald was able to make it over to the windows facing the street, which were in the kitchen. The glass had disappeared from one opening but he was able to clear out the cracked but still intact sections of two others, allowing more of the heat and smoke to dissipate. From there, he moved into another bedroom and vented it by pulling down the upper sash and raising the lower one so smoke could escape through the top and bottom openings.

By the time he moved back into the main living area, the room was overcrowded with jakes. Some were pulling open cushions from the furnishings, others were checking cabinets, drawers, closets and other concealed spaces for extension. Chief Macklin was in the corridor and was ordering that the sectional valve of the sprinklers be closed. The fire was knocked down.

Before they were dismissed, Desmond, who had been directing the overhauling process, gathered his crew and pointed out what was pretty obvious to them all. "Without those sprinklers in the hallways, it would have been a bitch trying to make it this far. We'd have probably needed at least one big line from each stairway inside and maybe even one over a stick to knock it down." They all nodded in understanding. "But remember—if the apartment had a couple of sprinkler heads in it, this would have been a piece of cake." He went on to explain that many builders intentionally kept the height of their structures under seventy feet. They knew that with the shorter floors of apartment houses, they could easily squeeze in six floors of apartments and be exempt from the protection required in higher buildings. It was frustrating to the fire department, but the law is the law. He smiled and said, "But, hey, we can't complain in this place. At least they put 'em in the corridors."

Down in the street, the Tower aerial was still extended to the fire floor. It had been effectively used to remove three occupants from the sixth floor in apartments adjoining the unit where the fire started. Fortunately, the couple living in the apartment of origin had made it out by themselves, so no one was seriously injured.

Ladder 17 had been extended to the roof and had opened the penthouses, while the second alarm ladder trucks had been elevated to the fire floor and were used to help ventilate because the floor was empty of residents by the time they were positioned.

Donald thought it was a very effective operation and commented on it in his journal. He also was grateful that the department high-rise SOP required the bigger hose in all such attacks. He didn't think Engine Ten's crew would have moved in so rapidly with the smaller inch and three quarter line some fire departments permitted in their operations in the larger buildings. Better to be conservative and pack a more powerful punch.

After he showered and changed, he went to the kitchen to get coffee and was surprised that nobody was around. He knew they hadn't had another run. He'd have heard the alarm and seen the house lights come on. He slid the pole and saw everyone gathered near the front doors, one of which was opened. He could just see the back of an ambulance as it turned onto Purchase Street, its lights flashing and siren starting to whine.

"What's up, Rick?" he said to Foster. "It's Lieutenant Grimes. His leg. I think it's his knee." He explained that while they were operating inside the apartment, the officer appeared to trip over some debris and fall. He got right back up and appeared to be all right. However, when they arrived back in quarters, after they had replaced their cylinders and serviced the apparatus, his left leg gave out as he was going upstairs to the second floor and he fell down a couple of steps, banging his head and causing a laceration over his eye. "He seems OK," said Rick. "He'll probably need a few stitches. But, Captain Hardy and the EMTs think he might have torn a cartilage in his knee. Jeez, I hope not."

By the time Donald got home, he was weary. The lack of work during the previous few weeks had spoiled him. Getting soft, he thought, as he put the key in his front door and stepped inside. Usually, the empty house seemed kind of lonely when Gena was at work and Nancy was in school, but today he was grateful. He stripped down to his underwear, slipped under the covers, and dropped into a deep and dreamless sleep almost immediately.

The sound of the telephone next to the bed awoke him and he glanced at his watch as he picked it up. Wow, two-thirty. The sleep of the just, he thought as he answered, "Hello, Nancy's not home yet." Phone calls were usually for Nancy.

"It's Rick, you shithead. Whatcha get?"

Donald frowned and said, "What did I get on what?"

"On the exam, you dope. The marks are out."

Donald stood up quickly. "They are? Howdaya know?"

He could hear a snicker. "'Cause I got mine, whaddya think?"

Donald could feel his breath quickening, "I gotta go check the mail." He started to hang up and then paused and asked, "Well, you must've done pretty well or you wouldn't be calling. What's the number?" They had been thinking about this day for three months and now it was here. It was usually just in the back of their minds, but every now and then the anxiety would appear without notice. What if I did worse than I thought? How far down would I finish? Shit—what if I flunked? No, no. I know I didn't...er I hope. All that studying for zero? Well, today we'll find out.

Rick paused dramatically before announcing, "Well, Hero, my friend, the number is—Ta Da—95.30."

Donald almost squealed, "Jeez, Rick. That's terrific. How do you feel?"

Foster answered, "Well, great, I think. But, that's why I called you. I haven't got anyone else's marks yet. So, even though it's high, I got no idea how anyone else did. Hang up, will you please, check your mail and call me back."

Donald threw on some sweatpants, rushed out, opened the front door and unlatched his mailbox. Amidst the stack of junk mail, he could see a couple of legitimate-looking envelopes. One was his credit card bill, but the other was from the state Division of Personnel. He closed the door, walked into the living room, sat in his favorite chair, and, his hands shaking, opened the official looking envelope. He took a deep breath, slid out the paper, unfolded it and read the official notice. He was advised that his test score, after his experience and two points veterans' preference were calculated, was 96.71. He almost dropped the paper on the rug, but held on and continued to read. He was instructed that if he chose to appeal this finding, he had seventeen days to do so. Appeal? he thought. Please! Just don't touch it. His next thought was, Oh shit, I have to call Rick back. Hope he's not pissed off at me.

Getting through to his friend was not as easy as he thought. The line was busy and remained so for the next hour. Why doesn't that jerk get call waiting, he thought in frustration. He tried to call Gena at work, but she was attending a seminar and was unavailable. Even his daughter was late coming home from school. Where the heck was she? Oh, yeah. Color guard practice today. Maybe I should call the information operator and tell her. Naw, even she's a recording now. No sense in telling a machine.

Finally, after Donald pressed the redial button on his phone for what seemed the twentieth time, Rick answered. "What the hell have you been doin', you jerk?" asked Donald.

"Gettin' marks, pal, gettin' marks. Everyone's callin'. Howja do?" When Donald gave him his mark, he thought his friend would be a little envious. "That's great, Donald, that's terrific. All these guys who been callin' are lower than the both of us. I think we're gonna be in great shape. Thank you, Desert Storm." He was referring to the two point advantage their military service during the war had produced. And it was true. As the afternoon wore on and the list of marks they were hearing grew longer, they found out that it was definitely an important factor. Oh, a few jakes had even higher marks, but not many, and those who were ahead were also veterans. The competition for promotion was so fierce that many students scored in the nineties, but not quite close enough to slip ahead of Donald. They'd know a lot more tomorrow, but for today, things looked great.

Gena and Nancy happened to arrive home together, and by then, Donald had worn out the floor, pacing back and forth. But, he decided to play it cool, if he could. As they stepped in the doorway, he said, "Good evening, ladies. I had a very busy tour last night and slept most of the day. I'm starving. Anyone like to hit the Farragut House for their Tuesday night turkey special?" Both of them squealed with delight as they pecked at his cheek, brushing by to get in out of the cold. "What do you think Nancy? How long before you're ready?" her mother asked. "Right now," replied the teenager. Eating out on a school night! She wouldn't even stop to call her girlfriends.

The neighborhood's favorite restaurant was crowded when they arrived, but after a ten minute delay, they were escorted by the hostess to a booth on the second floor. Donald could hardly contain himself, but he did. They worked their way through the chicken soup, Caesar Salad and the heaping portions of white meat, stuffing, mashed potatoes and squash. Donald's appetite was voracious from the day's excitement, but the girls' appetites seemed heartier than usual.

By the time they had finished their entrees, he couldn't wait any longer. He slid the envelope across the table top and said, "Oh by the way, I meant to show this to you."

"What is it dad?" Nancy asked.

"Aw, just some technical notice about the job. Nothing important." He gazed at Gena, who knew something important was up. The two women read the paper together. Nancy's mouth dropped open: "Oh, daddy, it says you got 96.71. I don't know anything about tests for your job, but in my school, that's awesome."

Her mother smiled and said, "In my school, too, honey. Donald, that's wonderful. I'm just absolutely thrilled. You must be, too."

Donald's face split into a wide grin: "Well, actually, I'm in shock and have been since the mail came. How about dessert? To heck with the diet. I'm having a big piece of carrot cake—and ice cream."

Nine

Whenever a list is established by the State Department of Personnel Administration, the fire department takes a certain number of those who finish in the top echelon and assigns them to the Pool. This headquarters facility is operated by the Personnel Division and contains a certain number of district chiefs, fire captains and fire lieutenants as well as fire fighters from the promotion lists. They are assigned there because the contract between the city and the fire fighters' union requires temporary vacancies in various ranks in the suppression forces, with a few exceptions, be filled by acting personnel from the various promotional lists as well as the newest permanently promoted officers and chiefs who are awaiting transfers to permanent vacancies.

Between vacations, which extend from February to the end of the year, as well as injuries, sicknesses and special assignments, this temporary force is never unemployed. Under the contract, those who fill in at a higher rank receive the same pay as those they are temporarily replacing, and they are granted the authority that the position requires. In the case of temporary fire lieutenants, they are brought to the Personnel Division for a brief period to become familiar with the company paperwork they will be required to submit during their tours of duty.

While most candidates for promotion are thrilled to get the dramatic increase in salary each level requires, they realize they will be gypsies for a period of time as they are shifted from company to company whenever the officer they fill in for returns and a new opening exists, usually at another firehouse. They live out of the trunks of their cars and feel kind of in limbo. However, they knew this was part of the program when they started studying; they just hope to get through the period quickly, as sometimes happens, and also hope they get a choice company when they finally reach the top of the assignment pool.

Following the training on paperwork, the deputy in charge of personnel addressed the group of fifteen candidates. The point he made quite forcefully was that they were now expected to operate as an officer—not a fire fighter any longer. "This means," he said, "we expect you to enforce discipline and comply with SOPs, just the same as anyone else. You will never be a fire fighter again, and, while it will probably feel unnatural to you at first, you are now in charge of four other people and you are required to attempt to safeguard them, not only at fires, but in quarters. In other words, you are accepting that responsibility starting now." He smiled softly and continued: "If you were well loved as a fire fighter, forget it from now on. While they might respect you, based on how you perform, there's a real good chance they're never gonna love you. And, don't try to win them over by being a good guy all the time. Just remember your own feelings towards your own officers. Did you love them? Probably not. I hope you had a boss that you respected and, if you did, try to model yourself after him." Donald thought about Desmond and felt a warm glow come over him. He sure was an officer you could respect, but he bet not everyone had the same positive experiences he'd had. They're not all superstars.

Before they left for their assignments, each candidate had a personal interview with the deputy and the district chief of the headquarters division. Actually, both of these chiefs were relatively new in their assignments and were waiting for the day when they would be able to return to the field, but, in the meantime, they were doing the job required. Donald entered the office and saluted before sitting in the chair facing them. They were not strangers to him because he had worked with them at fires in the past. The deputy asked how he was feeling since the collapse and he said he was fine. The district chief wanted to know how his nerves were and if he had any nightmares or other residual effects of the incident. "Not really, chief. Oh, I was a bit nervous, the first couple of fires I went to. I was worried the buildings were going to fall down." He smiled and shook his head, remembering. "But, what I really recall the most is the effort the department made to get me out of there. So, while I know anything can happen on this job, they never just write you off. No, sir, no aftereffects."

They talked for quite a while and finally, the district chief said, "O.K., Holden. You're probably gonna be happy with where we're putting you. As you know, Lieutenant Grimes got banged up on Congress Street. They operated on his knee the other day. The cartilage got torn up pretty badly and he'll be off for quite a while." Donald was thrilled to get the assignment, although he was concerned about Grimes. The chiefs explained that it sounded like it wouldn't be a permanent injury, but, because of the damage done, it would be a lengthy recovery. As he rose to leave, the deputy said, "Just one word of caution, Holden—we expect you to perform like an officer from now on. I know I told all of the group the same thing, but, you'll be working with jakes in the same group and same house where you were a private. There's a danger to that and we don't usually let a guy stay where he was because someone will try to take advantage of him." He smiled and held out his hand, saying, "But, I got broken in by your uncle Frank on Engine 22, and he'll be keeping an eye on you. Good luck."

Out in the hallway, Donald chuckled to himself. Uncle Frank must have broken in half the chiefs on the job. He never even made it to lieutenant himself; he just kept going to fires and teaching young jakes. Today they'd call him a guru or a mentor, but everyone who worked with him just said, "Frank was a good jake." That's about as high a compliment as they pay anyone. Hope they say it about me.

When he reported for duty the next time, it felt very strange, almost like his first tour after drill school. But, at least no one had to show him around the house. Naturally, as he passed by the patrol desk on his way from the underground garage, Stoler was on patrol. "Hello, Luftie-Wuftie. Hey, your head does look different. Swollen from all that shit they filled you with up the street." He bent over the speaker and announced: "Engine 10, your new boss is here. He's a close, personal friend of mine and if I hear ya give him any shit, you'll answer to me." Donald rolled his eyes. Well, at least Stoler's on another group and won't harass me every day.

Members of both the offgoing night tour and the incoming day tour were having coffee in the mess hall, and they all greeted him just as though nothing much had changed, even though a few things actually were quite different.

Since Rick Foster had also been drawn into the personnel pool, he was gone to a fill-in assignment in District Six, South Boston. A new jake from the drill class that had graduated a few months ago was now on the group. Captain Turner of Engine 10 had kept him on his own group for a period of time but now was moving him into Rick's spot, knowing Foster would not be back. The ffop was a cheerful little guy, just twenty years old, named Charles Sole. As soon as he had reported for duty and Stoler heard his name, he immediately called him "Fish" after the popular flounder that was caught by the thousands in Boston harbor. Also, Lieutenant Desmond, who was creeping up on his own promotional list, was detailed as an acting captain on a truck in District Eleven, Brighton. Desmond was being replaced by Ray Frisoli, a new permanent lieutenant from the pool. But, jakes adjusted, whatever happened. They fully understood that if you're doing thirty years or so, nothing remains the same.

Soon after the daily chores began, Captain Hardy of Rescue One brought both new bosses into his office and had them take seats facing his desk. "Ray," he said to the new officer, "I'm delighted to have you here. You might find it somewhat different than where you came from." Frisoli had been a fire fighter on Engine 5 in East Boston, District One. "You were in a single company house, which really doesn't make any difference. Except that where you probably had a *few* characters on the company. I mean, every place does. We have three companies here so multiply that number times three." He laughed loudly. "But, like most places, jakes are jakes here, some exceptional ones, some ordinary ones and a few stiffs who are just along for the ride." He went on to explain that he felt Joe Desmond had a fine group of fire fighters who were highly motivated. "As you know, the Tower goes everywhere. Most of the people are on it because they want a lot of work, and you should have no difficulty in that regard. I just want to tell you that I'm pretty tough on substance abusers, whether it be booze, pot or harder drugs. I expect the house to be kept clean and the apparatus and equipment ready to go. You might find a little more horseplay here than where you were, I don't really know. I don't mind that stuff too much as long as they don't do anything cruel. If they get too loud, they know I'll shut them up." He continued: "One more thing. We have a woman fire fighter in this house. That's still pretty unusual 'cause there are still only a half dozen or so of them on the job" Hardy smiled as he said, "The one we got is terrific. Her father died on the job and all this woman wants to do is make him proud of her. She does her work as well as anyone and seems pretty happy to be here. We don't want that to change. She's not on this group, but she swaps time just like the rest of them, so you'll run into her. Because of the way she performs, I don't expect any problems and we're going to make certain none develop." He turned to Donald: "I know you're familiar with this as well as everything else in the house, Donald, but you're a boss now and I hope I never have to remind you of it. You know all the jakes on your group except the new kid and, I expect you to produce as well as Grimes does." He laughed. "You'd better, or he'll kill you when he gets back. Now, if either of you need any help on anything, I'll be around. And, Ray, we got Deputy Franklin and

District Chief Kinsella on this group. They never interfere with anything in the house and they're both good jakes. Long as you do your work at fires, they'll never bother you." He held out his hand to each of them. "Good luck. Now, let's go see how much trouble Dothead and the rest of this crew is causing."

When Donald descended to the main floor, it seemed strange, a kind of felt difference. He could see Steve Tucker, the driver of the Tower, and Vinnie Sterling of the Rescue Company just finishing the job of washing their respective pieces of apparatus. On his own unit, Engine 10, all four members of his crew, Jerry Nagle, Brows Brennan, Derek Burton and the new kid, Fish, were busily polishing the pumper with Simoniz. The truck usually looked spotless anyway but this was an extra, added attraction. "Jeez, Jerry, you guys trying to suck up to me because I'm the temporary head beaver?"

"No way, fool. We're suckin' up to the new captain. Besides, he left instructions that each group has to shine a certain section once a month and we're doin' ours today, so stand aside, please—sir."

The new captain had actually transferred in a few months earlier. Captain Leonard, who had been the previous boss, had been promoted to district chief and Turner, who had been trying to get to the downtown berth for a couple of years, finally had achieved his goal by seniority. He had spent the last decade serving on fire companies in North Dorchester and Roxbury, but, while he had enjoyed the heavy work load in those areas, he had a nostalgic yearning to get back to the district he had been assigned to when he was appointed. Something about the larger intown buildings appeals to one type of jake, while others hate the sight of them, and another breed doesn't care what size they are, just so the paycheck keeps coming. Now that he was where he wanted to be, he intended to stay and was placing his imprint on the company. If he had his way, Ten would be the best company in the department—and, it would also be the cleanest.

"Well, Jerry, if you don't mind, you can drop that rag you're waving for a few minutes, since you're not exerting as much energy as these other dedicated men." Donald swept his arm towards the rest of the crew, who chanted, "Right on boss, right on."

Jerry squinted at him and asked, "Whadya want, Loo?"

"Your expertise, pal. I've seen a lot of water coming outta this vehicle during the last few years, but now you have to show me how it works and where it comes from." Jerry Nagle beamed. Since Brows Brennan was the regular driver and treated the pump like he owned it, nobody asked anyone else anything. But, under the rotation plan

Captain Turner instituted, each other member of the company was required to occasionally become the pump operator to improve their skills and give them confidence in the operations.

Donald was aware of this and decided to let each member find out he considered them all to be equally important. He had Sole join him for the lesson. "Charley, I know you've had a lot of drills with the captain, but one more won't hurt, will it?" The eager ffop grinned: "Naw, Luft, besides it's better than polishing. And, you might as well call me Fish. Everyone else does and I don't mind. Stoler's got worse names for other guys."

Nagle was won over promptly and spent the next hour instructing the two jakes in the nomenclature of the relatively new fire engine. He learned it was a 1250 gallons per minute pumper with a 750 gallon water tank and a three inch tank to pump valve which permitted the use of either a one and three-quarter or two and a half inch attack line from the cross lays of lightweight hose flaked out for fast attack on a fire. It also had a deck gun connected directly into the fire pump which permitted immediate operation of a much heavier stream for larger fires. Along with this was a lightweight portable gun which could be easily carried to inaccessible locations where a heavy stream was needed and was also included for possible use inside high-rise buildings where the volume of fire required a more powerful punch than was provided by hand lines.

The remainder of the hose load included a much larger quantity of both one and three quarter and two and a half inch hose, as well as 600 feet of four inch feeder line attached to a hydrant assist valve to increase the supply of water obtainable from fire hydrants. The truck also had a front end suction inlet with a coiled roll of soft suction hose, other inlets on both sides and five outlets located on each side and in the rear. It also had a special chuck for connection to the Lowry hydrants that are peculiar to this section of New England, along with a pre-loaded high-rise cart for operations inside those structures. There were also several fittings, including cellar pipes, different kinds of nozzles, spanner wrenches and a supply of foam and equipment for flammable liquid fires. Hard suction hoses and two short, aluminum ground ladders were mounted on the sides.

Relatively new additions were a defibrillator and resuscitation paraphernalia. The department had decided to equip every engine company in the city with these life saving devices because there are more of these units than there are ladder trucks; consequently, they provide a better distribution throughout the various districts of the city.

The Rescue Companies also carry such equipment; as funding becomes available, all fire companies will have this kind of equipment.

This new unit was also the latest design with all members enclosed inside the cab, riding in jump seats with breathing apparatus recessed for ease of donning. Brows Brennan had finished his polishing duties and was standing with his arms crossed, listening to everything Nagle was telling Donald and Fish. When he saw that Jerry was finished, he said, "Hey, you guys are listening to an amateur. If this fuckin' snow ever disappears, I'll give you a real drill. Talk is cheap! You gotta do the hands on shit and I'm the best in the business."

When they broke for lunch, not only was the piece gleaming from the jakes' efforts, Donald felt much more confident about his knowledge of engine companies in general and Engine 10 in particular. He was whistling as he took the stairs two at a time. He remembered the advice Deputy Simpson had given him when they were discussing the best way for a new officer to insert himself into the team he was taking under his command. Other than working just as hard as everyone else does during fire fighting duties, Simpson said the officer should "give everyone a piece of the action." When Donald asked Simpson what he meant, he replied, "Well, remember, they know more about the company than you do. Don't be afraid to admit that to them, whether you're talking about the fire engine, response patterns, house work, patrol duties or anything else. If you let them tell you a lot of stuff they know, they'll feel like they're gonna be an important part of what you're trying to organize, and they won't be ignored." He smiled. "A piece of the action. Simple, huh?"

After lunch, he brought all of the crew into his office and invited them to sit down. He had been thinking quite a bit about what he would tell his first crew, and even though this was a temporary assignment, he decided he might as well start the way he'd planned from the beginning. He told them he knew he wasn't going to be here very long, but, since it looked like he'd get promoted before the year was out, he was going to try to learn how to become a good officer right from the start. "Since I've been working with all of you, except Fish" and he nodded towards the rookie, "you know me just as well as I know you. We've been to a lot of fires together, but, I'm smart enough to realize I've got a lot to learn. I would appreciate all the help you can give me. If you have any suggestions, I'll be glad to hear them." He advised them that he felt it was an officer's duty to take care of his jakes and he intended to do so. He also said it was kind of a two-way street: "What I mean by that is I expect you to do your work, as I'm sure you will, and, when I give you an order, to carry it out. You can second guess me privately all you want, but, unless you think I'm trying to kill you all at a fire or something, just try your best to do what I tell you." He asked if they had any questions and since none of them did, he dismissed them.

During the afternoon both Deputy Franklin and Chief Kinsella stopped by separately to see him and wished him luck. The district chief, who was an older man with years of experience, was friendly enough but had some advice that he delivered in a serious tone. "You're a good worker, Holden. I've watched you, like I do everyone, since you came here. I think you know what I expect. This is a big line district. Any fire we get, that's what I expect you to run. Also, if you get to a fire before I do, you're in charge until I get there. Any decision you make, I'll back you up, whether it's striking a multiple alarm or sending the all out. As far as your jakes, you handle them yourself. I don't expect you to come to me with any minor problems. Make your own decisions unless you feel it's so serious, you can't handle it. Then you come to me and we'll figure it out. Good luck. Hope you end up in my district permanently someday."

Donald was still whistling when he arrived home from work. The company hadn't responded to any alarms, but he felt it had been a successful first day. Gena and Nancy were filled with questions during dinner and he told them it was really quite exciting to be in charge, even though he expected to be nervous for a while. "Why, daddy?" asked his daughter, "You've been to lotsa fires, haven't you? You must know your job by now."

He smiled. "Well, I think I do. But before, there was always a guy to tell you what to do, and, you did it. Now, I'm that guy. I'm responsible for four other fire fighters and I want to do it right."

Gena laid her hand on his forearm, "Well, you've always been bragging about Desmond and those chiefs you work with. If they're as good as you've been telling us, you must have learned a lot from those people."

Donald grimaced and shook his head, concluding with, "Ladies, I'm sure going to find out pretty soon. Maybe tomorrow night."

After all of the worrying he'd done, Donald's first response to a fire as an officer was actually anticlimactic. Close to midnight on his first night tour Box 2285 was struck for a fire in a vacant two and a half story dwelling in the District Nine section of Roxbury. The chief reported a working fire shortly after reaching the scene, and Engine 10 was dispatched to cover another engine company on Dudley Street. Before they arrived, however, a second alarm was transmitted and they were ordered to respond directly to the fire on Haley Street.

It was a very serious fire, but by the time Engine 10 made it to the location the first alarm companies had made an effective exterior attack with heavy stream appliances and had succeeded in knocking down most of the visible flames. With the assistance of the extra alarm units, they were advancing into the structure and Donald and his crew were used to help extend and lighten up the lines until they were all placed and operating to kill the remainder of the fire.

While they didn't have much to do, Donald took Fish and walked him through the interior of the burned out rooms. "See how there are openings in the floors and how the banisters on the stairs are missing?" When the youngster nodded, Donald continued, "This place was being renovated. I saw piles of construction material outside." He pointed upward. "The fire was probably set in the rear living room on the first floor, but then took off through those holes, and the stairway, right up through the second floor and into the attic." The new jake said, "Boy, it's really charred to a crisp. They musta done a good job." Donald smiled: "I guess they did. They hit it with their guns because it was fully involved and it knocked the shit out of the fire." They were soon ordered to report out to the division commander and he had them help make up one of the big lines that had been stretched. When they'd finished, the company was dismissed and returned to quarters, stopping, of course, just like the Tower did, to pick up donuts.

In the mess hall, Donald felt himself starting to relax. Didn't realize how tight I was until now, Donald thought. But, it's over. One down and, oh, about a million to go.

On Sunday, the weather had moderated quite a bit. Piles of snow were still everywhere, but the bright sun was reducing them rapidly. Even though it was March, no one believed for a minute that this record breaking winter was over, but a least for one day, it was nice.

At the insistence of Brows Brennan, who was driving the pump—or *my* pump—as he called it, Donald called Chief Kinsella and requested permission to conduct a practice drill with the unit, across the channel on the South Boston side, in District Six. Kinsella laughed and said, "Sure, kid, go ahead. Just make sure the hydrant you use drains properly. Glad to see you're trying to teach that new jake." Donald replied, "Thanks, Chief, but that's just the excuse I'm using. I'm really trying to teach me. He just came out of drill school and probably knows twice as much as I do, but I'll pretend I'm smart."

Actually, when they got out onto the cement pier in the old navy yard property, Brows took over. He had Fish hook up first with the soft suction hose, which was rolled and stored in a recessed aluminum tray on the front bumper. The connection was made from the large outlet on the hydrant into the front end pumper suction inlet. The hydrant wrench was rotated clockwise until it was fully opened. The fire pump was engaged through the transmission, and Fish advanced the throttle at the panel, delivering water through the deck gun, which threw a powerful stream out into the channel of the harbor. Brows next had Donald, Jeff Nagle and Derek Burton stretch a hand line and they were soon operating the nozzle, shooting the solid core of water as far as they could, but falling far short of the larger device. Next he had them shut down and connect their line into the lightweight portable gun. "Hey, Fish," he growled at the rookie, "this is what we can do. We're an engine company. All those other outfits—rescues, towers and trucks—suck. If we don't show up, what they gonna do, throw tools and ladders at the fire? Bunch of phonies." Donald figured Brows was giving him the word, as well as Fish, but he wasn't going to challenge him today. He was learning too much to upset the grumpy but sincere jake.

He heard the sound of apparatus and saw Engine 39 approaching their location. They were from the D Street firehouse in South Boston and their boss, Captain Ronald Ramsey, descended from the cab when the truck stopped. He knew Donald as well as the others in the crew and said, "Hey, Holden, you stealing our favorite hydrant?"

Donald laughed: "Not really, Cap. Didn't figure anyone else would be nuts enough to drill outside in March."

Ramsey nodded, "Well, ordinarily I'd agree. But, we just got this new piece and, with a day like this, we wanna try a couple of things." They had recently finished training with their new fire engine, which was identical to Engine 10's, but the captain wanted more training with the Hydrant Assist Valve. This device is attached to the end of the four inch feeder line on each engine company. Whenever a connection is made by the first company to arrive at any hydrant, the HAV is used to make the attachment. The pump is then driven towards the fire, laying out feeder hose as it travels to get as close to the building as possible, without interfering with the ladder company, which is positioned directly in front of the fire building. Lines are then run and operated from this first engine. In the event that more lines are required from this one pumper, another engine arrives and utilizes the HAV valve.

During this drill, Brows became the professor because Ramsey enjoyed watching this usually morose guy display such enthusiasm. The jakes from Thirty-nine were making faces behind Brennan as he preached: "Now lissen, Fish, this is a good thing. See that hydrant? It can deliver about seventeen hundred gallons a minute. Good huh?" When Sole nodded, Brows continued: "Yeah, but when we stretch out a four inch feeder and fill it, we can only get about a thousand gallons through it 'cause the pressure comin' in is only about forty or fifty pounds. Now, if another company arrives, like these stiffs behind me," he waved at the Southie jakes who were now dancing a mock Macarena, "even these dummies know what to do."

He showed how a feeder line from the discharge side of the second pump connected into the left side of the HAV, while a feeder from the same pump was connected from the right side of the HAV into the suction inlet of the unit, through the Jaffrey Valve. "Now," he continued, "once you've done that, you got it made. See this rod?" he asked, indicating a narrow, foot long pipe attached on top of the HAV valve. "You just swing this to the right. This causes the water from the hydrant, except an amount which is still feeding the first pump, to go into your pump." He explained that when you did that, now your pump could increase its pressure as high as was needed and relay it through the HAV valve into the previously stretched feeder of the pump near the fire building. "So, pal, now you're pushing almost the whole quantity of the water from that hydrant, right down to the front of the fire building. You can run up to six lines from that pump now, and man, you can put out a lot of fire with that much water. Who the fuck needs them trucks?"

"Hey, Brows," said a jake on Thirty-nine, "how come you didn't give us shit in our line over Charlestown?" He was referring to a third alarm both companies had worked at during a bitterly cold night two weeks earlier. "I told you pricks I hadda frozen hydrant," Brows replied, his friendly mood rapidly diminishing. Captain Ramsey patted him on the shoulder: "Brows, my friend, don't listen to these yahoos. Any time you get sick of that downtown stuff, I got plenty of room for you."

Ramsey took over the instructions and had his own crew re-familiarize themselves with the procedure because it was infrequently used and, as he explained to Donald, "I don't have them practice much with what they do every day, just stuff that they can forget if they don't do it for a while. When the good weather comes, if you want, we'll use up some of this foam we all lug around. That's always an interesting drill. I've been on the job twenty years and I bet I haven't used it five times. It's kind of a nuisance, but once we had a fire in the bilge of a mothballed submarine and it worked great. You never know, you know."

When Donald arrived at work on the next night tour, it was around fifteen thirty hours, which has become the usual relieving time in the downtown district. If you don't let your partner get on the road home before 4 p.m., he'll most likely get caught in the massive rush hour traffic. The twice daily horror show has been further complicated in recent years by the construction activities associated with the Big Dig. This ten year, ten billion dollar public works project, the largest in the country, has been ongoing since the late eighties. It has already exceeded its estimated cost several times and its completion date is seldom mentioned anymore. Its purpose is to construct a vehicular traffic tunnel directly under the present Central Artery. The tunnel will descend to a depth of ninety feet and extend for some seven miles, and upon its final completion, the overhead and antiquated artery structure will be removed. This ambitious plan envisions a much more beautiful eastern edge to the downtown area, with gardens, parks and fountains as well as extended shopping and recreation facilities and, hopefully at least, a much smoother flow of traffic.

In the meantime, as Jeff Stoler succinctly put it, "It's a fuckin' mess." Not only has access to and from work become more difficult, even the response routes of the fire companies have to be altered, sometimes resulting in delayed arrivals at alarms. Actually, some members who live outside the city have given up the battle and transferred to fire companies in less congested areas, but the majority have hung on because of the spirit that continues at a high level in the station.

After buzzing Engine 10's room and notifying the officer he was in quarters, Donald put his gear on the apparatus and checked his SCBA. Tonight, he was relieving Captain Turner and they shook hands when they met in the company quarters. Turner wished him luck and offered any help he could and said he was glad Donald had already been conducting a drill. "That new kid I gave you, Sole, I like him. Even though we haven't had much work on my group since he got here, he's got the right attitude. Eager and pretty cheerful. I'd have kept him myself, but I don't know anyone on my group I wanna lose. So, Donald, stay in the books, become a captain and pick out whoever you want when you get your own outfit."

Donald laughed along with Turner. "Yeah, Cap, I got ya. But you sure didn't put any stiffs on my group. Brows, Nagle, Burton. Can't do much better than that."

Turner nodded in agreement. "This has always been a good company. And a good company attracts good jakes. I think I'm gonna lock myself in here for a long time, maybe 'til I run out the string. See you later." He zipped up his winter jacket and departed.

After changing into his station uniform—which, since the introduction of the new turnout gear, now consisted of dark blue tee shirts and pants for fire fighters and a gray tee shirt, dark blue pants for officers—Donald sat at the desk and looked over the morning reports and other official papers, getting a sense of the daily routine. He also checked the latest general and special orders from headquarters, but there were no new ones since his last tour.

He was closing his locker, heading for the mess hall for coffee and to check on his crew for the night tour when the radio speaker blared an alarm signal and the fire alarm operator announced, "Attention, Engine 39, Ladder 18, District 6, respond to a building fire, 368-372 West Broadway, we are striking Box 7164, Fire Alarm at 1627 hours." The house alarm sounded as Rescue One was dispatched to the incident, the location being part of its first alarm response. Donald continued towards the kitchen but before he reached the coffee urn, the radio spoke again: "Engine 39 to Fire Alarm, we have heavy smoke showing, top floor, corner of Broadway and E Streets." The chief of the district confirmed the report and added that it was a four story, brick and wood building, occupied as a private club. Fire Alarm dispatched the Tower unit on the strength of the report. Hm, Donald thought, sounds like the Lith Club, which is the South Boston nickname for the building owned by the South Boston Knights of Lithuania. He envisioned it easily because it stood on the corner of the two streets and was frequently rented for all kinds of community functions, two of the floors having large auditoriums. Donald was quite certain it didn't have a sprinkler system because, since his appointment to the job, and after working so long with Desmond, he was in the habit of looking for such protection whenever he entered a restaurant or a large building. He had been in the club within the last year to a charity function and was quite certain he was right. Yeah, plus the fact they're reporting heavy smoke showing.

He slid the pole to be ready just in case they called for more help and was pleased to see his own crew milling around the patrol desk, as well as the deputy's aide, Hank Greenfield. They didn't have long to wait. The next message from the chief was an order for a second alarm and the house alarm instantly sounded. Actually, since everyone was present on the main floor, except the deputy, who was sliding the pole, no announcement was necessary. Just get on the piece and take off.

The multiple response route for the company required them to turn left on Congress Street, cross over the Central Artery and the bridge across the Fort Point Channel into the industrial section of South Boston. While they crossed the bridge, black smoke was visible above the tops of the many multi-storied structures in the former wool district, but the size of the buildings prevented an unobstructed view of the location towards which they were driving.

Just before they swung right on A Street, Donald's eyes caught a flash of figures running from the Boston Fire Museum towards their cars. The museum occupies a former fire station that is owned by the Boston Sparks Association. It is fully equipped with radios, tappers and pagers as well as a variety of antique apparatus and equipment. While it is usually unoccupied because its members all have professions, on weekends it attracts many of its members. Donald knew they would be speeding towards the fire, probably faster than some of the responding units, but he wiped the thought from his mind and concentrated on the radio messages, trying to anticipate their assignment.

The radio blared, "Car 6 to Fire Alarm!" The call was acknowledged. "Have an engine company run a big line in from Third Street and over Nineteen's stick on E Street. Two other engine companies to bring big lines from Broadway to supply the Tower." The Fire Alarm operator confirmed the order and then called, "Engine 10, respond by way of Third Street. Bring a big line from Third to be run over Nineteen's aerial. Acknowledge." Donald already had the remote mike in his hand. "Engine 10 has the message," he said and repeated the instructions word for word.

Brows Brennan was driving the unit and said, "Listen, Luft, we can get a good shot right from here into Third. I know there's a hydrant right on the corner of Third and E." Donald started to ask the veteran jake how he knew that but decided not to say anything. This guy's been around so long, he probably knows every hydrant in the city.

They passed the U.S. Post Office facility on A Street and took a sharp left onto Third. Now they had an unobstructed view of the fire building because the size of the structures in the area, mostly residential had dropped to three or less stories. Brownish smoke, punctuated by flames was pouring from the top floor of the hundred foot long building. Actually, it was three buildings that many years before had been converted into one. Two sections were brick and wood, and the front end, which faced West Broadway, was a combination of granite exterior and wood interior. It didn't really matter though, because all three sections were burning intensely.

As they crossed the D Street intersection, Donald spotted the black hydrant with its yellow bonnet just where Brows said it would be. So far, no other company was on it. Because the hydrant was less than two hundred feet from the fire building, they chose to connect the five inch front end soft suction directly to the large outlet of the plug. Donald assigned Derek Burton to help Brows hook up while he, Jerry Nagle, and Fish started stretching the two hundred fifty feet of big line from the cross lay on top of the pump. Donald stared up at the building. Facing him was a solid blank brick wall which extended two floors above the adjoining wooden dwellings on Third Street. Ladder Nineteen's aerial was extended to a point just opposite the end row of fourth floor windows that faced Third Street, but it hadn't been lowered into the building because of the volume of fire licking outward. Further up the street, the Tower Unit had a similar position and had not started to operate its gun yet, probably awaiting its water supply. A couple of figures were partially obscured by smoke, but apparently they were jakes from another truck attempting to vent the roof over the fire.

Hank Greenfield was at the base of the aerial as ten's crew climbed up to the turntable: "Ten, the deputy wants you to operate from the stick right where it is until you can knock it down. Then we'll drop you into the window." Donald nodded at the instruction.

Nagle pulled the pipe and hose over his shoulder and started climbing up the steep angle. Donald waved Fish after him, the rookie allowing several feet of slack hose to dip between his legs. Donald smiled wryly; the kid's doing it just like they taught him in drill school. Donald followed with his own footage, emulating the procedure.

As soon as Nagle waved to him from the top, Donald pressed the mike on his portable and ordered Brows to start the water, while he and the others lowered down the slack and attached rope hose lines to the hose and the right side of the aerial. This kept the center of the ladder rungs unobstructed and prevented excessive pressure from whipping the hose and possibly knocking one of them off. When Brows reported the supply was "on the way", all three members, now much closer together, slipped their right legs through a rung and hooked the knee of the leg over it, effectively locking them in safely.

The smoke was now enveloping them and they could feel the heat from the fire, but when the water arrived and Jerry Nagle opened the pipe of the straight-tipped nozzle, he drove it right into the flames, aiming it upward, attempting not only to cool the fire, but also to strike the ceiling of the interior and break the stream up into a heavy spray to provide a good distribution. This caused the smoke to intensify somewhat, and Donald turned his head to the right and leaned his helmet into Fish's hip, just in front of him. He could see the Tower was also plugging away, the unit's stream even more powerful than his own. Just to his right, he could see a fire escape that extended from the second floor to the fourth, with a cantilevered ladder that one of the truck companies had pulled down to the street. Where the fire escape terminated at the top floor level, fire was blowing out the entrance doorway. Since Nagle seemed to be knocking down a lot of the flames ahead of them, Donald told him to try to swing the stream over to that entrance momentarily. When he did so, even though the water was entering at an angle, it succeeded in pushing the fire back inside.

Hank Greenfield was just below Donald on the ladder and he said, "You guys seem to be knockin' the shit out of it. Let's have Nineteen lower you into the window sill. I'm gonna see if the deputy wants to run a line up that fire escape." He descended rapidly and soon the aerial was lowered gently onto the wooden sill.

Donald moved up almost next to Fish. The smoke was still dense, but it seemed to be a great deal lighter in color. He tapped Jerry on the shoulder and said, "Give Fish a shot at it." Nagle shut the pipe down while he changed positions with the rookie and soon Sole was joyfully operating the line fully open, swinging the pipe back and forth and shouting, "We're killin' it, killin' it." And they were. The combination of heavy stream appliances and big lines quickly placed and properly supplied was having a positive effect on what could have been a lost cause.

Two engine companies, each with a dry big line, were trudging up the fire escape, getting into place to advance into the top floor, whenever the deputy gave the order. As he positioned lines for an interior attack, Franklin was shutting down the larger, outside streams. When he was able to determine that the heaviest fire had been contained, he directed that the inside attack commence.

Donald said to Sole, "OK, Fish, here we go. Put your facepiece on." Donald moved past him, hooked his leg over the sill and said, "Give me the line, just for a minute." He wanted to determine if the floor inside was intact, so he pulled enough hose to let him drop the nozzle down until it struck a solid surface. Next, holding onto the top of the aerial, he backed inside and placed his feet down lightly, his elbows supporting much of his weight. Good, everything felt strong. Apparently the fire didn't involve the floor itself. He couldn't see anything, but he brought Fish in and had him open the nozzle, once again aiming it upward and moving it back and forth.

The heat was greatly reduced, but they didn't attempt to move forward immediately. Donald could hear voices now, over to their right and shortly afterward, the sound of hose streams pounding the overhead, just like they were.

As it continued to get cooler, the three jakes wriggled forward, deeper into the building. The floor they were crossing didn't have many furnishings and he remembered it was an auditorium without fixed seating. The smoke was getting whiter, the more the lines kept hitting the fire, and after going about thirty feet horizontally, Donald could see light in the distance. It was coming through the windows on the opposite side of the building. Actually, the wall opposite them was solid brick except for the back section, which did have window openings, all of which had been cleaned out by truck companies working on that side. A line of hose was also being advanced from that side.

Above them, the skylight openings became clearer as the smoke continued to vent upward. Soon they were able to see what had been burning. Tons of clothing, apparently being collected for charity, had been stored in a huge area at the rear of the building and had somehow been ignited.

The rest of the job was a lengthy overhauling operation, and the interior lines were reduced for this phase of the operation. Fish was all smiles. He met a jake from his drill school who was on a truck company and was digging into the piles of charred clothes with his rake. Donald could hear Fish bragging about how he personally had knocked the fire down; the other jake responded with, "Sure, mackerelhead. I suppose you told the chief how to run the show, too. You ain't changed a bit since we graduated." Donald chuckled. His rookie sounded a lot like Cueball Justice. Guess every class has its own.

Soon their task was reduced to just standing by with the line and spraying the materials the truckies were separating and exposing so extinguishment could be completed. Donald, remembering Desmond and his constant inquisitiveness, took Fish on a brief tour of the top floor. They noted how the high metal ceilings in the area of the fire had been pulled down by the truck, rescue and Tower crews to expose the burned sections up above. Donald was able to show Sole how they removed all of the overhead covering until a generous unscorched area was exposed and it was determined the fire hadn't extended any further towards the front of the building.

They also noted how the skylights had been smashed and cleaned out, which was the key to the effective attack, drawing up much of the heat and smoke and allowing advancement into the interior. He took him out to the front where they could see aerials extended to the roof and view the lines of twisted hose covering West Broadway, the main thoroughfare in the district.

Fish was obviously thrilled with his own performance, but Donald was just as happy himself. This was his first major job as the boss of a company and he hadn't screwed it up. While they were making up the hose in the street in the gathering darkness, Hank Greenfield tapped Donald on the shoulder: "The deputy says you can take off as soon as you're made up, pal." When Donald nodded, Hank added, "Yeah. He also said you did a hell of a job." When Donald smiled, the aide continued: "I guess he likes ya."

Fish was leaning forward, eavesdropping. "Er, Hank. Did he mention me at all?"

Greenfield said, "You bet, kid. He said he always knew where Ten was on the top floor. He could hear you yapping from the street, even with your mask on. That's pretty good. You're gonna be a superstar—just like Dot-head and Stoler." Sole beamed an uncertain smile. Was that good or bad?

Shortly after midnight on the same tour of duty, Donald was just preparing to turn in. He had spent most of the Sunday evening, after eating, completing his report on the fire and entering notes in his journal. He had decided to start volume two with his experiences as an officer, even though he was just acting and he wrote down everything he thought could be important. Brows, when Donald asked him how he knew where the hydrant in Southie was, responded, "Jeez, boss, you got any idea, how many times I've been over that way? I been here a lotta years now and there ain't too many places I haven't been to a few times." Of course, Donald thought. I think they call that experience.

A box alarm was sounded for a fire in the Mattapan section of District 12 at 0036 hours. The district chief reported a working fire and ordered a second alarm shortly afterwards, and the Tower Unit was dispatched, causing the lights and alarm system to operate. Shortly after the apparatus departed, another box was sounded for a location in the Beacon Hill-Back Bay area, resulting in the dispatch of both Rescue One and the deputy. Ladder 17 reported smoke showing on Beacon Street, apparently a one room fire. Engine Ten remained in quarters.

At 0052 hours a box was struck for a fire in a housing project in East Boston; when the alarm transmission was completed, Fire Alarm dispatched Engine 10 to cover Engine 9 in East Boston, District One. The route took the company up onto the Central Artery northbound, then through the Callahan Tunnel that passes under the harbor and exits in District One. Just as they regained communications after traversing the cylindrical tube, Donald could hear the district chief at the housing project reporting he was holding all companies for a two room fire on Border Street.

As Brows swung the pumper in a semi-circle to prepare to back into Engine 9's quarters just off Maverick Square, Derek, Fish and Jerry Nagle descended to the street to stop any traffic until the vehicle was clear of the street. Donald was walking towards the entrance, intending to use his alarm box key, which operated every firehouse door in the city. He would go to the patrol desk and operate the switch to elevate the massive overhead doors, which had closed automatically, three minutes after the local units responded to the project.

A car, its horn sounding rapidly, pulled up almost onto the sidewalk, causing Donald to jump sideways. Before he could shout at the driver, the guy yelled, "Fire, fire. I seen smoke comin' outta a house down on Jeffries Street." Donald wanted to ask him where the street was because he didn't know, but the car sped off down Maverick Street, heading in the direction of Logan Airport. Donald waved everyone back on the apparatus and grabbed the mike. "Engine 10 to Fire Alarm, we have a report of a building fire on Jeffries Street, no number, and are responding." He was about to ask the operator for directions when Brows said, "I know where that is. Just down the end of this main drag."

It was a misty, overcast night and the street lights gave off very little light as Engine 10 rapidly gained speed, Brows jamming the pedal to the floor. Box 6112 was struck for their report and after the methodical beat of the blows was completed, the Fire Alarm operator called Engine 10. He reported that they now had received a call for a fire at 11 Jeffries. He also said that all other units being dispatched would be delayed. Although Donald wasn't aware of it, the combination of all the other fires that were being worked and two medical emergencies that required the use of fire companies, had temporarily stripped a wide area of the city of protection until adjustments could be made, and the ladder truck they were getting was coming from District Six in South Boston.

The closer they got to the end of the road they were traveling, the visibility decreased because a haze of smoke was permeating the drizzle. Donald thought he could smell the distinctive odor of a burning mattress, and as Brennan swung the apparatus into Jeffries Street, the last three decker in a row of six had an open, second floor window with grayish smoke pushing out horizontally into the street. Donald, the mike still cupped in his hand, depressed the talk button and said, "Engine 10 on Jeffries Street. Smoke showing, second floor, three story wood, occupied." He shouted to Burton, who was fastening his mask straps in the cab behind him, "Derek, inch and three quarter, front stairs."

Brows had stopped the truck at the corner and Fish remained there, looping the feeder line and HAV valve over the hydrant and commencing to make the connection as the four inch line was paid out, pulled to the street by the movement of the apparatus under the hand guidance of Jerry Nagle. Brows pulled the pump up beyond the fire building, allowing room for a ladder truck to position directly in front, whenever it arrived.

Donald started to jog towards the rear of the pump in order to help Burton advance the line, but he hesitated as the thought *no ladder truck* flashed through his mind. He opened the compartment door on the side, reached in and pulled out the Halligan bar. Usually when an engine and truck arrived simultaneously, one jake on the truck was the open-up man. His primary duty was to help the engine company crew get its attack line to the seat of the fire and he was equipped with devices to open any door or anything else that hindered their advance. However, every engine company carried at least one manually operated door opener for cases just like this one; Donald tucked the steel bar under his arm and followed Derek up the stairway and through the already opened front door. As he passed through the opening, a man, dressed in pajamas was just inside. His speech was slurred and he was coughing, but he managed to say, "My bed's on fire. Put it out, would ya! Put it out."

Donald grabbed him by the shoulders and demanded, "Anyone else in there?" The guy shook his head negatively. "How about up stairs?" This time, the blurry eyes widened: "Ah, Jeez, I don't know. Maybe."

Derek had reached the second floor and leaned over the railing. "Tell him fill the line. I got enough," he yelled. Jerry Nagle was just coming in the door and he waved to Donald, turned and shouted, "Brows, fill the inch and three quarter." Donald sprinted up the stairs and soon joined Derek who was kneeling in the hallway, his mask covering his face and his regulator making a rhythmic sound as his exertion operated the pressure-demand supply valve to match his requirements. The door was unlocked, and was actually slightly ajar, smoke curling out along the length of the crack.

Donald started to slip on his own facepiece, but said, "Derek, I'm going up to the third. When you get water, don't open that door until I give you the word." Burton nodded. Nagle joined them on the landing as Donald moved swiftly up the dozen steps that turned at the mid-point and then continued to the next landing. Directly in front of him was one closed door and another one just to his left. He reached for the knob of the one on the left and it was locked, so was the one to his front. He deftly slipped the adz of the thirty inch bar between the jamb and the door just above the knob and, moving so his right side faced the door itself, pulled forcefully on the steel shaft. Gratefully, the latch popped easily and the door sprung inward. He dropped to his knees as clouds of smoke enveloped him. Moving swiftly across the short, narrow room, he managed to get to the window and quickly opened it. He moved out rapidly, not able to see anyone and performed the same operation on the other door. The smoke was of the same intensity and this time he saw that there were no furnishings in this larger area. Vacant. As he moved down the stairs, Nagle was about half way up towards him. "Anything?" he asked. "Nope. Tell him to open it up," Donald responded.

Donald and Jerry crouched beside Burton as he pushed the door open slowly. A tongue of fire shot up towards the ceiling but was quickly drowned as the powerful stream bounced off the plaster overhead. Derek and Nagle crawled inward on their knees, as Donald, satisfied they were making progress, mumbled he was going down to report to a superior.

He saw Fish coming in the front door and asked him if anyone else had arrived. The rookie shook his head and said, "I can hear sirens but they seem to be a long way off." Donald paused and considered the circumstances, "O.K. Fish, we'll start a big line from the cross lay." He figured that even though they appeared to be controlling the fire effectively with the smaller line, there was no one here to provide a backup if for some reason they couldn't hold it. Actually, with Brows lending a hand, it wasn't that difficult to stretch the lightweight two and a half inch line with its preconnected nozzle. The pump was just a dozen feet beyond the fire building and the destination was only to the second floor.

Fish had the pipe over his shoulder and Donald said, "OK, just pull enough slack up on the landing to make the third floor and flake it out in the hallway. We're not gonna fill it unless we have to." He could see the small line pulsating as Burton and Nagle continued to operate inside the room of origin. "Fish," he said, "I'm goin' back out front. Let me know if anything happens."

In the street, he was surprised that there was still no one else at the scene. Many of the occupants of the adjoining buildings were milling around, some of them in doorways, others with umbrellas out in the street. He reached for the mobile radio on the pump and transmitted, "Engine 10 reports we have a line operating on a one room fire, second floor. Is there a ladder company responding here?" He could hear electronic wailers in the distance, but didn't know if they were responding to his location. A voice came over the air, "Ladder 18 to Fire Alarm. We are about three blocks away from Jeffries Street. Be right there."

Donald told Brennan, "I'm going back up. Tell them I think we got it but it's still kinda juicy. Maybe they can get the roof scuttle. We'll need some rakes, too." On the second floor, Burton and Nagle had effectively controlled the fire. The king sized mattress had become fully involved throughout its length and the fire had consumed the wooden headboard and baseboard, a chair, the curtains and was extending to a bureau when they cut off the flames. Donald turned to go back down and almost bumped into a lieutenant from the truck company. "What do you need, champ?" he asked.

Donald smiled: "Glad to see you, Luft. We need the ceiling open and we better get another look upstairs again."

The officer nodded and said, "Two of my guys are gone up there and our stick is going to the roof."

In the next five minutes, another engine and truck arrived as well as Chief Kinsella from the downtown district. He had been dispatched to this district after he had completed his duties at his own fire. Donald reported the situation to him and he replied, "OK. Foreign service, huh, Holden?" He turned to the other companies assembled behind him, directed the second ladder truck to assist the one already working in the building. He had the second engine company run a line to be used for the debris that was being thrown out into the alley to be overhauled. Within a half an hour, the operation was completed. The fire, while it had licked across the ceiling, had not extended any further as a result of the effective attack Donald's line had made. The Arson Squad and the police were on the scene and it appeared obvious the guy who occupied the room had been drunk and accidently dropped a cigarette on the bed. The first floor had been occupied but the top floor was vacant, so it was a routine operation. Kinsella told Donald he had done a good job, and as he was dismissing him, he added, "You also ran that big line. I like that. You're using your head, kid. Keep it up."

The Boston Fire Department records forty fires of various types daily, quite a few of them similar to this one and with the same result most of the time. But, to Donald, it was anything but routine. He had been in charge of the first fire company at the scene and had to make some important decisions. First of all, did he report he had arrived and the conditions he found? Yes. Was there anyone trapped? No. He had determined that fact by asking the one occupant, but then by going above the fire himself to make certain. He didn't want Burton to open the door to the room involved until he had checked above because if the fire had gotten additional oxygen, it might have blown right out into the hallway and extended upward, cutting off anyone's escape. Next, should he call for additional help? Not immediately. Did he judge the size of the fire properly and choose the appropriate size line and method of attack? Yes. Did he provide access to the seat of the fire for the engine company? Yes. Could he determine if the fire was extending? Yes, but he ran an additional line to protect his crew, just in case. Did he keep Fire Alarm informed? Yes. Did he report his actions to a superior when he arrived? Yes. How did he feel now that he was back in quarters and in his room writing in his journal? Like he had just won the gold medal in the Olympics. On the way back to quarters, as they were entering the Sumner Tunnel for the crossing back to downtown, Brows had turned to him and his face twisted into what he considered to be a smile but looked more like a snarl: "Holden, for a truckie, you ain't as stupid as I thought you was."

Donald was beside himself with joy but said only, "Why thank you, Hoseman Brennan. Take the next three days off."

Brows squinted thoughtfully, then said, "Hey, we're off the next three days anyhow." The pair of them were still chuckling as they exited onto Cross Street and headed back towards the station.

The fierce winter continued and as March drew to a close, the newspapers and TV stations were now maintaining charts providing a comparison of snow amounts to previous years and they actually seemed gleeful that there was a possibility of exceeding a hundred inches of snow in the city for the 1995-96 winter. Jakes and other workers who had to operate outside in some of the horrendous storms were less than thrilled by the climatic conditions. Those are not the kinds of records that anyone really appreciates unless they are snow removal contractors, ski resort operators, or travel agents who get overbooked by people trying to get to warmer climates for a respite. Donald thought he had a fairly good knowledge of hydrant locations from his service on the Tower unit. But, this year, his interest was much greater because he was on an engine company. They were out shoveling almost every tour of duty. Post, Lowrey and High Pressure hydrants were scattered throughout the downtown area. Each time there was a significant snowfall, the plows would bury the upright plugs lining the sidewalks and ice would clog and obscure the ones located below the street, with access through a circular steel plate at the surface. Actually, each district was set up so that a limited number of companies were out of quarters at one time, so a two hour detail of snow clearance wasn't that difficult. Besides, Brows treated the hydrants like he owned them and no one wanted to challenge him if he made them take extra time making a wide enough path through the mounds of snow or insuring that all of the outlets were clear and accessible. There were no complaints, at least out loud and Donald liked that.

There were a number of fires throughout the city as the month ground to a close, but, other than covering at other stations during extra alarm fires, Engine Ten didn't make any of them. However, they did have some dumpster and automobile fires and responded to some vehicle accidents; each time they worked at an incident, Donald became more confident with being in command of the unit. Of course, except for Fish, the other members were so experienced that he seldom had to give an order. They'd frequently be starting to stretch the appropriate sized line by the time he had dismounted from the cab, and Brows would always know where the hydrant was located. He was beginning to enjoy what he was doing and could appreciate why Desmond, Grimes and Captain Hardy spent a lot of their time teaching their members. It sure made it easier when they could do so many things automatically.

The night tour that commenced on the 29th was very quiet. They had polished off one of Brows' fish chowders at meal time and, after they finished, Captain Hardy, Donald and two of the rescue crew had a great, uninterrupted workout in the fully equipped exercise room. When he finished, Donald showered and went into Lieutenant Frisoli's room. Ray was seated in an overstuffed chair, reading a golf magazine. He, like Donald, was just feeling his way along in his new assignment, although it was a permanent position for him. During the brief period they had been together, Donald really enjoyed his company. He was something of a comedian himself and had already managed to outwit Dot-head a few times during the endless banter sessions in the mess hall.

Earlier in the evening during dinner, Dot-head had been at his most outrageous. He knew the new officer was in the department golf league and Doherty's opinion of golfers was that they were actually non-athletes who should be wearing skirts. Football and hockey were Dot-head's sports; they were manly and required guts. As he always did, he pretended he wasn't aware of Frisoli's passion for the game and he casually said, "Hey Luft, ja see them nitwits on USA today? The Players' Championship. What the fuck is that? The season just started and they're havin' a championship already. Shit. The Bruins been playin' all winter and they ain't even finished the regular season yet."

Frisoli smiled before he replied: "You're right, Doherty. All those sixty games they play to do what? Eliminate a couple of teams so they can start all over again with the playoff season. How clever is that? The owners make a bundle and the troops just keep losin' their teeth. J'ever watch them on an interview? They got blow-out patches all over their faces and those beautiful red gums. Nice sport. Glad you enjoy it."

Dot-head growled, "I seen that golfer with the knickers and cream colored socks. Nice touch. And them other sissy-lookin' guys, too. They're always studying which way the putts are gonna go. Some of them have a big discussion with their caddies before they finally tap the ball. Yeah, and usually miss and then blame the poor jerk carryin' the bag."

"Well, you're right again, my friend," said the lieutenant, "but when that hockey championship finally ends, sometime in June, when the ice in all the arenas is like slush from the heat and those poor, dumb foreigners from Canada, Russia, Sweden, Slovakia and Finland win the Stanley Cup for their American teams, guess what they do.?"

Doherty frowned. He didn't appreciate the way the conversation was going. This new guy was too cheerful. And, he keeps agreein' with me. "I don't know what the fuck they do, Loo. Go back where they come from?"

"Not really, pal. Those slap shots they take all winter long are just getting them in shape for what they really want to be doing." He paused dramatically, "Playing golf. That's what those real men do all summer. They're all in the Celebrity Golf League, competing against Michael Jordan, John Elway, Dan Marino and all those other sissy non-athletes."

When Donald asked if he was busy, Frisoli shook his head and said, "No Donald, just thumbing through this magazine. Don't ask me why. I've been playing golf about a decade now and I read all this stuff, but I can honestly say none of it has ever helped my game. I'm pitiful. But, in just about another month, if this damned winter ever ends, I'll be out there, determined to beat all the rest of them. Have you ever played?"

Donald admitted he had, but was really just a beginner. He didn't get much chance last year because of his injuries and intended to get back at it this year. "I like the way you handled Dot-head, Luft. Is he a character or what?"

"Oh, he's great. It's guys like him that keep this job going. The only thing is, he's a piece of cake for me. On Engine 5, even though it's a single house, I had Manhole Mastrangelo and Lippy Liotta on my group. They'd out-talk Dot-head two to one in any kind of contest. They know enough about handicapping every sport. I'm not saying they're bookies, mind you, but the outside phone is sure busy whenever they're working."

"Where'd they get those names?" Donald asked.

"Well, Lippy is easy. He's got the biggest, juiciest, purple lips you ever saw. Mastrangelo leaned over a manhole that was really puffing smoke a couple of years ago. It blew straight up in the air and a sheet of flame followed up about fifty feet."

Donald shuddered. "Did he get hurt bad?"

"Naw, not really," Ray answered. "It knocked him on his ass and scorched his eyebrows. They were gonna call him Brows like your guy, but he didn't appreciate it and he can fight like hell. He kinda likes Manhole 'cause it sounds more virile. But he stands back pretty far whenever they respond to those Edison jobs."

Frisoli then talked for a while about his assignment. He was learning quite a bit during his brief time in the house. The Tower was altogether different than an engine company, and the fact that they traveled all over the city was expanding his knowledge rapidly. He was particularly happy the way they had performed at the Lithuanian Club fire and was starting to appreciate the awesome power the unit could unleash when properly placed. "But," he said, "every place you're assigned, you'll find something unique." He explained that in a single house, such as Engine 5 was, you are frequently the first-in to a fire and, you're all alone for a period of time. "You already had a taste of it when you were covering the other night. The officer has to make some quick decisions. With all the three deckers in East Boston, sometimes he has to just try to cut off the extension and hope to hold the fire in the building of origin until he gets more help. It's kind of interesting at times. I guess the most important thing, wherever you end up, is to learn your area and what's unusual about it. As they say, it's a business of surprises, but it's nice to be able to anticipate what they might be."

Donald returned to his room impressed with how sharp Frisoli was. You never know where you'll learn something. Think I'll jot down a couple of things he said. At midnight, he made up his hitch and went to bed. Jeez, not a run all night. Wonder if we'll get an "all night in." There hadn't been too many since he came on the job, but, whenever they occurred, the rule was you never told your wife about it. Whenever she asked what kind of a night you had, the answer was, "Tough. Four runs after midnight." If she replied that she hadn't heard anything on the news, the standard answer was, "Jeez, hon, you know you only hear about the spectacular stuff. We're in and out all the time."

He was snoozing softly when the beeper sounded and a box started striking. One blow, pause, two blows, pause, four blows, pause, five blows. He jumped out of bed, swinging his legs into his hitch and standing up. The lights came on and the house alarm sounded as the member on patrol announced, "Box 1245, everybody goes." He gave the location in the North End section of the district and, as Brows started the pump, Donald heard the radio announcement, "Box 1245 is struck for a fire, first floor rear, number 45 Fleet Street. Report of people in the building." Their route required them to cross over the Expressway on Congress Street, follow Atlantic Avenue along the waterfront to where it merged with Commercial Street. Fleet Street terminated at Commercial so they would turn left at that intersection. Engine 8, the first unit at the scene, reported fire showing in a block of five story, second class buildings. This area used to contain many commercial buildings that were used by meat, poultry, fruit and vegetables wholesalers and distributors. These businesses eventually moved to other areas within and beyond the city, and the structures remained largely vacant for years, although squatters and homeless people were frequent occupants. However, in the eighties, the area was revitalized and the former business buildings became apartment houses and condos.

Deputy Franklin arrived ahead of the other fire companies and ordered a second alarm to be struck, reporting people at the windows. Donald had Brows pull over to let the Tower unit proceed ahead of them and try to use their aerial for rescue purposes. Heavy smoke, flames and sparks were visible about three blocks away on Fleet, and as Engine 10 got closer, traveling along the narrow street, with mounds of snow on both sides, reducing the roadway to one, ice-rutted lane, Brows said, "There's a high pressure hydrant corner of Moon and Fleet." Donald replied gratefully, "Go for it." These hydrants have either three or four outlets and can deliver two thousand gallons per minute provided by massive stationary pumps whose operation is controlled automatically by the Fire Alarm office, whenever a box is struck for a fire in the high pressure area. At the location, Donald told the crew to start hooking up as he raced up the street seeking orders. Car 3's aide, Boley Raditz, waved to him and shouted, "Ten, big line, front stairs, second floor." That was all Donald needed to hear. He looked up and could see the fire was on the corner of Fleet and North and ladders were being raised by Ladder 1 and the Tower, with Ladder 24 positioning on North Street.

He started to return to the company but could see Nagle, Burton and Sole trudging through the snow towards him, a big line flaking out behind them. "Keep comin'," he shouted and moved up the street towards the fire building. Chief Kinsella was at the top of the outside stairs: "Ten, right up the front. Fire's goin' all the way up a shaft. Eight's on the first floor." Donald could see a big line disappearing down the hallway to his right and could feel the heat coming towards him along the ceiling as he started up the stairs, then he saw the line starting to swell as water filled it and knew it would be hitting the fire shortly.

He made it to the second floor landing and dropped to his knees as the smoke thickened. Nagle was just behind him with the line; Donald thought he could see a glow just inside the opened door in front of him. Pressing his remote mike, he spoke briefly: "Fill Engine 10's line." Brows acknowledged the message and Nagle kept pulling up more slack as they waited for the familiar sound of air escaping from the opened nozzle. It seemed to take a while but was probably less than a minute, but the heat kept getting worse and they had to back down the stairs as the fire continued to expand. When the water did come, they directed the stream right up over their heads and swung it along the hallway as well as into the room. Donald felt a tap on his shoulder and was startled to see Kinsella just behind him. "Ten! Eight is doing good down below. See if you can move into the apartment. We got other lines going over ladders up above and I want you to protect them." Donald didn't need any more urging. He spoke through his facepiece, "Right in, Jerry. Move it. Eight's got us covered underneath." His three jakes managed to wrestle the stiffly charged hose forward, doing a duckwalk as they advanced into the apartment. The fire had spread into two rooms from its original entry into the floor from the rear and they just kept plugging away, hesitating to direct the stream and then moving forward. Their progress was satisfactory and Donald slipped past them, trying to make his way to the rear windows. However, he thought he saw fire to his left and managed to get to a wall that had a square opening cut into it. Flames were racing upward through a shaft. He depressed his mike and called, "Engine 10 to Car 3. We have found a shaft, second floor, rear, fully involved." Kinsella answered, "O.K. We're aware of it. See if you can play up into it. Got another line coming to your location." His crew had succeeded in reducing the fire in the apartment to smouldering furnishings. The visibility was very bad but he worked his way over to them and managed to lead them to the opening in the wall. Soon they had twisted the line and were driving it at an angle upwards. Donald took Derek Burton and they worked their way to the rear windows which were shattered by the fire, but they cleaned out the shards of glass and broke the sashes to enlarge the openings.

They were joined by another engine company a few minutes later and continued operating up the shaft as well as killing all the fire in the apartment. Kinsella stopped by and said, "Just keep operating the way you are. We got it cut off on the fifth floor. That shaft is pretty big and it carried the fire right up."

"Everyone get out, Chief?" Donald asked.

The boss nodded. "Yeah. Lucky though. Those trucks and the Tower picked off several of them. Get a look at the ladders out back."

As the fire was brought under control, they did get a chance to look out at both the front and the rear. There was a maze of thirty-five and forty foot aluminum ladders extended in the rear that had to be hand carried down the alleys and over the fences. It was the same out front, although aerials were able to be used to reach the upper floors in those locations. The common shaft in the hundred year old buildings had allowed the fire to gain entrance into an adjoining building on

North Street and it required a three alarm response to rescue all the endangered occupants and control the fire. Nine engine companies, five ladder trucks, the Tower and Rescue Company were used in the successful operation.

When they were dismissed, they moved along the waterfront, watching the sun emerge from the ocean beyond the entrance to Boston harbor and it felt good to be alive. Of course, they stopped at Dunkin' Donuts on Commercial Street and had the usual argument about who would go in and beg for sustenance for the poor fire fighters. Fish lost because he was the new guy and he must have looked pretty forlorn to the two middle-aged ladies behind the counter because he came out with two bags of goodies instead of one.

Donald was relieved by his partner, soon after they returned; he was in the shower, whistling and he thought, well, I don't have to make up any stories for Gena today. We really were out after midnight, and boy, it was something.

Boston still suffered a few snow storms during the next few weeks of this record breaking season, but they were smaller compared to the snowfalls between December and March. It was, after all, April; the clocks were turned ahead and the temperatures didn't remain below freezing for long periods. The fires that did occur in the first few weeks of the month were either on other work groups or in sections of the city that Engine 10 didn't get to unless it required four or more alarms. But, there seemed to be an inordinate number of malfunctions and accidental alarms in the high rise buildings equipped with smoke or heat detectors. The downtown and Back Bay jakes responded to the most of these incidents by virtue of the fact the greatest concentration of larger buildings is in those areas. The incidents had a code name for official purposes, but the fire fighters referred to them as the "fuckin' bells." Some otherwise peaceful nights were interrupted frequently by these alarms and, unlike a false alarm pulled from a street box, these were much more time consuming and frustrating because of the extensive investigation required to find the cause of the alarm. Since about eight thousand of these incidents are recorded annually, it doesn't take long for the thrill to be gone.

One night just after Donald had relieved his partner, he was in the mess hall when Jeff Stoler began voicing his view of the system: "Fuckin' bells. We had three today. Soon as there's a thaw, every fucked-up system goes off. What a waste of talent. I'm gonna do something about it."

Dot-head Doherty offered no sympathy. "Those responses are

what keep you pricks in business. And, you're right, they're unimportant activities. If they were dangerous, they'd sent us rescue people to them. Besides, what can you do about it?"

"It's a working condition grievance," Stoler replied. "I'm callin' the delegate. We'll straighten this out."

Everyone hooted. The idea of the union leadership, who were always championing safety issues, trying to lessen a protective measure was unlikely. Actually, every year the department tried to reduce the numbers by instituting a series of fines to buildings visited the most frequently. But, there were always new buildings, new systems and appeals of violation penalties that seemed to keep the annual figures constant.

Stoler was working a tour for one of the Tower crew this night in mid-April and, as if to confirm his complaints, the engine and Tower responded to four such incidents before midnight. Each time Donald could hear him bitching as Ten stood by the standpipe while the Tower investigated the floor above. The last time, they could hear the voice of Lieutenant Frisoli, his patience at an end, shouting, "Hey Blubberbelly!" Stoler was easily offended at such a reference. "I think there might be a potential arsonist in this building setting off these alarms." Stoler could see he was getting the new officer furious so he said gently, "Yessir, Lieutenant, I think you may be correct, sir." Ray nodded: "Right. So, I'm leaving you here as a detail in the interest of public safety. Make a thorough search of every floor with the security people and let me know what you find out." He handed his portable radio to the dumbfounded jake and coaxed everyone else down the stairs. Donald and his crew heard the entire exchange and were laughing uncontrollably as Frisoli winked when they entered the elevator. In the lobby, the officer talked to Chief Kinsella and the rather serious older boss, frowned thoughtfully and then said, "I like it, kid. Good idea. Besides he's from that other fuckin' group anyway."

Not to be outwitted, however, Stoler was back in quarters in about a half an hour. He confronted Frisoli in the TV recreation room and said, "Lieutenant, sir, you're a genius."

"Oh, yeah. How come?" the obviously suspicious officer replied.

"I spotted that guy just after you left. Chased him all the way and got my hand on his shoulder right out on Federal Street." He grimaced in pain. "But, he karate chopped me right on the arm and got away."

"Why didn't you chase him, Stoler?"

Jeff dropped his eyes sheepishly: "Because, sir, you are right. I am a little overweight and I just couldn't catch him. I'm starting a diet tomorrow." Donald rolled his eyes, thinking, Boy it's tough to top an expert like Stoler. As Jeff started to leave the room, handing back the portable to his lieutenant, he said, "Er, any chance of writing me up for a commendation, Luft? I coulda been killed, you know."

Donald was delighted with Ray's targeted response: "I'll talk it over with Chief Kinsella, how about that? If he approves it, I'll let you know. Where will you be, in the exercise room?"

Stoler stormed out into the hallway, knowing he had a new and formidable opponent in this affront to his intellect. But, he thought as he strode down to the kitchen to check out the possibility of any leftovers in the refrigerator, he needed this type of challenge occasionally. The rest of the stiffs in this house were easy. He was whistling as he opened a brown paper bag carefully concealed in the back corner of the cold storage compartment. Hmm, carrot cake. He checked his watch. After 2300 everything is up for grabs. Besides, carrots are good for my eyes, especially on my new diet. Be too bad if this belonged to Frisoli, he thought, as he bit into the frosted dessert.

At 0230 hours, the engine and truck were dispatched to another report of an alarm signal for a location on Batterymarch Street, just a few blocks from the firehouse. When they arrived at the location, the front door of the six story office building was open but the security guard, who was required to meet them at the entrance, was no where in sight. A glance at the annunciator board indicated an alarm from the top floor and Donald activated the elevator service switch. This smaller sized, older building seemed to be intimidated by the much higher skyscrapers that abutted it, and as he watched the board, Donald could see that both elevators were at the top floor but were now descending. While they were waiting the arrival of their transport in the lobby, both he and Frisoli looked at each other. Was that smoke they were smelling? Without hesitation, the Tower officer depressed his mike button, "Tower Unit to Fire Alarm, strike a box for an odor of smoke 30 Batterymarch." The door of the first elevator to arrive sprung open and a cloud of smoke flowed out into the lobby along with the watchman and two cleaning women, all of them yelling in Spanish. "Fuego, fuego," one woman shouted. The watchman said, "Top floor, lotta smoke." Frisoli grabbed him by the arm and asked, "Anyone else up there?" The man shook his head negatively. The officer asked him what was burning, but he didn't know. One of the Tower crew set up the inhalator he carried as part of his response equipment and started supplying oxygen to the women, seating them on the floor against a wall.

Chief Kinsella and his aide burst into the lobby and Frisoli reported what they knew to him. The chief nodded, "OK, Luft. No sprinklers in this place. Check the fifth floor before you go to the top. I'll start a big line up the stairway from the street."

As the elevator rose, the smell of smoke became stronger. Frisoli pressed the button for number three floor and, as the doors opened there was just a faint haze visible. They continued up to the fourth and as they exited, it was still just a haze, but a little more dense. Advancing up the stairway, Stoler, who was open-up man, took his glove off and cautiously felt the metal-covered entrance door to the fifth floor cautiously. "No heat, Luft," he said, and Frisoli nodded to him to force it, because it was locked. The hydraulic Rabbit tool made quick work of the door fastenings and, while smoke drifted towards them, it wasn't under much pressure.

While the Tower was making a cursory check of the floor, Donald and his crew were connecting their hose to the outlet, unrolling the hose down the stairs and then joining each of the three lengths together. Meanwhile, the aide, Boley Raditz had continue up to the top floor and now was waving to Donald: "It's pushin' up here. Tell the truck the door's locked." Frisoli was just exiting the fifth floor and said they hadn't found any fire. He started up and said, "Donald, ease that standpipe open and be ready to move right up."

As soon as the top floor door was cracked, smoke filled the stairway. Ten's crew donned their masks and stretched the line rapidly up the stairs. Nagle was on the pipe and he had it open so that the trickle of water in the line pushed out any remaining air. On the landing, Donald could see the extended legs of one jake as the Tower crew crawled slowly inside. It was dark, but not completely black inside the doorway. Overhead lights were still glowing through the smoke, although they were growing dimmer as the smoke became more dense. Before they advanced the line inside, Donald had the standpipe valve opened fully. This made the hose swell and become solid. It made it more difficult to move, but at least they had a full supply of water to protect the operating personnel. From ahead of him, he heard a voice he assumed to be Frisoli's shouting, "Bring the line right down the corridor. Rear room, plenty of fire." Donald rose to a crouch and followed Nagle, with Fish just behind him. It seemed to be quite a distance, because it kept getting hotter, but it was only about thirty feet. Nagle bumped into someone and dropped to the floor. Raditz, Frisoli and Stoler were huddled behind a partition. "Around the corner, Donald," said Ray, "we got the door just ajar." Donald now had his head almost touching the floor as he looked around the edge of the wall. He could see fire through a door whose opaque glass was splintered from the heat. He pulled at Nagles's coat and they wrestled the big line around the corner. "O.K., pal, open it up. Blast it right through the door," Donald said. Nagle pulled the lever slowly toward him and the stream pounded the door open and continued traveling, driving into the overhead. In just a matter of seconds, they were able to move forward to the doorway itself. Donald could hear glass breaking from a number of sources. Some of the sounds came from overhead, where he assumed jakes were getting the skylights, while more noise came from directly in front of them, probably from fire fighters working off aerials, providing cross ventilation.

The line they were operating had tremendous pressure and it reduced the heat dramatically in just a short period of time. As Nagle cut back on the flow from the tip, Frisoli, Stoler and Raditz made their way inside and over to the windows. Those that hadn't been cleared away from outside they managed to open so that the smoke escaped and they were able to see what had been burning. It had been an executive's office with a huge desk as well as two leather couches and chairs, a bar and a coffee table. There was also a walk-in closet, stocked with clothing, but most of it had been destroyed. The fire appeared to have started somewhere under the bar where a charred electrical cord and some types of appliances were located, but the investigators would have to determine the cause because the destruction was total in the area.

Another big line appeared at the doorway, one that Kinsella had ordered up the stairway as a backup for the standpipe operation. It was Engine Four's line. Their station is on Cambridge Street, Beacon Hill near Government Center and also houses the district chief as well as Ladder 24. Richie Chasen, a character in his own right, shouted in the door, "Hey, Tower?" and Frisoli said, "Over here! Whaddaya want?"

Chasen replied, "That fat fuck Stoler from Group Two. Ask him is he goin' through on that grievance." For the first time in memory, Jeff was silent, but he glowered at Raditz whom he was sure had spread the word on his earlier detail. Next time Steve Tucker asked him to work a shift for him, he'd tell him to pound sand up his ass.

Donald, who was really starting to enjoy his role as a teacher, took Fish on a tour of the floor while the truckies were opening the ceiling and Nagle and Burton stood by with the line which had been reduced for overhauling. This type of operation didn't happen very often so, for his own benefit as well as the ffop's, he followed their route back to the standpipe outlet, explaining why the SOP required them to connect at a floor below the fire in order to protect the jakes opening the door, in case the fire attacked them and to provide a secure base for their own operation and advance. He also told him that as far as he understood, this occupancy would be equipped with sprinklers shortly under the new state law requirements. Perhaps, in the future, the type of fire that had occurred would have been controlled before they even got here. "Yeah, the way those sprinklers work, the water would be hitting the fire before we left the house. But, in the meantime, we better keep doin' what we're doing." Fish laughed and said, "I guess we ain't gonna support Stoler on his grievance then, huh, Luft?" Donald shook his head: "Nope, I think Fatso met his match tonight. But, don't worry, he'll be back. He's always thinking."

A couple of days before the end of April, Donald reported for a night tour of duty and, when he went into the room to relieve Captain Turner he was surprised to see Lieutenant Grimes sitting on the bed. He and Turner were talking about Grimes' injury and Donald found out that this was to be his last shift on the company. Grimes was really happy to have gotten clearance from the department medical examiner to return to duty. "Donald, I know it seems crazy with the lousy winter we've had, but I'm so glad to be coming back. I was going nuts at home and I was even getting nostalgic for shoveling hydrants, for cripes sake." He laughed. "I'd probably get over that in a hurry, but boy, for now, I'm as ready as I'm gonna be." The three of them had a lengthy discussion about the fires that had occurred during Grimes' absence and the lieutenant said, "Well, you must have done O.K., my friend. Even Brows said you're not too bad for a truckie, and that's about as far as he'll go with anyone. You're supposed to contact the Personnel Division tomorrow for re-assignment, but thanks for keeping my seat warm. Hope you get another good berth." He snapped his fingers, slapped his forehead lightly and said, "And oh yeah, I forgot the most important thing. They said at headquarters they'll be making some promotions in June, including four lieutenants." Donald gulped at this news before saying, "No kidding. Kind of unexpected, isn't it?" Like everyone on every promotional list, Donald had a computer printout that identified the mandatory retirement date of every officer on the job. Since all promotions were on a one for one basis, a jake on a list could figure out just about when or if he would get a job within the two year life of his list. One of the vacancy possibilities that couldn't be anticipated was when the city retirement board would act on injured officers who were awaiting disability pensions. Another one was if an officer died. And, finally, the nicest vacancy of all was when an unanticipated guy just walked into headquarters and said he was leaving. This was usually a member who had his time and age in place but hadn't reached the sixty-five year maximum. What a bonus this was for jakes on lists. And, if it happened to be a deputy, *wow*, four guys would move up to fill the table of organization.

After Grimes and Turner left, Donald placed a few phone calls and was able to confirm what Grimes had said. This development could leave him number six on the list. And, scheduled mandatory retirements made his promotion date in November. All right!

The evening was fairly busy because some nut was on a rampage of pulling street boxes throughout the downtown area. Since no box is struck unless a telephone call is received confirming a fire, one engine and one truck are dispatched to these incidents. Between midnight and 0300 Engine 10 and the Tower responded to four false box alarms. Since the rescue company didn't go to any of these runs, the returning companies made as much noise as possible each time they arrived back in quarters, just to keep the prima donnas from getting any rest. On the fourth incident, however, Captain Hardy was standing near the patrol desk, his arms folded across his chest, glaring at Donald and Frisoli. They both got the message and the apparatus glided in as soundlessly as possible, Donald nervously touching his helmet with his right hand in a sheepish salute. "Everything OK, Cap'n?" he asked.

"If it isn't, I know you're gonna make sure it is. Right, Acting Lieutenant Holden?"

Donald nodded his head vigorously: "You bet, sir. Next time, you won't even know we're responding."

The next run was for Rescue One, however. At 0344 hours, Box 1533 was struck for a fire on Beacon Street in the Back Bay portion of District Four. Dot-head Doherty had the electronic sirens and whistles sounding in quarters and was jazzing the motor of the rescue van vigorously just in case anyone on the Tower and engine had managed to doze off since the last response. But the gamesmanship became moot when Ladder 17 arrived at the location at 0345 and Lieutenant Walsh ordered a second alarm to be struck. When the district chief arrived moments later, he ordered a third alarm. By this time, Ten and the Tower were on the way; as they sped up Summer Street to Winter to Park and to Beacon, a fourth alarm was being transmitted. The fire to which they were responding originated in one of two vacant five story, brick and wood apartment houses in a densely populated area. As they approached the scene, driving down the hill of Beacon Street and crossing several intersecting streets, the fire looked enormous. Flames were roaring at least fifty feet above the tops of the buildings involved with sparks and flying brands being carried even higher.

The Tower was directed to proceed to a position at an angle in the street to operate on the main body of the fire. Ten was instructed via radio to utilize their deck gun on the adjoining structure to the left of the original fire building. This structure was not vacant, but the occupants had managed to escape. The fire had already entered into the second floor of this building, and extended upward, breaking out and fully involving the fifth floor and roof. To the right of the original two fire buildings, extension had been to a corner building of the same size and then into a four story brick dwelling on Berkely Street that abutted Beacon.

Once again, Brows knew where an unoccupied hydrant was located, within two hundred feet of the fire, and, with everyone working feverishly, in just a few minutes after arriving, Ten was arching a solid stream of water through their extremely powerful deck gun which was equipped with a special inch and three quarter tip, into the fifth floor windows of their assigned building. In spite of the massive amount of water they were discharging, and, with another engine company soon joining them with a similar stream, the fire just continued to roll out of every opening on the upper floor. Within sixteen minutes of the initial alarm, a total of six alarms had been sounded, totaling twenty-three fire companies. These included the Tower, six ladder companies, the rescue and many engine companies. The force soon had ladder pipes, deck guns, Tower streams and many hand lines surrounding the complex of buildings and cutting off further extension. However, Donald was amazed that the fire just continued to burn intensely for almost two hours before they began to get control and it started to darken perceptibly. It made him appreciate the fact that while sometimes properly placed lines resulted in early effective control, every now and then, fire would just let you know how tough it could really be and who was really in charge. He remembered something Jeff Stoler said after one particularly frigid all night stand: "In spite of our efforts, the fuckin' fire finally decided to go out." Now he understood what old fatso meant.

At least the weather was much milder now that May was only a couple of days away. As the sky started to lighten to the east, Donald was able to send half his crew for coffee from the canteen trucks located a couple of blocks away. When Derek and Fish returned, Donald, Brows and Jerry Nagle took their turn and joined the lengthy line of wet, sweaty and dirt stained jakes. As usual, people from various fire companies were harassing each other. At times like these, when most of the work was being done from outside with heavy stream devices, there was less danger than operating inside. The possibility of an additional collapse was, of course, always a factor, but generally speaking, the force could be kept at a reasonable safe distance. The two original fire buildings had, in fact, collapsed in a huge heap, but nobody was endangered when it happened. After the fire intensified briefly when the floors and roofs tumbled , it soon quieted down in those areas as the big streams were able to strike the uncovered sections more effectively.

Donald wished he had a tape recorder as he listened to the cast of characters from the different districts and divisions jibing at each other. Dot-head Doherty and Gap Keefe were shouting at Cueball Justice, and he in turn was jabbing away at Swishy Baron from Engine 3, who was trying to goose Holy Lynch from the Lighting Plant. Poor Lynch felt most fire fighters were corrupted and doomed to perdition. He spent most of his time praying for their souls, but, he actually believed it was a hopeless cause.

Jerry Nagle, who had his own wry sense of humor said, "Hey boss. This is really a big fire."

"How can you tell, smart ass?" Donald responded.

Nagle smiled and said, " 'Cause the four heads are here."

"Who?"

"Just look at this line. There's Hydrant Head Kurpinski, Fish Head O'Farrell, Empty Head Steadly and Bucket Head Buchanan. That's a lotta heads and they're from four different districts. Why I even saw B.P. Bernstein here. He's from out in Readville, so you know this is big stuff. He probably hasn't been this far in town in years."

Donald grimaced, shook his head and said, "O.K., I'll bite. What the fuck does B.P. stand for?" which was exactly what Jerry was waiting for.

"Boy, you don't know shit. You never heard of Broken Promises Bernstein?" Donald waited patiently for what he knew was going to be pure fiction. "Sure. That's why he's out on Forty-nine. He used to be on Thirty-three in the Back Bay and he got hooked up with more of those co-eds from Berklee and B.U. You know, in the good weather, there's a regular parade of female talent from those schools passin' by quarters over there. He was always gettin' engaged. Then he'd meet someone else. Finally, one dame's father showed up one night and, after he had a long talk with the captain of the house, B.P. was transferred—for his own safety—I might add, the next time orders came out."

Donald was staring at the culprit Nagle was talking about. He had to be the homeliest guy on the job. He was short, stoop shouldered and had a nose that never quit. He also had a bad case of acne and was shuffling along, looking like the original Sad Sack. "You know, Jerry, you must think I just came off a farm somewhere. That guy couldn't attract Miss Piggy."

"I'm tellin' you, Luft, he's got hidden talents...if you know what I mean."

Donald stepped out of line and tapped the forlorn looking jake on the shoulder, "Hey, pal," he said, "you look familiar. What's your name?" The guy looked around, wondering what he had done wrong. "Er, Lieutenant, I'm Thomas Quentin, sir, Engine 49." Donald was surprised to hear the guy call him an officer until he remembered the temporary shield he had on his helmet. "Oh, O.K. Thomas. Nice to meet you." He looked back at Nagle, who was by now near the head of the line, but before Donald could say a word, Jerry said, "They even made him change his name when he went out there, Lufty. Do you want cream and sugar?" Donald wrapped his hand around the back of Nagle's neck and squeezed. "You are full of shit. Just cream, thank you."

While the fire was contained, because of the size and number of buildings involved, the companies were still operating by the time the shift changed at 0800. It would be another twenty-four hours before the last of the detailed companies were finally dismissed. Donald's crew rode back to quarters in one of the relieving jakes car. After showering and having coffee, Donald packed his gear into the trunk of his car and took his leave of Brows, Nagle, Fish and Burton. He was pleased as he started to drive away when Brows said, "If this Grimes don't work out, we'll bring you back." Since Brennan actually worshiped his regular officer, Donald knew he was kidding, but it sounded good to hear this crusty veteran sound like he had accepted him.

Ten

During the next six months Donald came to appreciate how lucky he had been to spend a few months acting on one company. He now became a gypsy like most of the other temporary officers were. He didn't stay more than two weeks in any berth, replacing officers who were off duty for injuries, illness or administrative absences. While it was a nuisance to live out of the trunk of his car, he had to admit it gave him a much better knowledge of how the department operated. During the four years he had been in one house, he had come to believe that every house was about the same. It became apparent during his sojourn that he had been mistaken.

Not that there was anything particularly wrong with other houses, but in reality, every place has its own flavor. Some houses are great and at least the equal of the one he left; others seemed bland, without much personality. And a couple of places he couldn't wait to leave. He was able to determine that this was usually related to the leadership of the house and the fire companies. Not every captain or lieutenant was a superstar; nor did they all have the same gung-ho attitude he had seen on his own work group. There were guys who never cared if they went to a fire and just really wanted to put their time in and go home. But, there were also others, no matter what house he went to, who wanted to work all the time. They are the type that make a company succeed at operations and are a joy to work with.

Like all other floaters, Donald felt a little uncomfortable filling in and sometimes wished he hadn't studied, particularly when he was required to discipline somebody. He didn't actually encounter any real serious problems, but there was always something that needed correcting. The jake who irritated him the most was one who spent most of his time in bed. They called him "Numb-nuts" because he always seemed to be in a fog. Donald knew he wouldn't have much luck correcting this long standing problem during his brief stay and chose to ignore the fact that the guy laid in the rack except when he was required to respond to alarms, drill, do company in service inspections, patrol desk watches and house work. He really had no interest in anything except reading paperbacks and watching late night TV.

One morning, however, as Donald was in the hallway on the second floor, he was starting his tour of the house to see how the work was progressing. He glanced into the bunkroom and there was his champion, stretched out in bed, one leg crossed over the other, reading the paper. It was 0830 hours. The guy glanced at him and turned another page, concentrating on the sports page. Donald felt his face redden, turned and went back to his office. He sat there for a few moments trying to regain his composure. He wanted to go in, flip the bed and dump this shithead on his ass. But, he realized one thing—if he did that, he'd not only be admitting he had lost his temper, he'd probably be charged with some kind of assault. He knew he had to do something because this was a challenge he couldn't ignore. He was looking for some kind of inspiration and, as he glanced around the room, he spotted a can of simonize. It flashed into his head how when Captain Turner took over Engine 10 he had the whole company do over the pumper, not that it really needed it, but as a form of indicating the type of leadership he wanted to project for his tenure.

Donald pressed the house phone button to the patrol desk. When the jake on watch answered, he told him to have the guy report to his room. The announcement came promptly, "Hey, Numby, report to the officer's room, immediately."

At least five minutes passed before Donald heard a knock on the door. By then, he was mad all over again because of the delay. The guy was just defying him. "Come in," he said. The jake frowned as he entered. He was in his mid-forties, and Donald had found out by looking at his record that he had been on the job for ten years. He had his hands in his pockets as he yawned and said, "Whaddya want?"

"What do you think I want, Thayer?"

The jake smirked. "I supposed to be a fuckin' mind reader?"

Donald ground his teeth. "OK, Tell me why you aren't doing your housework, just like everyone else?"

Thayer shook his head before he answered, "Why don't you just collect your extra dough and stay in your room? You new world beaters come on, get a little lucky on an exam and think you're gonna run the world. Relax, kid, the fuckin' job's been goin' on for a coupla hundred years and it'll be here after you and me is gone."

Donald had been anticipating such a response. "Sit down," he ordered, "right there!" and he pointed to the barrel shaped wooden captain's chair. Thayer slouched down and glared at him. "Well, I have to admit, you're right. I did get lucky on the exam, although I think I studied my ass off. But, whether I did or I didn't, if you think I intend to take any cheap shit from you, you've got the wrong idea." He paused. "Yep, they're payin' me to do what I'm doing, just like they're paying you. Now, I know I'll be out of here in a week or so, but while I'm here, you better get used to doing what I tell you, in the house and at fires." Thayer started to speak but Donald held up his hand. He passed him the can of polish and said, "I am now giving you a direct order. Report to the main floor. I want you to start shining that pump, commencing with the cab. Keep doing it until I tell you to quit."

Thayer laughed nervously. "What are you fuckin' crazy? You'll make me look like an asshole. What if I don't do it?"

Donald walked over to the door, glanced outside to make sure no one was listening and said, "You already are an asshole, brother. You know when I was doing all that studying, one thing I learned really fucking well was the Progressive Discipline Guidelines. If you don't do exactly what I tell you, I will start the process to charge you with a violation of the code. And, I'll keep adding counts until I leave here. Because believe me when I tell you, I really don't give a shit about *you*, but I care about the job."

Thayer grabbed the can and stormed out the door and Donald breathed a sigh of relief. He felt a little nausea and was already questioning whether he had handled this correctly. He started going over what he had done and what he could have done, agonizing over his first attempt to discipline another jake. A knock came on his door and he shouted, "Come in." He was startled to see that it was Thayer. "What do you want now?" he asked.

"Wanna talk to you for a minute, Luft." He sank back down into the chair, looking much more subdued than he had during his initial visit, "Lissen, Holden," he began, "I, er, don't wanna do that polishing job." When Donald started to speak, Thayer said, "Wait a minute, will ya. I, er, I don't wanna look that bad in front of the troops. I got some kind of a reputation around here. It ain't a good one, but I don't wanna lose it. Know what I mean?"

Donald sat there for a few moments and finally said, "Well, what do you suggest? I'm not going to let you ignore my orders."

"Lookit," he said, "I'll do my housework right now. And, the rest of the time you're here, I won't give you no shit. I'll do what ever you want. But, please, don't embarrass me this way."

Donald nodded at the proposal and said, "O.K. Get going." Thayer almost smiled and walked quickly out of the room, gently closing the door.

Donald was so relieved he actually felt a weakness in his legs. He had a distaste for the entire incident and wished it hadn't occurred; but it made him understand what Billy Simpson had told him during one of their talks at Castle Island. The retired deputy, philosophizing about the duties of an officer, had said, "A new guy getting promoted probably doesn't realize it at first but he can find out the easy way or the hard way. Once you become an officer, they ain't gonna love you anymore, if they ever did. Oh, they may grow to admire and respect you, based on your treatment of them and how you perform at fires, but, you're still a boss." He continued, "So, if you want to play up to them and mother them, hoping to look like their best friend, they can read that like a book. They'd much rather you just treat them fair and be consistent with what you do. No favoritism. Treat everyone the same. But, when you tell them to do something, make sure they do it." He went on to explain that when he was a fire fighter he had worked for a captain who was completely unpredictable. One day he'd be so solicitous of everyone he'd make them nervous because they knew that it wouldn't be long before he'd become a tyrant and nothing would satisfy him.

"Whatever happened to him?" asked Donald.

"Nothing. He did his whole career and retired, acting just the same until he left. He could never understand why guys kept transferring outta his house. As a matter of fact, he was even kind of surprised they didn't have a going away party for him when he left. What he never found out was that they did. They just didn't invite him."

The rest of his stay in that house was uneventful. Thayer didn't become friendlier, nor did Donald enjoy working with him. It was an armed truce. Thayer did his job and didn't put as much time in bed, but he never showed much enthusiasm for anything either. At one of his other assignments, one of the officers said, "Howja like working with that asshole, Thayer?" Donald was noncommittal in his reply. "Well," said the lieutenant, "he came on the job like a world beater. He took a couple of promotional exams and flunked. Never studied, for cripes sake. But he felt he got screwed and has had a chip on his shoulder ever since. He ain't the only one. Some of them just can't understand the effort it takes and so they can't accept the fact that non-geniuses like us can beat them."

During this period, Donald had continued taking the required courses to become an EMT and, at the end of the sessions, passed both the written technical and practical tests and got his certificate. It was fortunate that he did, because, with his detail to several engine companies, he was much more confident when they were dispatched to medical calls and really felt he was making a contribution in helping to save the lives of citizens.

He worked at a variety of different fires and on different companies, including engines, trucks and, for a week on Rescue 1, back in his own quarters. In early June he responded after midnight on Engine 8, located in the North End of downtown, to cover at Engine 5 in East Boston on the report of a fire on Putnam Street. Before entering the Callahan Tunnel to cross under the harbor the chief ordered a second alarm struck on Box 6167 and they were ordered to go directly to the fire. When they exited the tunnel in District One, a third alarm was being transmitted as they regained radio contact. Heavy smoke, sparks and brands were filling the night sky as they sped up Chelsea Street to the location on Putnam Street. They were directed by the chief's aide to set up a portable heavy stream appliance in a rear yard. The fire had originated in two vacant, wooden three deckers, both of which were in a state of partial collapse when they arrived. The fire had already entered three other buildings, one more on Putnam and two around the corner on Bremen Street. Donald and his crew, one member leading with the lightweight gun, advanced down a narrow alley to the rear, dragging their hose, and climbed over a five foot fence to get into position. In a short period of time, they had one two and a half inch line connected and filled and were delivering a stream onto the rear porches of one of the structures. The pressure was inadequate, so they ran another line of the same size into the gun. It took a while to accomplish this task, but the results were dramatically different. They could see the powerful force the two lines created, and the effect it was having. Pretty soon they were not only killing a lot of fire, but actually peeling away part of the roof covering over the porches, as well as stripping some of the asphalt siding that had been burning vigorously.

They were soon joined by other companies responding to the eight alarms that were struck and the combined actions finally cut off the extension. It was a great job in a neighborhood where any delay could have resulted in a conflagration. When they were given a relief to go and get coffee, Donald made a point of observing the location of the mass of equipment. Some companies had used hydrant assist valves to increase the supply and others relayed lines from three blocks away. Four aerial ladders, as well as the Tower Unit were strategically placed and the elevated streams were very effective.

It was a very warm night, and, when they were dismissed around 0700, the sun was already making it clear that summer was finally coming. Donald felt great returning to quarters. They had complied with the orders they had been given and he was pleased to note that the jakes he was working with on this company were just as eager as any he had seen in his own house. He reflected how difficult it would be to express the tremendous feeling of accomplishment jakes got on the completion of a successful operation. They had just helped save a whole neighborhood!

He was also pleased to see that Engine 8, just like Ten, the Tower and the Rescue, were just as effective in scrounging donuts from the local shop on the way back to quarters. Yeah, it sure can be great at times. Fuck Thayer.

The expected promotions took place in June, and there were others in July and September. When these were completed, Donald was now number one on the list; his promotion should come in early November.

He reflected on the strange period he had been going through, not exactly an officer and moving from house to house. Well, while it was unlikely he'd get a permanent berth for a while after he was sworn in, at least he'd have the job permanently. It is a major step in anyone's career and he was fully aware of it.

He, Gena and Nancy escaped for a long weekend over Columbus Day in October and went to Harwich Port on Cape Cod, staying in a large motel equipped with both an indoor and outdoor pool. The weather was wonderful, warmer than usual for the early fall. The summer season crowds had thinned out considerably, as it always did after Labor Day, and they had their choice of many great restaurants.

Nancy was in the pool as soon as it opened. She had made another two week visit to Gap Keefe, his wife Marion, daughter Bethany and son, Fred Jr.., back in July at their place in New Hampshire. Since then, though, her activities had been confined to the South Boston Yacht Club's junior program. Nancy treated this trip like a well-deserved holiday. They not only visited Provincetown and went on a whale watch cruise, they also took the ferry over to Martha's Vineyard and spent a day at the beach, remaining for dinner on the waterfront and returning on the last boat. The moon and stars were bright as they crossed Vineyard Sound, and Donald felt really relaxed for the first time since he had begun his acting assignments months earlier. It was a wonderful break for all of them.

Nancy fell asleep as soon as they got back to the motel and her parents repaired to the lounge where a woman piano player played softly as the half dozen couples moved across the small floor. Gena and Donald talked about his coming change of status while they sipped chardonnay. They both reflected on how the job had changed their lives and wondered pensively what the future would hold for them. It was a wonderful evening and they enjoyed the romantic music as well as dancing to slower rhythms than they were used to when they went out with their friends at home.

When he reported to the Personnel Division for assignment the day after they returned, he was notified that he was to be promoted on November 1st. Wow. They always said, never believe anything they tell you until you read it in orders, but this sounded like it was for real. He was instructed to go to the Clothing Department to get an order for being measured for an officer's uniform. It wouldn't be ready for some time, but he was to pick up some white dress shirts and wear one to the promotion ceremonies at Memorial Hall in the headquarters complex.

George, the jake in charge of clothing, has become something of a legend in the department largely because of his friendly demeanor, but also because he always manages to slip in an extra Tee shirt or shoulder patch or a dress hat or shirt. He must be a whiz at creating his budget requests annually because most jakes leave his office smiling. And, he has a great memory. As soon as Donald stepped into the cramped enclosure that served as an office, George said, "Hey Donald, you back already, huh? Seems like last week I was suiting you up as an FFOP. Time flies doesn't it? Let's see, sixteen and a half oughta do it." He handed over a box of shirts, marked "Dress White/Short Sleeve" and had Donald sign a receipt. He then handed him a blue slip authorizing him to go to a clothing firm that had this year's contract to be measured for a dress uniform. As he was leaving the section, Donald paused to study the huge, glass enclosed series of bulletin boards that lined the hallway. George was forever collecting shoulder patches from fire deferments all over the world and he displayed them in the area near the medical examiner's office. Jakes who had been injured and were reporting to the doctor for their required weekly visit spent time reviewing the inventive and colorful identification markers, but most preferred the Boston patch that had been established some thirty years ago. Donald grinned as he thought about it. Someone like Thayer wouldn't care what kind of tag they put on him, as long as that paycheck kept showing up each week.

The swearing in ceremony at Memorial Hall—the same place he'd been sworn in when he came on the job—was great. It was also quite a reunion, what with Desmond and Andy Novak making captain and Donald, Goat Hitchcock, Cassius Murphy and Rick Foster all being appointed lieutenant on the same day. Each member was allowed to bring his family and guests so the Memorial Hall was almost filled to capacity. The chief of operations made a congratulatory speech and then the fire commissioner, in full dress uniform, had them all raise their hands and repeat the oath after him. He told them how proud he was of each member who had the desire and the fortitude to make what was at least a year long commitment to study for the exam. He also told them that because of the system in the department, they didn't owe anyone anything. It was a competitive contest and they were being promoted in the order they had finished. He also congratulated their wives and families for cooperating with the members by allowing them to put in the essential time required to cover the mounds of material they had to learn in order to compete as well as they had. Finally, he advised all of them to continue with their efforts. They had already proven they could do it and, besides the responsibility they had chosen to accept as a leader, the financial rewards were also a major factor.

Each member was then given their hat and devices. Their wives were invited to pin on the shiny new badges while the department photographer clicked away, making certain the procedures were documented. The commissioner made himself available for pictures with all of them and then a luncheon was served to finish off the memorable event.

Donald and Gena had a wonderful reunion with every one of the new promotees and their families, because, actually, they knew all of them. Donald was extremely happy to see Goat Hitchcock and Cassius Murphy because even though they had been his classmates in drill school, they had hardly ever run into each other at fires since they had graduated. It was a heartwarming day. That evening, Donald and his two ladies completed the celebration by dining at the Bay Towers at the top of the highest office building on State Street, downtown. Nancy squealed with delight when they were seated at the huge picture windows which gave a panoramic view of the city down below, as well as the airport, harbor, Quincy Market and the Customhouse. When Donald finally went to bed, he reflected on all that had happened to him since his appointment and throughout his years as a fire fighter. Well, that was all behind him and a new adventure would be starting in the morning. Wonder where I'll be five years from now!

Eleven

Donald was pleased with his first assignment as an actual fire lieutenant. Of course, it would only be temporary because he was still in the pool and would continue rotating from house to house until his turn came and he got a permanent berth. As with the promotion, this was done in order, and while it was still somewhat uncomfortable, he knew his day would come.

In the meantime, he wouldn't mind staying where he had been sent for quite a while. It was to Engine 50 in the Charlestown section of District Three. He was filling in for a lieutenant who had been injured during a seven alarm fire in Chinatown; he wouldn't be back for at least a month. Fifty is a very famous company in the department for many reasons. It is a single engine company house in the mile square community, and is one of three fire companies located in the town. It is probably as good a place to serve as any house in the department. The morale in the place is always at a high level. The captain has been there for almost two decades and is well known, not only as a good jake, but as a man who takes care of his troops. While he himself doesn't live in the district, most of his members do. And all of them have a lot of experience because they've been on the job for many years before they can transfer into the station. All transfers are by seniority, so most of these jakes waited patiently for years to get "back home" to the town and they really appreciate being there. They are a most cooperative bunch who know what to do and do it without complaint; so Donald didn't expect any personnel problems during this stay.

One other major factor that contributed to the morale of the unit dated back to the beginning of the eighties. At that time, the fire department was decimated because of enormous budget cuts that were imposed by an unfriendly city administration. Twenty-two fire companies were deactivated, some districts were eliminated and many young jakes were laid off. One of the companies that was put out of business was Engine 50. The usual procedure was that all members who weren't being terminated were transferred elsewhere and their apparatus was removed and the building boarded up. This time, however, it didn't work out that way. The people of the neighborhood, including many wives of fire fighters, took over the property and refused to let the apparatus be taken away. Citizens manned the station twenty-four hours a day and couldn't be evicted. They generated tremendous publicity over the next few months, just as a fire company in Brooklyn had done when the FDNY faced similar cuts. Fifty's quarters became known as "Peoples Fire House #2", and it was a tremendous demonstration of the strength and determination of the people in the community. Needless to say, the mayor eventually gave in and ordered the company restored to service and the entire district celebrated. They also have long memories and it was probably a smart move when the mayor chose not to run for what would have been a fifth term, a couple of years later. Their opposition served as a beacon of encouragement at the time, and within a year, all of the laid off jakes city-wide were brought back on the job through the efforts of the fire fighters' union leadership.

Along with all of these other factors, Fifty is a company that goes to many major fires because they are assigned to most multiple alarm responses on the running cards which list the units dispatched to all building fires in the city. They also are a designated Mutual Aid unit and spend a lot of time at fires in towns outside of Boston, particularly in Chelsea, which experiences many serious incidents during the year. It is one of the poorest cities in the country and has a fire department that has been understaffed as long as anyone can remember.

The firehouse itself is over a hundred years old but has been completely renovated and continues to be a neighborhood focal point. It is unlikely anyone will ever attempt to eliminate this place in the foreseeable future. What mayor needs that kind of grief?

When Donald reported, he was relieving the captain and they had a nice chat. It seems that this guy, like so many others, had worked with his uncle Frank on Engine 22 and he was another admirer of this legendary jake. He showed Donald around the house with great pride, including his storage locker of replacement equipment for the company. Donald was amazed at the number of new nozzles, lights, spanners, wrenches and other gear that was systematically arranged in the walk-in closet. When he mentioned it to the captain, the officer smiled, "Been here a long time, Luft. Got a couple of friends up the street. They know I'll put this stuff to good use. Keep that in mind when you become a captain. The department buys a lot of gear every year, and, just like the military, there's always a little extra, if you know how to get a hold of it." He mentioned there was another room in the basement with plenty of hose and paint. When they looked over the gleaming pumper, one of the newest ones in the department, Donald remarked that there seemed to be an awful lot of feeder line arranged in the hose bed.

"Well, son, we go out of town a lot. Never know when you have to make an extra long stretch into a fire. If we do, we got it." After the captain left, the jakes with whom Donald was working explained that in order to get the latest pump into quarters—since the building had been constructed back when horses pulled the apparatus—the captain had managed to get the doorways redesigned and elevated to accept the ten foot travel height of the apparatus. Donald, who kept his journal with him in his travel kit, made a few notes that day that weren't about fire fighting. Nope, he thought, as he scribbled away, this is about management and common sense.

There was no difficulty getting the jakes to do their housework. Everyone, including the member assigned to patrol duties, hung out in the kitchen at the back of the house. Over the course of the years, they had surreptitiously installed an extension of the alarm system, public and department phones into their haven so no one was ever lonely on watch. They just all remained in the kitchen when they weren't doing something else. It is a neat clubhouse where most local, national and international policies and politicians, and all the local sports teams are scrupulously dissected and sometimes totally eviscerated.

Donald was pleased to see on his first tour that at 0815 the jakes headed for their house work assignments without complaint and before he finished doing his morning report and other paper chores, everything was completed. By the time the boss of the District, Chief Marty Kinsella arrived, the place looked spotless. In one of the deactivations that occurred well over a decade and a half ago, the Charlestown district chief was eliminated and the three companies were added to downtown, District Three, located just across the High Bridge. This resulted in eleven companies being assigned to one on duty district chief; the paperwork is more than double that of most other districts. Consequently, when the on duty chief stopped by, he wanted all of the submissions of reports to headquarters to be ready because he had a lot of other stops on his route. Donald was well aware of that requirement and was waiting at the door for the boss when he arrived.

Kinsella surprised him, however, by stopping for coffee and talking at great length to the on-duty crew. Some of them had to be almost as old as the chief, and the relaxed atmosphere made Donald think that all of these jakes had been through many difficult times together and that they must have been united in their common goals when they were fighting the political battles because they seemed to get along so well. Oh, they had their character, just like every other house and every other group. This one was called Fance. His name really was Francis Copeland, but his nickname came from his finicky and meticulous demeanor. He was the pump operator, and just like Brows Brennan, that truck was his baby. Maybe a little too much. He would polish it every day and couldn't stand it if someone was careless around his piece. Naturally, even in a friendly place like Fifty, a half filled coffee cup or a few orange peels would show up on the running boards just as he finished his chores and he'd be furious. Or someone would accidently turn on the garden hose and manage to spray a little water on Copeland. This would infuriate him because as soon as he had completed his house work, he'd shower and change, making certain the creases in his station uniform were knife-edged. If he was on patrol, he would stay inside the tiny office at the front of the house and greet the neighbors as they passed by, nodding to the men and bowing gracefully to the ladies. His nickname was actually Fancy Pants because he looked so perfect, but it had been shortened to Fance in the course of events.

In his youth he had spent a couple of years in a monastery, after serving as a medic in Nam, but he eventually left and came on the job when he discovered that not all the monks shared his views on neatness or silence either. He was looking for more military-like spit and polish and the fire department sure looked the part, whenever he saw the members marching in a parade or protesting to settle a labor dispute. To his dismay, once he was permanently assigned, he discovered that they weren't anywhere as neat as the religious folks—and their morals fell a little short of his expectations as well. But, he realized he had to work somewhere and maybe he could change the jakes he lived with by setting a fine example. Now, some twenty years later, all of his hopes had been dashed so he just settled in to complete his service, get his pension and then maybe have a delayed vocation into the priesthood. Goodness knows, he could spend the rest of his life praying for some of these jakes, especially Gigi Michlin. There is a man who spends all of his waking hours thinking and talking about women. He is in the throes of his third divorce and can't understand why. Fance thought that maybe if Gigi stopped ogling every woman that passed by the house, he'd have a better chance. At his last wedding, just a year ago, the members of the company attended the short ceremony by a justice of the peace, and as the happy couple was leaving the courthouse, Fance could see Gigi checking out the bridesmaids, probably looking for his next conquest. Yes, prayer was the only thing left for this hapless lout.

At 1342 hours that first day Box 7433 was struck for a fire on K Street, in District Six, South Boston. The location is just a block from a fire house and the first company at the scene reported heavy fire showing from the rear porches of a residential block. Within another minute the chief of the district reported a working fire and then ordered a second alarm struck. Fifty was out the door promptly and headed towards its covering assignment at an engine company's quarters in Southie. Long before they reached their destination, however, a third alarm was ordered and they were dispatched directly to the fire as part of the response.

When the deputy arrived he ordered a fourth alarm. He reported that a fire, which had originated in a first floor rear room of one occupancy, had extended out the back windows, igniting the wooden porches and then had taken off. He described the structure as a three and a half story building of brick and wood construction. It was the fourth unit of a block that included twelve such occupancies. There was a common cockloft, five feet high that ran unbroken from one end of the block to the other. When these buildings were erected at the end of the nineteenth century, the brick walls that divided each residence terminated at the top of the third floor, thus leaving the wide open space overhead. A grandfather clause in the building and fire codes prevented the department from having the proper protection installed. While there had been a few multiple alarms in the block over the years, none had extended any further than three units. Today, the ignition of the porches and a high wind, along with the rapid upward extension through the interior of the building to the cockloft, created a much more serious problem.

As Fance deftly maneuvered Fifty down K Street from East Broadway, Donald could see heavy smoke rolling across the street and was startled to see charred pieces of wood and shingles twirling through the air towards them. Fance stopped at a hydrant that already had a four inch feeder line extending towards the fire over a block away. Donald told him to stand by there with Gigi and commence making a connection to the Hydrant Assist Valve. It was obvious they couldn't advance the pump any closer because of the apparatus and hose blocking further passage on the narrow street. He shouted to

Fance, as he started jogging down the street with Tony Scotia and Mike Kurpeski, the remainder of his crew, "Don't hook up yet, Fance, in case they want us somewhere else. But be ready." The pump operator waved acknowledgment and began getting ready for the connection.

At the intersection of Fifth Street, where the block began, there was so much smoke banking down into the street, it was difficult to make out the fronts of the buildings. But, through the haze Donald spotted the deputy's aide, Hank Greenfield. "Luft, he wants a big line, off anyone to the rear of the buildings and down the alley. They're throwing ladders out there now." Donald nodded and turned to look for an engine company from which they could run a big line. Mike Kurpeski was at the rear of a pump, starting to pull a line off before Donald gave him an order. Tony Scotia had a two and half inch combination nozzle tucked under his arm. He had anticipated what was going to happen and took it from Fifty's pump when they arrived.

Donald raced up to the alley. It was about eight feet wide and ran from Fifth Street to Sixth Street. He looked up at the buildings and could see the fire had not only gained control of several porches, it had also entered the top floor and lofts of the adjoining buildings. Heavy smoke, under great pressure was pushing out of the eaves of the entire block.

A multiple alarm district chief directed Fifty to run a big line, which was already being dragged by Mike and Tony, up over a thirty-five foot ladder into the third floor of the second building from the corner. He said, "Luft, it's already into the one on your right. Try to cut it off, but watch yourself. That cockloft overhead might be gone already." He also told Donald that another line had been started up the one stairway in the building from the front. "Protect each other up there, but be ready to bail out if we tell you."

Other fire companies were arriving at the scene and being given assignments as the fire had now grown to a seventh alarm response. The line they were starting to advance up the rungs of the ladder to the balcony fire escape became easier to drag as someone around the corner was providing additional slack. Tony climbed over the iron railing onto the metal flooring, the nozzle hanging down over his chest. Donald landed beside him and took his helmet, smashed it into the top pane of the blackened window and ducked to the side as brown smoke billowed out and vented upward. In a matter of moments, they had cleaned out both windows that were accessible from their position and, after tearing the curtains and shades from the rods, dropped onto a narrow bed in the room. The visibility wasn't too bad at this point and there was no fire in the room, although they could feel heat coming from somewhere. Donald ordered the line to be charged before they advanced any further and, as they waited, he could hear all kinds of sounds. Breaking glass, an axe pounding overhead, the sounds of a power saw somewhere in the distance. He went through the room and found a hallway connecting to other rooms both front and back.

Tony shouted he had water and he and Mike, along with a district chief's aide, stretched the stiffened line and moved after Donald into the corridor. As they were slipping on their facepieces, the last thing Donald saw was a broad streak of brown immediately discoloring the ceiling of the room they had just exited. "Shit," he thought, "it's behind us."

He pounded Tony on the shoulder and said, through his facepiece, "Turn around and open the pipe into the bedroom." Suddenly, they were completely enveloped by smoke and heat. They could hear the sound of the falling plaster and strapping in the room. Tony opened the pipe fully as they all were driven flat to the floor. Donald leaned into him and helped him to hold the nozzle. The pressure was more than adequate, but it took the two of them to control the force that was surging into the overhead. Back and forth, back and forth, they kept sweeping the line, pouring 250 gallons per minute upward.

Mike moved up beside him and Donald wriggled along the hallway. He could see daylight coming through the windows of the next room, but, once again, the stain appeared and he knew this ceiling would drop as well. He pressed the button on his remote mike and reported to the chief that they needed another line right away or they'd have to retreat. The same chief who had directed them up the ladder, replied, "Ten is on the stairway from the front. It should be to your left. See if you can locate them. If not, shut down your line and get out."

Donald found the stairway just beyond the second room and to his left. Great! He could see Grimes and Brows Brennan halfway between the second and third. "Ten," he yelled, "get your water, will ya. We got plenty of fire here." Grimes answered, "On the way. Just show us where you want it." The sound of air escaping from the open pipe was music to Fifty's crew's ears and, in few minutes, Ten was working one room while they worked the other. Now Donald wanted to check for further extension behind them, leading to the Fifth Street side, while Tony, Mike and the aide kept plugging upward at the ceiling and into the loft. Thank God, thought Donald, the water hitting up above prevented their charged line from burning or they really would have been screwed.

He couldn't find any evidence of fire spread towards the end of the block, but a ladder company crew arrived behind Ten and the officer had his jakes open all the overhead ceilings in the hallway and beyond. Ten had managed to find a short ladder that led directly into the loft and, when Donald crawled up beside them to take a look, he was startled. As far as he could see, there was badly charred wood extending along the length of the space. Fire companies were operating lines over half way down and maybe even further, but the now lightening smoke prevented him from seeing any further.

Gigi came up the front stairs and gave Tony and Mike a spell operating the line, which now was only operating half-gated to reduce the pressure. Donald took the two jakes out into a front room where they could look down on the scene. The commissioner had assumed command early in the fire and was talking to reporters from the print and TV media. What impressed Donald and his crew the most was the number of aerials that had been crowded into the narrow area to provide overhead ventilation throughout the block as well as access for hose lines to the upper floors. The Tower had also been well placed and he could see his old crew hooking rakes onto the protruding window frames in the pitched roof, opening them up so they could wash down the glowing embers.

When overall control was finally gained, Donald took his jakes and walked, hunched over, the length of the cockloft. He realized there were probably very few buildings in the entire city that had been constructed in this manner, so many years ago and he wanted to learn all he could before they left. The fire had extended to seven buildings through the loft and had dropped down into the third floor of five of them, just as they had in the one Fifty had entered. Some of the stairways from the second floor right up to the loft had been burned out and collapsed. It was a tremendous loss of property in a very stable, tree lined neighborhood and there were many distraught residents milling around in the crowd on the opposite sidewalks.

Of course, now that the job was almost over, up where the companies were the usual chatter was going on. Guys from other companies and other districts, even though they were stationed a long distance from Charlestown, knew all about Gigi and his latest marriage difficulties. "Hey, Golden Balls," yelled Eddie Knowles, the pipeman on Twenty-one, "why don'tcha give up on broads. Get together with the Fance, shave your heads and go to Tibet. No dames, no sex, no alimony. You don't even have to talk to each other. Just keep chanting."

Gigi was offended. "Eddie, you been married to the same woman ever since drill school. Must be pretty boring. I, on the other hand, am striving for perfection. When I find it, you'll be the first jerk I'll show it to." Another voice off in the haze said, "I seen a bumper sticker the other day that said, 'If you've been married to Gigi, beep three times.' There was fuckin' horns blowing everywhere. Keep lookin' and keep payin', Lothario." Gigi tried to worm his way through the crowd to find the rude fire fighter but never made it to the source of the voice.

When they were finally dismissed, Donald was thrilled when both the commissioner and Deputy Franklin told him they had done a good job. The big boss said Fifty's line had cut it off on that end and saved the last building in the block. At the other end, Rescue Two and another engine company had held their ground in the loft. As a result, five homes were spared in what seemed like a hopeless task in the beginning.

As they walked up the street toward the pump, the aide to the district chief said, "Hey, Luft, my boss says your pump operator got on that Hydrant Assist Valve just in time. There was about four big lines running outta water and your guy filled them all."

Donald spent the next few weeks on the company and really didn't have any serious fires during the period. A few dumpsters, a few stolen vehicle fires and a covering job in the city of Everett on Mutual Aid. Just routine work. But, he was so pleased to learn what an experienced fire company could do under difficult conditions. Hooking up the pump was great, but the way his line had been advanced so rapidly was a bonus. And they brought the pipe with them, *without* him ordering it. Most of all, when they were up in the hallway and the ceilings dropped behind them, that was really hairy, but no one panicked. They just kept moving that line, killing the fire and protecting themselves. Boy, I love it. And how about the characters, Fance and Gigi, or Golden Balls as he is also called. As a contrast, Tony and Mike, who are about as normal as anyone I've met. Yeah, but they know how to stir up their two friends, just for practice when things get a little boring. I'm jotting down each one of them in my notebook. If I keep this up, by the time I retire, I'll have a list of characters no one will believe.

Thanksgiving and Christmas came and went without any of the usual tragedies that seem to occur around the holiday season. Donald was bounced to several companies, including ladders and engines. He was starting to feel like a will o' the wisp. Bring your gear, meet your crew, do your paper work, respond wherever they send you, pack up and move out. He was pleased at the number of jakes he already knew no matter where he was assigned, but it sure would be nice to get his own berth.

The winter—in contrast to the record breaking snows and severe cold of the previous year—was quite mild. The accumulation of snow was only measured in inches rather than the nine feet recorded in 1995-96. As a matter of fact, in the middle of January it warmed up so much for a few days that the golf nuts in the house to which he was detailed headed out to the city course at Franklin Park following a night tour of duty. The next day they worked they were complaining that they had to wait for a starting time. It seems jakes and anyone else who could skip their day jobs were not letting this temperature bonus slip past.

Donald was notified to report to the Personnel Division as January, 1997 drew to a close. He was a little surprised because he still had a week to go filling in for a lieutenant in Brighton. When he was admitted to the deputy's office he knew something was up. Deputy Fire Chief Stephen Lawton was seated behind the main desk with District Fire Chief Andrew Polin standing at his shoulder. Both men were smiling and gazing down at some papers spread out before them.

Both of these chiefs had been promoted to their present ranks about a year earlier. As happens constantly when the newest gain their ranks, they get assignments that are being vacated by other bosses who can't wait to get back to the field from headquarters. It's almost become a tradition that the most junior—or new ducks—go to personnel. The reasons are obvious. They become responsible for maintaining the ever changing assignments of all personnel in a department of over sixteen hundred. They also monitor members absent from duty on sick or injured leave, each of whom must report to the personnel chiefs once a week unless they are physically unable to do so.

But, they also get to meet and dislike the "five percenters". These are the real fuck-ups on the job who are constantly in trouble. When they eventually have to face charges for serious infractions that can no longer be handled in the field, they'll show up here. Or when they are AWOL or end up in jail for being drunk or disorderly, personnel will find out about them. A few have been involved in robberies, rapes, and once in a while, even a murder or two. These folks are usually discharged following a department trial, but like all legal activities, it takes time with charges, counter charges, appeals, etc. They're called "five percenters" because that is the percentage of jakes who constantly "surface on the computer" at personnel. They are mostly repeaters. Donald remembered having a discussion with Billy Simpson on the subject during their conversations at Castle Island. The retired deputy was well aware of the term and said, "In a way we're pretty lucky. Five percent isn't as large as the fuck-ups in other jobs. Most of our jakes are pretty good people. Oh, even a normal guy can make a mistake once in a while and that's when you have to temper justice with mercy. But, a real fuck-up? Don't waste your time worrying about him. He's on a count down to being fired anyway and you can only do so much rehab. We used to say that with all the breaks you get on the job, by the time a guy is bad enough to be fired, he really deserves it. By that time, even the union has given up, and when they do, just wave goodbye." He smiled and was quiet for a moment before he continued: "I used to agonize over a couple of my superstars when I was a new officer. I'll never forget one night, many years ago. I had this drunk who would be all right for a month or two and I'd think I was having success with the way I handled him. Then, sure enough, he'd end up shitfaced in the middle of a tour and I'd have trouble. One night he disappeared from the line during a cellar fire and we couldn't find him for a while. We almost got killed lookin' for that asshole." Donald asked if he had been injured badly. "Naw, I wish he was. We were scared shitless 'cause the fire was all around us. He was passed out in a corner with a stupid grin on his face."

Simpson described another time when his champion fell off the apparatus just as they were leaving quarters on a run. Landed on his head and knocked himself for a loop. When the company returned from the alarm, Simpson spent the rest of the night putting ice on his head and making sure he was breathing, at least.

"Jeez, Chief," said Donald, "why didn't you just take him to the hospital?"

Simpson laughed. "Well, I know it sounds stupid now, but if I did it would've meant serious charges for sure. I kinda felt sorry for him. He had served at Guadalcanal during World War II and probably had what they now call Post Traumatic Stress Syndrome. I'd been in the Pacific myself and had more compassion than I should have. He also had a wife and four kids, and I knew they'd suffer worse than he if he lost the job. Oh, I'd punish him in-house quite a bit—extra watches and house work—but it didn't really work. I mishandled the whole thing. But," he chuckled, "I was new and pretty stupid."

"Whatever happened to him?" asked Donald.

"A funny thing, but a good lesson for me. He was detailed to the ladder truck one night and we had a tough fire in a six story apartment house on Boylston Street. There were a lot of people hanging out the windows. The officer on the truck was raising as many ground ladders as he could to try to pick them off. He lost sight of our hero who actually went in a third floor window and got lost. Nobody knew he was missing until he was found by the captain of another company. He was wandering around in a corridor about half way back in a hundred foot deep building." Simpson described how he was taken out and removed in an ambulance. When the fire was knocked down, the deputy in charge went to the hospital to see him. This old boss was born in Ireland and was a rigid disciplinarian. When he smelled the booze on this jake, all his charitable demeanor disappeared. He was reported to have shouted, "I almost killed good men to find the likes of you. You are a besotten wretch. I will have you discharged from this job immediately."

Donald shook his head. "Wow. That's big stuff. So, was he let go?"

Simpson laughed loudly. "Naw, that's not how the job was in those days. The head of the union was Marty Pierce. He could charm just about anyone. He went to see the deputy, hat in hand, the next day they worked and described in great detail, the suffering the jake had gone through during the war. He waited for the inevitable question from the boss, 'Er, Marty, lad, what branch of the service was he in?' 'Why the U.S. Navy, sir.' Pierce wasn't sure if that was the case, but he knew the deputy had served with the Atlantic fleet himself during the war.'"Navy man, eh? Well, he's still a disgrace. But, get him out of my division and I won't pursue this incident. I never want to see him again.'"

When Donald asked what finally happened to this guy as the years passed, the deputy replied, "Well, what happened turned out to be the best lesson I ever had in handling jakes. His next boss was a tough captain out in Dorchester. The first time the guy screwed up, he told him that was it. One chance and the next one was charges. And the captain was a man of his word. The next violation he was suspended for a month. While he was off, he joined Alcoholics Anonymous. It was quite a transformation. He stayed dry for the rest of his life. This sounds like a fairy tale, but it's true. He eventually studied and became a lieutenant. Then he started getting jakes into the AA. He became the first leader of the program that evolved into our current Employees

Assistance Plan."

Simpson concluded his tale by telling Donald that he reflected on this case many times whenever it became necessary to discipline anyone. It was like a guideline for him throughout the rest of his own years on the job. "Donald," he said, "I could have cured that jake years earlier than it happened if I just had guts enough to come down hard on him in the beginning. It would have saved him and his family a lot of grief. I always admired that captain who hit him hard. He was the best friend the jake ever had." Simpson became friendly with the lieutenant as time went by, and he always remembered one particular thing this unusual man had told him: "When you're a drunk, *you* always come first. When I got paid, my bar bill came before my family. I was as selfish as could be. Once I stole change from my kids' piggy banks. They and my poor wife suffered a lot more than I did. Keep that in mind, my friend." Billy always did.

Donald found out the reason the bosses were smiling in short order. Chief Lawton said, "Holden, you're getting a good berth." Already? He didn't expect a permanent assignment for another year. "Here's the story, pal. Two deputies and two district chiefs are retiring. And, you know what that means—everyone moves up and out. As a matter of fact, Chief Polin and I are out of here next week and we couldn't be happier. But, you don't care about that."

He explained that the department was assigning four fire lieutenants to assume control of the department Command Post. This unit had previously been staffed by Fire Alarm Operators and responded to all major incidents to maintain communications. It had been determined over a long period of time that it would probably be wiser to have fire officers rather than civilian staff operating at the scene of incidents because, among other reasons, they had better job security if they became injured in the line of duty. In addition, their experience in fire fighting would be more valuable in performing the duties.

"So," said Lawton, "there's a lot of vacancies and a lot of people moving around next week. You, my friend, are going to Engine 22. The fact that we both worked with your Uncle Frank has very little to do with it. Just the luck of the draw." The two officers laughed as Donald saluted and stumbled out of the room. To get a berth this quick is a miracle. But, to get Twenty-two, required intervention less deified. Thanks Uncle Frank, I'll take it, he almost shouted as he flew down the steps and out to the parking lot.

He was so excited when he got home, Gena and Nancy couldn't

contain him. Neither of them attempted to interrupt him as he babbled on about his new assignment. They were both wise enough to understand that such enthusiasm would result, at the very least, in going out to dinner, and, sure enough, when his chatter died down, he said, "Hey, let's go get the biggest steak we can find." They nodded rapidly even though they were not big beef fans. They understood, though, that this man they loved would head for the Hilltop Steak House in Saugus, just north of the city. This restaurant is world famous because of the quality and the quantity of the meals they produce as well as their reasonable prices. At one time it was the largest single owner restaurant operation in the country. The two girls also knew that the menu was so varied, they could easily satisfy their desires for red meat alternatives. Heck, Donald wouldn't even notice what they ordered, he was so zeroed in on the news he had received.

It was a wonderful evening for the three of them. Of course, Nancy wanted to know if this meant they would no longer see the friends he had on the Tower during his years in that station. She was primarily concerned about her close relationship with Gap Keefe's daughter, Beth,—and of course her burgeoning interest in Fred, Jr..

Donald laughed softly before saying, "No, not at all, honey. This job is so much like a family. It's a pretty tight knit circle of people, and while you move around quite a bit in your career, particularly if you get promoted, you never lose touch with those jakes who are your close friends." He explained that with a few exceptions, you just didn't see them as much because you worked different shifts and in different districts, but guys like Gap, Rick Foster and Joe Desmond, you frequently get together with or just talk to them on the phone. It helps you retain your great memories. "I mean, look at me. I still see my first deputy, Mr. Simpson, and he's thirty years older than I am. But he's great. He knows so much about the job, and he seems to always have an upbeat approach, not only about work, but about life in general." He concluded by telling her that he expected to meet other equally interesting jakes, and that he expected his assignment to expand the number of his friends, as well as his knowledge of fire fighting.

When they returned home, his message machine indicated several calls. Even though the orders wouldn't be out for another day, the pipeline was in full working order and he heard from not only his friends in the Purchase Street house, but a couple of his drill school buddies as well. The second last call he returned was to Joe Desmond, his first company officer, who now was a captain in the personnel pool and was bouncing from place to place, just like Donald. Desmond congratulated him on his permanent berth and said, "Yeah. It's great. But, like everything else, there's good news and bad news. The good news is that you're going to Twenty-two. The bad news is a double header."

Oh, oh, thought Donald, the other shoe is going to drop. "What is it, Cap?" he asked.

"Well, Captain Dave Tilden is leaving. He's accepting an assignment in Personnel. He's had a lot of problems with arthritis in his back and he's gonna finish out his time up at the Pentagon."

Donald immediately felt a let down. This outstanding jake, with whom he had worked at so many fires, wouldn't be there to guide him along. He had become very fond of this well respected black officer. He remembered him from way back at Uncle Frank's funeral, but much more recently when Donald was buried in the debris on Newton Street and how Tilden not only began the attack that resulted in saving Donald's life, but ordered additional alarms and prompt medical assistance as well. His transfer would be a big loss to the company and the district. "What's the other bad news, Cap?" he asked.

"Oh," replied the officer, "the guy who's taking his place. What a stiff. He's one of those know it alls from the pool. Just because he was lucky on the last exam, now he thinks he's God's gift to the South End district."

Shit, thought Donald. Well, Chief Simpson told me they're not all perfect. "Who's that?" he asked apprehensively.

"Got it written down right here. Fire Captain Joseph Desmond. What a loser!"

Nancy was already fast asleep and Gena must have turned in as well because she wasn't in the living room or kitchen and the door to the master bedroom was closed. He had tell someone! He had jotted down the one remaining call from the machine and wasn't sure who it was, but dialed it anyway. When he identified himself, he knew instantly who it was by the piercing voice. Cueball Justice. "Hero Holden," shouted his friend. "Finally joining the real fire department. The South End jakes. And not only that, but the best company in the district. But, even more important, the best jake in the country, yours truly." Donald couldn't shut him up as he rattled on about how good he was. But, he wasn't sure he wanted to. He had always enjoyed the little twerp in drill school, and would never forget how shattered the usually self-assured redhead was when Donald was trapped.

The rumor-monger with all the inside dope kept chattering away:

"Oh, yeah, my good pal, Bad Ankles Brosnahan got transferred, too. So, Captain Tilden, being the genius he is, knew a dummy like you would need the best hoseman and more important, the best pump operator in the department, so he shifted me over to your group. You oughta get down on your knees tonight and thank God that wonderful man is so compassionate. He musta really loved Uncle Frank." Before Donald could reply, Justice continued, "'Course I don't know how that new duck boss, Desmond, will do without me but, shit, I can't be everywhere. Too bad. He's from that Tower, just like you, so you know he don't know nothing."

Donald figured he'd never stop so he casually said, "Well, listen, Cueball, my friend—"

Justice cut right in: "Hey, hey, pal! Let's get one thing clear. That drill school nickname don't play in the real world. Besides, I think my hair's comin' back."

Donald smiled. "Good night, er, Peter. Be on time Wednesday."

When he entered the bedroom, he didn't turn on the light. He could hear Gena's rhythmic breathing, indicating she was fast asleep. He slid gently beside her and closed his eyes. What a waste of time that was. They popped open again immediately as so many thoughts crowded into his head. He kept squirming around until his wife said, "Well, now that you've managed to cut into my dreams about our honeymoon in Maui, what's on your mind, Lieutenant?" He gathered her into his arms and said, "About a thousand things, gorgeous but none of them as important as you." When he put his lips to hers, he could feel that she was smiling, and then responded with the same passion, mystery and inventiveness she had displayed back on that Hawaiian trip fifteen years ago, and Donald knew he was hooked forever.

Over the weekend, a warm spell drove the temperature up into the fifties. Gena and Nancy took the car and went to visit Marion and Beth Keefe—Nancy, naturally, hoping Fred, Jr.. might also be at the Keefe home. Gap was working the day tour, so Donald stayed at home. In the afternoon, he took his most familiar stroll around the lagoon and out to Castle Island. He didn't expect to see Chief Simpson; it was the beginning of February and his retired boss should be working on his golf game down in Naples on the Gulf Coast of Florida. He was really surprised to see his friend on his usual bench, eyes closed and face elevated towards the weak sun in the winter sky. "Chief, what on earth are you doing up here in the frozen north?"

Simpson twitched; he had obviously dozed off. "Oh, hi, Fire Lieutenant Holden," he said with a grin. "Just working on my tan before we leave." He explained that a death in his wife's family had delayed his departure for a few days, but they'd be on their way by mid-week.

Donald sat down and sputtered out all of his news, with Simpson smiling inwardly as he remembered back to his own first assignment as an officer. It had actually been to Ladder 13, which was paired with Engine 22 in an old firehouse on Warren Avenue. During his tenure, the companies had been moved to the then new, one story house at 700 Tremont Street. Yeah, he thought with a shrug of resignation, that was thirty-six years ago.

When Donald finished, he expressed his delight with his young friend's good fortune. He also offered his praises about Joe Desmond, whom he considered to be as good a fire officer as he had met during his own career. "As you know, that man is a wonderful teacher, and it's not just restricted to his fire fighting knowledge. You shouldn't have any qualms about seeking advice from him anytime. He's wise beyond his years, Donald.

"But," he continued, "I'm pretty certain you won't be running to him with every problem you have. Reserve that for when you don't know what else to do, and hope it never happens."

He then went on to review so much that they had discussed in the past, but in particular, how a new officer should present himself to his jakes. "I have to reiterate that so many new bosses think they have to ingratiate themselves to their troops. They start off spoiling them and then, at some point, when they are required to be really tough, they are surprised when everyone gets pissed off 'cause they leaned on them. Donald, once you become an officer, if you treat them fairly, and set a good example, they will respect you. There are certain rules that have to be enforced and there are unpopular orders you are required to give. I wish I had done what I'm going to tell you now, but like most young guys, I had to get screwed a few times before I understood. I can tell you, that every mistake I made as a new lieutenant, which I've told you about, I didn't make as a new captain. That's what I guess you call experience."

He continued: "As a captain I gathered my members together right in the beginning, including my three lieutenants. I established the rules for how I wanted the house to be run. I don't mean it has to be by rigid discipline, but more by common sense. I told all of them, and I'm advising you to do the same with your own group, 'No booze, no drugs, no stealing, either at fires or from each other, no women on duty—or vice-versa if you have a female fire fighter assigned to you. Keep the house clean and the apparatus and equipment in good condition and ready for use. If you do these things, this will be a nice place to work. If you give me a screwing, I will give you a much bigger one.' "

Donald gulped. "Jeez, that's pretty hard-nosed stuff, deputy. Is that really what you did?"

Simpson smirked slightly and said, "Well, that's the way I remember it, now that I'm much older. I probably wasn't quite as direct as that, but I did make my point. Now, once you do that, someone is going to challenge your rules, just to see if you really mean them. The absolute best thing you can do is come down hard on that dope who wants to be a test case. It usually straightens him right out, but gives the word to everyone else that the new boss means it. You will never know how many problems that will prevent in the future. But, in my case, I had far fewer ones as a captain than I did as a lieutenant, so I think it worked." He went on to tell Donald that it must be perceived that even as an officer, you work as hard as anyone else on your company. "You know, today, you have far few members on duty than when I came on, so as an officer, while you must be making the operating decisions for your crew, you have to pitch in and get your hands dirty. But you broke in under Desmond, Grimes and Captain Hardy, so you know what I'm talking about."

The chief then reminisced about Twenty-two and the eleven years he had spent in the house and district. He talked about the riots back in '67 and '68 and how frightened they were at first, when the people who had always been so friendly started using jakes as targets. He mentioned the huge number of arson fires in the sixties and seventies and also talked about the Vendome fire in 1972. His eyes glistened noticeably as he said, "I was with another truck then. But, you know, Twenty-two and Thirteen had always been considered pretty lucky outfits. Of course, plenty of injuries, just like everyone else, but no deaths. At the Vendome, that ended. Five of the nine jakes killed that day were from the house and that ended the talk of good luck charms."

He mentioned many other major incidents the companies had been involved in and finally said, "Boy, am I rambling on. I'll tell you one more thing and then send you on your way. Twenty-two went to an auto fire back in November of 1942. As they were making up their line, a civilian tapped the pump operator on the shoulder, he said, 'Hey fireman, I think there's smoke comin' outta a building around the corner.' When they investigated, they found the guy was telling the truth. It was coming from the Coconut Grove nightclub. As everyone in the fire service knows, four hundred ninety-six people died that night. However, few people know that Twenty-two was the first fire company to arrive. Plenty of occupants were pulled out by those jakes from the company in spite of the fact so many others couldn't get out."

"So, you're going to a great place, you'll get plenty of work there and now that I told you all about being an officer, keep studying. Remember, though, it is a business of surprises and the more you learn about the job, the less often you'll be surprised."

Twelve

When Donald reported in for his first tour, which proved to be an evening shift, he was relieving Captain Desmond. He had arrived at about 1500 hoping to spend some time with the officer who not only taught him so much about the job, but nagged at him and several others to study. This was kind of a culmination to so many things his first boss had emphasized during their years together.

They shook hands in the company office and Donald left to put his gear on the pump, check his mask and light and be ready to respond. When he returned, Desmond was sitting in the secretary chair leaning back with his feet up on the desk and hands clasped behind his head.

"Well, Donald, here we are. I'm just as surprised as you are. I've always been harping on the jakes I work with, as you know, to study and try to get promoted. While I believe it, I also know that it doesn't exactly happen just that way because of so many imponderables. But, with you and Rick Foster getting made, I'm almost starting to believe what I preach. Yeah, and even myself and Andy Novak moving up. Not bad, my friend. Now I'm tempted to tell you to keep going, but," he laughed, "I think I'll give you some time to get your feet wet first."

They then talked about the company, the district and the members they would be working with. "I know you've got your drill school buddy with you, but I can't say I know the rest of your crew. We'll just have to feel our way along. And, in your case, you even have a new chief from the pool, Andy Polin, and a new deputy, Steve Lawton. I never worked with either of those guys, but the word is they know the business. If they're as smart as they're supposed to be, they'll kind of lay back a bit, see how everyone performs and then gradually insert their own personalities into their operating procedures and other requirements. Takes time. You have any questions for me?"

Donald talked for a while about his meetings with Billy Simpson and the advice he'd been squeezing out of him dating back to when he had been injured on Newton Street and was rehabbing by trudging around Castle Island. Desmond laughed and said, "Donald, I pumped that guy all the time I worked with him and I hope what I do is a reflection of his views. As far as I'm concerned, he was the man."

Before he left quarters, Desmond came back in his civilian clothes. "One more thing, Donald. I started today taking my jakes out on a tour of our sub-district. I know they know a lot more about the streets and buildings than I do, so I'm going to milk as much dope out of them as I can. It's still too cold to do much outside drilling, but since they all ride inside nowadays, it's no hardship to have them take me on a tour."

Donald shook his head after Desmond left. He had been thinking along pretty much the same lines. On his way in to work he had driven along Tremont Street, one of the main drags that ran from the downtown District Three, through his new District Four and continued into District Five, in the lower Roxbury section. While he had been to some fires in the area, this time he took a more thought-provoking survey. The main street had a variety of businesses on the first floor of many five and six story apartment houses, and block after block of the side streets were jammed with three and a half and four and a half story brownstones. Most of them had basement apartments with windows at ground level. The main entrances were mostly up fifteen cement stairs to a double door, then another inner door to the hallway. Inside, they had, either to the left or the right, a wooden stairway ascending to the upper floors. Just to the side of the stairway is a corridor with rooms lined one after the other towards the rear, terminating directly ahead at a rear bedroom. A stairway leads downward, underneath the front stairway, leading to the usually four rooms below street level. Some of them have a crawl space under the basement, often used for storage on the dirt or mildewed wooden strapping.

Since the main stairway is really the only interior exit, all of these structures have balcony fire escapes in the rear. There are usually about fifteen buildings of pretty much equal height and depth in a block, and the balconies, while they don't descend to the street, permit occupants to cross to the next building, which is across the other side of the fire wall. When fire fighters do their annual in-service building inspections in their sub-districts, some of the things they try to concentrate on is seeing if the windows aren't nailed shut to the balconies and whether these secondary means of exit are not lined with plants and are not hopefully, starting to disintegrate from oxidation and rust.

Unlike the Back Bay section of this district, there are very few alleys that permit the passage of motor vehicles, so access to the rear is either over fences from the main avenues, or through the adjoining structures, if there is no other way. Yeah, Donald thought, I got a lot to learn here. Not exactly like downtown where the Tower is located.

After changing into his station uniform and nervously attaching the quarter sized red discs, each with its single silver bugle centered to indicate he was definitely a lieutenant, he took a deep breath and walked from his room along the main floor of the one story structure and entered the kitchen. Instantly, Cueball jumped up from a bench at the small table, hooked his left arm around Donald's shoulder and said, "O.K. you twerps, Lieutenant Donald Holden and Assistant Lieutenant Peter Justice from the Class of '92 are now in charge. When either one of us gives you an order, you better shape up or we'll ship you out. Right, Lufty?"

Before Donald could reply, a husky looking black jake, who was poised over a frying pan on the gas stove, with a fork in his hand, smiled and said, "Shut up, you asshole. The only reason you're here is 'cause Captain Tilden didn't wanna screw up his relief with a yapper like you."

He reached out his hand and said, "Glad to see you, Luft. You have my sympathies. How'd that class ever graduate a blowhard like him?"

Donald covered his mouth with his hand: "Just lucky I guess." The jake identified himself as Jacob Larrabee and the other fire fighter seated at the table as Oregon Glenburne. Donald didn't remember seeing that name on the roster but the jake, who appeared to be in his late forties, said, "Hi Luft. No-o-o, that's not my real name. It's where I'm from. My real name's James. I married a girl from here when I was in the army. I'm really from Portland, but most of these Easterners think I'm from Maine, so I hadda explain to them there really is another town, same name out west. Oregon keeps reminding them, so that's what it is."

Donald grabbed a cup of coffee and, when asked, told Jacob he'd like to be in on the evening meal, which was to be steak tips, some kind of rice, and spinach.

He carried his cup and walked out towards the patrol desk, which was about a hundred feet away, facing Tremont Street and diagonally across from the kitchen. On the way, he looked fondly at the pump which he knew was the latest model. 1250 GPM fire pump, 750 gallon water tank, all aluminum body, the standard load of four inch feeder, two and half, inch and three quarter hose, pre-connected deck gun, portable gun, limited supply of foam. Yeah, just about the same as Ten and Fifty. Standardization sure makes it easy to learn.

At the patrol desk, the jake seated in the chair didn't glance up as he entered. Just sat there, staring out the window that gave a view of the front apron. No attempt to rise or even say hello. "My name is Holden. I'm the new officer on this group." He held his hand out. "Yeah. I know who you are. I'm Lansing." His manner was curt and he didn't respond to the offered handshake. Donald felt his face redden. Keep cool, he thought. "Stand up for a minute, Lansing," he said. The jake shuffled to his feet and asked "For what?" "Just wanted to see how tall you are. Sit down." Donald turned and walked out, crossing in front of the apparatus and returning to his office.

Back in his room he slid into the chair at his desk. Well, this is it, he thought. Now, I'm an officer and it looks like I'm going to be challenged early. Have to think this through. At least I didn't bite like I wanted to. I hope he's over there wondering why I'm interested in his height. Shit, I don't know. It was all I could think of at the time.

Before they had dinner, Chief Polin entered quarters. By this time, Cueball had assumed the watch and he went into his usual act of greeting the new boss and telling him how lucky he was to have not only Twenty-two in his district, but the best jake in town. Polin and his driver, Bobby Stearns, were laughing by the time Donald led them out to the kitchen to meet the others. Thankfully, Dan Lansing wasn't around.

Later, in Donald's office, Polin waved him to a seat and sat in the old overstuffed leather chair in the corner. "Luft, we're both new and it will take a while to get to know each other. I can tell you I have no interest in studying for deputy. I had enough of headquarters to last me 'til I retire. I'm delighted to get this district. I served here as a private on Engine 3 and I always wanted to come back. So I expect to be around a long time. Just a couple of things I want to mention in the beginning. Since this is a single house, with no truck, I will keep you running with one and four as much as I can." The department minimum was an officer and three fire fighters, but in places such as this, where they often were at a fire all alone for a least a few minutes, it was a good decision to allow them an extra jake.

"Thanks, Chief, I appreciate that," said Donald.

"But," Polin continued, "I learned when I broke in here, if you get a fire, run a big line right away. These places really can take off and you have to hit them with your best punch right away. I don't mean if it's obviously a mattress or inside rubbish or an investigation for the odor of smoke. No, I mean if you can see it or smell wood burning, know what I mean?"

Donald nodded, "I think so, Chief. I can't argue with that, sir."

Polin smiled. "Good...'Nother thing. When you're first in, you're in charge 'til I get there. You wanna send the all out, go ahead, if you're sure you know what you got. If you have a fire, I don't care if you strike a second or a third or whatever you do. You're the boss and I'll back you up. I'm gonna trust your judgment 'til I learn otherwise, which I hope I never will."

The first shift proved to be fairly routine for the district. Three runs for the company. One was a false alarm. One was a dumpster fire and Twenty-two was first in. It was fully involved but was not exposing anything else. Justice said as they approached the location near the railroad tracks separating the South End from the Back Bay. "Hey, Luft, let me whack it with the gun, will ya?" In a matter of moments, Cueball had transferred the transmission into pump gear and Jacob had sprung up on top of the piece. The tank to pump valve was opened and the water was soon spurting from the pre-connected deck gun into the large rubbish storage container. The fire disappeared and turned to whitish smoke instantly. Donald called Fire Alarm and told them to return the ladder truck that had been dispatched. The dumpster was rapidly filled and it was extinguished completely, although Donald had them carefully sift through the stacks of charred material to make sure it was out. Don't want a rekindle on my first job, he thought.

When they were returning, they drove along Carleton Street, which bordered the railroad, and as they passed the streets that terminated at that point, Donald could see that each of them had the standard brownstones, all attached, just like so many other sections of the district. He also noticed that at the end of each street, almost down to the railroad, there was a post hydrant. Since they always entered these streets from the main thoroughfare, Columbus Avenue, at the opposite end of the block, this could be a valuable piece of information some time. Yeah, file it away.

The final response of the tour was to a mattress fire in the Back Bay. Engine 33 and Ladder 15 were first at the scene and, by the time Twenty-two had arrived in response to the box alarm struck for a building fire, those companies had already run a line to the second floor. The aerial was almost to the roof and laddermen were opening the windows in the room of origin. Polin had Donald stretch an inch and three quarter so that when the smouldering mattress landed in the street, the line could complete the extinguishment while the second due truck, Ladder 17, tore it to pieces with their rakes.

As he showered in the morning after he was relieved, he was whistling. His relief was Phil Cummings who was in his mid-fifties. He had been on the company for almost two decades and was a cheerful, grey-haired string bean who overwhelmed Donald with his enthusiasm. "Hey, Holden. Glad to see you. This is the best company in the city. It must be. I've been here forever. If I had found a better place, I'd have been gone. All you gotta remember is, do your work and they won't bother ya. Not too much bullshit from the brass. Those West Point martinets would get too dirty here, so they stay out in the country with the grass fire jakes. Good luck, pal."

The next day tour they were on duty, after the house work was completed, Donald brought the four jakes into his office and invited them to sit down. Cueball immediately chose Donald's seat, leaving his friend half-seated on the desk with his feet on the floor and arms folded. "O.K., Lufty, here we are. Any chance of gettin' Saturday night off?"

Donald smiled. "Geez, er, Peter, it's a little early for that. You've already been telling me how great you are, but I haven't seen anything yet." Jacob and Oregon chuckled. Dan Lansing just sat in a chair, elbow on the armrest and fist resting on his jawbone.

Donald had almost memorized the script for what he was going to tell them. His biggest worry was that he'd seem like a jerk, but he was hoping to set the right tone for the jakes he was now responsible for. Before calling them into his quarters, he had reviewed their folders in the company file. Other than a listing of their occasional injuries, none of which resulted in too much lost time, Cueball, Larrabee and Glenburne had unremarkable records. No suspensions, no reprimands, no commendations. Hm, just like the other ninety-five percent, he thought.

While Lansing's record was almost the same, Donald noted he had just recently transferred into Engine 22 and that at his previous company he had been off sick a number of times, although none of the absences were with loss of pay. It was interesting to note that he had gone off on two occasions on New Year's Eve and only missed one tour each time. Not really enough to establish a pattern of abuse, but worth noting. Most jakes would like to be off through the holidays but they knew the job requirements. Some years your group just wasn't scheduled and other times you hit them all. The luck of the draw. But it all evens out mathematically in time. There also was a listing of an oral warning for tardiness a few months ago. Under the Progressive Discipline Guidelines, such a warning is supposed to be given immediately when there is a violation of rules under non-emergency conditions. In reality, though, most officers didn't use the procedure very often, unless a jake was becoming a pain in the ass. Therefore, it was worth considering that Lansing, for whatever reason, had been getting on his leader's nerves. But, thought Donald, he gets a fresh start with me. Take them like you find them, not how someone else does, is not bad logic. Might've just been a personality clash, who knows?

"O.K. men, now that Peter has grabbed my seat, I just want to go over a few things with you. I don't have to tell you I'm brand new; you read the same orders I do. Up until now, other than during this period when I was floating around without a berth, the only real responsibility I had was to myself. Do my job, collect my pay and that's about it. Now, though, I am responsible for how this company operates while I'm on duty. This responsibility includes being concerned for the welfare of the people I have been assigned to command. That's you guys. I accept that duty without any reservations. I know that I'll probably make mistakes, not only in how I treat you, but at fires too. I hope you'll have patience with me, and I hope I have it with all of you as well. I want you to know that I love this job and expect to stay on it until I'm too old to work.

"Now, my own limited observations, not only on the job, but in the service, is that men would much rather know where they stand with a boss than to try to outguess what he wants done. I don't think that will be one of my faults. So, I'm gonna lay out a few things for you today and we'll see how things go. I have no interest in what any of you do when you're off duty. That doesn't mean I won't try to give you a hand if you get in some kind of difficulty, financial or otherwise. But, every one of us has another life besides working here and you're entitled to lead yours however you want. I have no interest in your morals as long as it doesn't affect your performance during your forty-two hours with me.

When you report for work though, I expect you to be fit for duty. I won't allow any booze, drugs or any thing like that while you're here. No stealing, either from each other or at fires. No women in quarters unless they're here on business or," he smiled, "are jakes themselves and are working here." He realized none were presently assigned to the company, but they could be detailed in from other houses.

"Do your work at fires. Keep the house, the apparatus and the equipment clean. If you do, I will take care of you for sure. If you

decide you want to give me a screwing—I will give you a bigger one."
He managed a smile as he gave them these rather strongly worded
concluding remarks. "Anyone have any questions?" None of them said
anything. Even Cueball was gazing at his folded hands in his lap. Ugh,
Donald thought, must have fucked this up for sure.

"O.K. Now, I know that Brosnahan was the regular pump operator
on this group. I'm also aware Captain Tilden shifted Justice over here.
But I'd like to know if any of you would prefer to drive the piece. You
three are senior to Pete. As time goes on, and I get to know you all,
I'll make my own decision on this, but I'd like to know your views."
Jacob said, "Naw, I don't care about the pump. I like bein' on the pipe
as much as I can." Oregon nodded affirmatively. Lansing just sat
there, said nothing. "O. K.," said Donald, "for now it's you, Pete. But
I want all of you to remain familiar with every job on the company. I
plan on rotating each of you so that one week a month Pete rides in
back and someone moves up front."

Before he dismissed them, he said that at eleven hundred hours
they would be leaving quarters to drive around the sub-district. "I
know you all are very familiar with it, but I'm not and I want to look
around. You guys must know where the best subs are at least."

After they left, he shrugged his shoulders. Not much response.
Just wait and see, he thought. Bet that's exactly what they're doing. He
walked out to the apparatus and climbed into the officer's seat. He was
pleased to see that on the panel in front of him were affixed the splits
for the main streets. He understood that someone had taken the time to
list the numbers of the streets as they were approached from the
centrally located fire station. So, if they were dispatched to a certain
number on say, Columbus Avenue, by responding up the narrow
thoroughfare diagonally across from quarters, they would know which
way to turn to reach their destination. While many modern cities and
towns were laid out in a methodical and probably boring fashion to
facilitate ease of access, the founding fathers in Boston seem to have
decided to follow the cow paths. The fact that one street may have a
certain number at an intersection is no guarantee that the avenues
paralleling it will be anywhere close to that designation. So, you had
to know. He also found a well worn notebook that listed every other
street in the district in a similar fashion. Yeah, these guys know what
they're doing.

Cueball slid in beside him. "Hey boss, you don't need that stuff.
You got me. I know every fuckin' street, alley and pathway in this
town. I told you I was the top driver the army had during the Gulf

War. Schwarzkorpf checked with me before he kicked off the attack to make sure they'd head for Kuwait." The little redhead looked around nervously, then said in a hushed voice, "Well, pal, you got the troops worried. The last guy they worked for never told them shit. Now you lay out all that jarhead talk and they're kinda puzzled." He laughed and said, "So am I. I think you done right. But we gotta wait and see. And, pal, I mean me, too. First of all, I'm a fire fighter. And second of all, you're an officer. That's a dividing line. I know you're not lookin' for it, even though we're friends, but I'll never be a stool pigeon, running to you with stories about them. 'Cause, you see, I am them."

Donald appreciated the advice and spent the rest of the day questioning his decision to lay out his ground rules. They seemed friendly enough during their tour of the district, at least Jacob and Oregon. Lansing just stared out the window from his jump seat, and never said a word.

At home in bed that night, he stared up at the ceiling, wondering how many other times he would be doing the same thing, now that he was a boss. I don't know. Well, I sure gave them the word. But, I think Cueball gave it to me as well.

The next night tour they were dispatched to a report of a building fire on Rutland Street, which is just a block from the station. It was shortly after 0100 hours and, as they turned from Tremont, Donald could see grayish smoke oozing from the top floor of a three story brick and wood building. He had Cueball stop at the hydrant where Oregon jumped off with the bag and looped the four inch feeder over the bonnet. As they stopped near the building Donald reported light smoke showing, top floor. He shouted to Lansing, "Inch and three quarter, front stairs, top floor." He was quite certain he smelled a mattress but he wanted to be sure it wasn't something worse. As he slung his mask over his shoulders, he heard Car Four announcing their arrival at the box. It flashed through his mind that he was now free to enter the building instead of remaining in the street, in command until relieved. The front door was open and he charged up the stairs. As he was entering an elderly Hispanic woman said, "Bed on fire. Up, up." He asked if anyone was in there but she didn't reply, just hurried out the door and down to the street. Three other people followed closely behind, but they were just chattering to each other and leaving the building. At the second floor level, the smoke was growing thicker, but he still couldn't smell wood burning. On the third floor landing, he almost breathed a sigh of relief. One door was wide open, and, as he bent forward to slip on his mask, he could see flames, not really intense, skipping along the top of the tumbled bedclothes. Yeah, a mattress.

He worked his way across the room and waited for the line to arrive. He could hear Lansing shouting for it to be filled so he turned to the windows, and, as soon as he heard the discharge of water from the pipe, pulled the top sash down, opened and raised the bottom one to meet it, allowing the smoke to vent outward towards the street. Next he used his gloved hands to pulled the rotted wooden moulding away from the frame, and carefully lifted out each window, enlarging the opening to its full size. He placed the windows along the wall so they wouldn't be broken unnecessarily. He pressed the button on his mike and reported to Car Four that it was a mattress, top floor and they were checking for extension.

In a few minutes they were joined by members of Ladder 17 who dragged the dripping mattress over to the opening, shouted to watch out below, and heaved it into the street. Car Four's aide, Bobby Stearns, reported the status to the chief and, shortly afterwards, after finding no extension to the wall or furnishings, the line was made up and they were dismissed. Routine. There'd be countless others just like it, but when they got back and had repacked the hose and changed their cylinders, Jacob nudged Donald as they headed for the kitchen and some coffee: "Nice job on the window, Luft," he said. "Love those big openings." Not bad, not bad, thought Donald. Made the right call on the size line to use, so I guess the chief was content. Didn't say anything anyway.

The next few weeks of February saw the winter plowing along. There were a few snowfalls, but no major ones or blizzards. Even so, as soon as the plows were out, the fire companies followed shortly afterwards, checking hydrants and digging out any that were buried by the piles of snow that were pushed over them. Donald actually enjoyed the duty. It was a great excuse for going up and down the various blocks in rotation. He soon learned that there was usually a hydrant at each end of a city block and one in the middle. Unlike downtown, there was no extension of the high pressure system to this end of the district. Hydrant pressures varied somewhat but averaged about 50 psi. The mains were large and there were no dead ends so the most important duty was to clear the hydrants and make sure they weren't frozen.

There was no discussion in the kitchen about Donald's

introductory message. Probably a lot in the other areas of the house, but things seemed pretty normal. Although the building is good-sized, it has only housed one company since the massive deactivations that occurred in 1981-82. As far as Donald was concerned, it was an awful lot of room for one officer and four fire fighters. Except for the member on watch at the patrol desk, the remainder, often including himself, congregated in the kitchen and the adjoining TV-rec room at the rear of the building. The single pumper would have looked quite lonely sitting just inside the middle of the three overhead doors. But, of course, everyone brought their personal cars inside to guard against theft in the relatively high crime area. It also protected them from being plowed in by the city trucks when the storms came. Just as in Donald's first house, one jake, in this case Oregon, was a good mechanic. Whenever he was doing a tune-up or changing someone's oil, Jacob, Cueball and Donald would stop by to give him unneeded advice and very little assistance.

It became a friendly atmosphere and Donald was pleased that there was no residual tension apparent. Of course, he was working hard to place his own personal stamp on the unit. At each fire they went to, it soon became apparent that he could work, probably as hard as any of them. He would be constantly lighting up on a line as it was advanced and always carried a claw hammer and a large screwdriver in his pocket. He had noticed Lieutenant Grimes always had the same tools on Engine 10. When he asked him about it he said, "Yeah, well, most of the time we have a truckie with us, but if we don't, it sure comes in handy. You can open a wall or punch a hole in a ceiling if you have to, shut off a gas main, disconnect an electric fixture or even pound through a locked door. Nothing worse than seein' a bunch of hosemen with a line, waiting for someone to get them in somewhere." He also showed him an inch and an eighth straight nozzle tip that he carried in case they needed a more penetrating stream than the usual combination attachment.

Over a period of time, Donald also learned, just by keeping his ears open when he was with his jakes, that apparently the last boss wasn't all that aggressive, either at fires or in quarters. One night they were dispatched as a working fire company to an apartment house in the next district. The chief's aide directed them to take a line into an attic over a forty foot ladder. Lines were operating on the lower floors and seemed to be gaining control, but the attic window, which was still intact, had volumes of dense brown smoke under pressure pushing through the frameworks it was set in. As they were about to start climbing the ladder with Jacob leading, the pipe and hose draped over his shoulder, Donald grabbed his arm and said, "Hold it a minute." He directed Oregon to grab the extension halyard of the ladder while Donald and Lansing pulled the ladder away from the building until it was vertical. "Pull it up three clicks, Oregon," Donald oredered. This brought the tip of the ladder level with and opposite the top of the upper window sash. "OK, Dan," he said to Lansing, "we'll lean it out and then drop it right through the glass." As the weight of the aluminum extension smashed through the pane, he yelled, "Keep your head down!" as shards of broken glass slid down the ladder. The effect was dramatic as the pressure was released. He then had them slip the ladder down so it broke the lower pane as well. Then they jammed it into the sill and slid it over to the left side. Now he told Jacob to start climbing and, as the jake reached the upper rungs and hooked his knee over one of them, Donald ordered Cueball via radio to fill the line. He was just behind the pipeman when the line was filled, and leaning on him as he opened the nozzle, they drove the stream upward and rotated it several times. Donald then had the line shut down and, when no fire came towards them said, "O.K., pal, let's move it in slowly." Jacob straddled the sill as Donald took the weight of the charged line. Soon they were both on the floor inside, the stream operating again, sometimes directly over their heads to reduce the heat that was trying to envelop them, but the volume of the water and the force it was distributed under knocked down the fire in a matter of minutes. They were joined by the other two members, who took over the line, while Donald made his way over to the top of the narrow stairway, leading downward. He was pleased to see a jagged two foot square hole up near the ridge line, indicating the truckies had gotten the roof. "Hey," he shouted, "tell Car Five that Twenty-two's in the attic and is knocking it down."

While there was nothing unusual about what they had done, the chief nodded when he came up to make a survey. "Nice job, Luft. Some of you Division One jakes aren't too bad." The fire was across the Massachusetts Avenue boundary line that separated the department's two fire divisions. The rivalries, while mostly good natured, have been going on since jakes were operating with bucket brigades a century and a half earlier.

Back in their own quarters, Donald could see that the members were pretty upbeat. They knew they had been the key to cutting off the fire and bringing it under control and they had that feeling jakes got that was really inexplicable to civilians with less exciting and demanding jobs.

As he left the kitchen to make out his report, he heard Jacob say, "Boy, this guy's better than old Numb Nuts, isn't he. Don't mind gettin' dirty either." He beamed as Cueball's piercing voice said, "I told you assholes. We got Hero Holden, my old pal. Better shape up or I'll have you railroaded outta here." The only one of the four who made no comment was Lansing. He did his work all right, but he showed no enthusiasm for much of anything. Donald shrugged. Deputy Simpson had told him they aren't all superstars. "Listen, Donald," he said at one point, "the fact that you love what you do is great, but don't think it's unanimous. Nothing is, kid. Actually, I've met a few jakes over the years who never should have been on the job. They hated it. You might wonder why they stay. Well, many times it's economic circumstances. You just can't throw away a good job 'cause you don't like it and immediately get another one. Look at all those poor stiffs in private industry who can't wait for the end of the week. That phrase, 'Thank God it's Friday' is no joke." Then he laughed: "Hell, fire fighters never know what day of the week it is, they just keep comin' into work, and, if they love it, they couldn't care less what time their tour ends." He said he worked with one guy who would report for duty, do whatever was asked and then spend most of his time staring into his open locker. Nobody bothered him, just as long as he made all the runs and did his share.

"Whatever happened to him?" Donald asked.

"Nothing. One day, much to every one's surprise, he announced he had his thirty-two years in and was leaving. No goodbyes, no parties. Never saw him again. Nowadays they'd want to have him analyzed or something, see if he hated his mother or was abused by his father. Back then they just shrugged it off. I'm not sure what's better, then or now, but I wish I knew what he saw in that locker."

March finally arrived, and it was great to see it getting light earlier. And, still no really bad storms. Looks like we'll have an early spring, Donald thought. So far, only about twenty-five inches for the whole season, well below the average annual accumulation. But, old time New Englanders, ensconced in their nursing home rocking chairs, swayed rhythmically to and fro and murmured, It ain't over 'til May.

Donald worked the day tour on Sunday, March 30th, and while there wasn't any action to speak of, the weather forecasters on the noon time news were talking about snow coming in for the start of the week on Monday. Of course, in the Boston area, people really don't give the meteorologist much credibility. If you planned a summer picnic based on their optimistic prediction for the next day, you might very well spend your outing at some lakeside retreat huddled under pine trees with water dripping on you and the family. You'd be trying to decide if you should wait it out or get everyone to safety before the lightning strikes, but it would be hard trying to concentrate with the dear wife and kids bitching and blaming you for the disaster. It's better to rely on how your arthritic knees are performing than to watch the weather channel. However, the radar had a mass of green showing by the time they were relieved from duty and the wizards were talking about the Monday morning commute being screwed.

Well, it wasn't, but there sure were some ominous clouds as Donald prepared to leave for work. He decided to take his car rather than the MBTA because if it really was a big storm, it's better to stick it inside the fire house than leave it at home out on the street. On the way in, flakes started falling and grew in intensity as he drove along Broadway. They were the heavy, wet kind that were loaded with moisture and that was about normal for springtime. The sun would be out tomorrow, the temperature would jump up to fifty and, if you're lucky, you won't even have to break out the shovel.

By 1900 that evening it was obvious the storm wasn't going to quit for quite a while. Donald even had to get all hands out on the apron to keep it clear of snow so their response wouldn't be impeded. The department activity increased dramatically as companies were dispatched to calls for electric wires down, trees falling onto buildings, limbs obstructing street passage, power failures and all the other incidents related to major storm damages.

The city trucks and the contractors who normally would be prepared for such an event encountered significant delays. The mild winter had disarmed them into complacency and many of the plows had been already detached for the coming warm weather. At 2000 hours the deputies of both divisions ordered companies to start clearing hydrants. Donald's boss, Chief Polin, arranged so half the companies would be on the road and the others remain in quarters just in case some of them became snowbound. Even the main roads became difficult to maneuver, and some of the side streets were becoming impassable. When Twenty-two got on the road at midnight, it was pretty frightening. This was certainly near blizzard conditions. The wind had shifted so it was what is described as a Nor'easter, which means the storm has circled out to sea and was now driving ashore with velocities nearing the hurricane range. Donald started listing the worst streets and made certain the hydrants were cleared on each end of the block. While only a few plows were traveling, and these on the main thoroughfares, abandoned cars would have prevented them from clearing the smaller streets and avenues. Boy, he thought, if we get anything, we'll have to drag lines a long way.

The number of incidents also continued to rise. Soon after 0100 hours, Fire Alarm directed them to return to quarters. By listening to the radio, Donald understood why. Everyone in this district and the next one were tied up at alarms, except Twenty-two. It was a good move to get them into their centrally located house.

There was a building fire in Chinatown, and while it didn't seem like it would become a multiple alarm, Engines Seven, Ten, Three, Ladders 17, 18, the Tower and Rescue companies were operating at that incident. Thirty-three and Ladder 15 were somewhere in District Five, there was a building fire in East Boston and wires down all over the rest of the city. Not much help available. When they arrived back at the house, the apron already had a few more inches than when they had left. Cueball swung the pump out into Tremont Street, waited until the door was raised high enough and then revved up the powerful diesel, released the foot brake and roared right through the snow into the station.

"Nice going, Ace," said Donald.

"Please, mon lieutenant, I told you I was the best driver the army ever had. I whipped those trailers right through avalanches in Turkey. This storm is nothin' to a wheelman like me."

Jacob said, "I thought you said you were advising the generals when to attack during the war. What the hell were you doin' in Turkey?"

The redhead shook his head from side to side: "You poor non-vets don't know nuthin'. We were strategically located in case Saddam tried to escape in that direction."

"Well, you sure did a good job, Peter" Jacob responded. "He ain't left yet."

The crew reluctantly broke out the shovels again, but while Donald, Lansing, Oregon and Jacob were outside digging methodically, suddenly the house lights came on and the doors started to open, indicating they had a run. Cueball, who was on patrol shouted, "Building fire, 33 Holyoke Street. They're striking Box 1552, Columbus and Holyoke." Donald jumped into the front seat and grabbed for the notebook. Holyoke started in the four hundred block of Columbus and ran down to the railroad barrier on Carleton Street.

"Up West Newton, Pete, then right on Columbus." Justice nodded, "Know it, Luft." Donald was trying to think rapidly. He had chosen Newton because he knew it was a main artery and had been plowed at least once. Now, he squinted his eyes in concentration, thirty-three, he thought. Starts with number one at Columbus, odd numbers on right. Only about fifteen buildings on each side. Gotta be down the other end. Hope it isn't blocked. The snow was driving so fiercely that Cueball had to reduce speed as they approached Columbus. It was really difficult to see. The avenue had been narrowed dramatically by cars that had pulled over and become stuck. Cueball crept along the street. Donald was counting intersections because they couldn't identify streets. They passed through Columbus Square where it intersected with Warren Avenue. Next on the left should be Braddock Park and then, hopefully, Holyoke. Fire Alarm called, "Engine Twenty-two, we're receiving calls now for that location. Your first due truck is Ladder 19 from quarters." Donald gasped, Nineteen was at the City Point section of District Six, a long way off. Everyone else is tied up. Cueball swung over to the opposite side of the divided highway at Braddock Park and they crawled along to Holyoke. Shit! It wasn't plowed. It couldn't be because two cars were stuck right in the narrow roadway, covered with snow. As Donald stared down the street, the visibility was so poor he couldn't see any smoke or flames, but he thought he got a whiff of wood burning. "Keep going, Cue," he shouted, "West Canton Street's next. It's a main drag. Hope it's been plowed." He crossed his fingers; he couldn't think of what else to do. To try to run a line from Columbus through the deep snow all the way down to the end of Holyoke would take forever. Have to take a chance. He wished they could see more, but the snow kept driving at them.

Here's the intersection. Swing to the left and pray. Ahh, someone's been through here. The roadway was already rutted but they could maintain traction. They still couldn't see much but so far, as they moved forward, no cars were blocking their way. Now, Donald thought, if only the plow guy had hit Carleton Street, we have a chance. Oh boy, he did it, he did it. "Go left, Cueball, go." By now, the smell of smoke was powerful but they still couldn't see the fire even though they were less than a hundred feet from the Carleton-Holyoke intersection. Keep going.

There. They were approaching the alley dividing the Canton Street dwellings from the ones on Holyoke and suddenly they could see fire blowing out of a first floor window at the rear of the second building from the corner. Donald told Cueball to drive right up to the intersection. He remembered there was a hydrant just a few feet in on Holyoke on the same side as the fire building. He grabbed the mike to report to Fire Alarm: "Twenty-two to Fire Alarm. Fire showing on Holyoke. Have responding companies come West Canton to Carleton. I need a ladder truck as soon as possible." He jumped from the piece and waded through the snow-filled street to the front of the building. Cueball and Oregon were racing to the front of the engine, dragging out the five inch soft suction from its tray on the front bumper. Jacob and Lansing were at the side of the hose crosslays adjusting their mask cylinders. Donald yelled, "Big line." He couldn't see where the fire was but there was smoke banking down everywhere. There were footsteps in the snow leading down from the house and he could see a couple of people moving rapidly away from the building, He shouted to them to ask if anyone was inside but they were bent over, leaning into the wind-driven snow and kept trudging away from the building, through the deep snow on the sidewalk.

OK, OK, he thought. Size it up. Basement apartment with three stories over it. Brownstone with three bay windows on each floor extending up to the right of the outside stairway which had some dozen or more cement steps leading to the double-doored entrance and foyer. One window on each floor directly over the stairway.

Heavy smoke pushing out on all floors beginning at the first one at the top of the stairs and obscuring the building, right up to the roof. Lansing, the big line draped over his shoulder, shouted, "Where do you want it, Luft?" Donald waved Lansing and Jacob up the stairway and ordered, "First floor, don't know which room." They moved rapidly up, bent over against the wind and snow. They no sooner disappeared inside the building than Jacob reappeared and shouted, "Water. Two rooms in back, fully involved."

Donald relayed the word to Cueball who was at the pump panel. The soft suction was swelling as Oregon kept rotating the hex nut on the bonnet clockwise with the steel wrench, admitting water from the underground main to flow through the four and a half inch outlet of the hydrant, through the large diameter hose and into the pumper. Donald could see Cueball wave acknowledgment and start breaking the hose at the next thread to connect it into the discharge outlet. The crash of glass and a piercing scream caused Donald to swing his head back towards the building. The middle window of the second floor bay was shattered and a woman's head and shoulders were protruding outward. She was gasping for breath as the dark smoke swirled around her. Shit, he thought. Ladder. "Oregon, help me get the twenty-four." He was referring to the size of one of the two ladders strapped to the side of every engine company in the city for just such an emergency. The two of them reached up, unlocked the release and moved back towards the sidewalk. Donald shouted to Cueball, "Second alarm, my orders. People in the building." As Donald set the butt of the ladder into the snow and faced it towards the building so Oregon could push it upright, Cueball, who had just opened the discharge gate and was filling the two and a half inch attack line operated by Lansing and Jacob, picked up the remote microphone from the holder on the pump panel: "Engine Twenty-two to Fire Alarm. Orders of Lieutenant Holden, strike second alarm Box 1552. People in the building."

While Oregon held the ladder vertically, Donald rapidly pulled the rope halyard hand over hand until the extension reached its maximum height. The two of them then dropped it towards the building, and thankfully, it just touched the bricks directly under the sill. The woman was now pitching forward, trying to dive out of the building. Donald clambered up the rungs and grabbed her under the armpits, her head bumping precariously against his shoulder. No chance to get her turned around. He started to descend, hoping she wouldn't somersault back over him. Oregon was just below him, leaning his own weight against Donald as a means of support.

It was not a textbook rescue, but they made it to the street, all three of them landing in a heap. The woman appeared dazed but otherwise uninjured. Donald told Oregon, "Get up on the line with the others." He led the woman over to the pump and shouted to Cueball, "Call for ambulances. Put her inside." He turned to go back to the front of the building, paused, pressed his own mike and said, "Fire Alarm. This is Engine Twenty-two. Tell the first truck to park on Carleton. They can get the roof from the adjoining building. We also need ground ladders in front and rear."

He knew he should now remain outside in front as the officer in command until relieved by a superior, but he ran up the stairs. He knew he had to keep sizing up and find out where the fire was going. He moved in through the foyer to the hallway. The inside stairway was directly in front of him, leading to the upper floors. Just to the right was the corridor and his charged big line, which disappeared into the blackness. The heat was twirling around him by convection and he had to drop to his knees to continue deeper inside. He wriggled along until he bumped into a prostate figure that was lying on top of the charged line. He pounded his fist against the buttocks of the jake and, as the smoke rose momentarily, thought it was Oregon. "How you guys doin'?" He shouted through his facepiece. "Holding it. Fire's in two rooms. Could use another line!" was the reply. "But, listen, Luft. Dan's gone upstairs. Thought he heard someone screaming and just took off."

God. That's bad. Gotta get up there. "Try your best to hold it, Donald mumbled. "I'm going up too." He thought he could see Jacob flat on the floor, moving the pipe back and forth, trying to contain the fire in both rear rooms. Donald pressed his mike against his mask facepiece and said, "Fire Alarm, we need another big line, first floor, front stairs and lines up above. People still inside. Strike third alarm, Lieutenant Holden, Engine Twenty-two." He was so engrossed in what he was doing that he never even heard them reply. He started ascending the narrow wooden stairway, one step at a time. At the ceiling level of the first floor, where the stairway started to bend to the right, the heat struck his face and right ear as it was rising, seeking to extend upward. Keep going, was all he could think. Lansing's up there somewhere.

Because people were trapped inside, Cueball was now the only member left out front and he was thrilled to see Ladder 19's apparatus burst through the snowflakes and pull up near the intersection. He waved to the officer and started to give him a report, but the captain said, "We got the message." He turned and ordered the aerial thrown to the top of the building they were adjacent to and shouted, "Get the roof, second building in from the corner." He pointed to two other jakes. "Forty. Front. Third floor." He himself raced to the front, looked up and called to Fire Alarm: "Ladder 19 at Box 1552. Orders of Captain Hillary, I want everyone to come in West Canton to Carleton. I want two big lines to the front as a priority. Have a ladder company get ground ladders to the rear, through the alley. Tell them the snow is deep."

Cueball yelled from the pump panel, "Cap, I can take all the lines you can get." Hillary relayed that information to Fire Alarm. Justice was thrilled to see how rapidly the aerial was extended and, in front of the fire building, the captain was helping to push the heavy forty foot extension ladder upright so it could be elevated to the top floor.

Donald flopped on the second floor landing. He had to catch his breath and as he sucked on the regulator of his mask, the unit responded to his demand. Hot. Yeah, and juicy. Can't hear anything. He shouted Lansing's name but wasn't surprised when he couldn't detect any response. The speaking diaphragm didn't project his vocal cords as effectively as they would have traveled if his face was uncovered. He took a breath and slipped off the mask. Ugh. It was juicy. "Lansing!" he shouted, and quickly refastened the neoprene seal. Wow. Was that a voice from upstairs? He crept back towards the front of the building in the hall until the stairway started up again. Still hot and even more smoke, it seemed. Hope they're holding it down there. The doors to the rooms on the second floor were all closed. Hope there was no one in there but the woman we got out. But Dan must have kept going or he would have left a door open. Make the turn half way up and pull yourself, hand over hand to the third floor landing. Donald flopped on the flat surface. He reached directly in front of him and his hand didn't touch a solid surface. Door must be open, he concluded and moved forward. Now, he heard the rhythmic sound of a 4.5 breathing regulator as it operated to supply air to the mask. "Dan! Dan! Where are you?" he shouted and moved towards the sound.

Lansing was on his knees, bent over a prostrate figure. He was attempting to move the body back towards the door, but was having a difficult time. As Donald drew up beside him, he understood why. The victim was a woman, but she was huge. He had apparently moved her from her bed, some ten feet away, but was just about exhausted himself.

Donald grabbed him by the arm and said, "I'm with you, Dan. Let's keep dragging her together." Lansing nodded, but didn't reply. Together they were able to move towards the doorway and, just as they were about to enter the hallway, they heard a crash from above. Shards of heavy glass started hitting the stairway and splintering into even smaller pieces. They could actually see the smoke dart upward and feel the pressure abating. Donald started to say "Thank God," but then checked himself. "Hold it here, Dan," he said. He was hoping the overhead ventilation didn't draw the fire right up to where they were. While he was hesitating, he heard more glass breaking. Sounds like it's the front windows on this floor breaking out. Boy, I hope they have charged lines down below or we're screwed.

He would have been relieved if he'd been able to see what was transpiring. Captain Hillary was fully aware of the situation and not only had another charged line operating in the rear rooms beside Jacob and Oregon, but he also had a line in position on the second floor landing, just in case of extension, and another line advancing over the forty foot ladder to the now broken out middle window at the top floor.

Apparatus was pouring in from various districts in response to the third alarm. Even though some of them had to come from great distances under terrible driving conditions, it wasn't long before there was plenty of help at the scene. Both Deputy Lawton and Chief Polin had completed operations at their fire and responded, and the commissioner was en route. However, before anyone else had made the top floor, Donald heard a gasp and Dan Lansing released his hold on the woman and tumbled down the stairs, rolling to the bend and leaning upright against the outside wall. Donald requested help immediately to his position and reported a fire fighter was down on the stairway between the second and third floor. Members of Rescue One, who had just arrived on the scene, ran pell-mell into the building and three of them picked up Dan and descended to the street. Other jakes arrived, one with a resuscitator, and before he knew it, Donald was unencumbered by the victim, who had also been moved downward. He sat on the middle step, one elbow resting on his knee, completely exhausted.

He was still sitting there, his mask warning bell now signalling that his supply was running low. His eyes were closed, and he was somewhat at peace. The heat was dissipating rapidly and he knew they had gotten the fire. He had to determine the condition of the woman they were trying to rescue, but he was much more concerned about Lansing. He felt a tap on the shoulder and raised his head. It was Chief Polin. "Lieutenant, are you all right?" Donald straightened up before replying: "Uh, sure, Chief. Just a little punched out." The district chief smiled: "Well, you should be. You guys did a hell of a job."

Jakes from other companies walked past him. They were entering the top floor rooms to complete ventilation operations and to determine if the fire had extended up this high. Donald stood up wearily and placed one foot in front of the other as he descended. At the second floor level he glanced into the rooms. A charged line was in position in each of the rear rooms. He stepped inside and was able to determine that, yes, the fire had worked its way up to here. The walls had been stripped and the ceilings were opened, revealing some extension into the overhead, but not too much. On the first floor, the damage was much more severe. Not only had the two rear rooms been completely destroyed, but the fire had traveled towards the front of the building in the hallway and along the ceilings of two of the front rooms. The area was crowded with several jakes who continued to remove laths, plaster and strapping, while engine companies with lines now reduced for overhauling were directing controlled streams to wash down and complete extinguishment.

Donald thought that Jacob and Oregon must be out front because jakes from another company were handling Twenty-two's line. He found them sitting inside the compartment of the pump, each clutching a steaming container of coffee.

"Uh," Jacob said, "the deputy told us to take a break, Luft. You want us back in?"

Donald smiled: "Naw. Not yet. Take your time and finish your coffee. You two hung in there and really saved our asses. If you'd backed out, we were screwed. Any word on Dan"

They both shook their heads: "We didn't know where either of you were. They told us Dan was breathing OK, but his eyes weren't open when he left. He was on his way to the hospital when we got relieved."

Cueball's worried face appeared in the doorway. "The Command Post says Dan's at the BCH. I just seen the commissioner leaving the fire. Think him and the deputy's on their way over there."

Donald wanted to take off himself, but it just wasn't possible yet. The storm was still raging. It had grown even worse, if anything. Holyoke Street was still unplowed, although they said tow trucks were working at the Columbus Avenue end to move the abandoned vehicles so plows could clear a passageway. Apparatus were lined up bumper to bumper on both West Canton and Carleton Streets, as well as on Braddock Park, the next adjacent street that ran from Columbus to the railroad barrier.

He had coffee himself, then he and the remainder of his company took over their line on the first floor. He managed to make his usual survey and was thrilled to see not only that another aerial had been extended to the rear of the roof from Carleton, but three ground ladders had been wrestled through the snow clogged alleyway and had been elevated to the rear of the building. None of them were long enough to reach the location where he, Lansing and the victim were because that was well over fifty feet above the rear yard. But, by God, they were trying. He loved this fire department. Nobody quits.

He had been a little concerned about striking a third alarm because the building wasn't all that massive. However, after seeing the difficulties encountered in getting lines and ladders in position under such conditions, he felt he had used the right judgment. This was confirmed when he talked to Chief Polin as the force was being rapidly dismissed, now that the fire was knocked down. "Lieutenant, I just want to re-emphasize how well I think you and your company performed. I told the deputy and the commissioner what you accomplished. When the boss left here he was telling Chief Lawton he wants a full report. Far as I can see, you made a lot of good moves."

Donald said, "Well, thanks boss, but I have a great crew. These guys really know what they're doing."

Polin smiled, "Yes, but it was you who made the decisions. You all did fine getting the line and ladder in position, but you're the guy who told us what you had and called for plenty of help. That's good judgment." Donald hesitantly asked if the third alarm wasn't a little bit of overkill, but the district chief shook his head: "Listen, kid, when human life is in danger, no amount of help is too much. I wouldn't care if you struck a half a dozen more alarms. You recognized the danger and didn't hesitate." He continued: "You know, there are twerps in this business—including some chiefs—who have too much pride to call for help. They're either too stubborn to want a superior coming in on them, or they're just too dumb to know the difference. There's an old saying that someone smarter than us must have come up with: 'You can always send them back if you don't need them. But, if you ain't got enough, you can lose the building, the jakes and the people you're supposed to be saving.'"

Polin, somewhat philosophically, said, "Now that I've got my own district, I can put all my own theories into practice. One of the things I know I'll have in mind as a chief is, whenever I have a fire, I personally am not doing any physical labor. I'm just standing out front trying to make the right mental moves. I will not work the asses off of my own jakes when I actually need more help. If I'm too proud to call for it, would that make me a brilliant leader? I don't think so. There are about a couple of hundred other jakes on duty, sitting in firehouses around the city, most of them just hoping to go to work at this fire. I'll tell you, Luft, they'll get their chance to do that when I'm the boss. You just keep doing what you did tonight and you and I will get along just great."

Back in quarters, it took quite a while to get the piece back in service properly. The hose was frozen and had to be replaced. The pumper was completely covered with snow and chunks of ice and had to be drenched with hot water. The mask cylinders had to be changed and the harnesses and facepieces cleaned and made serviceable again. The fire company that had been covering them during the fire had managed to keep ahead of the storm by shoveling the front apron constantly, but by the time Twenty-two was back in service, the other unit had been dispatched to another fire and the snow was piling up again. They had to attack it once again, hoping the blizzard would finally start to abate. It didn't. They had two more runs before the tour ended but neither were for fires. One was an automatic alarm in a high rise and Donald laughed at how rapidly the crew advanced into the lobby to get out of the storm. The other response, believe it or not, was to a false alarm from a street box. Donald stayed a little longer at the location than was usual because he just couldn't believe some screwball would make the effort to get out of a car and pull a box maliciously in such weather. However, someone did and they returned to quarters.

The radio told them Logan Airport had closed at midnight and that by dawn the number of inches on the ground totalled well over a foot. At 0700 the signal was struck keeping all members, except fire officers, on duty. This was the usual procedure for a big storm, although no officer could leave until his partner arrived and would be paid overtime until properly relieved. No buses or surface street cars were running on the MBTA—just trains and trolleys in the subways. Cueball shouted over the P.A. system, "It's April Fools' Day. This is just someone's idea of a joke. We'll all wake up in a while and it'll be gone."

They would learn that it was not a fake storm—just New England doing what it does when it wants to. Eventually three quarters of a million people were without power, some for almost a week. Schools across the state were closed for a minimum of three days. In Boston, the snow, which didn't quit until that evening, accumulated to over twenty-five inches. The town of Millis reported three feet. And, unlike most spring storms, it didn't go away the next day. The temperatures remained below freezing for an extended period before the big thaw finally arrived.

Donald's usual relief, Phil Cummings, arrived right on time. He had done what many fire fighters do when they know things are screwed up. He started walking on the main road from his home in the Brighton district. It wasn't long until he was picked up, first by a contractor driving a snow plow, next by a Boston police car, and finally, by a Health and Hospital ambulance that deposited him at the front door of Twenty-two's house.

Donald quickly showered and changed into his street clothes. He knew where he was headed. Right to the Boston City Hospital. He had to see Dan Lansing. He had been unable to get any information because Fire Alarm was still swamped with emergency calls. His intention was to walk out to Mass. Ave. and then trudge the half dozen blocks to the massive medical center. Cummings wouldn't hear of it: "Donald, soon's you're ready, we'll deliver you first class in the pump. Your crew won't complain. Shit, they're all on O.T. I'll be in the kitchen getting coffee when you're ready."

Donald was just about to leave when there was a knock on his door. It was his superstar, Peter Justice. "Speak to you a minute, Luft?"

Donald smiled at his friend and said, "Sure, pal. Just like I said before, you performed like the champion you are. A real Class of '92 jake. What can I do for you?"

"Well, sir," he said, quite formally, "those two twerps, Jacob and Oregon, think you're so cool. Never got excited or anything. I for one disagree. You lost complete control of yourself and I'm the only one who knows it."

Donald swallowed nervously before asking, "Why, Cueball? What did I do wrong?"

The short redhead shook his head. "There, you just did it again. If I told you once, I told you a thousand times. Never call me Cueball on duty. These guys never heard that name. You know that jerk, Alan Hitchcock, gave me that tag in drill school just to get even 'cause I named him Goat. I got plenty of hair left. Just look at it."

"What the hell are you talking about!" Donald said. "I always call you Pete on the company, don't I?"

Justice, his face in a tight grimace, said, "Sure. Until the crunch comes. Tonight we get that fire and there you are, yelling at me, '*Cueball*, do this, *Cueball* do that, *Cueball* get a second alarm.' See, Luft, under pressure you just fell apart and forgot my instructions." He swung around to leave the room, with Donald standing there, his mouth agape. Justice turned back: "Well at least nobody else heard it, so I forgive you. And now that you are off duty and are not currently my leader, Donald you are truly Hero Holden. I'll follow you anywhere, boss." He wrapped his arms around his taller friend, leaned his head against his chest and then fled the room.

At the hospital, the department hospital representative told Donald that Lansing was doing pretty well. He was conscious, but was suffering from exhaustion and had an irregular heart beat. They were going to keep him for a couple of days to run a battery of tests and attempt to determine if there was any permanent damage. Donald asked if he could see him and the rep said, "Yeah, sure. The bosses were here but they've gone along now. His wife is up there. I picked her up and brought her in. Boy, is she pregnant."

This information was a surprise to Donald. Of course, Lansing had been completely uncommunicative during the two months Donald had been assigned to the company. His record indicated he was married, but didn't mention much else. No children were listed.

The door to the private room was just slightly ajar when Donald arrived. He peeked in and saw a woman's form bent over the figure in the bed. He knocked and there was a pause before she said, "Come in." The first impression Donald received was that the hospital rep didn't use any understatement. The woman looked ready to deliver any time. His second glance told him she was not a young woman. Her serene face, surrounded by hair more grey than black, spread into a smile as she watched him enter. "You must be Lieutenant Holden," she said and reached out to shake his hand. "Daniel has told me all about you. I'm Rosemary and I'm very pleased to meet you. He's asleep now. Would you like to step outside for a few minutes."

Donald spent the next half hour in the visitors' reception room, listening to this truly remarkable woman. She said, "First of all, I want to thank you for what you did for Daniel." He started to protest, but she stopped him. "I don't mean just tonight. I'm sure you've found Daniel to be uncommunicative since you were assigned to his station." She talked about when they had met, about a decade earlier. She was ten years his senior and met him just after he had been appointed to the job. She had worked as a dental technician for several years, but now they both agreed they wanted to have a family. "Well," she continued, "we haven't had much luck. Three early miscarriages and it has been very difficult for us. Daniel's parents died when he was a kid and his only brother had already died in Vietnam. He was brought up in foster homes and none of them seemed to be that great. He was determined to get the type of family he never had."

As the years slipped by, it appeared they would never succeed and he had withdrawn more deeply into himself. "He also became disenchanted with his job. In the beginning he had loved the fire department, but I guess he had a couple of officers at other assignments he didn't really respect. He never gave me any details of why he wasn't happy. He just decided to put his time in and get out as soon as possible.

"But then, a couple of things have happened that I'm pleased about. First of all, this pregnancy. As you can see, I'm due anytime. And all of my tests indicate I'm going to make it all the way. Those other three ended in the first trimester, but this time things are looking up. That is one thing that seems to be bringing him out of his shell."

Donald said, " I'm-uh glad to hear that, er, Rosemary."

She held up her hand: "Yes, it's wonderful for us. But, the

other thing is you."

He blinked his eyes before saying confusedly, "What do you mean?"

She explained that her husband came home a couple of months ago and said he had a new boss. His first impulse was that he'd be just like the last couple he had. "But then you made some kind of a speech to them when you started. That hadn't happened before. Dan figured you were just making talk and trying to impress him and the other fire fighters. As time went on, though, he told me you seemed to be pretty sincere and at least you tried awfully hard."

Donald said, "Well, I don't know. He never seemed to change much to me. Don't get me wrong. He does his work, but he sure doesn't respond much to attempts to reach him."

She laughed. "No, no, but, believe me, you were getting there, Lieutenant. I think you would have noticed a difference pretty soon. Now, I know you will. Why don't you go in and see him."

Donald walked down the corridor and quietly entered the room again. This time Lansing was awake but still lying flat. The nurse had explained he still had a residual headache, probably from some CO he had absorbed when he had shared his air supply with the woman he was attempting to rescue. Nevertheless, when he saw Donald he smiled and said, "Hi, Luft. How you doin'?" Donald answered that he was fine but was concerned about Lansing. "Gonna be OK! Boy, was I pooped. Thought we'd never get outta there. How's the woman doin'?" The hospital rep had reported to Donald that she was going to make it, so Donald passed on the information.

He said, "Look Dan, I'm not going to bother you. You get some rest. I just wanted to tell you, you are a terrific jake. When you went up above that fire, you didn't know if you'd come back." Lansing started to say something but Donald stopped him. "What you did know, though, was that someone was up there and you never hesitated. I'm proud to be working with you."

Lansing's eyes became watery and he rubbed them with his hand that wasn't encumbered with an IV. "Thanks, Luft. That means a lot. But I was scared to death until I saw you. You look after your jakes. When you showed up, I knew we'd make it."

Donald laughed out loud and said, "If you knew how scared I was up there, you wouldn't have felt so confident. I thought we were all gonna be statistics."

Lansing smiled. "Yeah, but you came and you stayed. I'll be back when they get me outta here. Besides, I really want to straighten out that loud mouth, Justice. You know, he never shuts up."

When Donald arrived home, Gena and Nancy were waiting to see what kind of adventures he'd experienced during the night. There was very little mention of the fire, just a brief report about a third alarm, because all the news was about the storm, the damage and disruptions to most of the state, and the fact that it hadn't ended yet.

He told them about everything that had happened, downplaying his own role, but they could see he was really excited about what had been accomplished. He was particularly happy about Dan Lansing and what he had said to him. Finally, when he wound down, he felt his eyes starting to burn and realized he had to get some sleep. He was exhausted.

In the evening, he felt Nancy's hand gently shaking him awake. "Hey, Dad. Time to get up. Mom wants to tell you what's on the news." He slipped on his robe and stumbled out into the living room. Gena said, "They just had a great story on the news."

"What is it?" he said.

"Oh, it seems a woman had a baby boy at the BCH this afternoon."

He mumbled, "Wow. That must be a first."

Gena smiled sweetly at him and said, "Don't be sarcastic. This one's a little different. She was visiting her husband, who just happens to be a Boston jake."

Donald's eyes popped open: "Lansing? Was it Rosemary Lansing?"

"It sure was. They said her husband saved a woman at a fire in the South End. That's where you were, right?" He nodded. Nancy couldn't contain herself, "But guess what, daddy? Mrs. Lansing was just on. They asked her what the baby's name was going to be."

"Yeah. Well, what is it?" Donald asked.

Nancy chuckled: "She said, 'Daniel Donald Lansing' and she said *someone* would know the reason why!"